NEW YORK REVIEW BOOKS
CLASSICS

THE CORNER THAT HELD THEM

SYLVIA TOWNSEND WARNER (1893–1978) was a poet, short-story writer, and novelist, as well as an authority on early English music and a devoted member of the Communist Party. Her many books include *Mr. Fortune*, *Lolly Willowes*, *Summer Will Show*, and *Kingdoms of Elfin*.

CLAIRE HARMAN's first book, a biography of Sylvia Townsend Warner, was published in 1989 and won the John Llewellyn Rhys Prize. She has since published biographies of Fanny Burney and Robert Louis Stevenson. Her most recent book is *Jane's Fame: How Jane Austen Conquered the World*. In 2006 she was elected a Fellow of the Royal Society of Literature.

OTHER BOOKS BY SYLVIA TOWNSEND WARNER
PUBLISHED BY NYRB CLASSICS

Lolly Willowes
Introduction by Alison Lurie

Mr. Fortune
Introduction by Adam Mars-Jones

Summer Will Show
Introduction by Claire Harman

THE CORNER THAT HELD THEM

SYLVIA TOWNSEND WARNER

Introduction by

CLAIRE HARMAN

NEW YORK REVIEW BOOKS

New York

THIS IS A NEW YORK REVIEW BOOK
PUBLISHED BY THE NEW YORK REVIEW OF BOOKS
435 Hudson Street, New York, NY 10014
www.nyrb.com

Library of Congress Cataloging-in-Publication Data
Names: Warner, Sylvia Townsend, 1893–1978, author. | Harman, Claire, writer of introduction.
Title: The corner that held them / by Sylvia Townsend Warner ; introduction by Claire Harman.
Description: New York : New York Review Books, [2019] | Series: New York Review Books Classics | This publication is a reproduction of The corner that held them by Sylvia Townsend Warner, the edition published in London by Virago Press on 1988.
Identifiers: LCCN 2019017347| ISBN 9781681373874 (paperback) | ISBN 9781681373881 (epub)
Subjects: | BISAC: FICTION / Contemporary Women. | FICTION / Religious.
Classification: LCC PR6045.A812 C67 2019 | DDC 823/.914—dc23
LC record available at https://lccn.loc.gov/2019017347

ISBN 978-1-68137-387-4
Available as an electronic book; ISBN 978-1-68137-388-1

Printed in the United States of America on acid-free paper.
10 9 8 7 6 5 4

CONTENTS

Introduction

Of Sylvia Townsend Warner's seven novels, *The Corner That Held Them* was her favourite and one of the most popular. As she always wrote primarily to please herself though, no one of her books was sufficiently like another to produce the impression of coherence upon which a loud reputation depends. The nearest she got to being a bestseller was in 1926 with the publication of her first novel, *Lolly Willowes*, and anyone who knows that book would have difficulty drawing a line connecting it with *The Corner That Held Them*. In length, content, tone and technique they are poles apart. The only consistent element is the quality of the writing, particularly evident in *The Corner That Held Them*, which is a *tour de force* of worldliness, wisdom and controlled irony, though the two books share one theme characteristic of the work of women novelists, which can be called "the female condition." In *Lolly Willowes* it is the spur to action and rebellion; in *The Corner That Held Them*, the story of a community of women in the fourteenth century, it is one of many immutable facts of life: "I consume, I burn away, always lighting the same corner, always beleaguered by the same shadows; and in the end I shall burn out and another candle will be fixed in my stead."

Anyone could be forgiven, when reading the first few pages of *The Corner That Held Them*, for thinking that they had picked up a historical novel. The opening episode, brightened by passions and the colour of blood, is certainly in that tradition, but as the book progresses, the reader becomes aware that it is poised ambiguously between a history and a fiction, for *The Corner That Held Them* is a masterly piece of contrived realism. Once the narrative settles around the convent of Oby in the Fenlands, it loses itself in events, like the Waxle Stream which flows from the convent to the sea, "a muddy reluctant stream, full of loops and turnings, and constantly revising its course." There is no protagonist—five prioresses and four bishops come and go; novices arrive, grow up, die—and what story there is never strays further from Oby, the convent, than a horse could take it. Aware as she was writing it that this was no conventional novel, Sylvia Townsend Warner wrote to a friend, "I still incline to call it People growing Old. It has no conversations and no pictures, it has no plot, and the characters are innumerable and insignificant." Yet by abandoning the usual techniques of novel-writing in this way, she managed to bring off the novelist's supreme coup, to create a totally convincing fictional world.

Oby, "that epitome of humdrum," is a convent built on a rise of ground which was once an island, founded to pray for the soul of a twelfth-century adulteress and dedicated to Saint Leonard, the patron saint of prisoners. The land attached to the house is poor, the estate unproductive except of rheumatisms, and the convent, a remodelled manor, has to make do with a chapel which was formerly the cattle-hold and a converted dovecot for chapter-house: "allowed as a temporary expedient, and as such [the arrangement] became permanent." The shabbiness of Oby makes it expensive to maintain and dooms its inhabitants to lives of scrimping and wheedling. In an interview late in her life, Sylvia

Townsend Warner claimed that she began this novel "on the purest Marxian principles, because I was convinced that if you were going to give an accurate picture of the monastic life, you'd have to put in all their finances; how they made their money, how they dodged about from one thing to another and how very precarious it all was." It is Mammon rather than God who dominates the lives of the nuns at Oby, not because of any innate viciousness, but because so few of them have the leisure for spirituality.

The main action of the book takes place between the years 1345 and 1382, dates as arbitrary as everything else in the novel. Dozens of characters appear and disappear, drift into focus and then out again. There is a glimpse of every "point of view," often to no purpose whatever except that we will have seen the bishop's clerk looking at the sleeping bishop, or understood which of several possible thoughts triggers off an old nun's tears, or have heard, with the dying Dame Joan, her own death rattle, and wondered what it was. As in life, things are rarely tidied up to a conclusion; there is, for example, no indication of what finally happens to the man Jackie, the altar hanging, Dame Adela, the Lay of Mamillion, the lost altar vessels. When Dame Adela is manoeuvred onto a boat or Jackie disappears down a side street, no artifice is employed to follow them, and in the book's constant mistakings of meanings and motives, no pattern appears. In this oddly engaging chronicle of small things happening or half-happening, certain characters and episodes stand out; Prioress Alicia (a first cousin, surely, to Chaucer's prioress) in secular company at a christening; Henry Yellowlees discovering *Ars nova*, the new polyphonic music, at the leper house; the death of Bishop Walter; Ralph Kello's sermons, which owe more to Humanism than Christianity and are discounted because of his "madness"; the bereaved Dame of Brocton; the young nun Dame Isabel, possibly the most sympathetic character in the book, who dies young, and regretting to exchange "the ambiguity of this world for the certitude of the next." Music, vernacular poetry, needlework and architecture also make their way into the book, and humour, which though too wry for laughter, surfaces constantly, as in this description of the development of Bishop Walter's reputation:

> In the year 1351 many people were saying that Walter Dunford was a saint. Five years later twice that number was saying he was a man with a future. He became eminent enough to have slanderers, the retinue of eminence. He had the evil eye, it was said; he was leprous, he was crazy, he was a plotter, he was a sorcerer. Beyond doubt he was undersized, pious to eccentricity, ludicrously thrifty. His reputation spluttered, and hung fire. It did not seem likely that he would ever win more than a local fame. He was made an archdeacon, with every expectation that he would die of the office, but he did not die. All of a sudden, as startlingly as a grounded heron displays its wing-span, he was in every mouth as a man who should by every right be a bishop. There is only one statesmanly answer to this sort of challenge, and in 1374 he was given a mitre.

The most immediately noticeable thing about the style of *The Corner That Held Them* is that it is free of what Sylvia Townsend Warner once called the "arthritis of antiquarianism." There is no quaint language and no scene-painting. Detail is kept to a minimum by drawing our attention only to what people in the fourteenth century might themselves have found noteworthy. The Black Death, which terrorized the age, is always described in heightened language, as vivid as the hold it had over every fourteenth-century imagination:

> It travelled faster than a horse, it swooped like a falcon, and those whom it seized on were so suddenly corrupted that the victims, still alive and howling in anguish, stank like the dead. The short dusky daylight and the miry roads and the swollen rivers were no impediment to it, as to other travellers. All across Europe it had come, and now it would traverse England, and nothing could stop it, wherever there were men living it would seek them out, and turn back, as a wolf does, to snap at the man it had passed by.

But the Hundred Years' War and the Peasants' Revolt, to which history has given names, do not feature prominently in the book. The wars with France are translated as another set of taxes and levies; the Peasants' Revolt means, for Oby, a night of fairly mild damage in a year of rumours and wild fears. There is no mystification of the past in *The Corner That Held Them.* The author is more interested in what links us with the fourteenth century than what separates us from it, as she wrote to Marchette Chute, apropos "those people who prefer their fourteenth century at a more gothic degree of perspective. It is wounding to a strong twentieth-century *amour propre* to admit that the course of time has not made vast differences in the development of human nature."

The illusion of real life which is created in the book is completely beguiling. The American novelist Anne Parrish wrote to Sylvia, "each page has its actual shock of someone really known, really seen," and it is just that, a shock, almost a charge, which the best of the writing produces. The impression that the book consists largely of fact when it is singularly devoid of fact is another measure of how well-imagined the novel is. The authority which it carries derives in great part from the author's restraint, the way in which she presents her material to us rather than chaperoning us round it, so that the reader falls in easily with the tone of the book. The lack of a protagonist and a plot frees the author from the pressure towards significance and enables her to absent herself from the writing to a remarkable degree and create those realistic illusions. The best example of this (and a trick she wisely uses once only) is on page 354 when Ralph Kello leaves his bedchamber and "As the door closed behind him a brimstone butterfly fluttered in at the open window." This has no bearing on anything, and beyond a suggestion of ephemerality, no meaning. It is simply a butterfly flying through a window six hundred years ago; doing nothing, seen by no one. As a piece of bravado on the part of an author, it takes some beating.

When *The Corner That Held Them* was first published in 1948 many readers found Sylvia Townsend Warner's portrait of the religious life scandalously irreverent. Writing back to one complaining Californian, Sylvia defended herself on purely historical grounds:

> Even allowing for a perceptible male bias against houses of women (and though this was certainly felt, I think it was held in check by most of those who felt it) the evidence of contemporary ecclesiastical records makes it inescapably plain that the monastic establishments (of either sex, but we will keep to nunneries) displayed all the characteristic faults of community living—as well as grosser faults. On this evidence I could have made Oby a much worse place, and still have had the support of contemporary ecclesiastics.

For all that—Sylvia Townsend Warner was a learned woman, a music scholar in her youth and the daughter of a historian—I suspect that her own eyes and ears were as important a source of information for this novel as any number of accounts of Episcopal

Visitations or fourteenth-century church strictures. *The Corner That Held Them* was written between 1941 and 1947. "All the characteristic faults of community living" must have been particularly evident in wartime Dorset, simmering as it was with provincial womanhood. The Maiden Newton Civil Defence Unit, the Dorchester WVS and the Winterton Mothers' Union must have provided a wealth of detail for Sylvia's book.

"Anyway," Sylvia wrote of her work-in-progress, "it has a remarkable vitality, for it has persisted in getting written through an endless series of interruptions, distractions, and destructions, it has been as persistent as a damp patch in a house wall." She finished writing the novel in the winter of 1947, "to the accompaniment of green snow," parting reluctantly with the world which had been so engrossing and sustaining. Soon after, she decided to continue the story in a sequel, but the second volume never got past the early stages. Properly, *The Corner That Held Them* cannot be said to have an ending. It just stops. Nothing could be more suitable to a book which conveys so clearly the pulse of life.

—Claire Harman
Manchester, 1988

THE CORNER THAT HELD THEM

For neither might the corner that held them keep them from fear

THE WISDOM OF SOLOMON XVII 4

To Valentine Ackland

I

Orate Pro Anima

Alianor de Retteville lay on her bed and looked at Giles who was her lover. She did not speak. She had nothing to say. He did not speak either. They were not alone, for in a corner of the room an old woman sat spinning, but she was no more than the bump and purr of her wheel. It was summer, and late afternoon. The rain fell and birds were singing; they had their summer voices, loud and guttural. The rain had come unobtrusively, breaking up a long spell of drought. For leagues and leagues around it was falling on the oak woods, dripping from leaf to leaf and taking a long time, because the foliage was so thick, to reach the ground. It would be pleasurable, Alianor thought, to lie naked in the oak woods now, feeling the rain on her skin. Each drop would be a small separate pleasure. But only the pigs and a few foresters were in the woods, creatures whose skin has little sensitivity.

It is going to thunder, thought Giles, noticing how dusky the room had grown and seeing the leaden hue of the sky above the vivid green of the oak woods, a narrow picture in the window that because of the heat was unscreened. Instead of the thunder which he expected to hear a wood-dove began to croon. He closed his eyes and stretched and fell asleep again.

They were both sleeping when the old woman jumped up from her wheel and hobbled towards the bed, softly calling on them to waken. A moment later the spinning-wheel was knocked over as the door was forced open, and Brian de Retteville and his two cousins, Piers and Richard, burst in. Giles awoke and saw the old woman at the bedside holding out his sword. She proffered it blade towards him, poor old fool, and in snatching it he cut his hand. That was the first bloodshed. Immediately the three were upon him. He fought, not to defend himself, there was no hope of that, but to die fighting and quickly.

After the first start of waking Alianor did not move. Recumbent, stiffening in the posture of her sleep, she watched her lover being butchered. What would have been the use of moving? She could not save Giles and in a little while she would be dead herself. So she stayed as she was, the braid of hair lying across her breast, her long arms and narrow hands spread out on either side as she had laid them for coolness, for the air, cooled with rain, to refresh her ribs and flanks. Even her seaweed-coloured eyes were motionless, attentively watching her lover's death.

It was this immobility which saved her life. Turning to the bedside Brian de Retteville supposed that now he would kill the woman too. But seeing her lie there, so calm, so arrogantly still, his anger was arrested by the horror a man feels at a woman's immodest individuality. He began to call his wife whore and strumpet. The impulse to kill her was overwhelmed in a flood of reviling, and only emerged later in kicks and blows.

Meanwhile the two cousins were dragging Giles's body towards the stairhead. The old woman reproached them for their unchristianity, saying in her rasping dialect that they should show pity for the dead even if they had none for the living.

Looking down on the young man's bloodied face, which seemed to express an indignant and slightly supercilious astonishment, she crossed herself and began to pray. He had given her many presents and joked with her. It was a sorry thought that now for lack of a little grace of time and a priest he was almost certainly damned.

Piers and Richard were in no mood to stomach pious reproaches just then, being excited with bloodshed and embarrassed by Brian's stockishness and Alianor naked on the bed. Bundling the old woman up between them they tossed her downstairs.

'So much for you, Dame Bawd!'

There was no reply. Peering down they saw that she lay at the turn of the stair, her head wried to one side, a thin vomit trailing between her lips. She was dying, and they felt relieved, and as if the situation had been bettered. Even if that oaf Brian could not follow the example, an example had been set.

That evening the three men got extremely drunk. The house rang with their brawls. Alianor, listlessly stirring to and fro, trying to find some attitude in which she could forget the pain of her bruises, heard the cousins telling Brian what they thought of him, and Brian shouting out that he knew how to manage his wife, it was no business of theirs.

'Since you've left the slut alive,' hiccuped Richard, 'you'll have to send her to some nunnery.'

'I'll do what I'll do,' Brian roared.

He won't do much, she thought. There will be no nunnery, for he will never part from my money. If I had the energy I could soon cuckold him again and serve him right. But remembering Giles and his love and how she had loved him, and how deeply they had embraced and how little they had spoken, it seemed to her that all possibility of love was over, that any other love she might entertain would be flawed with deliberation, and specious;

and she wept silently, biting her hair to prevent herself from crying out.

Her forecast was right. Beyond some more outbursts of temper, and dismissing most of the servants, Brian did no more. Life went on in the former pattern. Brian rode out to hunt, the horns squawking through the oak woods. Within doors the long afternoons were silent as ever except for the buzz of the lazy autumn flies and the bump and purr of an old woman's spinning-wheel: only it was a different old woman, and there was no lover. By Christmas Brian had squared matters with his self-respect. If he had omitted to kill his wife it was because such a wife was not worth the trouble of killing: a sensible man does not take women so seriously. The sense of ignominy which might have fretted him he sublimated by seeing the funny side of his misadventure. With roars of laughter he entertained company by recounting how he had sneaked home to find Giles and Alianor snuggling. A rude awakening ... God's blood, how chopfallen they had looked! At dinner, at supper, the story was repeated till in the end even the sturdiest senses of humour found it tedious.

And so for another ten years they lived together, Brian countering all suggestions that he should take the cross in defence of the Holy Sepulchre by the plea that he must stay at home to keep an eye on Alianor's virtue; and he would recount again the tale of that summer afternoon to anyone unwary enough not to get away in time. In summer the woods were green, and full of flies and deep shadows, and the wolves lived quietly, the she-wolves bringing on their cubs from the teat to rabbits and badgers. In winter they gathered into packs and ravaged the open country night after night. In snowy seasons their large footprints showed how they moved in companies, where the scouts had gone out from the main pack, and how cunningly they had skirted the wolf-traps; or the blurring of footprints told how a carcass had been dragged back to the outskirts of the wood where it could be eaten in privacy. All night their voices rose and fell, sharpening into quarrels like the voices of men. So time went on, every year a little more draggingly, as though time itself were growing middle-aged. Alianor bore two more children, both girls. Then it was time to find a bride for Gilbert, the eldest son. Aged ten, she came to live with her new parents. She was a highbred hoyden, wealthy, frank, hating all music except the sound of the horn – a daughter-in-law after Brian's own heart. Once again Alianor was with child, and unwontedly timid, oppressed by the girl's hearty, careless curiosity and pebble gaze. And in this childbed she died, having given birth to a large dead boy.

What followed astonished everyone – perhaps even Brian himself, who had become the astonishment. Whether it was he dreaded Alianor's ghost, or whether in some dull crevice of his heart he still loved the woman who had once dishonoured and always despised him, or whether her death released him from the bondage of feeling and acting like a dolt, no one could say; but suddenly he was a different man. Alianor's funeral was a nine days' wonder. She lay unburied for a fortnight while the preparations were heaped up; and because there were few serfs on the manor, for he had cleared away two hamlets in order to have more room for his wild boars, he sent a general invitation through the countryside for all beggars, scholars, jugglers, and broken men to come and share in the funeral feast and receive alms and new clothes in her memory. He commissioned the best craftsmen in England to carve her tomb, and sat beside the effigist as he worked, telling him that the nose must be a trifle narrower, the left eyebrow a hair's breadth higher than the right, while he watched for the likeness to emerge as sharply as in better days he had watched outside a thicket.

Meanwhile Alianor's body, in a lead coffin, waited till it could be transferred to the nunnery which he intended to found in commemoration of her soul. For months on end his intercourse was with bishops and lawyers, and through the long negotiations his hunter's patience was inexhaustible and no detail escaped him. He chose to have a priory of the Benedictine order. All Alianor's fortune he gave to its endowment, and made a will leaving it half his own property, though Gilbert and Adela and Adela's relations complained furiously and threatened alternately to bring a law-suit or to write to the Pope. The site chosen was a manor called Oby. Oby had been part of Alianor's dowry, and in the early days of their marriage they had often lived there, for it was good hawking country along the Waxle Stream; but as his taste in hunting turned to larger quarries the manor house had fallen into neglect and now only the shell of it remained, housing several families of serfs and countless bats. Now this shell was made weatherproof, whitewashed within and partitioned into dormitories and chambers. A chapel was constructed and a bell hung in the squat belfry, the barns were re-roofed and the moat was cleaned. The dedication was made to Our Lady and Saint Leonard, patron of prisoners, and the choice of this saint was perhaps a little acknowledgement towards those acquaintances who had urged Brian de Retteville to take the cross, since several of them had actually done so and still awaited ransom. The nuns arrived, bright as a flock of magpies, and into their keeping he gave his two younger daughters; and then, when everything was finished, he went back to his oak woods and his hunting, and died in 1170.

The Waxle Stream flowed north-east through a poor country of marsh and moorland: a muddy reluctant stream, full of loops and turnings, and constantly revising its course, for the general lie of the land imposed no restraint on its vagaries. In some places it had hollowed for itself long pools where the current seemed to have ceased altogether, in others it skulked through acres of rushes and spongy moss. Every second year or so it spread itself into a flood. When the flood-water went down, the Waxle Stream had changed some part of its course and the former channel was filled up with a false brilliant herbage that had little or no nourishment in it.

Such a stream makes a very contentious boundary; and if the land had been of more value one generation or another of Alianor's ancestors might have set their men to embanking. But their manor of Oby was a small part of their possessions and lying far away from any other de Bazingham property, so nothing was done. The only indication of man's will to thwart nature was the high earthen causeway running to the town of Waxelby on the coast. This was made long before the first de Bazingham came into England. It was called the Hog Trail, and people said that long ago all the hogs of Oby, and of Lintoft on the further side of Oby Fen, had been driven along the trail to Waxelby for slaughtering because in those days men were so foolish that they took their hogs to the salt instead of fetching the salt to the hogs. Whoever made the Hog Trail, and for whatever purpose, it was well made and still serviceable, though the willows, that had rooted in the ditches and grown to huge trees and split and rooted again, had weakened the earthworks and sooner or later would pull them down. When the floods were out the Hog Trail was the only way to get from Oby to Waxelby: a bitter nine miles, with the wind from the sea beating over the floods like a skater. But in summer, when Brian de Retteville came to the manor for some hawking and to remind his bailiff that if the Martinmas beef were to be worth eating the beasts should now be fattening, the place was well enough: he, at any rate, had liked it. When he chose to found his nunnery there it did not occur to him that nuns live in a place all the year round, and must feed through the hungry half of the year as well as through the plentiful half. There was land, and water, and a population of serfs, not many but enough; there were buildings and outbuildings, a fish-pond, an excellent dovecot. What more could women, holy women, desire?

Negotiations with the house in France which was to supply his first batch of nuns enlarged his notions of what holy women desire. The abbess, a notable woman of business, sent him a long list of requirements, including a boat; for the title deeds of the manor, expressing Oby's condition in the more watery past, used the term *insula*. Even after assurances that the manor was on the mainland she extracted a great deal more from him than he had thought to give: yearly loads of timber, carriage free, from his oak woods; half the profit of one of his mills to cover the purchase of wine; a yearly consignment of dressed fox-skins, to make coverlets; a good relic; books for the altar and for account-keeping; the complete furniture for the convent priest's chamber over the gate-house and the tolls of a bridge over the Nene to pay for his upkeep and salary; a litter; tin porringers with lids to them; and a ring for the prioress.

Even so, the nuns arriving to take possession felt that they had come a long way to worsen their lot. They saw their new home at its best, for it was midsummer, and under the enormous vault of sky their manor, perched on the little rise of ground which gave the place its old name and half-circled by a loop of the Waxle Stream, looked like one of those maps into which the draughtsman has put every detail and coloured the whole to resemble life. The river was blue, the fields were striped in the colours of cultivation and fallow, there was a small mill, a large barn, a brewhouse, a fish-pond, also blue, and the house itself, a scramble of low buildings newly roofed with reed thatch, with a small chapel to one side of it and to the other a large dovecot, banded with black-faced flints. Further along the ridge were the huts and sheds of the hamlet. To the east there was a belt of trees, warped and stunted by the wind from the sea.

Everything was poorer, smaller, clumsier than they had expected. The rooms were dark and poky, and seemed thrown together at random. Food had to be carried across the yard, for there was no covered way between the kitchen and the refectory. They must take their exercise out of doors or not at all, for there were no cloisters. Even their newly built chapel – they had been told it was newly built – was a squat, cramped building with a disproportionately large west door, a low roof supported by stumpy pillars, and a floor two foot below ground level (it was, in fact, a reach-me-down conversion of what had been the dungeon and cattle-hold of the original manor house). Like all people of bad taste, Brian de Retteville had saved on the structure in order to spend on the fittings. Altar, screen, stalls, canopies, were highly ornate and bright with paint and gilding. As for the one bell, it was so clumsy that it took two women to sound it.

With dubious hearts they sang their Te Deum.

A good convent should have no history. Its life is hid with Christ who is above. History is of the world, costly and deadly, and the events it records are usually deplorable: the year when the roof caught fire, the year of the summer flood which swept away the haystacks and drowned the bailiff, the year when the cattle were stolen, the year when the king laid the great impost for the Scotch wars and timber for five years had to be felled to pay it, the year of the pestilence, the year when Dame Dionysia had a baby by the bishop's clerk. Yet the events of history carry a certain exhilaration with them. Decisions are made, money is spent, strangers arrive, familiar characters appear in a new light, transfigured with unexpected goodness or badness. Few calamities fall on a religious house which are not at some time or other looked back upon with wistful regret. 'In such an out-of-the-way place as this anything might happen,' said the first sacrist of Oby, staring at the listless horizon towards which the sun was descending like a lump of red-hot iron. 'Anything or nothing,' replied the first prioress. It seemed to her that Brian de Retteville's choice of site had been unrealistically too close to the mind of Saint Benedict – since it was a nunnery he had founded. Men with their inexhaustible interest in themselves may do well enough in a wilderness, but the shallower egoism of women demands some nourishment from the outer world, and preferably in the form of danger or disaster. While appeasing grumbles and expostulations, she realised that the inconveniences of the new house were in fact providential, and that when they were remedied (and for the good name of her order she must strive to remedy them) her nuns, exercising themselves dry-footed and eating meals which had not been spoiled between the kitchen and the table, would complain much more, and with better reason; since they would then be able to give an undivided attention to the mortifying tranquillity of their lives.

As things turned out, the providential inconveniences of her house lasted longer than she did. With a manor abounding in reeds and supplied with a sufficiency of timber one might think it an easy matter to make a covered way between kitchen and refectory and some makeshift sort of cloister. But the wood was not seasoned, the reeds were not cut or were not dried, the labour was not available, the time of year was not suitable: in short, the newcomers were unwelcome. The families which had been turned out of the manor house when it was made over for the nuns were, of course, related to all the other families on the manor; and the evicted were scarcely more resentful than those into whose hovels they packed on the plea of cousinship and christian charity. Under an absentee lord and a careless bailiff the manor serfs had achieved a kind of scrambling devil-take-the-hindmost independence. Though the new state of things included fresh livestock, repairs to roofs and carts and ploughs, and all the advantageous pickings which flow from an occupied manor, the Oby serfs unanimously disapproved of the nuns, a pack of foreigners who had come to feed on them, a gaggle of silly women, more tyrannical than any de Bazinghams or de Rettevilles, and ignorant into the bargain. The de Bazinghams had at least known better than to plant fig trees. To this enmity was added, after Brian de Retteville's death, the enmity of Gilbert and Adela, who suffered as sharply as any of the evicted serfs from the pangs of dispossession. Brian's legacy to the convent was indisputably legal and spiritually meritorious; but this did not prevent them from holding on to it as long as they could and wrangling over every piecemeal transfer. Neither did this prevent the convent's mother-house in France becoming increasingly unsympathetic towards an offshoot whose revenues on paper now warranted filial offerings rather than these perpetual begging-letters. Meanwhile the first prioress had died of a fever and her successor was that same hopeful sacrist who had thought that anything might happen, and still preserved the same illusion (it was she who enfranchised two families, the Figgs and the Torkles, in order to raise enough money to build a new gallows). In 1183, twenty years after its foundation, the convent of Oby was in such a state of confusion and indebtedness that the bishop of the diocese began to talk of dissolving it. Then Richenda de Foley interposed her strong secular arm. Richenda was Alianor's younger sister, a widow and a seasoned harridan, who having quarrelled her way through all her nearer relations had now worked down to quarrelling with Gilbert and Adela. What love is to some women and needlework to more, litigation was to Richenda. Gilbert and Adela were withholding Brian's legacy, were they, and imperilling the soul's welfare of a beloved sister and, for the nonce, a beloved brother-in-law? She would hunt the last farthing out of them; and in addition she would shame them by finding other and better patrons for the house, and better dowered and more creditable nuns than Gilbert's two wretched sisters. In order to conduct these operations she settled herself in the nunnery, where at that time there was room and to spare for boarders. She brought several servants, a great deal of household furniture, three dogs, one of the Magdalen's tears in a bottle, and twelve chests stuffed with law-papers and inventories. She also brought a great deal of method and efficiency. For the first time the manorial dues were properly enforced, and the serfs, working as they had not worked for years, became almost reconciled to the convent, since one of the old family, who in shrewdness and obstinacy might almost be one of themselves, had taken it under her wing.

In 1194 a wandering scholar, very old and shrill, came begging for a meal. As he sat munching his bread and a salt herring he talked to the wicket-nun about the properties of numbers, and of how Abbot Joachim, analysing the arithmetic of the prophecies, had discovered that the end of the world was at hand. He himself expected much of the year 1221, a date whose two halves each added up to three. In such a year, he said, one might look for the reign of Antichrist to be fulfilled, or else it might betoken the coming of the kingdom of the Holy Ghost, as the number six expressed a completion of two-thirds of the Trinity. Something, at any rate, he said, might be expected. Under his arm he carried a monochord. To make himself clearer to the nuns (for several of them had gathered to pity the old man, so wise and so witless) he explained to them about the Proportion of Diapason, the perfect concord which is at once concord and unity, and showed them how, by placing the bridge of the monochord so as to divide the string into a ratio of one and two, the string will sound the interval of the octave. Thus, he mumbled, was the nature of the Godhead perceptible to Pythagoras, a heathen; for it lies latent in all things. He sat on a bench in the sun, but overhead the wind howled, tormenting the willows along the Hog Trail and clawing the thatch, and the nuns could scarcely hear his demonstration of how the Godhead sounded to Pythagoras. It was really no loss, for his hand, shaking with cold and palsy, had failed to place the bridge correctly, and the diapason of the Trinity was out of tune. Then, brushing the crumbs out of his beard and plucking a sprig of young wormwood to stick behind his ear, he sang a lovesong to entertain the ladies and went on his way towards Lintoft. The lovesong had a pretty, catchy tune: for some days every nun and novice was humming it. Then Dame Cecilia began to have fits and to prophesy. This infuriated Richenda de Foley, to whom any talk of the end of the world after she had worked so hard and successfully to put the convent on a good footing for the next century seemed rank ingratitude. But the itch is not more contagious than illuminations, and throughout that summer Oby resounded with excited voices describing flaming bulls, he-goats of enormous size floating above the lectern, apparitions of the founder and shooting pains. In a fury of slighted good intentions and outraged common sense Richenda de Foley packed up and went away, but as she was generous as well as authoritarian she left a great deal of household stuff and provisions behind her. The community, after one universal gasp at finding itself unclasped from that strong and all-arranging hand, settled down to enjoy an unregulated prosperity and comfort; and prosperity and comfort wielding their usual effect, the spirit of prophecy flickered out, and by the close of the year they were looking for nothing more remarkable than improvements to the fish-pond.

In 1208 came the Interdict.

In 1223 lightning set fire to the granary.

In 1257 the old reed and timber cloisters fell to bits in a gale. It was decided that the masons who came to build the new should also build on a proper chapter-house. When it was half-built a spring rose under it. Rather than throw money away, the head mason suggested, why not finish the new building as a dovecot, a wet floor being no inconvenience to doves, and convert the old dovecot, so solid and weatherproof, into a chapter-house? This suggestion, too hastily accepted, led to discomfort all round. The pigeons refused to settle in their new house. Some flew away for good, the others remained in the lower half of the old dovecot, whose upper storey, remodelled with large windows and stone benches, made a very unpersuasive place of assembly. However, the arrangement was allowed as a temporary expedient, and as such it became permanent.

In 1270 there were disastrous floods, and this happened again seven years later. In 1283 hornets built in the brewhouse roof and the cellaress was stung in the lip and died. In 1297 the convent's bailiff was taken in the act of carnality with a cow. Both he and the cow were duly executed for the crime, but this was not enough to avert the wrath of heaven. That autumn and for three autumns following there was a murrain among the cattle. After the murrain came a famine and the bondwomen of the manor broke through the reed fence into the orchard where the nuns were at recreation and mobbed them, snatching at their wimples and jeering at such plump white breasts and idle teats. For this a fine was laid on the hamlet, and the last remnants of the *pax Richenda* broke down. Tithes and dues were paid grudgingly or not at all, and going along the cloisters to sing the night office the nuns would strain their ears for the footsteps of marauders or the crackle of a fired thatch.

In 1332 a nun broke her vows and left the convent for a lover. Misfortunes always go in threes, was the comment of the prioress: they might expect two more to play the same game. But after a second apostacy there was a painful Visitation by the bishop, when the prioress was deposed and Dame Emily the novice-mistress, a better disciplinarian, nominated to be her successor. Unfortunately Dame Emily was unpopular, being both arrogant and censorious. Dreading the rule of such a prioress the nuns refused to elect her and chose instead, out of bravado, Dame Isabella Sutthery, the youngest and silliest nun among them. The young and silly can become great tyrants. Dame Isabella proved fanatically harsh and suspicious, scourging the old nuns till they fainted for anguish and inventing such unforeseeable misdemeanours that no one could steer clear of offending. The convent waited, languishing, for the next Visitation, when each nun in her private interview with the bishop could make her report. But though the bishop came and heard, he was still nursing his wrath about their rejection of Dame Emily whom he had nominated, and though Dame Emily herself was the greatest sufferer under Prioress Isabella he answered every plea for a fresh election by saying that the convent having chosen must abide by its choice. It was not till 1345, when Prioress Isabella choked on a plum-stone, that peace and quiet returned, followed by four ambling years of having no history, save for a plague of caterpillars.

In 1349 the Black Death came to Oby.

When Prioress Isabella first began to gasp and turn blue Dame Alicia de Foley framed a vow to Saint Leonard, patron of the convent and of all prisoners, that if their tyrant should die of her plum-stone a spire, beautiful as art and money could make it, should be added to their squat chapel. In her mind's eye it soared up, the glory of the countryside, and she was so absorbed in contemplation that Prioress Isabella's eyes were lolling on her cheeks before Dame Alicia remembered to add to the saint that she would also undertake to pray daily throughout the time of the spire's building for the repose of Isabella's soul.

Persuading the rest of the convent to support her in this vow, working on her relations in the world to contribute towards the expenses, manipulating the bishop into expressing approval (his approval was not really necessary but after the business of Prioress Isabella no one at Oby was going to risk slighting a bishop), arranging for the supply of building materials and making a contract with a band of travelling masons took three years – though her election as prioress enabled her to do all these things more easily. She had been praying for the repose of Isabella's soul for just under a twelvemonth, and the spire, after several false starts and buttressings of the existing tower which was to be its base, was beginning to rise, when at the news that the pestilence had reached Waxelby the masons with one accord scrambled off the scaffolding and went away.

It had been pleasant to kneel on alone after the end of mass, hearing the noise of her spire growing: the whine of the pulleys, the scrape of trowels, the jar as stone after stone was set in its place, the songs and outdoor voices of the masons. But now there was no sound except the March winds hoo-hooing through the gaps, and the thought that the second part of her vow could still be kept was cold comfort. Besides, could she be sure even of that? The pestilence might stop her mouth. Already her treasuress was making it difficult for her to find much time for praying. In the leanest time of year the convent had to be victualled and provided as though to stand a siege. There was wood, meat, meal, fish, oil, spices, candles, serge, wool, and linen to get in, wine and honey, and medicines in case the sickness penetrated their defences. There was fodder for the beasts to be thought of, vinegar for fumigations, charcoal for braziers, and the roof of the infirmary to be re-thatched. The running of the household must be looked into and tightened up, and dues still owing must be got in, and somehow she must increase the convent's stock of ready money, for in times of calamity people will do nothing unless they are paid on the nail for it. Then, too, there was the problem of how best to prepare for the assaults of the poor and needy: these would troop to the wicket, crying out for food, for medicine, for old rags for their sores: they would bring the pestilence to the very gate, and yet they could not be denied, Christ's poor and the plague's pursuivants. Her musing was interrupted by the sound of horses being halted outside the gate-house and a fluster of unfamiliar voices. William de Stoke, whose daughter was a novice in the house, had sent to fetch the girl away, having heard that the pestilence was already at Oby. He had sent a large retinue of servants, and all of them were hungry and required feeding.

While the de Stoke people ate they talked. Though there had been pestilences often enough there had never been, they said, such a pestilence as this. It travelled faster than a horse, it swooped like a falcon, and those whom it seized on were so suddenly corrupted that the victims, still alive and howling in anguish, stank like the dead. The short dusky daylight and the miry roads and the swollen rivers were no impediment to it, as to other travellers. All across Europe it had come, and now it would traverse England, and nothing could stop it, wherever there were men living it would seek them out, and turn back, as a wolf does, to snap at the man it had passed by.

The roads were filled with people fleeing before it. The riders cursed at the travellers on foot, and lashed at them to make way. A fine litter had gone by, said one of the men, and he had asked who was inside it: it was an old Counsellor, one of the retinue answered, and for a long time he had been dying with a slow death that fed on his vitals; but even so, he wished to preserve the live death within him from that other death. Lepers broke out of their hospitals and crutched themselves along with the rest, and people scarcely feared. them. Townsfolk who all their lives had lived in comfort now ran to the forests and fed on snails and acorns and rabbits, tearing them apart and eating them raw; but the Black Death was in the forest, too, and the outlaws lay dead beside the ashes of their fires. There had never been such a press of men going to the ports to take ship for the wars in France: for it was better to die in battle than to die of the Black Death. But in the ports and in the crammed holds of the ships the Black Death found them and killed them before they could be killed by their fellow-men.

Wherever they went, another voice broke in, they would find this new Death waiting for them. Better to stay at home than be at so much trouble to go in search of him. For if you went to another town you heard the bells tolling, and saw the kites gathering, and smelled the stink coming from the burial-pits; and if you went afield, the same stink crossed your path, the ploughman lay rotting under a bush and the plough stood near by, with the spring grass growing up around it as though this year were the same as other years. People were fools, he said, to go in search of a death which would come in search of them. Better to stay under your own roof. Yet that was dismal, too, to sit waiting with your hands dangling between your knees, not daring to pull off your shirt or handle yourself for fear of seeing the tokens come out on your flesh: sometimes like spots, sometimes gatherings as big as plums, but always black because of the poisoned blood within. There was no comfort or pleasure in neighbourliness now: friends scarcely dared look each other in the face, for fear of seeing there the look of death or the look of one who looks on it.

Death drove the best bargain at the market, drank deepest at the tavern, walked in processions, married the bride at the church door. The priest said his *Ite missa est* and already his lips were parched and blackening. The server's *Deo gracias* slid between teeth that chattered with fear. The congregation hurried away, silent, each man staring before him.

But the foot-loose have the best of it, the prioress said to herself, hearing all this talk beyond the window. Better to be one of those masons and run into the jaws of death than to sit behind walls and wait for the Black Death to enter. When the little girl was brought in to make her farewells she said to the child, as desperately as to a grown woman: 'Remember to pray for us here at Oby.' The child burst into tears and clung to her skirts, saying she was afraid. 'Afraid of what, my child?' – 'Afraid of the horses.'

Early in April the pestilence was in Lintoft. It broke out in the miller's house, and immediately the miller of Oby went off with his family and belongings, none knew whither. His departure was no hardship to the peasants: for many years households had dodged the manorial mill-dues, grinding their corn in their private hand-mills; but it was a blow to the convent, and though Dame Blanch, who as cellaress ruled over kitchen and storeroom, said jauntily that when they could no longer make bread they must eat frumenty and be thankful for it, many saints and christian garrisons had thanked God for a handful of parched grain, the other ladies muttered about starvation and the weakness of their teeth. Presently more people in the hamlet began to flit away and another novice was removed by her parents. At each new departure the nuns drew closer together, whispering in corners and hunching up their shoulders as though a cold wind blew in on them, as though they bodily felt the cold breath of rumour, the many stories now current of how the Black Death had dealt with other religious houses. It crept in, and laid a finger on one person; and his sickness spread through the community like fire through a faggot until the smell of death was stronger than the smell of the boiled meat in the kitchen or the incense in the quire. For a while the Rule held out, the imperilled lives were lived to measure, the dark figures shuffled into quire and out again. There were no straying glances, no one spoke to his neighbour: never had the ordinance of silence and self-immurement been better obeyed. But at last the Rule itself faltered, and sagged, and was lost, and the altar was only greeted by desperate visitors, solitary figures grovelling in silence or perhaps suddenly thrusting out a frantic shriek for mercy.

In one house, every monk had died. In another, every monk but one. And that was the worst – that desolate figure on whom the brand of life was scored like an inversion of the brand of death.

If it were I, the prioress thought – if I were left alive and alone under my unfinished spire ... Overcome by her imagination she forced herself to go and sit in the parlour, where the nuns were telling each other that this pestilence was unlike any other, for it killed men rather than women.

The first two to sicken were Dame Emily and a novice, and they died on the same day. That evening Sir Peter Crowe, the convent priest, walked uninvited into the prioress's chamber, where she sat with the treasuress, Dame Helen, and Dame Blanch the cellaress, talking calmly (as one does when all hope is gone) about the quality of some vermilion paint, newly bought for an illuminated book of hours which had been commissioned by Piers de Retteville, descendant in the sixth generation of Gilbert and Adela.

'I am leaving you,' he said.

Her first thought, that he was running away from the pestilence, could not be sustained in the face of his bleak self-assurance. He must have gone out of his mind. He had always been sombre and given to austerities.

'I shall set out tomorrow, as soon as it is light. I am going to Waxelby.'

'To Waxelby?'

It was on the tip of Dame Blanch's tongue to say that they did not need any more dried fish. She blushed, thinking how nearly she had said it, while Sir Peter spoke of how heavy the plague was at Waxelby. Since it had declared itself there two rectors had died, the second only ten days after his predecessor. Most of the friars were sick, of the two chantry priests one had gone mad, the other had run away. And the common people were dying unattended.

'You are going to shrive them? It is a most christian intention – but we here may be dying also. Will you leave us to die unshriven?'

'You must find someone else.'

The prioress stared at her hands. She had never found it easy to brook bad manners.

'I think you should have consulted us before deciding. Like you, we are sorry for the poor people at Waxelby. But in your anxiety about their souls . . .'

'It is not their souls I am thinking of!' he exclaimed. 'I am thinking of the faith. I can't stay idling here while heresy is spreading faster than the pestilence. Do you know what they are doing at Waxelby? – yes, and all over England! Do you realise what they are doing?'

'Dying without the aid of the Church. But how is that a heresy?'

'They are confessing to each other! Yes, and shriving each other, too, I'll be bound.'

'I hope not.'

'It's bound to follow. Give presumption an inch and it will

take an ell. Hodge confesses to Madge and Madge gives Hodge absolution. What is let loose on us, I say?'

'But if there is no priest confession may be made to a secular – for instance in battle. My father once received a confession on the battlefield from another knight, and if he had not heard it a great wrong would have remained without amendment.'

Dame Blanch drew herself up and looked round sternly. It was her pride that she came of a warrior family.

Drawing his hand over his chops Sir Peter assumed an air of patience, and began to expound in easy language the doctrine of the sacraments, of the sacramental virtue which sets the priest apart from the ruck of the world. Pedantic fool! thought the prioress, saying courteously: 'Of course. Undoubtedly. How clearly you put it.'

'We shall miss your explanations,' added Dame Helen with sturdy malice.

'God knows,' cried he, 'I say this without arrogance. Humility is inherent in the priestly office, what can be more humbling than to know that the sacramental work is efficacious without regard of him who performs it? In the hands of the vilest priest, a fornicator, a blasphemer, a sodomite, the sacrament is as much sacramental as in the hands of a saint. But the distinction must be kept. And if the saint were a layman his administration of the sacrament would be void.'

'Surely a saint would know that?' Dame Helen said.

His fingers twitched in his wrath.

'All this is beside the point. The point at issue is . . .'

'Whether you go to Waxelby.'

'No. That is decided. The point at issue is whether we are to leave Holy Church undefended while heresy stalks the land. Yes, and when even a pastoral crook is raised against her, when a bishop himself, a bishop! . . .'

In a horrified whisper he told them how the Bishop of Bath and Wells had written allowing that those at the point of death might confess to a lay person if no priest were available.

'But whom shall we confess to?' asked Dame Blanch. 'For while you are giving absolutions at Waxelby we shall be dying unconfessed and unshriven.'

'That is a secondary consideration. How often must I tell you that I am not concerned with individuals? What matters the ease of a few souls more or less when the faith itself is in danger? It is no longer a matter of who dies shriven or unshriven, comforted or comfortless. What is at stake is whether the Church is to keep her hold over the souls of her children. Think of the future, or try to. Consider the frightful possibility – an England where men and women will die, will die quite calmly, without the assistance of the Church!'

They considered it, moved by his eloquence. Such a future was hard to imagine. It seemed to them that Sir Peter would do better to trust in God and remain at Oby. But they saw it would be useless to say so.

Their silence appealed to him. Presently he began to speak on a milder note, saying how deplorable it was that though God's providence sent these catastrophes upon mankind, mankind was not, as a rule, any the better for them. Then, asking for their prayers, he said farewell.

The convent and its manor lay in the parish of Wivelham. The rector of Wivelham was a young man of good family. He had celebrated one mass in his parish church, looking round with horror on the gaunt grey building in the flat, tow-coloured landscape, and then returned to Westminster. His curate, elderly and decrepit, was not likely to have much time to spare for Oby. A mass a week was as much as they might expect of him; and to supply that he must travel seven miles fasting and seven miles back, or wade the short cut through the marshes. A messenger now sent to him returned with the news that he was sick with an ague. As soon as he could get about he would come to them.

The graves were dug for Dame Emily and the novice; and the prioress told Jesse Figg, the bailiff, that he had better send up a man from the village to dig other graves in readiness. 'They can always be filled up if they are not needed,' she said. The bailiff assured her she need not worry on that score, the graves would soon fill; he added that it would be more satisfactory to dig a large pit, the more so as he could not promise to supply labour for long. After the first two graves had been smoothed over life crept on as usual for a few days. The messenger again returned with word that the curate's ague was abating, that he hoped to come early next week. He did not come, and another nun sickened.

'Sir Peter might just as well have stayed. He would have found plenty to do,' remarked Dame Susanna, the infirmaress. She spoke to a nun called Matilda de Stapleton, who was helping her to powder dried lizards and centaury roots. Presently they began to discuss the convent's latest difficulty, shortage of labour. Being a poor convent Oby could never keep its servants for long and having the village at its door it had come to depend on day-workers. Now these came no longer, the kitchen was reduced to old Mabel and poor Ursula, who was more afraid of what the world could do to her than of any pestilence. Milk was carried as far as the threshold, wood was thrown down in the outer yard, and once some compassionate person left a dozen fowls there, but the rats spoiled them. To Dame Matilda this desertion seemed like revolt. Dame Susanna saw it as lack of christian charity and so was more philosophic. She pointed out that though the Black Death kept away their servants it also kept away beggars. It was some days now since any poor traveller had troubled them for a dole.

II

The Tuft of Wormwood

(*April 1349–July 1351*)

Nowhere does news travel faster than among vagrants. For miles around every wandering beggar knew that the pestilence was among the nuns of Oby. If Ralph Kello had not got drunk he would have known it too. Not that he had drunk either well or deeply; but being cold and hungry the liquor had mounted to his head, and he had spoken so cantankerously that the company at the alehouse let him depart unwarned, thinking, as they watched him stagger off in the moonlight he mistook for morning, that if a clerk took the sickness it would be one proud beggar the less and a seat by the fire the more.

It had been very bad beer, and after walking a few miles he was sick. During the last mile he had seemed to age with every step, his features growing pinched, his jaw drooping, his eyes sinking into his head. Now, even more rapidly than he had aged, he grew young again. The rabbits coming out to feed in the sunrise looked scarcely more innocent and candid than he. Hunger, and another hour's walking, smudged out this glory and by the time he reached Oby he looked his true age, which was thirty-five.

Seeing the unfinished spire he crossed himself and greeted the Virgin, partly in thankfulness that a meal was in sight, partly in thankfulness that this time the pestilence had not got him; for till the vomit had risen in his throat, tasting so unmistakably of sour beer, he had believed himself stricken.

There were some faggots of small wood lying before the gatehouse. He stepped over them and knocked. A party of crows flew up from the roof and one by one returned and settled again; but no one answered. He knocked once more. He noticed a tuft of wormwood growing near by, and he broke off a shoot and began to snuff at it – for his head ached violently. A weasel reared up from the grass and studied him.

At length there was a creaking overhead. A window had opened and an old nun was looking down on him.

'A breakfast, my good man? Yes, if you are not afraid of us. We have the pestilence here.'

His impulse was to run for his life. But self-esteem compelled him to muster up a few words of compassion.

'Yes, we are all shut up here, like knights in a castle. The enemy has broken in, but we aren't overcome yet.'

Later he was to find Dame Blanch's military fantasies as tedious as everyone else did. But now the contrast between the warlike words and the piping voice touched his heart; and looking up (for after her first speech he had stood with head hanging) it seemed to him that the old nun had a face of singular goodness and honesty. She for her part saw a large, raw-boned man with a hooked nose and thick lips; and discerned, as she said later, unmistakable traits of a noble character. He heard himself asking if he could help them. It was a relief to learn that the help required was to carry a message to Wivelham.

'To the curate there, if you will. Beg him to come to us, if only to say one mass. Our priest has left us, for ten days now we have had neither mass nor shriving.'

'My daughter, I am a priest.'

He had thought to himself: Enough to comfort them, and then be off – off before they rise from their knees and begin to ask questions. Perhaps, too, there entered into this hare-brained falsehood an element of superstition; as though by going to meet the pestilence he would insure that it would fly him. Waiting to be let in he had time enough to examine every aspect of his folly, and to quake with fear and to remember that there is no beast of worse omen than a weasel. And yet at the same time he was saying to himself: I am certainly fasting.

Weeping with gratitude, she let him in.

In the sacristy a thin short-sighted nun awaited him with an armful of clothing.

'Is this your largest chasuble?'

'Forgive me! Our sacrist died last week.'

'This one is better. Who will serve the mass?'

She pointed to a boy who stood in the doorway, picking his nose and swaying from foot to foot as he gazed at the silks and embroideries. A nun's child, no doubt: a pupil of the convent would be better disciplined and better dressed. But this was one of those little creatures which trot through a household of women like a pet animal, accepted and neglected as a matter of course. Thirty years ago on just such terms another boy had picked his nose and stared at fine raiment – only it was Fat Maggy he watched, or Janet, or Petronilla, instead of a priest. Between their quarrels they were kind, and when his mother died Petronilla replaced her just as Janet would come forward if Petronilla had gone with a client. But a little boy grows lanky and out of place in a brothel, and so, remembering his mother's ambition, the whores of the establishment clubbed together and sent him to the Canons across the way to be educated and made a clerk of.

The sacrist came forward with the stole. My first mass, he

thought, kissing it. And my last. And of all my sins the deadliest, and of all the negligent idiocies I have fallen into the most idiotic. If I had not grown bald it could not have happened, for I suppose not even the shadow of death could blind these ladies to an untonsured head; but causation tunnels like a mole under the surface of our free will, and because of an attack of ringworm in Toledo I am about to say mass in an English convent where they are dying of a pestilence. And here, very probably, I shall die too. The stole settling round his neck seemed to noose him and lead him on into a new life.

A few hours later it was as a matter of course that he sat with the prioress and the older ladies of the convent telling them of his education among the Black Canons, and of his travels and studies; and falling asleep that night the priest's lodging over the gate-house seemed as familiar as an old cloak.

Long after he was abed Ursula was on her knees in the kitchen, offering up thanks to the Virgin. The glow of the embers silhouetted the cooking-pots on the hearth and lit up the curve of the boy's cheek as he lay before the fire. Now they were safe again, there was a priest in the house, and a man. Her child had served his mass, and so already he and she were linked. He would certainly take notice of the boy, and so in time become aware of the boy's mother. He would speak to her about Jackie. She would not be able to answer, but he would have spoken to her – priest and man he would have spoken to her about her child.

She was cold, and tired, and ageing, and disgraced. Three times she had left her convent for love, and twice she had crept back and lived in penance. Again a craving for love had haled her out into the world, where with a child in her belly and afterwards with the child on her back she had wandered from place to place, the creature of any man who would look at her with a certain look, speak to her in a certain voice. And then, just as before, Christ her bridegroom had waylaid her, more mastering than any man, and she had gone back, cowed, to woo him with abject repentance. This time her convent would not re-accept her: she was sentenced to live in mortification and obedience, but without the veil, and presently she was sent with her child to Oby to live there as a servant. She was a good cook and a feverishly hard worker, and the Oby ladies did not trouble her with any reproaches unless they found insects in the salad – which happened occasionally because lust and tears and wood-smoke had weakened her eyesight; and was serious because in swallowing a live insect one may swallow an evil spirit inhabiting it. Sometimes, when a fit of hysteria took her, Dame Helen would urge her to resist Satan whose bargains, as Ursula must know from experience, were so little worth the purchase; but Dame Helen's exhortations, as Ursula also knew, sprang as much from anxiety lest the convent should lose a cook as concern lest the fiend should gain a soul. This assurance that she was of some value in the world did more than any prayers and fastings to keep her safe in the convent kitchen. For the rest, they were kind enough, and tolerant to the boy; and no one suspected what she suffered at the hands of the Oby laity – the miller's wife with her scorching tongue, the boys who threw stones at the child and scattered dung on her hair. Six years of virtue and security had almost tamed her. Then news of the pestilence came like a yelling of hounds on a renewed scent. At one moment it seemed to her that she had not repented sufficiently and that death might take her before she had had leisure to win God's mercy (there had never been so much to do, even when the bishop came, as now); an hour later the thought of dying without one more taste of the sweet world drove her frantic. Then Sir Peter left; as a man of no account, but his departure created the most frightful of all voids; for the priest stands in the place of God, and when that place is left empty God steps into it, God unmitigated and implacable.

But now the strange priest was lying in the room over the gate.

She crept on her knees towards the child and began to kiss him, furiously and inattentively. Only by kissing or shrieking could she slack the strain of so much thankfulness. The child woke and struck at her with a sleepy arm.

'Don't kiss me so hard, mother. It hurts.'

'Tell me, Jackie, tell me about the new priest. What does he look like? Has he got white teeth?'

'He's got an ugly nose,' said the child. Burrowing into her lap he fell asleep again. For a long while she sat there, staring at the embers with her weak eyes, holding the hot bony immature creature that would one day in his turn become a man.

A man; but being a bastard, never a priest.

'Yes, it is a pity he is a bastard,' said the prioress, answering commendations on her server. 'As you say, he is a clever child. And what could be better than to return as a priest to the house that nurtured you? Such a priest would feel a son's care for everything about the place, he would be interested in its upkeep, see to the repairs, drive the work-people, carry out, may be, projects he had seen others begin. Such a priest,' she added, smiling, 'might even finish my spire.'

She liked Ralph Kello. He was educated, and discreet, and she was grateful to him for arriving when he did, and remaining.

'But who can talk about the future now? Yet if any of us are left alive, and if the world remains, and if Sir Peter dies at Waxelby – which I suppose he is very likely to do – how convenient it would be if you should take his place! Why not, indeed, since God has sent you? We are all convinced of that.'

'I might have been sent by the devil. How are you to know?'

He had woken with a splitting headache and with it a strange feeling of some inner exhilaration and ferment. It must have been that which allowed him to speak so incautiously.

She looked at him and sighed.

'You are too polite to say so. But I can see that you have other ambitions than to bury yourself at Oby.'

He let it go at that. Whether he spoke discreetly or recklessly either way seemed to lodge him more securely in his imposture. For now it was his second week at Oby, and Dame Joan, the short-sighted nun who, all in a flurry at finding herself in the place of the dead sacrist, had tried to fit him with the smallest chasuble, was herself dying. He walked up and down the infirmary, nursing the flask of oil in the crook of his arm. Each time he walked towards her she seemed to have grown smaller and shabbier, like a dying cat. She had lain senseless for many hours; but at the anointing of her feet she had suddenly quivered, making an intense effort to come out of her stupor, and the hand which had been clawing the pallet was extended, blindly caressing the air. That tremor, and that enamoured gesture of the hand, had revealed such an intensity of love that he had stayed by her, thinking that if she recovered her senses it would please her to be godspeeded towards the God she loved so fervently. Or was it that she was ticklish? The vocabulary of the body is full of ambiguities. Be that as it might, he had stayed. The prioress had lingered to thank him, and Dame Susanna, the infirmaress, coming in and out with medicines and linen, gave him esteeming glances. Every action now must fasten him more irrevocably into his perjury.

Perjury, and imposture, and sacrilege. His thoughts, running with unusual lucidity (for by nature he was a heavy and confused thinker), were like a transparent stream. They ran by, and by; and beneath them, like the river-bed, were the facts. He was no priest, and he was here in a house of nuns, absolving the dying, saying mass. The absolutions were void, the rite was sacrilege. He was damning himself and abetting the damnation of others. There, plain enough, was the bottom of the matter, the bottom of the river. But between him and the facts ran this glassy process of thinking, this flow of apprehending how it had all come about.

How could it have happened so? – and again, how could it not? He had not wanted to impose himself on the convent. He had never even felt any particular desire to be a priest. Learning his music-note and his Latin at Holy Cross, enduring so many beatings, so many chilblains, so much hunger and cold and so many bouts of the itch, it had never occurred to him but that he would grow up to be a priest as naturally as he would grow up to be a man. But he had taken it merely as a matter of course, there had been no vocation in it; when he understood the impediment of his bastardy he felt no great regret, and growing up into a man seemed good enough. The Canons had assumed that he would take lesser orders or become a friar; but quitting them he had said only that he would bear it in mind and decide later, after he had ripened his judgement by travel and study. In time the impetus of his schooling had carried him on into lesser orders; and that was reasonable enough, a tidy completion of a course of learning, a practical measure towards a livelihood. The sow's ear does not expect to become a silk purse, but to become pigskin it submits itself to singeings, tannings, and thumpings. In the same way the thumpings of theology had suppled him, and proximity to the priesthood had coloured him; and some of the pigskin he had seen in Spain was really very fine indeed, and when stamped and gilded almost indistinguishable from damask. So he had travelled on into his middle age, with poverty always at his heels and his wits generally contriving to outpace the beast, until that morning when he had stood knocking on a gate, thinking of nothing more blameful than a breakfast. Then an old woman had looked out of a window, and had spoken some fanciful brave words in a piping voice, and his voice, loud and clear and confident, had answered her. *My daughter, I am a priest.* For no reason; he had not even said it as a jest or a cheat. He had just said it – out of complaisance, as one soothes a squalling child, not even troubling to ask what it squalls for. And then Satan, weasel-shaped behind him, had watched him cross the threshold of Oby, walking with priestly dignity and making large signs of the cross.

The dying nun grew smaller and shabbier, but still she did not die. God makes woman to have more endurance than man, because of childbearing. Even in a virgin this endurance is valid. But was it thus in the original creation, God providing even in his unfallen creatures for the Fall, or was it added to Eve at the time of the sentence upon her to obey her husband and bring forth in sorrow? Again, has the bitch more endurance than the dog? And if so, why? For animals are soulless and without either sin or merit, merely obliging or disobliging, which makes it a simple matter for the devil to go in and out of them whenever he pleases. He turned once more towards her, and still she lived. And here he walked up and down, waiting to comfort her departure with a fraud – out of complaisance, as one pats a squalling child.

He began to think of a sermon he might preach one day, showing how if a man be too timid, too scrupulous, too indolent, to run into any mortal sin the fiend can trip him in an act of merit: an alms to a beggar, a cloak thrown over a naked back – but damnation lies at the bottom of the cup. *Thou hast made them to drink of a deadly wine*. That could be the text of the sermon he might preach one day – on the day he was made pope, perhaps!

The woman from the kitchen – she was called Ursula – came to the door with a cup of broth. Catching sight of him she started, and dropped the bowl, and began to wring her hands and cry out that she could see the pestilence in his face. The infirmaress came forward. She too stared at him, and caught her breath. Ursula's cries brought other nuns hurrying. Not since his childhood had he lived among so many women. That, too, and the begetting in some hasty forgotten bed, lay at the bottom of the river. But now the river ran too deep. He could see all these things, but he could not plumb to them.

A little before she died Dame Joan became conscious. It seemed to her that she was floating in a dark place and that a very slow and fitful wind was propelling her westward. Somewhere near by a woman was weeping. She thought she knew the voice and said at last: 'Is that you, Dame Salome?' But as she could only speak in a whisper the other did not hear her and wept on. Dame Joan began to think that she was dead, in which case the weeper must be some poor soul, who naturally would not hear or answer. Yet it did not seem to her that she was rightly dead. Then another noise came into the room, the noise of the death-rattle; and an unmistakable Dame Salome began to call out: 'Come, come! She's dying, Dame Joan is dying!'

They hurried in and took their places round her and began to say the prayers for the dying. One and all they were thankful to be on their knees, murmuring the familiar words. There was nothing in this death to shock them, nothing furious or unmanageable. They were still vibrating from their experience with Sir Ralph. It had been as though their recognition of his sickness had in an instant changed him from a man in his senses to a madman. His knees had given way, he had grovelled on the floor, tearing at his bosom and shuddering. Worst of all, he had seemed incapable of understanding anything they said to him, tossing their words out of his ears like a wounded animal. In the end there was nothing for it but to take hold of him and drag him away to his room over the gate, hoisting and hauling him up the stair.

Staring round on the room, he suddenly freed himself. 'No one is to come near me!' he shouted; and fell face downward on the bed and sank his teeth into the bolster.

He had no idea of sparing them the sight of his agony, it was because he hated them that he roared to them to go away. These women, fluttering and whispering, had done enough with him. It was through them that he had damned himself and lay dying. Even the bolster smelt of them, a shabbily sweet smell.

'No one is to come near me!'

His head was so heavy that he had to lever it up with his fist. The room was almost dark, and it sounded empty. But as he rolled his eyes heavily it seemed to him that a child, a little boy, was there, always flitting away just before his sight could take hold of him.

'No one is to come near me!'

Furious, senseless, melancholy, his roars echoed through the house. It was as though a bull were tethered by the gate-house. Such an heroic man, said Dame Blanch, could be sure of heaven and a good end. Just now Satan was trying him. This only proved how nearly Sir Ralph was a saint, for God constantly permits Satan to have his sport with the saints in their last hours on earth, just as when one has fixed a partridge on the roasting-spit one throws the feathers to the cat.

But shout and command as he might, the kitchen-woman always came back. He knew her by her shuffling gait, and by the smell of smoke and grease that came in with her. She came and went. Her hands were hard, like tongs. Sometimes she cajoled him, sometimes she spilt broth down his neck, sometimes she cried.

She was the kitchen-woman. She came and went. The other

one, the black man, never stirred out of his corner. The other one was Death. Death was a burly man-cook, who breathed heavily. His hair was frizzled; between his black lips the tip of a red tongue wandered like a flame among charred logs; at his girdle dangled an iron hook. Hour by hour he watched the cauldron boiling and scumming, and when the right time came he struck his hook into the pot and lifted out a lump of meat. No sooner was the meat lifted up through the steam than it putrefied, and began to quiver with worms and then to shrivel and then to fall into dust. Death watched the pot patiently, biding his time. The hook was plunged in again, seeking and finding. Though there was no fire under the cauldron it boiled perpetually, for it was licked invisibly by the breath of hell-fire.

'I am damned, damned, damned!'

They sent for the curate of Wivelham but he was dying: of his ague, said the messenger, laughing foolishly. Dying of ague, think of that!

'How the priest roars out that he is damned,' said Mabel the scullion to Ursula.

'It is his fever burning him.'

Jackie, chewing a bone in his corner, looked up and asked: 'How can a priest be damned?'

'Easy enough,' Mabel answered. 'Why, have you never seen the picture in Waxelby church, the picture of the Last Judgement? There is a priest there, tied in a faggot with naked women, and the devils are wheeling them away in a barrow. A priest can be damned.'

Ursula wandered about the kitchen, picking things up and wiping them and setting them down again, restless with the mechanical industry of exhaustion.

'Presently he will leave off bawling. Then he will die.'

'No!'

The word had broken from Ursula like the twang of a bow-string. It echoed in the smoky roof of the kitchen. She brushed the back of her hand across her lips, and crossed herself. With her round eyes, her long face, her long yellow teeth, she looked like a hare.

'Yes, Ursula, he will. Simon Ragge died just so. For three days he bawled and burned. Then on the fourth day he died. He too was a big strong man, just such another as our priest.'

Ursula took an iron pot and began to scrape the grease off it. The pot sounded hollowly; as she scraped harder and faster it gave out a continuous groaning boom, and so neither of the women heard Dame Susanna come in. Her face was exceedingly pale, and she crossed herself repeatedly.

'Ursula, Ursula! He is saying it again.'

'I'm coming, I'm coming. Leave it to me, madam.'

She threw down the pot and hurried after the infirmaress. Still resounding, the pot rocked to and fro like a dying animal.

Half-way up the gate-house stair the infirmaress turned back. She leaned close down over Ursula, and seized her wrist and cried: 'But suppose it were true?'

'That he is damned, madam? How can we tell? Many are damned. Sir Peter told us that out of seven six will go to hell and burn everlastingly. It is God's will, and no affair of ours, if the priest be damned.'

'No! Not that! The thing that is worse – the thing he says over and over again: that he is no priest.'

'But he talks about a blackamoor cook standing in the corner. He points to him and says, "Now he has it, now he has it!" That is not true.'

'N-no.'

'Neither is the other. Now let me go in, for I understand a man.'

He was lying on his back staring at the flies that buzzed overhead. In a reasonable voice he said:

> *'Ipsa dies alios alio dedit ordine Luna*
> *Felicis operum.'*

She had never been a learned nun: the flesh had given her no time for that; and in the long years of drudgery all her Latin had fallen away and it was as much as she could do to muster up a creed and a *Salve Regina*. There was a louse crawling on his cheek. She pounced on it and nipped it between her nails.

> *'Septima post decimam felix et ponere vitem*
> *Et prensos domitare boves et licia telae*
> *Addere. Nona fugae melior, contraria furtis.'*

Dame Susanna would have been edified by all this beautiful Latin. But the cowl does not make the monk. For all his Latin the man who lay there was no priest. The admission came out, tumbled among his other ravings, among the black cook and the Black Canons and the forge where the two Catalans laboured at the bellows, and the bear, and the deadly wine, and the weasel; and there was nothing to distinguish it from the rest of his nonsense, only that it was true. She knew in her bones it was true. She began to smooth his black hair. The fever had scorched it, it was harsh as dried bents, and stank. He moved his gaze and looked at her with a dull half-recognising mistrust.

'My love, my sweet falcon!' she said.

The bell began to ring for compline. Doors opened and shut, the nuns were going into quire. He started and sat up in bed, striking her away.

'Do not hate me, do not fear me! I swear I will never tell it.'

For a moment he seemed to look at her with his full senses. Then wearily he lay down again and turned his face to the wall and began to weep. She squirmed on to the bed and lay down beside him, caressing him and pulling out her breasts as though for a child. For a while he tried to shrug her off, at last he resigned himself to her, and lay sighing in her arms.

'My falcon, my heart's comfort, my love!'

She heard the nuns singing and the wind stirring the willows, and ruffling the flood-water in the ditches that bordered the causeway. While compline lasted she could hold him in her arms and be appeased. No one would miss her. And there was no great sin in it for he was no priest and she was no longer a nun.

It was true, no one missed her; and if anyone wondered that Ursula should take such pains over a dying man, the answer was easy: for Ursula, poor soul, was always a hard worker. To scour the grease off a platter that will be greasy again tomorrow, to scrub a board till it is clean enough to be dirtied once more, to wheedle a dying man into swallowing broths that he will presently vomit up again, such labours were what one associated with Ursula. It was true that she persisted in saying that Sir Ralph would recover; but Dame Susanna declared that he would die; and as she was the infirmaress she must be the better judge.

He would die. Everyone would die, for it was the end of the world. The bailiff's wife was dead, Roger the wood-reeve and three of his children, Ragge and his two sons. Two more nuns had died: Dame Helen the treasuress (an invaluable nun, for she kept all the accounts, never forgetting a sum or a date); and Dame Alice Guillemard who was to have made the book of hours for Piers de Retteville; and another novice was dying.

'Very soon,' said Dame Agnes the novice-mistress, 'there will be none left but us old hags.'

The prioress started. Though she was in her forties she did not feel herself a hag. Dame Agnes apologised for disturbing her meditations.

'No, no! You did not disturb me. A flea bit me in the breast. As it happens, I was just about to remark that God calls those whom he loves best.'

For all that, Dame Agnes's words had startled her from a meditation. She had been reflecting that both the novices had brought good dowries, and therefore the house would be the gainer by their early deaths. Such speculations are unseemly in the shadow of death, yet it is usually in the shadow of death that one is forced to entertain them. Provisioning her household to resist the pestilence she had bought in a rising market, and to buy at all she had been forced to pay money down. Summer was coming on, but because of the pestilence on the manor no work had been done, and there would be little revenue from crops or livestock this year. She would not get much from the convent's outlying property either: tithes, tolls, rents – the pestilence would be reason or excuse for their non-payment, and she dared not go to law for them; Prioress Isabella (for whose detestable soul she must still pray God's mercy) had given Oby its stomachful of lawsuits. Then Dame Beatrix and the other Dame Helen and the novice Cecily, who had had the sickness and recovered from it, would need dressings, salves, extra diet and strong beer, and the same must be given out among the work-people. Then there would be the cost of a new priest. This must needs be a considerable item; she would scarcely find another who would tolerate the shabby hangings and broken floorboards of the gate-house lodging which had appealed to Sir Peter as a mortification and which Sir Ralph had not been granted time to complain about. Indeed, as the pestilence wrought such particular havoc among men, priests would be at a premium and able to demand whatever they wished – and the same would apply to masons and carpenters. She had been counting on the book of hours to bring in a good sum, but this was crossed off by the death of Dame Alice Guillemard, while the colours and the gold leaf had still to be paid for. It was possible, of course, that in this downpour of deaths some legacies would come to the convent, and bequests for the saying of masses for the dead; but these were possibilities only; and at best time must go by and many formalities before they could be paid. Thinking of her spire she said to herself that jackdaws were likely to be the only builders she would see on it.

Till now she had never had to face poverty. Oby was not a wealthy house, but it generally had a margin between its revenues and its outgoings. Lying far from any city, cut off from the world by marshes and heathland, its expenditure on transport was disproportionately high, and she had often listened to Dame Helen and Dame Blanch discussing whether it was worth while to send further in order to buy cheaper; but they always concluded by agreeing that isolation benefited them in the long run, for it kept away visitors and pilgrims, and allowed them to be shabby without being shamed.

It had been an easy house to rule; remembrance of Prioress Isabella lasted on and reconciled the nuns to leading a humdrum life, a life stagnant but limpid. So they had lived. So, now, they were dying. For the extravaganza of death that was sweeping their world away suggested no changes to them except the change from being alive to being dead. They kept to the Rule, punctually offering God his regular service of prayer and praise. In the same spirit they also expected their meals to be as plentiful, and punctual as before. 'It is bad enough to be without a priest. Surely we need not be without purslane,' she had heard Dame Agnes remark to Dame Salome, who answered with a story of the piece of eggshell she had found in her pancake. If they had panicked, she could have been braver. If they had rebelled and disputed, she could have felt sure of her power to rule them. But with a meek desponding fortitude they went on waiting to die while she with her knees knocking under her was asking herself how they could manage to live.

When the worst of the pestilence was past she called a meeting in chapter. Ninety years' tolerance had not made the converted dove-house any more tolerable. It was cramped, and full of cross-draughts, and between the lofty roof and the empty room below such an echo was created that it seemed as if every dove ever hatched on the manor were haunting it. Consequently, it was seldom used, and only for the most formal and unpleasant occasions, a bishop's visit, the announcement of a new impost, the administration of rebukes and punishments. The nuns now climbed the stairs and sat themselves down on the cobwebbed benches. No doubt they would hear an admonition on the narrow space of time left them on an earth where, as in the time of Noah's deluge, the waters were rising, and of how that space should be filled with prayers and final meditations. They were surprised to hear themselves urged to be more economical: to darn little holes before they became large ones, to be sparing of fuel, to keep a sharp lookout for moths. Their prioress's voice, which was thin and reedy, contended with the flustering echoes. 'Poverty, my daughters, is nothing to fear. As the brides of Christ it is our portion. We must prepare ourselves for poverty.' Her eyes, set shallowly in her pale, plump face, desperately perused their stolid ranks, but saw no answering alarm.

She talked on and on, darting from one precept of housewifery to another, the high price of pins, the extravagance of little loaves, the wastage of candles. She told them how much wood was thieved yearly off the convent lands, and how the cost of living must certainly rise and how the convent's income must as certainly fall. She spoke of the increase in beggars they must look to face, and of the cost of a priest which must now be met from their general income as the bridge over the Nene had given way, and the de Rettevilles, not getting the profit of the tolls, naturally refused to repair it. And again she asserted that poverty was nothing to fear. Being so appalled by what she had to say she found it hard to leave off. When at last she had ended, her senior nuns assured her that they did not fear poverty in the least.

A sensation of unmitigable loneliness crushed her spirit. She lived with these women and she would end her days among them; yet she understood them no better than they understood her. There can hardly be intimacy in the cloister: before intimacy can be engendered there must be freedom, the option to approach or to move away. She stared at their faces, so familiar and undecipherable. They are like a tray of buns, she thought. In some the leaven has worked more than in others, some are a little under-baked, some a little scorched, in others the spice has clotted and shows like a brown stain; but one can see that they all come out of the same oven and that one hand pulled them apart from the same lump of dough. A tray of buns, a tray of nuns . . .

After a difficult silence Dame Agnes suggested that they should proceed to appoint a treasuress to take the place of Dame Helen. She suggested Dame Salome. Dame Salome begged that she should not be chosen, saying truly that she had no talent for business. But the appointment was unanimously urged: plainly because of a general realisation that the position of treasuress was going to be uncomfortable, and Dame Salome one of those mild pillowy women who can be squeezed into tight places.

Irked by the sense that a responsibility which they had never bargained for had been imposed on them the nuns left the chapter-house in silence. When they began to talk again it was all of religious matters; relics, vows, and cases of conscience. By the evening it had somehow been agreed that if death spared those still alive they should go in pilgrimage to Walsingham.

Dame Blanch began to rub her hands up and down her thighs, a trick of hers when she felt pleased or excited. In fancy she saw herself riding under an archway, and heard the horse's hoofs ring on the pavement. This, too, would come of the pestilence, just as the pestilence had brought about the chivalrous and miraculous arrival of Sir Ralph. Sir Ralph was still alive. He might even seem to be recovering, Dame Susanna said, but in truth he was only lingering. Though he could not lead their pilgrimage his soul would benefit by their prayers, unless, indeed, already released from purgatory he watched them from some heavenly turret. Craving for adventures, Dame Blanch had enjoyed the Black Death. She had been excited, dauntless, and even sought-after. Her chatter about knights and fortresses had suddenly seemed heartening and authentic, and when she assured them that the battlefield smelled much worse than the infirmary because of all the entrails, no one remembered to remember that in fact she had entered religion at the age of ten, having seen no nearer approximation to warfare than a provincial tournament.

The pilgrimage of thanksgiving did not, of course, take place. Except to Dame Blanch it was merely something to talk about and a path of escape from thinking about economies. Sir Ralph's recovery took its place as a subject for conversation, for soon even Dame Susanna admitted that he was better, and well enough to leave his room and sup in the prioress's chamber. They made a little feast for him, and Dame Blanch as cellaress could not be prevented from assuring him at every mouthful how carefully it had been chosen for him and how much good he would gain from it, nor from reminding him jocosely how he had first come to them for a breakfast. He grew paler and paler. His face twitched; he put down a chicken-wing only half-chewed. Supper being ended Dame Salome and Dame Susanna rose and asked leave to retire. Dame Agnes sat on, and so did Dame Blanch. There was an awkward pause.

'Well, well,' said Dame Blanch too genially, 'now that supper is over, why do we not come to business?'

Thinking of the expenses at stake the prioress looked at the window where a white cloud sailed peacefully above the insignificant horizon. A little more geniality, a few more encouragements, and he would refuse. Already there had been Dame Agnes's stories of her squirrel and Dame Salome's conundrums. How could an educated man, fastidious, too, with sickness, contemplate a future of such company? Still looking at the cloud, she said in a flat defeated voice that they now had definite confirmation of Sir Peter's death, and wished to offer him Sir Peter's place. In a voice equally flat and defeated he accepted the offer. He seemed to be accepting because it was the quickest way to end a painful evening and get to bed.

To Ralph Kello it also seemed like that. He had entered Oby on an impulse and on an impulse he now engaged himself to stay. But the first impulse had been something spontaneous and hardy; this was a mere trickle, as though the last very small drop had sidled out of a tilted cask. He felt like an empty cask. Nothing was left him but an enormous consciousness of fatigue and a few ghostly sensualities: the relief of lying down, momentary pleasures from the smell of wine or spices, a momentary sensibility to colour. In the body's combat with sickness his mind, a poor ally, had gone down and been trampled to death. His conviction of damnation had lost all meaning, and so had his old ambitions, his curiosities, his resentment against that fatality of being a nobody's bastard which had barred the chancel door against him. He would stay quietly on at Oby, doing a priest's duty since that was what they required of him, and being housed and fed. And what would be, would be.

Having secured her priest the prioress could give a more judicial mind to examining him. Perhaps he was not quite all she had supposed: not so sympathetic, not so capable – in fact, slothful and rather glum. But she had got him, and he seemed prepared to put up with his floorboards till he fell through them, and her nuns liked him, and – perhaps his greatest recommendation – he had become hers with very little trouble. As the Black Death moved northward and its shadow rolled away she looked round on her landscape, summing up what was lost and what remained. Of her twelve nuns four had died, and two novices; and two other novices whose parents had taken them away to escape the sickness had died at home. However, she could reckon on their dowries, their parents could scarcely default on such an obligation. Of the four dead nuns two had been under twenty. As Dame Helen would have said, they had eaten very little of their provender. Were Dame Helen alive now, how shrewdly and with what impartial pleasure she would be casting her balance of profit and loss! No doubt she would be allowing for many more losses than were apparent to the prioress; even so, the final balance might not be altogether discouraging. On the manor the Black Death's encroachments were unequivocal. Many of the best men were dead and many of the ablest women: Big Roger, the three Ragges, Baldie Shipperson, the cooper and his boy, Anne and Katharine Noot, the best reapers on the manor, and Emme who washed sheepskins and made candles, and Joan Scole and Joan Pick. Later on, when the hay was in, a requiem must be said for the repose of all these souls. But what sort of hay crop would it be? For months the cattle had been straying where they pleased, eating what they found: hay, rye, or winter barley. Her thoughts having taken a more cheerful turn since the affair of a priest was settled, she supposed that if the beasts had eaten the crops they would at least be the fatter for it, so that what was lost one way was gained another.

She felt less confident, and more than ever regretful for Dame Helen who had been so clever at overcoming difficulties, when she had talked to Jesse Figg, the convent's bailiff. The hay, he said, wasn't so bad. But who was to win it? She ran her finger down the roll whence the names of the dead had been scored off. She repeated the names of the living.

'They wouldn't do it, Madam Prioress. Not now. Flog, flay, or fine, they wouldn't do it.'

'Not do it? What do you mean?'

'They're thinking of themselves. They're behind-hand on their own work, and that's what they'll do first. Pease and beans, that's what they'll plant – pease and beans to stay them through the winter.'

'But work for the manor must come first,' Dame Salome interposed.

'Not this season, Madam Treasuress. If they cheated the sickness one year, they say, it wasn't to starve the next. That's what they're saying. And it's the same everywhere. Ours are no worse than any others. Maybe they'll come along after they've looked out for themselves,' he added. 'But I daresn't drive them.'

Why should they be driven, she thought maternally. They are only stupid children. Persuasion will bring them back. And she took particular pains over the three masses for the souls of the manor's dead. The nave was cleared of its lumber. Garlands were hung along the screen and the boy Jackie was sent up a ladder to dust the rood-loft. The west door was forced open, its rusty hinges whining like an old dog with rheumatism; for the nave was so small, Brian de Retteville having thought only of the nuns' quire beyond the screen, that it would not hold all the worshippers, and the later comers would have to kneel outside.

The summer air streamed in, warm and purifying, and the garlands rustled and tapped against the wood. She heard the people coming in, whispering among themselves. They were comparing the convent's church with their parish church at Wivelham and with the friars' great church at Waxelby. They snuffed approvingly. She had ordered that the incense was not to be spared; but even so it could not mask the odour of sweat and poverty that came in with them. The candles on the altar burned with a pure scent, their smoke and the clouds of incense spun a visible blue on the air. The singing, too, was excellent: a small body of tone but very pure and accurate. Only Sir Ralph did not strike her as doing his part as well he might. His voice was as carelessly pitched, and he gave an impression of being hurried.

Afterwards there was a distribution of small mutton pies, and a child was heard crying because he had not seen the convent ladies. 'I want to be a nun, I want to be a nun!' he lamented.

This innocence was often recalled among the nuns, the more tenderly because at that time the children on the manor were being peculiarly tiresome and ill-behaved. With parents either dead or still sickly, they were running wild, thieving, maiming, and destroying. They killed the convent's doves and roasted them on spits; they swarmed through the reed fence into the orchard and broke the trees; they overturned the beehives; they threw a dead dog into the fish-pond; during office hours they marched up and down singing lewd choruses to an accompaniment of bird-rattles and old cauldrons. At first they had come to the convent to hunt Ursula's Jackie. Though he was better-grown than most of his peers, being better housed and fed, he was timid and backward. When he heard them coming he turned pale and ran. But one day when his mother was not there to protect him they caught him and dragged him away, saying that they intended to pluck, skin, and roast him. Late that same evening he came back, bruised, filthy, tattered, and a changed boy: bragging of all the mischief he had done and all the enormities he had witnessed. After that there was no keeping him from their company. He feared them as much as ever, but his fear had turned itself inside-out and now he was a ringleader among them.

Ursula's complaints became so tedious to all who listened to them that finally the prioress decided that it was time Sir Ralph took the boy and made a clerk of him.

At this time she was making many decisions. Early in the new year Dame Blanch had a fit, and became childish – a noisy and rollicking childishness which imposed a great strain on the decorum of the younger nuns. As she could not fulfil her post as cellaress she was retired and the other Dame Helen took her place. Dame Blanch's relations in the world had not troubled about her for years, but in that summer, as ill luck would have it, Humphrey de Fanal rode to Oby to visit his aunt and to present a small reliquary containing a tooth of one of the Holy Innocents to the house where his daughter had ended her short life. Dame Blanch happened to be in one of her more rational moments. Humphrey could see no reason why she should have been deposed and put away in the infirmary and she, in her rambling explanation, chivalrously defending the prioress's decision, did not supply him with one. His aunt was ill-used. His daughter was dead. That too was a form of ill-usage. He left Oby in dudgeon, taking the reliquary with him.

To lose so interesting a relic, even though one had never really possessed it, was bad enough. A more serious loss was to follow. One of the two novices who had been taken away at the time of the Black Death and who had afterwards died at home was the daughter of William de Stoke, and Humphrey and William were brothers-in-law. Presumably Humphrey said something to his sister about the treatment of their aunt. The de Stokes, who supplied a yearly provision of wine as part of their daughter's dowry, defaulted. This was the more disquieting as the parents of the other novice who had died at home had from the first demanded her dowry back, alleging that between leaving Oby and dying the girl had changed her mind and been betrothed. These parents were of no great social standing, there was little hope of shaming them into a more religious frame of mind. With the de Stokes it was different. They had a reputation to keep up; moreover, by sending one consignment of wine after their daughter's death they had admitted the obligation. So argued the elder ladies of the house, supporting their prioress in her sharp if rather sketchy conviction that something must be done about it, and could best be done by means of the bishop.

Sir Ralph was asked to give his advice, and said that they had best get a legal opinion. Dame Agnes, who always preferred to disagree with her prioress, now reminded her how in the days of Prioress Isabella, God rest her soul, the bishop had been worse than useless to them.

'That was the old bishop. There is a new bishop now.'

'A new broom sweeps clean,' Dame Salome pronounced. 'Which reminds me, dear Mother, we must have a new broom. The passages are really quite filthy. Of course Ursula is growing very short-sighted.'

'I have treated her with euphrasy water, but I don't think it has done her much good,' said Dame Susanna.

'Sea-water is best. If only we were near the sea!' Dame Beatrix exclaimed; and she was telling them how the Cornish fishermen preserve their sight with sea-water when Dame Agnes interrupted, remarking that they seemed to be wandering from the point and adding that as the bishop was a new man he would probably be too busy just now to spare much attention for a nunnery.

The prioress stiffened. She was loath to give up the bishop, because if he would not act for them they would have to pay fees to a lawyer.

'I remember, my daughters, that in the time of Prioress Isabella the bishop was prejudiced against us because he thought we had shown too much independence in refusing Dame Emily. We don't want to get a name for independence.'

'But as you yourself pointed out, dear Mother, this is a different bishop. It is unlikely that he would know anything about Dame Emily's affair.'

'I still maintain that we were justified in . . . '

Haled back from Cornwall they were now heading towards a discussion of the rights and wrongs of Dame Emily. Sir Ralph folded his arms and coughed.

'There is another consideration to bear in mind. We do not know how this new bishop feels about dowries. He may not approve of them.' They were silent, their attention riveted by this extraordinary surmise.

'Obviously, dowries are expedient. Ladies cannot lead the religious life with decency if they are to be beggars and paupers. But nevertheless there are some extreme churchmen who deny this, and say that monastics should be apostolically poor. Fancies of this sort delight the laity, who are only too willing to learn that they have no obligation to support the religious. All this is in the wind now, and perhaps our new bishop may not wish to mix himself up in a squabble about dowries.'

They are all the same, thought the prioress. I might be listening to Sir Peter. She said:

'I really do not see how we can live on air.'

At the same moment Dame Salome began to explain how very galling it would be for those families who paid dowries to see others going scot-free. In the end, she pointed out, no one would pay anything at all.

'That is why I advise you to consult a lawyer, who is less likely to act opportunistically than a bishop. Make ye friends with the Mammon of Unrighteousness and he will receive you into everlasting habitations.'

'And do you really think that the bishop might refuse to take up our case?'

'I think he might even forbid you to proceed in it.'

Sir Ralph went back to his lodging and sat down with a sigh of relief. He thought that the bishop had been fended off for the present. He had no wish to obtrude himself on bishops.

Having sighed with relief he grinned with pleasure. It had been enjoyable to throw this cat among his ladies, whom just now he was finding almost intolerable. His grudge against them began when he had to teach Jackie. He did not mind the boy so much; but teaching Jackie exposed him to Ursula's gratitude, and he disliked Ursula a great deal. His dislike was increased by a morbid apprehension that he would come to dislike her more and more. It alarmed him to be feeling such loathing for such an insignificant person, to catch himself avoiding the sight of her, leaping aside from the thought that a hair in the soup might be one of her hairs, or sitting in his room like a prisoner because he fancied he could hear her breathing outside the door. Once, when Dame Susanna had spoken of how devotedly Ursula had nursed him during his sickness, he had been compelled to lean from the window and vomit.

In songs and romances an apostate nun may be a romantic figure. God's Mother becomes her proxy in the convent and pins up the curtain before her frailties; but in real life she is a drab like any other drab, nursing her baby and eyeing her lover and the tankards from the tavern doorway. Ursula at Oby, among loyal nuns, Ursula with her sly sad glances and her hot breath, was an indecency. She was there like a grub in an apple. What about yourself? – asked a rapid voice. True enough; and reason enough why he should hate the sight of her. Now she was for ever pestering him with hopes that Jackie was a good scholar, and fingering him with gratitude and little services. So it was no wonder that his exasperation enlarged itself, and took in the nun's boy and the loyal nuns as well. When the prioress invited him to make one of the expeditions to consult a lawyer he felt as much relief at a holiday from Ursula as on the score of evading the bishop. The bishop could not be everlastingly evaded, sooner or later he must come to Oby on a Visitation; but half a loaf is better than no bread; and every month that postponed the bishop weathered him more naturally into the Oby landscape. He had done all in his power to encourage the prioress to make this expedition. Being a woman and a natural gad-about she had not really needed encouragement. Being a woman in authority, though, and a natural featherhead, nothing could nail her to a decision, and not till the morning when they set out, the prioress, Dame Helen, and himself, did he feel secure that things would go as he hoped. For a long time the problem of a suitable bower-woman to wait on the ladies had kept them dangling over the bishop's lap: then in the nick of time came Pernelle Bastable. Pernelle was a widow, childless, and with just enough wealth and more than enough high spirits not to want another husband. She boarded herself at a convent, till the convent was rebuked for keeping too many boarders, when, as Pernelle was only a small-fry person, she was sent away. After trying the amenities of two other convents she applied to Oby. The money she could pay for her board was not much, but the agility with which she took a swarm of bees during her interview of application convinced Dame Salome that Pernelle would prove a good pennyworth. She had too her own horse and saddle; and scarcely had she done with exclaiming over the delight of being settled and tranquil at last before the horse was saddled and Pernelle hooded for another journey.

The August sun was climbing lazily out of the mists when they set out. Watching their departure, Dame Blanch received her last disillusionment: Sir Ralph had a deplorable seat. The thought of that pilgrimage to Walsingham returned to her, her fancy of riding under an archway, hearing the horsebells jingle and smelling the wholesome sweat of her mount. Now they were riding towards the Lintoft heath and she was left behind, an old woman supping gruel and supported by pillows. There would be no pilgrimage to Walsingham, no adventures by the way, no fording of rivers, no wandering through forests, no castles. She would end her days still a prisoner, among silly women a silly old woman. She ripped open her pillow and began to throw handfuls of feathers about the room, weeping and screaming as she did so. The feathers flew into her open mouth. Then the usual pattering footsteps came patiently pattering to the infirmary, and Dame Susanna bent over her, holding her wrists with her soft hands and saying that she really must not excite herself, that no harm was likely to befall their prioress even though she was obliged to go on a journey. When she lay back exhausted, Dame Susanna began to pick the feathers out of her mouth.

The prioress had decided that the lawyer should be consulted in York, saying that it would not be judicious to be consulting lawyers in the cathedral city of their own bishop, and adding that though York seemed a long way off she had a cousin there with whom they could lodge with no expense beyond a few gratuities to the household. In fact, she wanted to examine the minster.

Though it would be painful to see fine architecture while her spire was halted and unlikely to go further, the pain would be a small price for the pleasure of seeing something new. She looked back. A rise of ground had already obliterated Oby. A spire would be visible from here, giving a soul and a reason to the country, and any traveller would bless her for it. But her spire, however lovely from a distance and lovely in itself, might disappoint that traveller as he came nearer, and saw it in its relation to the body of the building. That is the curse of having to work on someone else's foundation. The awkwardness of an earlier generation will assert itself through later additions, like an original sin. It might be possible to lengthen the nave, or seemingly to lengthen it by adding a portail to the west door. If the nave were lengthened, the spire would be more nearly centred and the disparity between height and length less apparent. Meanwhile Pernelle Bastable was chattering about Lincoln. She had been there, it seemed; but only to eat eels and buy a lined gown and visit a nephew.

'No Jews now,' she chirruped, 'to waylay poor little lads and hang them up in cellars. It was a good day for England when they were packed off. My grandfather – he was a ship's captain – saw a whole shipload of Jews spilled and drowning off Wittesand. The waves were speckled with their bales and parcels bobbing up and down. My grandfather cast a hook and line, and hauled up one of the bales, and inside it there was a gold cup, and baby-clothes of finest linen, and little padded caps with furred ears, little gloves – christian babies, my grandfather said, had no such gear.'

'Poor things!' Dame Helen said.

A hook . . . a hook fastening in a bale and dragging it up from the boiling surge. A hook dragging up a body, and the body corrupting as soon as the air touched it. That is what I dreamed of in my sickness, Sir Ralph thought. A moment later Pernelle Bastable dismounted, having caught sight of some mushrooms.

'They won't be here on our way back,' she remarked wisely.

By the next day they were well inland. A light rain fell, the apples shone on the boughs. Their road, mounting and descending through a rich rolling landscape, continually presented them with new things to admire; and after the sad fen country round Oby, to be travelling through this landscape so full of plenty and variety was like turning the pages of an illuminated psalter.

At the inns Pernelle Bastable showed all the wiles of an experienced traveller, calling for hot water, demanding chickens and pillows, following the hostler to the stable. 'It is wonderful what God sends us,' remarked Dame Helen. 'First a priest, now a Pernelle. We should have done badly without her, for we could scarcely shout and bustle as she does.' The prioress agreed, thinking that left to herself Dame Helen would indeed have done badly; for she always agreed with every statement and fell in with every suggestion.

It was a late afternoon when they first caught sight of the minster: dominating the city, as Pernelle pointed out, like a hen brooding her chickens. If it isn't a hen it's a goose, thought the prioress. The journey had been delightful, but now it was over, and the proximity of the lawyer dashed her spirits. She felt exhausted with travelling, and even more exhausted by the atmosphere of rustic inferiority which she must breathe, it seemed, whether she travelled or stayed at home. When her hostess, Marie de Blakeborn, whose first husband had been a de Foley, welcomed her with the news that cousin Thomas, the prior of Etchingdon, had heard she was coming and would sup with them that night, her first impulse was to plead fatigue and take refuge in bed. She had not seen Thomas for twenty years. During those years he had become more and more distinguished, while she had lived at Oby. But when she saw him the prior of Etchingdon was so little changed that she began to think that she might not be much altered either.

'Look at us! How well we've both got on,' he said, in the manner she so well remembered: a manner at once warm and insincere, but with an insincerity which was deeply flattering, since it implied a common indifference to what wounded less enlightened self-esteems. She laughed without a shade of mortification.

'The prior of Etchingdon! The prioress of Oby! Solomon and the Queen of Sheba!'

'The goose-girl and the goose-boy! But you are luckier, you don't have to herd a mixed flock of geese and ganders.'

He began to mock at the incommodities of the Gilbertine Order, telling of his quarrel with the nuns, who were supposed to see to the victualling of the monks, but supplied them with nothing but soup.

'I reminded the dear creatures of their vow of obedience. The next day the cabbage soup had radishes in it – two and a half radishes (we counted them) for each man.'

It was the same old story of kitchen and buttery; but as he told it the greed of his monks, the peevishness of his nuns, was transfigured into the grotesque. Fired into wanting to have something to recount also, and forgetting all about the lawyer, she began to consult him about the spire and the problem of reconciling it to the existing building. He pulled out his writing materials and she sketched the ground-plan with the belfry jutting artlessly from the north-west corner. She might lengthen the nave, he said, and balance Brian de Retteville's old stump by a porch to the south; then she would have balance and yet avoid that pedestrian symmetry which made so many of the new friary churches appear to have been designed by grammarians. He went on to say that the transition from the stump to the spire would call for management.

'I thought of doing it rather like this.'

The rest of the party saw the resemblance between the cousins, and felt that the tie of blood excused this monopolisation of the guest of the evening.

'And your country is flat?'

'Flat as a trencher.'

'You will bring it to life. What I like so much about your design is its unanimity. It looks as though from the very first you had seen it as a whole.'

'I did.'

She told him of her vision when Prioress Isabella choked on the plum-stone and turned blue, adding: 'But I shall have prayed her into heaven long before I can get on with the spire.'

God forbid, he said devoutly. If lack of ready money were the obstacle, that could be overcome tomorrow. York was full of the most worthy usurers.

She answered that she dared not incur any more debts. 'For I know how it would be!' she exclaimed, heedless now whether or no she exposed the poverty of her house. 'The interest would fall due, and just at that moment the floods would carry off our corn-shocks, or the King would ask us for three men-at-arms, or the roof would fall in, or our church at Lantock would burn to the ground and we should have to rebuild it.'

'I am sure that would be a great improvement. Have you many spiritualities?'

'One at Lantock near Northampton and one in Cambridgeshire.'

'That's not enough. I must find you some more.'

'I would rather you took those we have. They are the curse of my life. The tithes are never paid us unless we drag them out like teeth, and the vicars are always in some trouble or other. God does not wish his nuns to own spiritualities.'

He tapped his bald head with a bony forefinger.

'Listen, my dear prioress. All this can be managed. Etchingdon has just appropriated another church. We will do all the business for you, and you shall have half the revenues.'

'How much for the vicar?' she enquired.

'Nothing at all. We don't propose to put one in, at any rate for the present. Since the pestilence it is impossible to find a spare priest at a reasonable price. People think of nothing but money,' he said, 'and what do they do with it when they've got it? Spend it hoggishly on themselves, or endow chantries for their souls, which is really only a rarefied self-indulgence. No doubt we are much pleasanter people than our forebears. But compared to them how mean-spirited we are, how lacking in enterprise! Look at the old buildings! I daresay they seem uncouth, but what a grandiose imagination conceived them! Now we only tinker and ornament and enlarge windows and put canopies over tombs.'

'I like modern architecture,' she said.

'I like your spire, because it is ambitious. But if you were proposing to smother old Brian de Retteville in pleats and fancywork I would not give you a penny to further it. As it is, I offer you half the Methley great tithe and all the little tithe, for really it's too small to be worth dividing. And if that's not enough, then ask me for more. It will be a great satisfaction to me to think of some portion of a church revenue being properly spent.'

'But, Thomas, I am not easy about the little tithe. Surely it is very wrong to leave a parish without a priest?'

'Methley is a great scattered parish, inhabited by long-legged cattle-drovers. It will be no trouble to them to walk elsewhere for their mass. And no priest is better than a bad priest.'

'Do you really mean that?'

She had it in her mind to tell him about Sir Peter's departure for Waxelby, an example of a diametrically opposite way of thinking; but he had turned to the others, and was telling them how beautifully his cousin's spire would rise out of the melancholy flatness of the moors; and though she felt the falseness of their interest compared with his, their questions and congratulations smothered her uneasiness about the little tithe of Methley. After all, Thomas was prior of Etchingdon and must know what he was doing. To refuse the little tithe would seem priggish and ill-mannered, and be of no benefit to the Methley parishioners either, since there was to be no priest in any case.

III

Prioress Alicia

(*August 1351–October 1357*)

In his lifetime the Black Death, a sorcerer travelling from China, had shifted the balance of Christendom and killed half the folk in England. But to Ursula's Jackie it seemed that nothing new ever happened or ever would. The bell rang and the nuns went into quire. The bell rang and the serfs in the great field paused in their labour and crossed themselves, and then scratched themselves, and then went on working. The little bell rang and Christ was made flesh. One day the thought had risen up in him: Suppose I don't ring my bell – what then? This thought had come on a summer afternoon when the noise of the grasshoppers was everywhere. For an instant the sun had seemed to smite him with a tenfold heat, he felt himself dissolving like wax, and the butts of the mown grass where he lay pricked him like a thousand daggers. What then? The end of the world, perhaps. The bell silent, Christ not made, the world snapped like a bubble. Perhaps. But also a beating. Sitting up he shook the hair out of his eyes and saw a grasshopper and tore it apart and felt better. The sun was no stronger than before and all round him it was a summer afternoon and the grasshoppers were chirping and the dun horse feeding and everything was as usual.

The willows and alders cast their leaves, the clouds gathered, the earth darkened, the autumn rains began. One morning there would be a great bellowing of beasts. It was Martinmas, when the pigs and cattle were driven to the shed and slaughtered for winter meat. After that it seemed to grow dark very quickly, as though darkness steamed out of the great cauldrons where they made the black-puddings. A frosty day coming in December scratched one's eyes, the sunlight was so suddenly brilliant. Through Christmas and Epiphany there were sweet dishes, pastes of eggs and figs and ground-almonds that encrusted the spoon and the mixing-bowls. A pittance of unmixed wine made the nuns a little tipsy, they walked more swimmingly and were unwontedly polite, and when they spoke their voices were pitched as though they were just about to sing. This amiability made it difficult to tell them apart. But each face resumed its particular expression, and through February and March he was glad to stay in the kitchen, watching the wind ruffle the pool of rainwater that spread from under the woodhouse door, and eating the chips of dried cod that flew from under the mallet. Round and round went the days like a mill-wheel, and because it was Lent when penances are remembered, on Fridays his mother went barefooted to the cloisters to repeat the penitential psalms and be scourged by the prioress. No one much pitied her, neither did he; and hearing Mabel say that the bishop's sentence had ordained that the scourgings should continue throughout the year and that only the prioress's laziness restricted them to Lent he felt defrauded, as though his significance as a nun's child were belittled.

Being a nun's child distinguished him from the other children about the place, and even when they taunted him he knew he was more interesting than they, and that whatever future awaited him he would not, like them, live tethered to the sour soil of the manor. In spring, when all young animals play together, he played with them and was their ringleader, but when the days grew hot he left them and went to lie among the rushes, hidden, as he liked to lie. And so it would be full summer again, and he would be a year older, and this summer, surely, he would be old enough to go to Waxelby Fair.

But no summer is so long, so wide, as the summer before it. Time, a river, hollows out its bed and every year the river flows in a narrower channel and flows faster. Jackie was old enough to work now, and Jesse Figg the bailiff set him to weave hurdles or spread dung or keep the cows from straying into the young crops, and Mabel added that a cowherd has time on his hands, time enough to gather the tufts of wool that the sheep leave on brambles. Now, too, there was this new woman, this Pernelle. Sometimes she was a pleasure, for her clothes were coloured, and she could tell stories, and with a fine comb she would scratch the lice out of his head when they became troublesome. But at other times she was hateful, bustling after him and saying: 'Jackie, do this! Jackie, do that! Jackie, Jackie! Where's my little page?' Then he would have to help her set up her loom or pound ginger or pick over feathers for pillows, or she would send him out to collect dew for a facewash; for being a townswoman she was full of such notions. And her stories, after all, were not worth much. Though they were of different places they were all about herself; and wherever she had gone she had always been the same Pernelle, cleverer and more meritorious than anyone else. If she spoke of anyone else, it was always her three nephews, who were such fine brisk boys, no bookworms. You would never see them with their eyes reddened by crying over grammar.

'Grammar, grammar! Who's the better for grammar? The Apostles had none.'

'Saint Paul was a scholar,' said Ursula.

'So they say. But he was never Pope. That was for Saint Peter who was only a fisherman. Saint Paul's grammar never hoisted him so far.'

She plunged her smooth hand into the belly of a goose.

'If you had seen as much of the world as I have you wouldn't care to have the priest stuffing your boy with grammar. All this hickorum-hackorum never filled a belly yet. Look at my brother-in-law the armourer. He can neither read nor write but he can afford to pay two clerks to keep his accounts for him, and in his house there are three beds, one of green serge, one of russet, and one of a most beautiful blue. The abbess of Shaftesbury hasn't finer beds. But plenty of poor honest souls lie on rotten straw while these abbots and abbesses loll on goose-down, thinking over their Latin. Let them work, I say! Let them earn a living as other people do! Many's the day my brother-in-law has worked twelve hours at a stretch, forging link after link till the eyes stood out of his head. Quite right, too! We are put into the world to labour. Let them labour like the blessed Apostles, that's what I say. And if your Jackie were my Jackie I'd take him from those books and send him off with the masons.'

Jackie's heart assented to these last words. As learning went on it became less agreeable. There were fewer discoveries in it, it lengthened out like a midday road. Sir Ralph had ceased to teach him what he could repeat to the astonishment of others. There were no more anecdotes of the basilisk, the swallow curing her blindness, the virtues of precious stones. Instead, it was all proportions and properties, things impossible to remember. And there sat Sir Ralph, plucking at his lower lip, brooding some thought of his own, or endlessly, scornfully patient.

'The Proportion of Diapente, I said. What is the Proportion of Diapente? Pooh, you will never learn! And why should you?'

Among the masons it was different. They were kind jolly men, they always had a welcome for him and the fish they caught and roasted in coffins of river-clay tasted better than any food cooked by his mother, or Mabel, or the widow Bastable even. It was in the spring of 1352 that the masons came, and put up their booths in the shelter of Saint Leonard's wood – which had that name because the timber sold from it paid for the candles which burned before the figure of the patron saint. The convent supplied their main victuals, but they eked out the supply with what they poached from pool or thicket. In the convent it was all women living together, and in the masons' settlement it was all men. He liked the men better. For one thing, they made more of him. There was always something to eat and a knee to lean against, and the rough hands that stroked his head stroked unenquiringly, never pausing to ferret after vermin or tweak out tangles. They told stories, too, stories of wonder-working shrines and clever animals and the bands of wolves that came down from the Welsh mountains. They made the more of him because he was the only child who visited them. The manor people cold-shouldered the masons. They were thieves and strangers; worse, they were building the new spire with money which should have been spent in repairing houses and supplying ointment for plague-sores. Even now many of those who had recovered from the Black Death were limping about with open sores, though it was two years since the plague had left the manor; or where sores had healed rheumatism had followed, and cramps that disabled a man when he had worked for no more than a couple of hours. Straightening up from their toil in the field the labourers would see the stonework, white as bleached linen, new as nothing else about the place was new. To cart those stones they had been obliged to spend their days and the strength of their oxen tugging loads across the heath. All for nothing, all for display and vanity!

If the prioress must spend her money away from the manor let her buy some relic, something that would cure agues or avert cattle murrain or help a childing woman.

But those proud nuns knew neither the curse of Adam nor the curse of Eve.

Since the Black Death the relations between convent and its manor had been getting steadily worse. The work was still done, the dues were still paid – but with delays, cheats, interminable English arguments. The bailiff became more and more like an ambassador carrying terms from one camp to another.

The older nuns, whose lives had accustomed them to broils within the convent but only compliance from the dun landscape without, were troubled at these changes. It was not christian, they said, to have the sulks and grumbles of the working-classes so continually thrust before their noses. How could a nun contemplate when within earshot there was a dispute about whether or no William Scole would yield his ox on the Thursday to bring in a load of firing, whether or no the family of Noot should pay a fine for the loss of their son to the manor? – Mabel, who knew everything, and Jesse Figg both asserted that the boy had gone to find paid work elsewhere, though his family continued to declare that he had been drowned in the flood on Saint Luke's day. It was not seemly. It was not christian. The prioress was to blame for allowing it. It should be reported to the bishop.

But when the bishop next came for a Visitation he took it for granted that Oby should be experiencing labour troubles. Instead of condoling with them he said they were fortunate to have serfs who would still remain on their manor, and congratulated the prioress on being wise enough to know when to give way a little. Dame Margaret, a nun who was transferred to them about this time, bore out what the bishop had said with her story of the nunnery whence she had come. There, the serfs were so unruly that one day they had gone off in a body, leaving only the old and the infirm behind them. The abbess had been forced to hire labour, and this at such an exorbitant rate that the finances of the house had given way and some of the nuns had had to be redistributed, Dame Margaret being one of them. Her reading of the times, however, was opposed to the bishop's. There must be a firmer rule, she said, more penalties and more punishments, or society would fall to pieces and Christendom be the prey of heathen invaders.

The younger nuns disregarded these croakings. They said that things had never gone so well as now. There was the spire going up, a pleasure to watch, the exciting visits from the prior of Etchingdon, the revenues that were coming from Methley. Their prioress was really a fine woman of business. Instead of scraping like a hen in the manor acres, scratching up a grain here and a grain there, she had spread her wings in a longer flight and had come back from York with a whole new spirituality in her mouth – as it might be Noah's dove. That was how one should manage: with bold strokes, with a policy that fitted the times. In these days a convent could not afford to turn its back on the world, spin its own wool and wear it, live on eggs and salad through the summer, sleep through the winter like a dormouse, and never receive a novice who had not three aunts and a cousin among the nuns.

'Yet we are told to renounce the world,' said Dame Susanna.

'That is not to say that the world is to renounce us,' replied Dame Isabel. 'Besides, we are also told not to hide our light under a bushel. We cannot for ever go on in the old way, booming in our swamp like so many bitterns.'

Though she was young, Dame Isabel de Scottow was already a personage, and talked in chapter with as much weight as if she had been a nun for twenty years. She would argue her point so reasonably, so gracefully, that no one felt herself humbled by being talked round. Here, in embryo, was a most eminent prioress – if her fevers and shivering fits did not carry her away first. The prioress had already contemplated resigning in her favour, and was only kept from it by the assurances of some of her elder ladies that a prioress who spent half the year in bed would be worse than no prioress at all. Instead, a new post was created for her – the post of guest-mistress. Now that Oby was seeing so much company a guest-mistress was really quite necessary.

It was a pity that no post could be found for Dame Matilda, who was also of the stuff from which prioresses are made, though she had no outward graces and had come to the convent late, and under a cloud: a novice of eighteen who had been bedded with a husband, and only scrambled out of bed on a plea of nullity, causing Dame Agnes to mutter about fish, flesh, and red herrings. But Dame Matilda was still young and so healthy that she would certainly survive till a death or a resignation freed a post for her. If only Dame Salome would resign! She had proved a wretched treasuress. But people like Dame Salome never resign. Each time she exclaimed: 'If it were not for love of Our Lady and Saint Leonard I could not keep on!' one knew that only death would detach her from her burden.

Divided on a moral issue – the old nuns so naturally saying that one must be faithful to old ideas, and the younger nuns saying that one must live in the date where God has set one – the convent was preserved from lesser bickerings. Pernelle Bastable with her considerable experience of convents declared that she had never known such peacefulness, that one might be among holy images rather than among holy ladies. At other times she admitted that such tranquillity made life a little dull and that she felt herself growing old before her time – since without some small dissensions the blood grows thick, as in oxen, who age before bulls do. Fortunately she felt a great benevolence towards the masons, and was out on every sunny morning, warning them to be careful not to fall off the scaffolding. Pernelle's slope of mind towards kitchen and brewhouse made her a convenient boarder. From Pernelle being in the kitchen to oversee the cooking of some particular mess for herself it was a short step to Pernelle being in the kitchen filling sausages for them all. A good useful sort of woman, the prioress thought; suppressing the thought that followed it: that Pernelle among the masons was almost intolerable. It would have astonished the prioress to learn from some incontrovertible source, an angel, say, that next to herself it was Pernelle Bastable who felt the keenest enthusiasm about the spire: muddied, certainly, by pleasure in the masons, excitement to have something going forward, hopes of a day when the completed spire would bring company to admire it; but for all that springing from a true pleasure in fine building.

It was in 1351 that the prioress made her visit to York – where she took a lawyer's opinion on the disputed dowries but went no further. In the following year the prior of Etchingdon made the first of his three visits to Oby. Luckily he came at Martinmas, so there was plenty of fresh meat and stubble geese in good condition; and the darkening weather was really an advantage, for with a spirited fire rooms do not show their shabbiness as they do in summer. But even in a November dusk Sir Ralph's cassock could not pass muster; and among all her other preparations Dame Isabel found time to measure him for a new one, which the novices made up under Dame Agnes's supervision. After so much sweeping and garnishing it was a surprise that the great prior of Etchingdon, a man known throughout England, could be such an approachable figure, talking to everyone, speaking English like any peasant, smiling if he as much as caught your eye, sneezing without dissimulation and apologising to everyone for having such a frightful cold. At their first sight of this extraordinary prior the simpler nuns could not believe that this was indeed the man. It must be one of the others: the stout one, or the one in a furred hood who looked so very scholarly and ascetic. But, no! The stout one was the secretary and he of the furred hood was the Etchingdon clerk of the works, who had been brought because he was such a good man of business, delighting in costings and estimates. Further inspection of Prior Thomas convinced them that thus, and no otherwise, should a great cleric look, talk, and behave. His eccentricities were the sign of good breeding; his extravagances betokened a heavenly unacquaintance with ordinary cares. One forgot that the house was shabby, that one's skirts were narrow, that one's company manners were rusty, that the noises from the kitchen were too plainly audible in quire, that Dame Salome was again singing much too loud and had lapsed into her old habit of *et in saeclula saeclulolum*. Even his cold was gracious, and yielded to Dame Susanna's horehound with poppy seeds.

Listening to the subsequent praises Dame Isabel thought: And not one of you suspects that all this simplicity and spontaneity, and all those sneezes, represent the height of arrogance. She was wrong. Sir Ralph, travelling by a coarser route, had arrived at the same conclusion.

Perhaps being put into a new cassock had sharpened his insight. To be put into a new cassock in order to appear with decency before a great man who insists on treating you as an equal can be a mortifying experience. A prior of Etchingdon should not straddle the gulf fixed between him and the priest of an unimportant nunnery like a boy leaping back and forth across a ditch. What call has he to be so ingratiating? grumbled the lesser man. Questioning me about Toledo, envying me my travels – he knows well enough that all I saw in Toledo is what a poor man sees anywhere: a glimpse through a doorway, a garden behind a grating, and on a saint's day, six inches of a bishop going in procession. So he growled to himself, devouring the fine food which was served because of the visitor and which his resentment distracted him from enjoying.

His third winter at Oby was closing about him. He was lonely, uncomfortable, bored, and damned. For a quiet anteroom to hell he had engaged himself to Oby: a bargain with a weasel, a bad bargain. True, he no longer had to wonder how he should earn, beg, or steal the price of a breakfast; but instead of his own money troubles he listened to the money troubles of the convent. True, he had escaped from the company of rogues, pilgrims, and prostitutes to the company of good women; but he had as little in common with the one as with the other. As for his future, it was no more certain than before; for it seemed to him that he could not endure another year of his present life, and his thoughts trudged in a round of speculation as to how he should live next, whether he should go to a town and hope to pick up a livelihood as a copyist, or follow the plough (there was a demand now for any man who would work on the land), or load a pack with bones and beads and set up as a relic-pedlar, or go to sea, or become a soldier. He must do one or the other, one day or another he must set about it. Meanwhile he was still bewintered at Oby, and thinking: Tomorrow is Saturday, so we shall have beans and bacon. I hope there will be more bacon in my portion this Saturday.

The new cassock had a wider girth than the old one. He had put on flesh, he was broad now as well as long. All the more to frizzle, he had said, answering Dame Isabel's jokes as she measured him. He could talk so, and feel no more than a numb appreciation of the jest. Not that he doubted of damnation. He was as sure about hell-fire as any good simple old woman watching her pot boil. But having gone into his sickness in a frenzy of terror he had somehow come out again with only the formula of fear. From time to time he felt horribly afraid; but what he feared was not the ultimate hell-fire, but that nearer day, sure to come, when terror would rouse up again and take hold of him. Then he would go mad.

The Martinmas visit was a time of plans and talk, and one of the plans was that Prior Thomas and the clerk of the works should come back in the spring to see how the work was going on. Before Easter the nuns were talking of how they should receive their guests. Prior Thomas did not come till August – he had been busy in Westminster. When he came there was not much for him to see. At an offer of higher pay the chief mason had gone off with most of his men to another job. Such things happened now, the pestilence had made wage-earners freer than those who hired them. But what did it matter to Prior Thomas? He was affable as ever, affable as an immortal, telling diverting stories of how projects of his own had been frustrated by such petty accidents as death or disease. And so he was gone again, leaving a strew of gifts and largesse behind him.

'I shall come early next year.' The words rang in Sir Ralph's head, reminding him of King Tarquin's Sibyl, coming back with her diminishing offer, her rising fee. In the quick of his reason Sir Ralph knew that the prior of Etchingdon was his last chance. To such a man, insatiably curious in the oddities of human misfortune, he could tell his story. If he could once humble himself and get it out, Thomas de Foley was the man to hear him and help him. He might be quit of his sin yet: confession, contrition, penance . . . it could be done. In the end even he might be made what he was damned by feigning to be: a priest. Prior Thomas was very much his cousin's cousin: he would exert himself to cover up the scandal that for four years Alicia de Foley and her nuns had been without the body of Christ.

For they were like that, all calling each other cousin and sharing England among them. Even in their feuds they were united. They quarrelled among themselves and saw to it that no one should quarrel with them. He had listened to Thomas de Foley explaining to the prioress how deftly things were managed at Westminster, how by statutes and ordinances both wages and prices would be held down, how, though there should be but one labourer left, man and loaf should be as cheap as before.

During the third visit the quarrel blazed up between them. It was April. The party had been walking in the grounds to see how the spire looked from different aspects when the sharpening east wind brought a pelt of rain and they went into the nave for shelter: the prioress, Dame Agnes, Dame Margaret, Dame Salome, Dame Isabel. Thomas de Foley had a new secretary with him, a red-lipped smiling young man, and the clerk of the works. Sir Ralph was also of the party, half unwillingly, for he had been invited to join it by Prior Thomas; and yet it pleased him to be talking about painted windows and discussing the French cathedrals with the clerk of the works. The nave seemed very small and cramped with such a number of people walking about in it, the more so since the masons were using it as their storeroom and had blocked the western end with timber and bits of ready-made carving.

Prior Thomas continued to urge his cousin to lengthen the nave.

'There is nothing here you can want to keep. Your western arch – it is like some country sermon where the priest mumbles out: Good people, I will now begin. And then there is a long pause while he pulls up his hood.'

Dame Agnes expressed a hope that new doors would be better-fitting. The screen between nave and quire was no protection against draughts. Dame Isabel and Dame Salome took up the theme, describing the painfulness of mattins in winter, the wind howling, the nuns scarcely able to repeat the office because their teeth chattered so.

'The novices stamping their feet and rubbing their chilblains!' Dame Agnes cried.

'The candles wasting!' Dame Salome mourned.

Thomas de Foley glanced from one wrinkled face to another, thinking how much uglier they must look at two o'clock on a winter's morning. Every force of art was strained to beautify God's house and worship, but nothing was done to improve the appearance of his votaries. A religious order where everyone was young and beautiful . . . there would be no place for him in it. A new expedient for the nave sprang into his mind, and he turned to the prioress. Let them abolish that west door, since there would be a south porch in the remodelled nave. Instead, a simple arcading, balancing the screen, and above it a small rose window with modern glass.

'My vow was a spire. The spire brings a south porch, a lengthened nave, a window. All this must be paid for; and we are not Etchingdon.'

She spoke lightly, as good breeding demanded.

'Surely you are not worrying about money? If the Methley tithes are not enough . . .'

Dame Salome had begun to pant in a very strange way, and was turning purple. She rolled her eyes imploringly towards her prioress. The prioress shook her head.

'What's wrong?' asked Prior Thomas.

'It's nothing.'

Her tone of voice made nothing as good as a great deal. 'I believe,' said the secretary, 'at least I understood our treasurer to mention, that though it is perfectly understood that the Methley tithe is earmarked for Oby there are still a few formalities . . .' He paused, and added with a pout: 'People are such sticklers.'

Prior Thomas beat his forehead with his small fist. 'My fault, my fault! My mind was so taken up with your design that I forgot these accursed formalities. But nothing gets done unless I see to it myself. Steven! Make a note of this. Because of the great love we bear to Our Blessed Lady and Saint Leonard, and that the vow of my cousin the prioress of Oby may not be hindered, and so forth: half of the great tithe of Methley and all of the little tithe; for ten years, no, twenty. No, no! That's paltry. In perpetuity.'

The faces of Dame Agnes and Dame Margaret expressed at once their admiration of a man who could dispose so easily of a spirituality and their reprobation of such flippancy in money matters. Though they had suspected that the money was not coming in – otherwise, why should Dame Salome have sighed with such portentous secrecy whenever they referred to it? – no one had supposed that its payment had not even been secured. Sweet Trinity, he might have died meanwhile, and we should have been left with the cost of all this! At the thought of the peril they had been in Dame Margaret sat down and crossed herself with a trembling forefinger.

Embarrassed by feeling herself so much relieved the prioress began to veil the crudity of her sensations by a return of scruples about the lesser tithe.

'I do not like to think of those poor creatures without a priest.'

'I assure you the poor creatures wouldn't know what to do with him. When they had one the only use they could make of him was to pay him for charms to hang about the necks of their cattle.'

'It seems a shocking state of things in a christian country.'

'So it is,' he replied cheerfully. 'But one must look facts in the face. Say we send a priest to Methley. If he is a good man they will murder him. If not, they will do as they did before: turn him into a sorcerer, a water-diviner, and a weather-witch. I will waste no priests on Methley.'

'This is a very stewardly outlook on salvation. One can see that Etchingdon is a great priory, to have so economical a prior.'

Everyone looked at Sir Ralph, the speaker. He was leaning against a stack of timber, turning a little piece of carved work in his hands.

Prior Thomas flushed.

'As for salvation, I am modest enough to suppose that salvation comes from the Lord. But that is disputable, and if you please you may say it is heretical. As for Methley, you must allow me to know more about it than you do. And I do not intend to cast any more pearls before its swine. I have too great a respect for the priesthood.'

'A fine respect for the priesthood! You place a priest here, you withhold him there. What do you suppose you are doing? Playing at checkers?'

The secretary closed his notebook and returned it to his pocket.

'A very striking metaphor,' said Prior Thomas. 'I think you have mistaken your calling. You should have been a preaching friar. Metaphors are a great comfort to simple congregations.'

'And to talk of casting pearls ... that's not a metaphor, I suppose?'

'Not my own. I content myself with quotations from the scripture. In fact I am, as you imply, merely a humble administrator of the church's goods. A steward.'

He spoke with contemptuous good humour, and gave a little bow.

'Perhaps you would like to go to Methley yourself?' he added. He had meant to annoy; but he had not foreseen such a glare of resentment. He hastened to add that he hoped that Sir Ralph would think of no such thing, that Oby would be badly off without him. The nuns exclaimed that they could not do without Sir Ralph and the prioress told of how providentially he had come to them in their hour of need. Swept by the general impulse to make talk over an awkward interval the clerk of the works stirred himself to reply with an anecdote of how a cousin of his had seen, had seen quite plainly, a skeleton hand appear and scrawl *Hic* on the door of a house in Shrewsbury; and the next day plague broke out among the people of the house.

Sir Ralph stared at the floor. His face was of a uniform dull red except for the bridge of his hooked nose, which showed with a sallow whiteness. Even then all might have gone well if Dame Margaret had not taken it on herself to remark profoundly: 'Without a priest there can be no mass.'

Sir Ralph looked up. The prioress said hastily that no doubt there were masses within reach of the Methley folk. Plenty, said the secretary, and it would do them no harm to walk for the good of their souls. In the old days when masses were not to be found in every corner there was much more true devotion.

Praises of olden days seemed about to tide them to safety when Sir Ralph exclaimed in a loud tone that fury rendered doting: 'Feed my sheep!'

Losing his self-control the prior answered testily; 'Oh, very well, very well! Go and feed them yourself.'

The little piece of carved stone fell from Sir Ralph's hand.

'Why should I stuff up the holes you make?'

'You seem to make a practice of it. You stuffed up a hole here, did you not? By the way, what hole were you shot out off to be so conveniently ready to pop into this one?'

Another hailstorm was coming up. The wind howled, the sunlight was wiped off the window as though a cloth had mopped it. Sunlit no longer, they all seemed to dwindle and sink lower – like blown-out candles, Dame Isabel thought, pulling her veil closer about her face and peering out through the chink. Men fight like so many stags, and to live with them perpetually would be intolerable; but from time to time a male quarrel is refreshing, like hartshorn or catnip.

'No cloister, at any rate,' Sir Ralph bellowed. 'I did not sit caressing my belly in a cloister, robbing the poor and slighting the body of Christ because I was not able to make it.'

'They all talk like this nowadays.' Thomas de Foley turned to the secretary with a paternal air. 'Every boy, every beggar, can talk like this. It is the growth of learning and the spread of piety.'

Sir Ralph detached himself from the heap of timber and lumbered towards the prior. He walked stooping forward, his hands dangled, his mouth hung open. His face was blank of any expression except an intense animal attentiveness.

'A fit! He's going to have a fit!' exclaimed the secretary.

At this moment the bell began to ring for vespers. Beyond the screen could be heard the orderly steps and rustling skirts of the other nuns going in to take their places. With a sudden roar Sir Ralph launched himself on Prior Thomas. The prior stepped nimbly to one side, and simultaneously the clerk of the works and the secretary joined in the fray. The nuns clustered round their prioress, scandalised, excited, and inclined to giggle. It was ludicrous to see Sir Ralph charging to and fro, dragging the clerk and the secretary after him, and the prior so coolly whisking his skirts from under their feet. Then Dame Agnes asserted herself, pointing her lean forefinger to the door in the screen and signing to Dame Isabel, the youngest among them, to open it. There she stood, her snub nose in the air, her face rigidly composed, and marshalled them in their order through the doorway. One by one they went sedately into quire, and the door closed behind them. Just as it fell to the noise of scuffling ceased and was followed by a pitiable bellowing, the outcry of a beast struck down in the shambles; then that too died away and there was no more to be heard but the chant of the nuns in quire and outside the cry of the first cuckoo calling through a downpour of rain.

Two days later, riding through the flashing landscape, Thomas de Foley said to his secretary how glad he was that the priest had gone mad just then, enabling him to witness this performance: a perfect demonstration, he added, in proof of how women, despite all their weaknesses, perhaps, indeed, because of them, are best fitted to live under Rule. The Rule is a kind of dance to them, he exclaimed, a lifelong dance. The bell chimes, the music strikes up; and with the whole force of their sense of drama, their wilfulness, their terrific vanity, they give themselves over to a formal pattern of obedience.

'Don't doubt it, Steven! Those women going in to their vespers were experiencing a far greater excitement by doing what they were pledged to do every day of their lives than ever they could have procured from watching their maniac trying to strangle me.'

The secretary remarked that just as God had called Mary to be the vehicle of the incarnation, he called women to the religious life, choosing the frailest objects and the most unlikely to convey his intentions and to illustrate Our Lady's words about exalting the humble. His head was still throbbing from the blow Sir Ralph had given it, and he could not look back on the visit to Oby with any pleasure. Thomas de Foley's observations struck him as hyperbolical. Everyone knew that nunneries made hay of their Rule and needed constant supervision and rebuke. The house they had left behind was no exception, with incompetent finances, no proper servants, a prioress thinking of nothing but building, and a mad priest.

Sir Ralph had run mad, no doubt of it. What was equally disconcerting was that Dame Susanna chose this moment to run mad too. Instead of welcoming an opportunity to show her skill as infirmaress she refused to go near him, and to give any reason for her refusal, saying she could do nothing but pray. Prayer was all very well; but more than prayer was needed. Fortunately Dame Beatrix came forward, saying with decision that what was needed was a black cock. The message went into the kitchen, and Jackie had laughed till he cried, thinking how funny the priest would look with a black cock crowing in his ear like another Saint Peter. That would rouse him! – for Sir Ralph's madness was of the stupid kind, his bellowings and blubberings had ended as abruptly as though a key had been turned on them, and nothing remained but a heavy doting melancholy. The black cock, however, was killed, and bound to Sir Ralph's head. A black cock tied to the head was, of course, an old and sanctioned remedy, and no sooner had Dame Beatrix prescribed it than others remembered it too. But Dame Beatrix had remembered it instantly. There was a general satisfaction when Dame Susanna resigned her post and Dame Beatrix became infirmaress in her stead.

Till past midsummer Sir Ralph was mad. It was a remarkably fine season and every morning he was led out to enjoy the sun. There he would trudge up and down, blinking behind his feathers, and sometimes he would stoop and very carefully remove a twig or a pebble from the path before him. Sometimes he just sat still, a waterlogged bulk; or he would stare at a bush and tremble all over, and then utter a long thrilling howl like the howl of a dog which smells the approach of death. At other times he would chuckle and rub his hands together and then trot off to find a hearer, anyone patient enough to listen to him, and very earnestly recount some joke or funny story that had visited his mind. At meal-times he came in of his own accord, clambered to his room over the gate and sat there polishing his spoon and waiting for his dish to be brought him. Seeing how well he remembered his old habits they feared he might attempt to say mass, and on Dame Susanna's suggestion the quire door and the door of the sacristy were kept locked. But he never attempted this.

Several cocks had corrupted and been removed, and still there was no change in his condition. A mad priest became part of the routine of the house, an accustomed nuisance, like the wash-house door which for so long had been warped and would not close properly. Dame Helen and Pernelle and the novices were busy all through this fine weather with airing and cleansing the rugs and the furred winter hoods and mantles. Shaking them and beating them, and pouncing on the fleas that skipped out, they laughed and frolicked, and the madman was nothing more to them than his shadow passing and repassing.

When he had his fits of howling the nuns drew together and whispered that it was indeed an approaching death he smelled: the death of Dame Isabel. Throughout her short sickly life she had accepted the idea of an early death; but now she thought that, after all, she would be sorry to exchange the ambiguity of this world for the certitude of the next. There is pleasure in watching the sophistries of mankind, his decisions made and unmade like the swirl of a mill-race, causation sweeping him forward from act to act while his reason dances on the surface of action like a pattern of foam. Yes, and the accumulations of human reason, she thought, the proofs we all assent to, the truths established beyond shadow of doubt, these are like the stale crusts of foam that lie along the river-bank and look solid enough, till a cloudburst further up the valley sends down a force of water that breaks them up and sweeps them away.

Recently the prioress had made many references to the desirability of death, the comfort of being released from worldly cares and disappointments. Part of this, Dame Isabel knew, was on account of the convent's money troubles, the prioress's scruples about that lesser tithe of Methley, her uneasy conviction that the spire, somehow, would be the worse for it; but another part was meant for consolation. Studying the prioress's face, a round moon-face clouded with uncertainties as the moon's disk is tarnished with cloud-rack, the young nun assented to the consolations; but under her assent she reckoned the years she must forfeit, the events which would happen and which she would not see, the many thoughts she might have had – and no one else would think them. The world was deeply interesting and a convent the ideal place in which to meditate on the world. She was twenty-three. If she should live to forty, to sixty, her love of thinking would not be satiated. And yet Dame Agnes, who could remember the Jews in England and the Te Deums that had been sung at their expulsion, and Dame Blanch who was older still, so old that she remembered nothing, had never spent an hour of their lives in speculation.

Meanwhile, she also had to think about her money. The de Scottows had property in Guienne and though since the war and the increase of pirates in the Narrow Seas the wine trade was not so profitable as it had been the family was still wealthy, and Dame Isabel had not only brought a great dowry with her, but also received a yearly income from a vineyard of her own. 'To pay for a few little comforts,' her mother said, semi-apologetically, 'since the poor child is so sickly.' This was the sheepishness of the lay mind, still nursing an illusion that nuns lived on dew and a little porridge. The convent was less squeamish. Dame Isabel's private property shocked no one there, it was only the state of her health which made alluding to it a little delicate, since to enquire about its disposal was tantamount to talking about her death. Hints and enquiries observed a sideways decorum, as when Dame Agnes and Dame Helen spoke so regretfully of the draughts in the chapter-house which had, they felt sure, undermined her health. That she should bequeath her vineyard for the purpose of building a new chapter-house was the design of the majority. Dame Susanna, however, a chilly woman, attributed Dame Isabel's sickness to the fact that the convent burned so much peat. The smoke had made her cough, and coughing had worn out her lungs. It was peat-smoke, too, which was spoiling Dame Beatrix's eyesight. Was it not distressing to watch her measuring out medicines? She could be sure of nothing unless she held it an inch from her nose, and often the wrong ingredients must have gone into a potion. A little money laid on on improving the convent's woodland ... Dame Matilda said bluntly that what the convent needed was better housing for the labourers, and a new bull. 'Our own roofs are bad enough, heaven knows, but good or bad we have to stay under them. But nowadays a discontented serf just walks away from us.'

One other speaker matched Dame Matilda in frankness. This was Dame Salome, who urged the dying nun to devote the whole of her vineyard to masses, since of all sins spiritual pride takes longest to expiate.

'And now that Sir Ralph has recovered it can be managed so nicely, the masses said in your own convent where you can be sure nothing will be scamped, for we shall keep our eyes on that. The day he came back to his senses and went off to spear eels I said to the others, Now our poor Dame Isabel can die in comfort! It was my first thought.'

A different thought had come to Dame Isabel when they told her how Sir Ralph had suddenly come out of his madness, rosy and blinking like an infant awakening. Though she had never found him a congenial confessor her curiosity started up at the prospect of meeting someone newly returned from madness. Madness was a whole new world, and surely he would have some interesting news of it? Her hopes were dashed. The simile of the waking infant was only too true; he sat smiling at her bedside saying how wonderfully well he felt, and that in spite of the drought he had never seen the harvest so promising.

A nun has no property, she cannot make a will; but there is nothing to prevent her setting down her dying wishes. Dame Isabel's dying wishes were expressed in a letter to her father, and a signed copy of the letter was retained by the convent. It seemed to her, as it usually does to the dying, that her intentions would inevitably be misunderstood or disregarded. Still holding the copy of her letter she repeated what was in it. She had asked her father to grant to Oby the income from her vineyard for ten years after her death. For these ten years no penny of that income, beyond the charge of a decency minimum of masses, was to be spent. It was to be put out to usury, and the interest as it accumulated was to be put out to usury also.

'And when we get it, what then?' asked the prioress, flustered by all these directions. Sometimes it seemed to her that everyone was in league to talk of nothing but money.

Dame Isabel made a gesture of impatience. Another coughing-fit began to shake her, and Dame Beatrix handed her the spitting-bowl.

'Pay . . . off debts,' she gasped. A surge of blood swept away anything else she might have been minded to say.

She had a long agony. The weather was intensely sultry. Thunderstorms rattled overhead but did not break the drought. The little rain they wrenched out of the clouds had scarcely touched the earth before it rose up in a steaming mist. The nuns, exhausted by kneeling round Dame Isabel and repeating the prayers for the dying on behalf of a woman who seemingly could not die, found it hard to conceal their weariness and their disillusionment (for it is disillusioning to discover that compassion, stretched out too long, materialises into nothing more than a feat of endurance). The flies made everything worse. The smell of blood and sweat brought them in swarms, house-flies and bluebottles and horse-flies. The lulling of prayers and the buzzing of insects were broken by shooings, scratchings, and slaps at the flies which settled on cheeks and foreheads. There lay Dame Isabel, mute as a candle, visibly consuming away and still not extinguished. Every time she opened her eyes they were more appallingly brilliant. It was an exemplary end, but not a consolatory one. Even her patience seemed to take on a quality of deceit and abstraction, it was as though she were calculating the hours that must pass before they would leave her alone. When at length she was dead the reflection that they had done everything they could for her was confused by a feeling that they and not she had stayed too long. To crown all, the drought broke in such torrents of rain that the ready-dug grave filled with water and it was impossible to bury Dame Isabel till it left off raining and the floods drained away.

For many years the death of Dame Isabel, so young, so unusually gifted, was remembered because it coincided with the flood at the Assumption. Crops were spoiled, cattle were drowned, the river broke its banks and settled in a new channel, so that the mill was left high and dry, and finally fell into ruin. After the floods went down there was an epidemic among the masons, and several of them died. All these disasters enforced the disagreeable impression of Dame Isabel's death, and later on a legend grew up of a nun who was so wicked that death himself refused to take her and earth would not give her burial. Her wickedness was an excessive learning: all day she sat reading forbidden books, and sometimes barking like a dog, for such was her knowledge of grammar that she could change herself into animal shape. Naturally, all this was known in Lintoft and Wivelham and Waxelby before it was heard of in Oby, and the convent only learned of it through Pernelle's bringing it back from a lying-in, where, as she remarked, people will say anything to help pass the time. Dame Salome felt herself grow hot and uncomfortable. Once again, she realised, she had been guided by an angel when she had modestly supposed she was only following her own nose.

For the unbelievable had happened. Dame Salome's devotion to Our Lady and Saint Leonard had given out, and she had resigned her office as treasuress the day after Dame Isabel's death, alleging that she had scruples about usury and could not undertake sums *per centum*. Dame Matilda was appointed in her place.

It was high time for a change. At the last Visitation mild Bishop Adlam had observed that even conscientiousness can be carried too far and that Dame Salome's habit of glossing every entry in her books with a recital of how painstaking she had been to make it thus and not otherwise was, in the long run, tedious. He had also been obliged to point out several faults in arithmetic. Besides the relief of getting rid of Dame Salome the prioress was relieved to have Dame Matilda at last among the obedientiaries. She was a Stapledon, a family not to be slighted.

Just as the Scottows were eminently rich the Stapledons were eminently well-to-do. They had the name of being prudent, self-providing, strong-minded, and full of family affection. That was one version. The other version of the Stapledons described them as miserly, obstinate to the point of pig-headedness, and tribal as the Jews. The mother of Prioress Isabella had been a de Stapledon. To the convent groaning under her rule the arrival of a full-grown de Stapledon, and one who had already got the better of a husband, seemed a menace of the worst kind, and there were many allusions to that text in holy writ which promised that Rehoboam's little finger should be thicker than his father's loins. In the course of time she had plodded down most of the prejudice that met her; but the old nuns who still remembered Prioress Isabella continued to assert that Dame Matilda was only biding her time till she could leap into authority and become as frightful a tyrant as her aunt had been.

In 1354 when she became treasuress Dame Matilda was thirty-six, a tall, heavily-built woman, slow of speech and sparing of glance. When she raised her eyelids it was to look: a steady observing glance, wielded like a weapon or a kitchen implement, and, its purpose fulfilled, put by again. Oddly enough, she was extremely popular with the young.

This might be the reason why the prioress, constantly praising her, and supporting her in her new-broom measures, so plainly did not like her and had kept her so long without an office. Dame Agnes, explaining the convent politics to Dame Margaret, had another theory. The prioress was so absurdly fastidious and finicking that she could not stomach Dame Matilda's loud voice and cart-horse tread. The real explanation was so obscure that the prioress was the only person who could have given an account of it, though she would have been abashed to do so. In 1345, when she first vowed her spire, Dame Matilda was a raw-boned stockish creature, very shy, and looking much younger than her real age. Time went on, and she became self-possessed, massive, even stately, all without appearing to make any especial effort and with no one taking any pains on her behalf. The spire was still unfinished. Why should the most prosaic of her nuns have grown as smoothly as Solomon's temple while the spire lagged and pined like a rickety child? Because of this unfortunate association of ideas the prioress felt that somehow the one had grown at the expense of the other, that Dame Matilda was the spire's rival, and her indifference to it charged with ill-will where the indifference of the other nuns was merely due to stupidity. She had been used to console herself with the thought of Dame Isabel. Dame Isabel would recover her health – at any rate she would grow no sicklier; Dame Isabel would be the next prioress. It was probably God's design that what had begun because of an Isabella an Isabel should complete. While there was a Dame Isabel, Dame Matilda could never amount to much, her common sense could never be more than a foil for the other's brilliance. But Dame Isabel had died, Dame Salome (whom she had only tolerated as treasuress because she was an obliging stopgap) had resigned, and immediately the prioress had found she must submit to depend on Dame Matilda.

Yet the new treasuress showed no enmity towards the spire. It figured in her account-books along with butter and prunes and tallow and cattle-drenches. She made one or two very sensible suggestions about it, and she kept the men at their work, intervening whenever she could do so discreetly in the incessant quarrels that sprang up between the prioress and the head-mason.

'Why was Dame Matilda talking for so long with Edmund Gurney? I wonder she does not climb up on the scaffolding and spend the afternoon with him. What with Dame Matilda and Pernelle Bastable it is a marvel that any work at all gets done on the spire.'

'Talking of Pernelle reminds me that . . . ' But Dame Beatrix got no further in her tactful diversion.

'You were there, too, for part of the time. What was she gossiping about?'

'She was reasoning with him about the price of this new load of stone.'

'I might have known it. That is all it means to her – whether it can be done more cheaply.'

'She is reserved. You know she has always been reserved. And naturally she would not try to compete with you in matters of taste. But it is not true that she is uninterested. Only the other day I heard her say to Dame Susanna how much she was looking forward to seeing it finished.'

The prioress walked away, red with mortification. Plainly, Dame Matilda was not only indifferent to the spire: she made game of it, and rejoiced in its laggard growth. Nowhere could she find a sympathetic hearer for her ambitions, her agonising doubts. If she consulted the nuns, they agreed with whatever she said. If she consulted the master-mason, he disagreed. Just now she was ravaged with indecision about a crocket. If only Thomas would come!

But he did not come.

In 1356 the work on the spire was suspended, and the masons told to prepare foundations for the extension of the nave. Digging was none of their business. They sat about, chewing grasses, while old Richard Noot, lame ever since the pestilence, and Mary Ragge and Mary Scole spaded and carried earth in baskets. It was impossible, Jesse Figg said, to spare anyone else from the manor, and hired labour could not be had. Inwardly he was resolved that no man of his should waste his strength while those great idle masons lolled in the shade. Though strangers might cheat the prioress they would not get round the prioress's bailiff. Presently the master-mason took his men away, saying that they would do a small job at Waxelby and be back by Michaelmas, he did not suppose the digging would be finished till then. As it was now harvest the diggers also went away. The nuns said among themselves that the prioress would spin out the work till her dying day rather than lose the self-importance and sense of power it gave her. Fortunately there was the Methley money to pay for it, and Dame Isabel's money to come later.

She had now been prioress for almost twelve years – a long time to hold that office. If she had been a really good prioress, good by orthodox standards, she would scarcely have been endured for so long; but her faults made her tolerable: being self-absorbed she seldom interfered, and except where her spire was involved she was quite remarkably free from suspicions. The arrears of the Methley money had been paid, the tithes now came in punctually. Life had become very comfortable, in spite of the rising cost of living – or perhaps because of it. The rise in the cost of living brought a rise in the standard of living. When difficulties with the manor resulted in less home-grown produce the deficiency was made up by buying more at fairs and markets. What is produced for sale is naturally more luxurious than what is produced for home consumption. The nuns ate more delicate foods, wore finer wool, drank wine and cider when their home-brew ran out. The bad times, too, had increased the number of pedlars, and the competition among the pedlars had improved the quality of their wares. Pins were bought freely, gone were the days when a nun searched on all-fours through the floor-strewn rushes, saying: Where is my pin? Fur-lined slippers were bought, little cushions to slip behind the loins, comfits to sweeten the breath, and new spoons that did not stretch one's mouth till one looked like a gargoyle. New furnishings were bought, the walls had hangings, the tables had napery. About this time the book of hours, projected so long ago, was carried out by the young Dame Cecily Bovill, and found a purchaser (the de Retteville who had commissioned it had died of the Black Death). With the money that this brought in Saint Leonard's altar was done up in the latest style.

Pernelle Bastable had a say in many of these improvements. She knew where such and such things could best be bought, she travelled to fairs and came back with bargains and novelties.

Jackie saw fairs in plenty now, fairs which made Waxelby Fair very small beer. Pernelle needed a strong boy to carry bundles and scare off dogs, and Jackie was just what she needed.

He was now in his teens and by way of working for the masons, a big comely lout, fresh as a new painting with his crimson lips and green eyes. Pernelle had supplanted Ursula with her son just as she had supplanted her in the kitchen. For now, among the many servants which the convent's improved style of living called for, Ursula was a nobody. Almost blind and very rheumatic she had drifted back towards the cloister and lived pretty much as a nun, spending most of her days before the redecorated Saint Leonard whose lips were as bright as Jackie's. Her carnality had burned out at last, love had no more power over her than fire has over a clinker. And in the Lent of 1357 when Ursula limped into the cloister and knelt down for her penance the prioress, looking at her with embarrassment, said: 'The time is past . . . there is no sense in it now. Go in peace, my daughter.'

It was notorious that the prioress disliked scourging Ursula; and to Ursula it could have been no pleasure. Yet for some days after both women looked cast down, and the prioress began to speak of herself as an old woman. Only a week or so earlier Pernelle, riding home from Waxelby with the lenten provisions of dried fish and figs, had been lifted from her pony by Jackie and laid on the grass. She had yielded with little ado, for she recognised a talent. Afterwards, resettling her headgear, she studied his indeterminate English profile against the pure green sky of twilight. Watching him stand there in an isolation of bodily contentment she felt an almost virginal gratitude and humility.

This humility was followed by the reflection that a mature woman has great charms for a boy. What was more natural than that poor little Jackie should make love to her? She in return would bestow her stores of experience, treasures of amorous learning now immensely ripened and subtilised by keeping; for a woman, she said to herself that night, always keeps the best wine till the last. And she had always been kind to Jackie. Later that night she woke again. She heard a shuffling of feet, quiet yawns. The nuns, poor ladies, were coming back from their mattins. They knew no pleasure, their lives never quickened into real life. Taking it all in all they would have to expiate as many sins as secular women, being greedy, slothful, angry, and proud; and yet have nothing to show for it. Here lay she, still reverberating the pleasure long laid aside and never forgotten. Too long: she was old. Her body was wrinkled, hairs grew from her chin. Very soon Jackie would not want to set his teeth in this old keeping pear. He would quit her and go off after something of his own age. For two wisdoms never can keep company, and a boy is no sooner made wise in love than he wants to impart his wisdom to some ignoramus of a girl. There are girls everywhere, and here there were the nuns. The conviction seized her that she must certainly lose Jackie to one or other of them. They were ladies, their skins were smooth with idleness, they were virgins. At any moment Jackie might feel the desire for a virgin; and having neither shame nor modesty there would be nothing to restrain him. Neither would the nuns be likely to hold back. Think of Ursula . . . all nuns are the same.

The convent noticed that Pernelle had suddenly lost her looks and was always losing her temper. They also noticed that Ursula wept a great deal, as though the scourgings had been doubled instead of remitted. As for Jackie, they noticed nothing: he was outside their world, the subject of an occasional remark that he was old enough to work as a man, and that Sir Ralph's lessons had been wasted on him. At mid-Lent Pernelle announced that she would have to go to Waxelby to buy provisions for Easter, and that she would take Jackie with her. They were absent for a week.

It was the fifth day of their absence, the nuns, walking in the orchard, were talking about robbers and Dame Beatrix was recounting her dream in which she had seen Pernelle's horse rush out from a thicket, its eye-balls glaring, carrying, not Pernelle but a tall hairy man in a torn jerkin, when Dame Susanna exclaimed that a man was riding towards the convent. They pressed their faces to the gap in the reed fence. Sure enough, there was horse and rider. The horse was not Pernelle's horse, neither was it rushing, neither was its rider particularly tall or dishevelled. But Dame Beatrix talked of signs and portents and they listened, half-persuaded, till Dame Susanna spoke again, to say that the rider was Prior Thomas's secretary. They hurried indoors to wipe their faces and set their veils and clean the dirt from under their nails. A breath of festivities was in the air. What a pity Pernelle was not there to whip up one of her custards!

There was no sign of festivities about Steven Ludcott. His manner was cold and hurried, his voice had an edge on it. When they enquired after Prior Thomas he replied that Thomas was prior of Etchingdon no longer. He had resigned his office in order to devote himself to contemplation.

There has been some quarrel, the prioress thought, or some scandal. The partisanship of her girlhood boiled up in her, she felt herself throbbing with protective anger, and ready to exclaim that the whole world was in league to flout poor Tom just because he was cleverer than other people. She said:

'My cousin Thomas has always been deeply religious. His retirement will be a great loss to Etchingdon, but Christendom will be the gainer, for no doubt he will enrich it with some treatise of inestimable value.'

What's more, her thoughts continued, this fellow has had a

hand in Tom's downfall. Tom never had any discretion in his choice of favourites.

'Our new prior, Prior Gilbert Botley,' he said, 'has sent me to you with this letter. He chose me to carry it since I have been here before and know something of the circumstances.'

Prior Gilbert greeted his well-beloved sister in Christ, and while deploring the inroads of Mammon upon the religious life yet found it his duty to remind her that the interest on the Methley tithe since 1351 had not been paid. Some very exact and impressive calculations followed, and the letter closed with an allusion to the merit of the serving-man who converted his single talent into ten.

The prioress turned to Dame Margaret, who was present at the interview as a chaperone, and asked her to go and fetch Dame Matilda de Stapledon.

The dreaded name of Stapledon shook Steven Ludcott's reserve. No sooner had Dame Margaret left them than he said: 'Actually, the whole of this trouble was brought to a head by the Methley tithes. It was all so unbusinesslike, a family deal between Prior Thomas and yourself. The community objected.'

'The community,' she said, 'has been slow to anger.'

'Exactly! The community felt that it was time the whole matter was looked into and regularised. We could not have the late prior disposing of the community's goods as though they were his private property, handing over a considerable part of the Etchingdon income without consultation, without contract. Nothing at all, nothing beyond a mere note that the Methley tithes were to be paid to Oby.'

'Which you, I think, drew up? I recollect my cousin asking you to do so. We were all very unbusinesslike, that is true. For instance, I think we omitted any mention of the rate of interest, any mention of interest at all.'

'Very probably. We were interrupted, were we not? By the way, what became of your mad priest?'

'Thanks to Our Lady and Saint Leonard he is perfectly recovered.'

Entering, Dame Matilda received a meaning glance of comradeship from her prioress. It was as with one mind and soul that the prioress and treasuress of Oby conversed with Steven Ludcott. For the cloistered life develops in women infinite resources both of resentment and of intuition; or perhaps it merely develops their sensibility, from which arise both understanding and a delight in being misunderstood. Dame Matilda and the prioress might have been rehearsing their strategy for months. Though Steven Ludcott left Oby with every jot of his errand completed, the interest agreed on and his spleen vented, he rode away with the sensation of having been horribly mauled between the pair of them.

He was no sooner out of the house than a spirited defensive action became a defeat. The prioress had hysterics, Dame Matilda cursed like a crusader, and Dame Margaret, who had sat reading her psalter during the interview, sped off to tell the convent that Oby was certainly ruined and would most likely be dissolved by the bishop.

It was to the aftermath of all this that Pernelle Bastable returned, explaining that the Waxelby merchants were asking such exorbitant prices that she had thought it best to go on to Lambsholme, where she had bought such raisins as had never before been eaten at Oby. The price of the raisins was the only thing in her story that made an impression. Dame Matilda said it was much too high. The convent, she added, had to face an unexpected liability, and for some years to come must practise economy.

To Pernelle this meant one thing only: her Jackie would not

be so well fed. There would be fewer little marginal pies and pittances to hand through the buttery wicket. Feeding Jackie had become a precious duty – rather more than a duty, indeed; for she knew that to a young man the elderly woman he loves is sufficiently like his mother for nourishment to be part of the transaction. These virgins might economise if they pleased. They had nothing to lose but their suppers. She would lose Jackie. Reckless with agitation she began to huff and expostulate, saying that if, after all she had done for them, the ladies of Oby questioned her honesty there could be only one ending; go she must and go she would. Dame Matilda blandly agreed. Even so, Pernelle might have stayed (for travelling is costly, and ruin to a woman's looks, and there seemed little chance that another convent or her brother-in-law at Beverley would welcome her with a Jackie under her wing) if a Lent lily had not appeared behind Jackie's ear. A young man does not wear a Lent lily for nothing – unless he is a poet. It was during Holy Week, when the convent was busy commemorating Christ's death and passion, that Pernelle arranged her departure. While Dame Matilda was nailed down in quire Pernelle could do much as she pleased in the storeroom, explaining to the servants that she was getting ready for the great festival of Easter. On Holy Saturday she staged a quarrel, declared she would live no longer where she was not trusted, and rode off, her saddle-bags swinging, while the bells of Lintoft, Oby, and Wivelham stammered out their *haec*, *haec*, *haec dies*, assuring each other across the moor that Christ was risen. 'As for my bedding,' she cried over her shoulder, 'I will not wait for it. Jackie can ride over with it later to the inn at Waxelby.'

By the time Oby realised that Jackie was gone for good and had taken the roan horse with him it was too late to do anything. Several people had seen the woman and the boy riding southward, but supposing they went on yet another marketing expedition for those spendthrift nuns had taken no special note of it. Ursula wept. Jesse Figg cursed over the loss of the beast. Dame Salome, with one of those flashes of worldly wisdom which at times emerge from very stupid well-meaning people, said: 'Now we can expect a crop of slanders. For when people do you an injury they always slander you afterwards.'

No one can economise without arousing suspicion and dislike, and an economising community offends even more than an economising individual. Presently even the beggars and pilgrims who came for alms went on through the countryside proclaiming that Oby had grown so miserly that it provided nothing but sour beer and barley meal. Such news travels far. The parents of two prospective novices wrote to say that they found their daughters' vocations would be better suited under the Cistercian Rule. The convent's vicar at Tunwold complained to the bishop that Oby, while building fast enough for itself, had allowed the Tunwold parsonage to fall into shameful disrepair.

Tunwold parsonage came up at the next Visitation. The diocesan surveyor, sent to verify the vicar's complaints, had returned with the news that the roof was not only in tatters but sheltered, such as it was, a concubine and five small children. Though the nuns could not be held directly responsible for the concubine, such a state of things bore out the truth of what the prioress had said, half-laughing and in better days, to Thomas de Foley: That God does not wish his nuns to hold spiritualities. The bishop spared them this platitude, and went on to tell them how, when admonished, John Cuckow had pleaded that his house was infested by water-spirits, which was why he had taken a woman to live with him, it being better to go astray after ordinary flesh than after dracs and melusines. Smoothing his cheeks the bishop suggested that as well as having the roof mended the prioress might be well-advised to have the place thoroughly exorcised.

Dame Beatrix broke in with some hair-raising stories of phantom hounds galloping through Cornwall. Feeling that Dame Beatrix was displaying herself to be quite as silly as John Cuckow, the prioress put in a word to her credit, saying what a skilled doctoress she was, and how she had cured Sir Ralph with a black cock.

This jogged the bishop's memory. He had come intending to find out more about Sir Ralph, whom he had met and taken as a matter of course in an earlier Visitation. The scandal at Etchingdon had been a major one, and Steven Ludcott had felt himself sufficiently implicated in Prior Thomas's vagaries (they had gone as far as necromancy and raising the ghost of Avicenna) to avail himself of any red herrings handy. At the Etchingdon enquiry he had testified that Thomas de Foley had been seriously scratched by a mad priest at Oby, an alteration in his demeanour had been perceptible to the anxious Steven from that day onward: it was his opinion that Sir Ralph slavering at the jaws, howling like a wolf, and obviously under the dominion of Satan, had infected the prior. As a tailpiece he had added that nobody knew where Sir Ralph had come from. All this had come to the bishop's hearing. He discounted the dominion of Satan (the Black Death had roused up every superstition in England), but a priest from nowhere needed investigation. He questioned the prioress and some of the elder ladies. From all of them he got the same story. Sir Ralph was a man of sober life, a careful counsellor, a comfortable preacher. He had only been mad once, and then quite harmlessly. He was fond of reading and of fishing. Where did he come from? Dame Agnes said roundly: 'From God.'

She was now of a great age, leaning on a staff and quite bald. No amount of pinning could secure her coif, which sidled on her polished skull with every shake of her palsy.

'From God,' she repeated.

'Do you remember seeing his letters of ordination?'

'Dame Blanch de Fanal (God rest her soul!) saw them. She saw to it all. It was a terrible time, nothing but fluster and dying, and our priest had run away. If I live to a hundred I shall not forget it. Dame Blanch looked out of a window, and there he stood, and at the same moment there appeared a rainbow. He cured my squirrel, too, when she was scalded and all her fur came off.'

She hobbled away.

I may get more sense from a younger nun, he thought. Presently Dame Susanna Piers came in for her interview. She had been trying to nerve herself to speak of how Sir Ralph had raved in his sickness and had declared himself no priest. Her demeanour convinced the bishop that she was going to be full of scruples, and as he disliked scrupulous nuns and was feeling very tired he questioned her as briefly as possible, said nothing of Sir Ralph, and dismissed her before she could begin any confidences. The Virgin, thought Dame Susanna, smote my lips in the very moment when I was going to speak a slander. She went to the chapel and began to pray forgiveness for harbouring wicked thoughts. Meanwhile the bishop was back in the guest-chamber, still puzzling a little about this dull-looking man who had had the heroism to enter a house where the pestilence had entered before him and who an hour before, it seemed, had been wandering about at a loose end. No doubt there was some perfectly satisfactory explanation. The de Foleys were traditionally proud, Alicia de Foley was not reputed lacking in that family grace, she would scarcely engage a priest – even when priests were at a premium – without making sure of his credentials. And though there was no record of the transaction in the episcopal roll of appointments the Black Death had caused many such hiatuses. Perhaps they had neglected to apply to the late bishop for his approval. They were very unbusinesslike, that was obvious.

I will ask the man himself, he thought sleepily, while his chaplain sat at his bedside reading aloud from the Lives of the Hermits. That would be best, it would spare the prioress's feelings and save time. How pleasant to be in Egypt, sitting under a palm tree, plaiting a garment of palm fibre and speaking to nobody. Yes, he would speak to Sir Ralph tomorrow. But during the night his sore throat grew worse, and by the morning his larynx was so much inflamed that it was impossible to speak more than a word or two. All the voice he could muster had to be expended in thanks, in replies to condolences, in assurances that his cold had not been caught at Oby, in reiterated thanks for all the provisions being made to ease his journey. Dame Beatrix, hurrying forward with a linctus, dragged the priest after her. 'My Lord, pray take a sip of this every hour. Sir Ralph will tell you I am a good doctoress.'

'Yes, indeed, Dame Beatrix has much skill in medicine.' He looked round, saw Dame Susanna, and added: 'Dame Susanna, too, is most skilful. I should have died of the pestilence if it had not been for her care of me.'

'No, no! I did nothing, it was not I! It is Ursula you should thank.'

A modest nun, shrinking from praise, the bishop noted. A kindly tactful priest. The man had a loud roystering voice, yet he spoke with a certain crispness, an accent of scholarship. Speech, carriage, demeanour – everything was priestly, and he seemed, too, perfectly sane. A very worthy fellow, no doubt; running to seed a little, growing fat and forgetting his scholarship among all these women, possibly more inclined to follow Peter with a net than with a crook; but a good sort of man, and just where he was needed, and so providentially free from ambition that he might be counted on to remain at Oby.

A healthy man, too. One would need to be extremely healthy

to withstand such a cold lodging, such draughts playing over the altar, such a melancholy marish climate. No wonder if from time to time he went a little mad. There is no sin in madness, only God's wrath, and God's wrath often falls on the most estimable characters, as on, for instance, the prophet Daniel. Daniel's statements, so inconsecutive, so inconsistent – one must attribute them to God's wrath. When did order and reason slide into the world? – with Christ, *lux mundi*? Perhaps one might say a little earlier, a cool silvery intimation of the light to come glimmering through the heathen philosophers. So the bishop mused, shepherding his thoughts, trying to put off a recognition of an oncoming toothache. The litter creaked and swayed, presently the bishop began to fall asleep – a light sleep of old age in which he could distinctly hear himself snoring. Squeezed uncomfortably into a corner the chaplain looked at him with a malevolence so habitual that it was almost indifference.

IV

The Spire

(*November 1357–May 1360*)

This was in 1357. Bishop William Adlam, an unostentatious figure, went home to die, and Sir Ralph remained at Oby. His brief fillip of alarm was over. He did not think there was any further likelihood that an enquiry would rout him out from his place as nun's priest. He had exchanged the insecurity of being a man for the security of being a function; it was a sound bargain, though he sometimes regretted it.

The cassock in which he had fought Thomas de Foley was now rounded like a grapeskin, even when hanging on its peg it kept a flaccid rotundity like a grapeskin which has been sucked. But he said that it would last him out till the great day when the spire was finished and consecrated. The work on the spire was still going on – for economy's sake in the most wasteful manner possible: with one man and a boy.

'I begin to think there must be a curse on my building,' said the prioress, voicing to Sir Ralph what her nuns had felt for a long time already. 'Ever since I began it we have met with one disaster after another: the pestilence, the loss of that relic, Dame Isabel's death and those floods, and the vile behaviour of Etchingdon about the Methley tithe, and Pernelle Bastable's robberies, and those two novices being diverted to Culvercombe, and the cost of the repairs at Tunwold ... '

Her voice died away. She was tired of hearing herself complain and of hearing Sir Ralph's perfunctory consolations. Her laments rang false, because they always stopped short of the truth: the truth was Thomas. Since Steven Ludcott's visit there had been no news of Thomas de Foley. Thomas was lost and gone, his career ended, his light put out. She would never see him again, he would die and she would not know it. Her spire might be completed, but he would never come to praise it. And here am I, she thought, fixed in the religious life like a candle on a spike. I consume, I burn away, always lighting the same corner, always beleaguered by the same shadows; and in the end I shall burn out and another candle will be fixed in my stead.

She knew, too, who the next candle would be. Dame Matilda would succeed her as prioress, just as certainly as William Holly would follow Jesse Figg as the next bailiff.

In the spring of 1358 Sir Ralph found that he was tired of fishing, and wanted to go hawking instead. A strong horse would be needed to carry him, and since Jackie had gone off with the roan, horses were a painful subject. Rather stiffly – he had no talent for asking favours – he consulted Jesse Figg. Having said that it was useless to consult him about a horse, he had neither time nor heart for such frivolities, the bailiff met him a week later with the news that everything was arranged. The horse would be Peter Noot's dun horse, a raw-boned animal, but with feeding it would come into better shape and last for years; a horse taken from field-work is so grateful that it will give you another ten years' service. Peter Noot was due to die at any moment. When he died the convent would claim a heriot, its due of his best beast. The dun horse was not really his best beast; his young ox was better value. 'But do I say it is,' said Jesse, 'old Matilda will believe it.

And Widow Noot, she wouldn't complain at losing a horse and keeping an ox, an ox is work now and meat later. My cousin at Dudham has a hawk that will suit you. It's a sparrow-hawk. A sparrow-hawk for a priest.' Sir Ralph had looked forward to choosing his hawk; but he saw that he must take both or neither, and a hawk without a horse would be no use to him in this bare country. Peter Noot died, the heriot was claimed and curried, the hawk and her trappings arrived. When he felt her hard feet fidget on his hand Sir Ralph experienced an authentic happiness. At last he had something of his own.

The Oby people were pleased to see him ride out on Noot's horse. They had always liked him pretty well, giving him the meed of approval which an idle man who minds his own business is pretty sure to receive from the working Englishman. Now that he had a hawk they liked him better. It put her in mind of the old days, said Grannie Scole (pretending she could remember them), when the manor had a proper lord on it instead of a parcel of nuns. Those were the days: always something going on, hunting or hawking, hanging or whipping, always something to keep life stirring. Oby had never prospered since the nuns came to it.

Riding out with his hawk Sir Ralph began to have a hawk's eye view of his world. The river ceased to be a fisherman's river, a rosary of pools and shallows; from the back of the dun horse he saw it as a progress, winding like some wasteful history, with here and there the record of a forsaken channel, such as a row of alders sulking in a hollow, or a long ribbon of rushes. He began to see the shape of the hamlet, too, and how cunningly the hovels had been plastered to any shelter against the prevailing wind. Round and about them ran a network of footpaths, tending towards the common field and the common waste. Along one track went the Hollys, along another the Noots, and the girl driving a lame cow past the thorn thicket must be a Scole, for that was the way the Scoles went. The masons' settlement had added new tracks to the tracks of the village, tracks somehow different: one could see that they were made by strangers. Out of this network of footpaths, purposeful and well-trodden, ravelled the three tracks from Oby to the outer world. The southward one led to Wivelham, a wretched place, and to Dudham beyond it. Westward, past Oby Fen, a track went over the rising ground to Lintoft, and later joined the old road which brought you in the end to London, and was called King Street; and to the north-east the Hog Trail and the river twisted on towards Waxelby and the pale seaward sky. The Black Death had dealt hard with Waxelby, and still lingered on there like a dog worrying a carcass. The wharfs were rotting, the export trade of salted herrings had dwindled, the great church built by the friars was botched up and would never be properly finished. In twenty years' time there would be little left of Waxelby, so men said, but a byword.

Waxelby wealthy,
Wivelham wet,
Lintoft plenty,
Dudham sharp-set.

The dun horse and the Dudham hawk had drawn Sir Ralph into the company of the bailiff and his nephew, William Holly. He discovered that Jesse and William knew much more about the nuns than he did, and discussed them and their doings with dispassionate familiarity, always referring to them as Old So-and-So, regardless of whether they were actually old, middle-aged, or young. They might, in fact, have been discussing the peculiarities of the Oby cows – with no more reverence, and equally, with no more intention of disrespect. After the first slight discomfort of adapting himself to this outlook on religious ladies Sir Ralph enjoyed sitting in Jesse Figg's orchard, drinking cider and slapping away midges while the dews fell and the blackbirds sang through the dusk. His appearance was always greeted with the same remark: he must sit down and tell them about his travels. That was as far as his travels took them. Jesse and William then resumed their sober untiring arguments; sometimes about affairs on the manor or in the convent, sometimes about events that had happened during the time of the Danes. It was an everlasting dispute how far the Danes had travelled up the Waxle Stream. As far as Kitt's Bend, asserted William. Further by a mile, Jesse maintained; for at that time the Waxle Stream flowed in a straighter course, cutting down through Old Wivelham Fen where the ghost of Red Thane's daughter walked to this day through the osier-beds. Wrangling about the place of the landing, both men agreed as to what happened next. Whether at Kitt's Bend or further upstream, the Danes were welcomed by an old woman who gave them poisoned beer; half of them died forthwith and the rest were so weakened by sicking-up that the old woman's sons came out of the reeds and finished them off. Their boat was all that was left of them, and some of its timber was built into the roof of Lintoft church. If you licked on a wet day you could still taste the salt water in it.

Sometimes Sir Ralph tried to persuade them that they might be descended from these same Danish invaders. Swearing by Saint Olave they said they were English, nothing but English, and that no Danes had settled hereabouts, for the English had driven them off, as they would have driven off Duke William and his crew if Duke William had not been cunning enough to land in the south where men don't know how to fight. Then Jesse would call for more drink, and his wife would waddle out with it, and stand easing her bare feet in the orchard grass, staring round her with mud-coloured eyes. She was a Wivelham woman, born in the mud, she said. One shapeless garment covered her from neck to knee and her head was muffled in a dirty green hood. She had no air of being a bailiff's wife, even on saints' days she wore the same dingy clothes and the same dumb looks. For all that, she was a valuable woman to Jesse, the best of his three wives; she had an infallible gift of foretelling the weather. One evening as she stood there listening to the disputes about the Danes with her usual waterlogged expression the fancy came to Sir Ralph that she might have waddled towards them out of those same times, that with the same dull stare she had watched the beaked prow of the warship rearing above the osiers, and that if anyone could say how far the Danish ship had got, she could. The thought was so compelling that he half turned to ask her. But at the same moment she began to sidle away, clumsy and majestic as a goose.

Another drinker in Jesse's orchard was John Ragge, who fifteen years earlier had been one of the three men provided by the manor for the wars in France. An arrow had put out his eye, and though a one-eyed archer is still good for something, when the other eye began to fail he was turned off. There were many disabled men like him, going through the country in gangs, and he joined such a gang. One winter's night when he and his mates were busy in a dovecote a pair of great dogs came bounding out and attacked them. John Ragge, mistaking a frozen horse-pond for solid ground, crashed through the ice into icy water. There he remained; for the dogs sat watching him, he could hear them growl whenever he stirred; and in the morning the servants came out, noosed him, dragged him through the crackling ice to the bank, and thrashed him. To hear him tell this adventure one would think it was the most triumphant moment in his travels. It had taken him over a twelvemonth to beg and cozen his way back to Oby where, of all the tribe of Ragges, time and the pestilence had left only his sister-in-law and her two daughters, skinny muscular women who worked as thatchers. They had not much welcome for a blind man who spoke like a foreigner and was too lazy to trim gads or carry bundles of reed; but having once heard the story of the night in the pond William Holly could not hear it too often, and brought him to the orchard as a minstrel. Sir Ralph gave him an old cloak, and once a day he stumped up to the convent for an alms of bread and leavings.

It was through him that the novices began to practise levitation.

Dame Agnes died early in 1358. The new novice-mistress was Dame Susanna. She had neither the learning or the deportment of Dame Agnes, but her manners were particularly elegant, she was the cleanest eater in the convent, and her temper was so equable that even singing-lessons went by without ill-feeling. Noticing that the plain-chant was no longer urged on with thumps and stamps, and that no cries of 'Fool!' and 'Blockhead!', no yelps of pain, broke the flow of the melodies, the older nuns were inclined to say that Dame Susanna was no disciplinarian. But no one could dispute that she was a good musician, and that the novices' singing showed it. Another subject which every novice must master is the art of alms-giving: how to serve out doles at the wicket, whom to encourage, and whom to snub. Under Dame Agnes, who hated the poor, this had been chiefly a matter of snubbing. Dame Susanna, herself relishing a little gossip, enjoined politeness as part of the performance. Nothing loath, the novices chattered at the wicket like a troop of birds, practising, so they said, their French on John Ragge. Long after he had finished his victuals and turned his cup upside-down he lingered on, talking French and gibberish, and assuring them that the nuns in France were all very haughty and undersized. But it was in plain English (for really he knew very little French beyond the usual salutations and bawdry) that he told them how girls in Brittany have a game called Flying Saint Katharine, and how, if they sing long and earnestly enough, and are pure virgins, the girl sitting on the clasped hands of her four play-mates will rise and hover in the air.

'*Fly, good Saint Katharine*,' he sang in his weather-beaten voice. '*Fly up to your tower!* And up she goes like a feather. But it can only be done in Brittany, I think,' he added, his quick ears catching a little cough from Dame Susanna.

A few days later Dame Matilda, on her way back from inspecting some repairs to the brewhouse, heard giggles and a breathless singing coming from under the great walnut tree, and paused to ask the novices what wickedness they had hit on now.

Lilias le Bailey answered, rubbing her elbow: 'We are learning to fly, Madam Treasuress.'

She was thirteen – a tall girl, with burning hazel eyes, and the beauty among them. But they were all fine young women, Dame Matilda thought, straight and well-bred and likely to be a credit to the community.

'And where did you learn all this nonsense?'

'From Blind John. But there are not enough of us, only three. Sweet Madam Treasuress, buy us two more little novices, very little ones would do.'

It was one of those fine ripening days which come in mid-July. The air was pungent with the wild peppermint that grew along the ditches, and glancing up into the tree Dame Matilda noticed that there would be a fine crop of walnuts. Relaxed with heat and satisfaction she looked benevolently on the three girls and forgot to remember that games of this kind lead to torn clothes and sprained ankles.

'Romping and sprawling,' she said. 'Well, make the most of your time. No more of this when you are nuns, remember.'

Only as she walked on did it come into her mind to wonder where Dame Susanna might be. By rights, Dame Susanna should have been with her novices.

Dame Susanna was on her knees among some shallots which had been laid to dry. Her mouth was open, and she was staring upwards. Seized with foreboding Dame Matilda hurried towards her, though when she spoke it was to say rather casually: 'I'm sure you would be more comfortable in the shade.'

Dame Susanna scrambled to her feet. Dame Matilda's forebodings intensified themselves: only a visionary could look so distraught and so defensive.

'What are you looking at so earnestly?'

'I was watching the hawk – Sir Ralph's hawk.'

'And praying it may bring you down a snipe for supper, I suppose. Well, no doubt we shall all be in the air soon. I left your novices trying to fly. Perhaps you might go to them before they all take wing.'

As a rule Dame Susanna winced like an aspen under the slightest rebuke. Now she went off with only a surface apology, like a person answering out of a dream. Dame Matilda thrust aside her coif and scratched her head. All her pleasure in the brewhouse repairs, the fine ripening weather, the promise of the walnuts and the promise of the novices, was dissipated. A taint of the supernatural had mixed itself with the healthy odour of the drying shallots. Of all menaces to peace and quiet a visionary nun is the worst, and when that nun is the novice-mistress the worst is ten times worsened.

What had the woman been staring about for? More than Sir Ralph's hawk. How could she be brought back to earth? Dame Matilda scratched and pondered and walked out of the sun and into it again, wishing she could ask someone for advice, and knowing that there was no one whose advice she valued – for in this matter she could not consult Jesse Figg. That is the drawback of being so very sensible: one cannot take counsel because it is against common sense to seek it. The metal of common sense is so lonely and unfusable that for people like Dame Matilda there is no career except to be a tyrant or a superlative drudge. In the end she was reduced to the usual expedient of the despairingly practical: she would try what a chance augury might suggest, consulting the first person she met. The first person she met was Ursula, squatting in a doorway and rubbing a censer. Knowing all the household footsteps by heart Ursula did not look up, but asked if the censer were sufficiently burnished.

'Yes, you've put a good polish on it. Poor Ursula, you are almost blind now, are you not? How much can you see?'

'I can see light, and darkness. Sometimes, if I look at the sky, I can see a bird pass.'

'Can you see our faces?'

Ursula shook her head.

'I was going to ask you if you had noticed anything about Dame Susanna. She looks changed and sickly, to me.'

The blind countenance, attentive as an animal's, looked wise for a moment, and then became blank.

'She is busier now, being novice-mistress, perhaps.'

'Not so busy that she need sicken.'

'Oh, no, no! But you see her among young ladies. That would make her look older, would it not?'

Ursula kissed the censer, rubbed it where she had kissed it, and shuffled indoors. Dame Matilda knew that she had been put off a scent. She despised Dame Susanna for choosing such a confidante.

Meanwhile Dame Susanna had returned to her novices, and now they were practising an antiphon. The voices extended the tune like a silk canopy, and under that canopy one was safe from hearing the little bells fastened to the hawk's feet, which sounded so much like the little bell at mass. The antiphon was *Quinque prudentes*, from the parable of the wise and the foolish virgins. *And at midnight there was a cry made, Behold the bridegroom cometh; go ye out to meet him. Then all those virgins arose, and trimmed their lamps, and the foolish said unto the wise, Give us of your oil; for our lamps are gone out.*

Presently the sound of the hawk's bells began to pierce the singing like pins pricking through a piece of silk. It was Sir Ralph's hawk. Nine years ago she had stood at Sir Ralph's bedside, watching his hand clench into a fist and strike the wall till the blood spurted. A black stubble bristled from the spotted purple face, the air that steamed from him was foul with fever, and in the voice of someone infuriated by a long argument he asserted that he was damned, damned, damned, no priest and therefore damned. Ursula, who was with her, thrust a cup against his mouth. He whined and quarrelled with it like a child, and then, like a child, frowned and sighed and fell asleep. But later on he had cried out again, maintaining that he was no priest, and damned; and that time she had been by him alone. She had really been alone ever since, excommunicated by this fear she dared not express.

Once she had forced herself to speak of it to Ursula. Ursula had flown into a rage, saying that Dame Susanna should know better than to believe the witness of fever against a good man and a priest. Ursula did not believe it. But then, what is belief? A thought lodges in the mind, will not out, preserves its freshness and colour and flexibility like the corpse of a saint: is this belief, or is it heresy? Many times she had made ready to disburden herself in confession: to harbour such a suspicion was an offence against charity, and should be confessed, repented, absolved. But something always intervened: was this intervention diabolical, or angelical? Afterwards, looking at her fellow-nuns, seeing the small, familiar mannerisms which each one carried like a coat-of-arms, she had been appalled to think how she might have ruined them by suggesting that for all these years they had been served by a priest who was no priest. Even if it were disproved, and she for ever disgraced for having spoken it, how could Oby recover from such a scandal?

'*Exite obviam Christo Domino-o-o.* Shall we do it again, or is that enough?' asked the novice Philippa.

'Once more, I think. And this time try to be rather less noisy at *clamor factus est.*'

The hawk had missed her prey, and was mounting for another hover. But those bells only rang for the death of a little bird. One must not give way to accepting omens. One must stop one's ears, like the prudent adder. One must be silent. The sweat broke out on her face as she thought how easily she could ruin Oby. Who would bequeath manors or send novices to a house where such a suspicion could be breathed? The lamp must have oil, or it goes out. A convent must have money. And Oby was now a poor house: for the last ten years there had been talk of poverty, poverty and debt; the words had struck her the harder because she herself had brought a very little dowry, so little that if it had not been for her musicianship they would not have been able to admit her. She had impoverished them, was she to ruin them too? And for nothing more substantial than a fancy based on words spoken in a fever? It could not be true. It could not be possible. Heaven would not allow such a thing, and certainly not for so many years. There would have been a sign. A dream would be sent, a toad would jump from the chalice, the spire would fall. The spire! She turned and looked at it. It was tall now, pure as a lily-stalk in its cage of scaffolding. One could see how long it had taken to grow, this lily, for already the lower stages had begun to weather. It would soon be completed. Then it would be consecrated. The Virgin would accept the lily.

'*Exite obviam Christo Domino-o-o-o.*' The singers prolonged the last syllable till their breaths gave out. They did not want to go through *Quinque prudentes* again. They waited for Dame Susanna to tell them what to do next. But she seemed to have forgotten all about them. She had turned away, and was staring at the spire as though she had fastened her very soul to it. The novice Philippa tapped lightly on her white forehead with her white forefinger, and gave a condoling nod.

A few evenings later as the elder nuns sat in the prioress's chamber Dame Matilda loosed her arrow.

'By the way, I find our novices are learning to fly.'

The prioress frowned, for the arrow had twanged too sharply in Dame Matilda's voice. She made a languid enquiry, and was told that Dame Susanna could best answer it. Dame Susanna explained that it was a game.

'There is a song,' Dame Matilda pursued. 'I don't know how it goes. I have no ear for music. But no doubt Dame Susanna can sing it.'

In a timid voice, invincibly in tune, Dame Susanna began to sing. Instantly Dame Salome, not usually very musical, joined in at the top of her voice, and sang the tune through several times.

Since it really was not possible to praise such singing, the prioress praised the tune, and said that it sounded as if it were a very ancient one. Dame Beatrix remarked that much the same game was played by little girls in Cornwall, and added that as a child she had played it herself, and that if you were the girl in the middle you felt sick.

'Did you fly?' Dame Salome's voice was so solemn and suspicious that the others were abashed by her silliness. Dame Beatrix began to laugh, and answered that she had not been so fortunate.

Instead, she had tumbled, bruising herself badly, and had been beaten for dirtying her clothes. The prioress remarked that children lived in pain as in an element, so much so that beating was probably no real change to them. Dame Helen said that she had been a very well-thumped child, and told a story. Conversation had moved elsewhere when Dame Salome harked back, and said: 'You know, there are certainly some who can fly. At least they remain in the air quite a little while. And was not Saint Katharine herself carried all the way to Alexandria by angels?'

'There are so many stories of flying,' said Dame Beatrix, 'that no doubt some of them are true. But I think one would need to be extremely young or extremely saintly.'

'Not at all,' said Dame Salome. 'It can happen with quite an ordinary person – a good person, of course. But one need not be anything so very out-of-the-ordinary. Cleverness is not everything.'

Dame Helen agreed that cleverness was not everything. Many saints were simple enough. The prioress remarked that it was not till christian times that simplicity became a virtue; the good characters of the Old Testament were ingenious as well as virtuous.

'That was because they were Jews,' said Dame Beatrix.

Once more the conversation was turned away from flying. But Dame Salome continued flushed and thoughtful. Dame Matilda watched her. Though well aware that she had made a false step in her attack on Dame Susanna, Dame Matilda saw no reason why she should not follow up the false step with a better one. A dog-day demon had entered into her. She was determined to pull down her quarry, no matter who suffered by it. So she waited till there was a pause in the small-talk, and then remarked on the scarcity of miracles nowadays. As she had intended, Dame Salome instantly remarked on the scarcity of faith. After a couple of sentences Dame Salome was induced to say that faith could remove mountains.

'Come, come ... You are not as heavy as all that,' said Dame Matilda, and rose, putting back her sleeves. This was the difficult moment. But by exerting all her geniality, her air of good-fellowship and affable tolerance, she conjured Dame Helen, Dame Beatrix, and at last Dame Susanna, into her circle.

'Now then! Fly, good Saint Katharine!'

Amusement turned to embarrassment, embarrassment to a communal frenzy. '*FLY, good Saint Kathar-ine! Fly UP to your Tow-er!*' They sang at the tops of their voices, riotous as vintagers. Each felt another's gripping hand-clasp, their wrists ached, their fingers grew slippery with sweat. Thinking of the difficult moment when they must at last let go they went on and on; and Dame Salome jigged up and down on the swaying net of their hands, her features resolutely composed in a prim smile, like some enormously weighty doll.

'Oh! O holy Virgin!'

Someone had let go. Dame Salome sat on the floor and wept bitterly.

She wept unheeded because the others were looking nervously towards the prioress. The prioress sat with her eyes cast down, and her fingers closed so sharply on her little dog that it yelped and bared its teeth. Out of the past came Thomas de Foley's voice telling of the absurdities of the Gilbertine nuns, the cabbage soup with two and a half radishes for each monk. Out of the present came Dame Salome's sobs, which burst from her like hiccups because she was so much out of breath. At last Dame Beatrix took pity on her, wiping her face and thumping her shoulders.

'Is that better? Shall I get you some dill-cordial?'

Dame Salome looked up and said sullenly, 'I flew. I know you won't believe it, but I flew.'

Dame Matilda looked at Dame Susanna, and slowly shrugged

her shoulders. That night she fell asleep thanking her prudent saints for a good evening's work. She did not suppose that Dame Susanna would cultivate visions for some time to come.

When, after a decent interval, the question of John Ragge's deservingness was somehow raised in chapter there was a general sense of relief at the decision to feed him no longer. When there are so many cases of real need and genuine desert it was an abuse of alms-giving to nourish such idle roysterers. Throughout the convent there was a noticeable air of decorum and spring-cleaning. The incident in the prioress's chamber had a wholesome after-effect, bracing as doses of wormwood. Everyone felt with relief a tightened bond of discipline and convention, the sturdy tradition of the ordinary which had controlled for centuries and all over Christendom the cloistered life. In that life there was no place for aberrations of individuality. One monastic must resemble another, and all go the same way, a flock soberly ascending to a heavenly pasture, a flock counterfeiting as best it could under difficult circumstances the superlative regimentation of heaven. Even Dame Salome was subdued; and in Jesse Figg's orchard Sir Ralph was told how Old Matilda and Old Susanna had had another set-to, and now it was patched up again.

John Ragge's chatter at the wicket was regretted for a while and then forgotten. By the end of August the game of Flying Saint Katharine was forgotten too. There were the apples to gather, and the damsons and the elderberries and the blackberries. The fine weather lasted on into October, with frosts sharpening at night and dissolving in golden mornings. Quantities of wild geese flew over. Sir Ralph said that in all his years at Oby he had not seen a greater flocking of birds. It was a sign of a hard winter, and by such signs God warns his creatures to prepare against it. God's creatures were busy preparing as best they could. A great deal of firing was stolen from Saint Leonard's wood, several geese disappeared, and Joan Holly's wadded coat vanished from the thornbush where she had hung it to air. She said plainly that Elizabeth and Margery Ragge had stolen it to wrap their worthless uncle in. Now that Blind John was no longer fed by the convent he was less popular with his gossips.

On the eve of All Saints the masons began to take down the scaffolding – for at last the spire was finished; miraculously, one might say, considering all the mischances which had delayed it and, more potent than any mischance, the prioress's creative vacillations. But, just as at the end of a labour the child asserts itself and comes forth, it seemed that the spire had at last escaped from her whimsical control.

Walking in the cloisters Dame Beatrix and Dame Helen paused to watch the timbers being lowered.

'Who could have believed it? For all these years we have been expecting it. And yet, now that it has come, I feel quite astonished, quite taken aback.'

'Wonderful,' said Dame Helen more tranquilly.

'It makes me feel very old.'

It made Dame Helen feel very old too.

'Another wonderful thing is that we still have the same prioress. When you think of all the changes' – Dame Beatrix began to count on her fingers – 'and all the deaths . . . Dame Agnes, Dame Isabel, Dame Blanch. And Pernelle Bastable going away with our horse. And Bishop William. Well, God rest their souls! They were all very good people.'

'We must not forget those who died at the time of the pestilence. The spire was begun before that, you remember.'

'So it was. Dame Helen Aslack, Dame Emily—'

'Dame Alice Guillemard—'

'That poor little novice – what was she called? She was a hunchback.'

'Wait a minute. She was one of the Isabels. Isabel de Stoke.'

'No, Isabel de Stoke was taken away and died at home. She was tall and straight. No, I mean the novice who was to bring us the relic. Don't you remember, the tooth we were to have, the tooth of the Holy Innocent?'

'Quite true! The tooth of a Holy Innocent. That was a bad piece of work and I never perfectly understood how it all happened. I can't recollect the novice's name, though. She died first of all, just before Dame Emily. Isabel ... Isabel ... Isabel de Fanal.'

'Marie de Fanal. Not Isabel at all. The other Isabel was Isabel Goffin who was taken away by her parents and compelled to break her vocation and marry.'

'I suppose one can't count her in with the others. Now I am out.'

They began to reckon again, and had brought the count to eight when Dame Beatrix recollected old Dame Roesia who died before the pestilence and Dame Helen recollected Dame Joan.

'Though she was almost blind even then, you remember. Even if she had lived she would not have seen the spire. I hope that scaffolding will be split into firewood. It grows colder every day, it is as cold as mid-winter already. Here comes Dame Johanna.'

Dame Johanna was coming to fetch Dame Beatrix. Ursula had fallen downstairs again and cut her head.

She gave the message in a detached well-mannered tone of voice which conveyed a readiness to overlook. As the infirmaress hurried indoors Dame Johanna paused beside Dame Helen, huddling her hands in her sleeves, and remarked graciously: 'How delighted you must be to see your spire finished at last! And how fortunate you are to have the means to build it! At Dilworth we only saw things falling down.'

'We have been counting up all the ladies who have died here while it was a-building.'

'Indeed. Are they many?'

'Yes, a great many. But of course it cannot interest you, since you have known none of them.'

'I imagine that a great many of them must have died of cold,' retorted the newcomer. 'At Dilworth, even in mid-winter, it was not as cold as it is here.'

Dame Helen began stumping towards the house. Dame Johanna, keeping up with her, imparted a few details about the state of poor Ursula's head.

During these last few months Ursula had aged very fast and simultaneously she had grown tiresome and intractable. Though she was unwieldy with dropsy and crippled by a sore in her leg she would not stay quiet on her pallet, but roamed about the house listening at doorways, mumbling and crossing herself. She had a delusion that some danger threatened Sir Ralph, and this made her bent on sleeping outside his door – crawling up the stairs, bumping her blind head, losing her balance and falling, and making her way up again, uncontrollable as water. He would wake, and hear her snoring and praying in her sleep, and if he were not too sleepy himself he would lead her down again to the nuns; but in an hour or two she would be back. One morning she was picked up dead at the stair-foot. It was a deplorable death – the death of an animal rather than of a christian; but everything to do with Ursula was deplorable, except the kindness she had received: a rather negligent kindness, no doubt, but more than her deserts, since for many years no one had reproached her or forced her to labour beyond her strength.

Perhaps such kindness was a mistaken kindness. Praying for Ursula's soul (about whose welfare Dame Johanna expressed a deal of unsolicited concern) the prioress asked herself if she had acted improperly in remitting Ursula's penance. Another twenty or thirty scourgings might have made a great difference. She submitted these doubts to Sir Ralph, and speaking in his dry professional voice he assured her that she was being over-conscientious. Her part in the business was merely instrumental, for since no penance is sacramentally efficacious unless it is accompanied by contrition it depended on Ursula and not on her whether the stripes were salutary. She hastened to agree, and did not add that in beating Ursula she had felt no more sacramental than if she were a laundress thumping dirty linen.

For all men are alike; if one asks a direct question they reply with a treatise. Edmund Gurney the mason had been just the same, wrapping himself in long discourses about the natures of different kinds of stone. That is how men are made, and that is what they expect women to put up with. Yet if she had failed to supply Sir Ralph with a dinner, replying to his hunger with a discourse on the breeding of cattle and the difference betwixt beef and mutton, he would scarcely be contented. Beef and mutton, clothing and firing, that is the life-work for a prioress. Not souls. Not even spires.

She did not try to hide from herself the sense of anticlimax which accompanied the completion of her spire. It was beautiful, but it was not as beautiful as she had meant, and her inability to carry out the extension of the nave left it awkwardly placed. It was finished; but 'over and done with' was the truer word. The exaltation she had looked for had not kept its tryst; even her nuns, who had never cared for it, and who now went about saying how pretty it was, how neat, and what an embellishment, had more pleasure from it than she. It was her life-work; but her life persisted, a life filled with beef and mutton, clothing and firing, cavils and quarrels. Life as prioress, however, would soon be over, for after the consecration of her spire she would resign her office. They were expecting it. Probably they were looking forward to it. It was impossible that anyone could look forward to it with such longing as she. To be freed from beef and mutton and misunderstandings; to sit silent in chapter; never again to be pursued with those account-books; never again to hear those accursed syllables, *Dear Mother, I am sorry to trouble you, but . . .* Cost what it might – and this present bishop, Giles de Furness, was rumoured to be a much sterner stickler for fees than the kind old Bishop William – there should be an election, and Prioress Matilda should replace Prioress Alicia.

Two dates suggested themselves as suitable for the ceremony of consecration: the patronal feast of Saint Leonard, or Candlemas. Saint Leonard's Day was the favourite choice until Dame Johanna took it on herself to point out all its advantages: this was enough to convince everyone that a late November festivity was out of the question, one could not ask people to wade through the mud. When Dame Johanna said that the mud would be just as much of an impediment in early February she was reminded that she had yet to spend a winter at Oby, and could not know what she was talking about.

Dame Johanna was a transferred nun, who had come to Oby from the house of The Holy Trinity at Dilworth. For years Dilworth had been notorious for its debts and confusions, and though Bishop William had been patient with it Bishop Giles had ordered its dissolution and the dispersal of its seven remaining nuns into other establishments. These unfortunate creatures carried no dowry with them, for their portions had been devoured in the Dilworth quicksand. Nevertheless, Oby had undertaken to receive two of them, Dame Matilda pointing out that to gratify a new bishop is always a good pennyworth. The bishop, returning kindness for kindness, had sent them his most advantageous pair. Dame Johanna Pyke was sickly, and not likely to cumber them for more than a year or so, and Dame Alice Sutton, though young and sturdy, was a skilled confectioner – so skilled that the little revenue left to Dilworth had been brought in by her exceptional marzipan.

Dame Alice's sweetmeats bore out the bishop's words. It was to be hoped that time would prove him as accurate about Dame Johanna. For Dame Johanna was disliked by everyone, and the more she tried to ingratiate herself the more she was felt to be an interloper, a meddler, and a bore. 'It would be better,' said the prioress to Dame Beatrix, 'if the poor scarecrow would not force herself to take such an interest in us and our doings. Surely it is quite unsuitable for a woman who is going to die in a year or so to attach herself to a mere temporary lodging-house!' – to which Dame Beatrix gloomily replied that being a bishop does not make one a doctor, and that there might be a long step between looking like a death's-head and dying.

'If I hear that woman utter another word of praise I really think I shall strangle her!' exclaimed Dame Margaret. 'She praises everything and doesn't mean a word of it.' Even Dame Helen was driven into a spirit of contradiction, and when Dame Johanna happened to mention that Dilworth owned no more than five books assured her that this could not be so, quite the contrary, the Dilworth library was cited by everybody as excellent.

Having discredited Saint Leonard Dame Johanna proceeded, all unwittingly, to compromise the coming election. Dame Matilda, she understood, would be elected unanimously: how very nice that would be! Unanimous elections are creditable to all concerned, they demonstrate to the world the favour of God, who makes men to be of one mind in a house. The Oby nuns were fortunate to have been spared such electoral squabbles as had taken place at Dilworth, where the sacrist had got herself elected in the very teeth of the bishop.

'It is so wonderfully peaceful here!' exclaimed Dame Johanna.

She meant it as a commendation, but her unfortunate manner made it sound more like a taunt. At Dilworth it was nothing to have half the ladies absent, one on a pilgrimage, one visiting a sick mother, another cheering a lying-in, a fourth searching for a little dog. The homecomings after such absences were as disrupting as the absences themselves: amid talk of heresies, fashions, family disputes, kid served with almonds, law-suits, adulteries, harp-players, and heraldic bearings, the offices were neglected, discipline was thrown to the winds, God was forgotten, and meals were late. Only those who had experienced such a state of things, she concluded, could realise what a comfort it was to find oneself in a house like Oby, where everything went on so quietly, month after month, and the bull *Periculoso* was so honestly observed.

As a result, Dame Johanna's hearers burned to flout the bull *Periculoso* as soon as possible; and when the prioress was invited to stand as godmother to a baby of a cadet branch of the de Rettevilles the indigenous Oby nuns insisted that she must go to the christening, and pointed out, as though it were something scandalous, that she had not slept a single night away from her convent since the August of 1351. The prioress, too, had smarted under Dame Johanna's commendations. She was admitting the various advantages of going to the christening – founder's kin, making new friends, picking up new novices perhaps, and making sure of that long-promised never-secured little Adela de Retteville, whom with any luck she could bring back with her – when Dame Beatrix happened to suppose that on this journey Sir Ralph might as well be left behind, he was really too shabby for visiting. Unquenchably shameful, the recollection of the scene in the nave overwhelmed the prioress: Sir Ralph lungeing and bellowing, Thomas skipping aside, his face bleached with fury. She exclaimed that going to the christening was out of the question. She was too old to ride through the winter weather, and the litter, a relic of Dame Isabella's days, lay mouldering past repair in the cart-shed, where the hens laid eggs in it.

But she was forced to give way when a grizzled squire brought a letter from Marie de Blakeborn. She too was going to the christening, and it would be only a day more in her journey to turn aside to Oby. 'Unless you have grown as fat as I have,' she wrote, 'the litter will hold us both, and it will be pleasant to talk of old times as we travel.'

Marie de Blakeborn arrived soon after sundown with a small retinue of elderly servants. She had grown unbelievably fat. Tottering forward in the January dusk, swathed in furs, she looked like a performing bear. She had also grown very deaf, and deafness had deformed her voice into a stately roar. The nuns found it hard to conceal their amusement. As soon as she had been taken to the guest-chamber they began to mimic her, mouthing hushed imitations of her roars, and Dame Cecily drew a sketch of Saint Michael weighing Marie and Sir Ralph against each other in his scales and staggering under their combined weight.

It did not seem to the prioress that there would be much talk of old times. Marie was absorbed in the present, bellowing about the latest shaping of gold hair-nets, a new sort of little woolly dog, and the progress of her law-suits and her grandchildren. Well, so much the better! Ten years had passed since their last meeting, and now she shrank from the prospect of any intimacy with this noisy, affable stranger. They set out immediately after mass. It was a dark morning, the sky was covered with smoky vapour, all the pigs were screaming in their sties. Deafened by the pigs, the shrill goodbyes of her nuns, Marie's torrential directions to her retinue, the prioress sat with closed eyes, cursing the moment she had consented to this expedition. As well drag a corpse out of its grave, she told herself, prop it up with cushions and send it off to stand godmother! Who wants a *larva mundi* at a christening feast?

She was aroused by an exclamation.

'Why, there's your spire! You never told me it was finished. Stop, stop, Denis! Stop the horses! We want to look at the spire.'

From the rise of ground they looked back across Oby Fen, darker than ever under the smoky sky. White and sharp-cut, the only thing with a definite outline in all the shaggy formless sad-coloured landscape, the spire seemed to be sinking, to be sucked down into the mud.

'Charming!' roared Marie. 'I should have known it was yours anywhere. You always had such good taste.'

The prioress was thinking: This is the first time I have seen it from a distance, seen it as others will see it; and it needed Marie's litter and the birth of a child to get me here. I had the enterprise, once, to begin it, and now I have not the enterprise to come out and look at it.

'Tell me, is Thomas dead?'

'Dead, my dear? Our Thomas dead? Very much alive, I assure you, and a great man again. Why, didn't you hear how he out-witted them all?'

She gave the order to ride on, and settled down to relate how Thomas had emerged from his spell of penitence as merry as a marmot and as vindictive as a hornet; how he had stayed at Etchingdon long enough to pay off all old scores, had got himself offered the priorship again for the satisfaction of refusing it, and now was in Lombardy, negotiating a loan for the King.

'They think the world of him at Westminster. And you really supposed him dead? Well, your convent is a most exemplary convent if you know so little of what's going on outside as to think Thomas was dead.'

To the deaf ears, to the sighing breeze, Alicia de Foley allowed herself to say: 'I see how wrong I was. I see now that it is I who am dead.'

Only good breeding enabled her to endure the christening festivities, the feasting, the display of gifts, the women exchanging childbed stories in one corner of the hall, the men getting drunk in a devil-may-care, no-business-of-mine fashion in another. Like a ghost she listened to the singing in Saint John's church, like a ghost she fingered the embroideries on bed and baby, half expecting to see her fingers leave a blight on what they had touched. The only thing like real life was the incessant tipping. Wherever she turned someone started up expecting a gratuity from a godmother, and by the third day she was compelled to borrow from Marie de Blakeborn. She saw her new novice, Adela de Retteville. The girl was very pretty, so pretty that it was a wonder that her parents had finally consented to part with her; but no doubt there was some sufficient reason why she should be given to God. Laying her finger – that blighting finger – under the warm chin and staring at the parted crimson lips, the prioress said: 'You will be very happy with us, my child. There is more contentment in the cloister than in the world.'

'And that there is!' said the child's mother, with a bitter expression on her discouraged face. 'And I hope you will be grateful to us, Adela, and pray well for our souls. It's time you did something more than romping and spoiling. When will you be going back to Oby?' she added.

'On the Tuesday.'

On the evening of the christening a band of musicians was hired, and the young ones of the party danced. Relieved of their company the elders had the supper table set close to the hearth and sat there quietly, drinking and eating nuts. Conversation turned on the infirmities of the flesh. Marie spoke of the encumbrance of her fat, describing her struggles on the close-stool, the terrific purges that were needed to drive a way through her bowels. Adam de Retteville replied that fat would be a comfort to him. His teeth had rotted in his gums, he could bite nothing without anguish, he was forced to live on broths and decoctions and no spices, no peppercorns, could mask the taste of corruption that haunted every mouthful he swallowed. But that, said his brother Steven, was better than a fistula. A man with a fistula could not be easy on a horse or on a cushion, and must wait, for all his pride and all his prowess, on the good pleasure of a body servant. Yes, but a flux of the lungs, imagine that! cried his neighbour: to spit, to stifle, to have, not only food and exercise, but the more common air denied you. An old de Retteville widow, yellow as saffron, continued to assert that the pains in her head would astonish anyone who could experience them, for sometimes it was as though the devil were stirring up her brains with a red-hot spoon and at other times as though three worms, bred in the nose, were eating their ways towards eyebrow and ear and jaw.

Since people will boast of anything and be glad to have the wherewithal, conversation in the ingle was happily competitive. The prioress took no part in it. She sat eating nuts with her eyes cast down.

'And you, my dear gossip?' enquired Adam de Retteville in a burst of cordiality. 'You too must have something to tell us, some hardening in the breast, some twinge in those white knees that are bent for us sinners on the cold stone?'

Marie answered for her.

'Not she! Look at her! Look at her colour, look at her smooth chin, smooth as a page's. Look how she sits there, stuffing herself with nuts, and not so much as a belch.'

Raising her eyes the prioress looked round on her contemporaries: on cheeks veined with purple or pinched and sallow, on rheumy eyes, grey hairs, brown teeth, knotted joints. How fat they were, or how thin! How hot, or how cold! How they belied their grand clothes and their grand manners! – a crop of toadstools could not look more garishly death-like.

'I must thank Our Lady,' she said correctly, 'for my good health.' And just as though she were running over her beads she felt herself reckoning up sight, hearing, touch, taste, smell, all perfect, her limbs wholesome, her blood pure.

'Look at her teeth,' continued Marie. 'The whole set of them, white as wolf's teeth.'

'One of them is chipped.'

She could hear the affected modesty of the words. Parting her lips she pointed to an eye-tooth that was minutely flawed.

'It's the same with all you de Foleys,' said Marie. 'There's Thomas, as brisk as a young hound. Not a grey hair in his head – nor in yours, I daresay.'

'We nuns are supposed to last out well, you know. There were two ladies in our house, both were near four-score, and except that one of them grew a little forgetful . . . ' Growing a little forgetful herself the prioress gave a coy description of Dame Agnes and Dame Roesia. Her companions listened with delight, melting with sentiment, nudging each other, rolling their bleared eyes, and saying that there was nothing so pleasant as the religious life, and that they wished they had given themselves to God instead of remaining in the world to be battered to pieces with care and sickness.

'Well, then, you must give me my god-daughter.'

Adam de Retteville pinched her arm.

'Nothing would please me better. But you must settle it with her father, you know, the dowry and all that. The girl is founder's kin, you ought to take her for nothing. You agree to take her for nothing – you can always get a double dowry from some scrivener – and she's yours.'

'But vocation . . . One must not forget vocation.'

Adam de Retteville looked across the table at the group of dancers at the other end of the room. 'What you eat's vocation,' he pronounced.

Marie de Blakeborn had planned to carry the prioress and little Adela back to Oby and make a short visit there. It had been raining heavily, the floods were rising, and Marie's horoscope declared that she would die by water. When Tuesday came she refused to set out. If the prioress were bent on swimming back to her nuns, she said – who no doubt were doing very comfortably without her – the litter was at her service, and one of Marie's waiting-women, a big hook-nosed Fleming, could go with her and look after the child. Painfully aware that she was disobliging a number of people the prioress paid the last gratuities and departed, farewelled by assurances that she would soon regret being so dutiful, and scowled on by Marie's retinue. It was a relief to look into Adela's beaming daisy-face, so very pink, so very white, so gaily turned towards the future. The floods were wide and turbulent. Clots of foam and swans speckled the water, and in the half-light of the January day the child amused herself by her inability to distinguish between them until a swan melted or a clot of foam rose into the air. The Fleming stitched on at a piece of embroidery, growling under her breath when a jolt or a stumble jerked the needle from its aim. The litter creaked and swayed and the prioress drowsed as if in a roughly-rocked cradle. Awakening she would find in herself a sensation like a wound, a sensation of being exhausted with bitter weeping; and then she would wake a little further and remember Thomas de Foley, who was alive and flourishing, and careless whether she died or lived on. Careless? No, it was more likely that he had deliberately put her out of his mind, she, and her spire, and her crazy priest, all detestably associated with his reverse at Etchingdon. But perhaps careless. She stroked one edge of the sword and then the other against her heart and it was impossible to decide which was sharpest.

On the second day they made better speed. The wind had got into the north, it had begun to freeze and the ways were harder. On the third morning it seemed likely that they would reach Oby before vespers, but flakes of snow began to glitter in the air, then the sun went in and the snow fell in earnest. The Fleming put by her embroidery and took the child into her arms, holding her close to warm her. Twice, bemused by the snow, the horsemen lost their way. At last they reached Lintoft, where the priest's housekeeper came out with a drink of hot beer. The floods had not been so bad, she said, no worse than any other winter; but the wind had been terrible, a biting north wind. During the night it had risen to a tempest screaming down on them like a troop of horses. Her master was sick of a fever, stifling, and black in the face. He would die tonight, she fancied ... would the prioress and her nuns pray an easy death for him?

'I will, I will!' exclaimed Adela, dancing up and down.

The prioress asked if he had been shriven. Yes, said the housekeeper; by a lucky chance Sir Ralph had ridden over yesterday, enquiring about his lost hawk, and had shriven him. He will be desperate if he has lost his hawk, she thought. He should never have loosed her in a north wind, hawks lose heart in a north wind. Thinking of a distracted Sir Ralph and of the prayers she must order for the Lintoft priest she felt herself suddenly reknit to her convent and interested to be returning. It always looked pretty in snow, a white landscape was a grateful change after the sallow monotony of the moors. Tomorrow they would throw out crumbs for the birds and she would ask the cellaress to provide some little extra delicacy for a dinner to celebrate her homecoming with one de Retteville novice in her hand and the prospect of another. If it continued to snow the litter could not be sent back to Marie for some days. Possibly the Fleming, so skilful with her needle, might be beguiled into mending the Trinity Cope.

'The sacrist must show you our vestments. We have one or two fine old pieces. But just now we are poorly off for needlewomen, none of our novices seems able . . .'

The litter canted over as the front horse swung aside. The beasts were halted with kicking and shouting. A voice said: 'There's something here across the track. One can see nothing for the snow, but I can see something there.'

The hinder horseman replied: 'You see and you can't see. I was nearly off.'

'It's a great heap of thatch. What a place to leave it! Now how are we to go on? The track is so narrow that we can't edge past it, and there seems to be a ditch here and a ditch there.'

'Well, we don't need to go on, do we? Here we are at Oby, in my opinion, for I can see a building in front of us, and people are coming out with lights.'

A moment later he added: 'Here comes such a nun! By God, she's fatter than our mistress!'

It was Sir Ralph. 'Which roof? . . .' she began. Grunting out something about the depth of the snow, he carried her indoors and set her down in the parlour. All the nuns were there, looking oddly formal, she thought; but of course nuns would look formal to an eye which had been studying the de Retteville christening party. She glanced round for the de Retteville novice. The Fleming had just carried her in and was unwinding her from her mufflers.

'See who I have brought.'

Dame Matilda came forward, kissed her ring, and drew her towards the fire.

'Dear Mother, you are very welcome to your poor daughters.'

'How solemn you all look! You must have been getting into some scrape.'

Up came Dame Beatrix with a bowl of mead. 'Drink this, dear Mother. Such . . . such a cold night!'

She sipped and looked round on them. After all, there was one missing.

'Where is Dame Susanna? I have brought her a novice. Half-frozen, but a novice for all that.'

Something was wrong. Not one of them could look her in the face. Now here was Dame Salome standing before her, crimson, opening and shutting her mouth like a fish. The instant I am back, she thought, this sort of thing begins. I suppose they have been flying again.

'Somebody must give the girl her supper, and put her to bed.'

Dame Salome flapped out of the circle, looking as pleased as a fish that slips out through the net, and beckoned Adela and the Fleming away.

The prioress finished her mead and then turned to her treasuress.

'Well? What has gone wrong now?'

'During your absence God has sent us a great sorrow. Dame Susanna is dead.'

Released by these words, the nuns now began to cross themselves flutteringly, to sigh, and to commend Dame Susanna's soul.

'How? When?'

'She died last night.'

'But how? How did she die?'

'She died suddenly. By an accident.'

'*Unshriven!*' The word was screeched out in Dame Johanna's most calamitous hoot.

'Where was that fat beast, then? Out hawking, I suppose?'

'No, he was in bed.'

'It was in the middle of the night.'

'He came at once, but it was too late. She was dead already.'

'She was buried!'

Together they could do what no one had the courage to do singly. Interrupting each other, contradicting, referring, harking back to make something clear, having theories as to how it happened and other theories as to how it might have been prevented, they pieced out the story of Dame Susanna's death.

They were in quire for the night office, scarcely able to hear themselves chant for the force of the gale. Then, following on a strong gust of wind, there came a noise of rending, and a crash. They looked round, they could see nothing to account for it; but at the same moment several candles were blown out and the air became icy cold. They went on with the office, and finished it, and were just about to leave the quire when the rending noises began again and this time, because the wind was not blowing so violently, they heard them more plainly and realised that they were close at hand. Dame Matilda opened the screen door and peered into the nave, supposing that a window had been blown in. The nave was flooded with moonlight, and overhead through a hole in the roof they saw the bleached clouds hurrying, the frosty stars, the outburst of the full moon. The nave floor was heaped with timber and rubble and blocks of stone. While they stood gazing there was a sharp patter, and fragments of mortar showered down, and then tiles and pieces of stone-work. Then came a terrible noise, like a lion's roar – no, said Dame Beatrix, like the noise a wave makes as it rears up against the shore and sucks back the shingle – and then, answering it from among them, a shriek that made the blood run cold, a shriek that was more horrible than anything else in all that horrible night, just such a shriek as a soul must utter when plunged astonished into hell-fire; and with the strength of a madwoman Dame Susanna forced her way through them and ran into the nave. Whether she fell on her knees or whether the falling masonry caught her and felled her it was impossible to say, but in that instant she had disappeared, lost in a cloud of dust, crushed under the falling spire.

The story was told but not finished. Dame Margaret had to recount all that was done afterwards, how comfortable Sir Ralph had been, how well Dame Matilda had kept her courage, how all the manor folk had heard the crash of the falling spire but not one had come near to help. Dame Johanna had to say how remarkable it was that within a minute or two of the calamity the wind had gone down, though bits of stone kept falling at intervals for some hours after. Having begun to talk, they were afraid to leave off. No one wished to bring on the silence into which their prioress must speak. Flustered, compassionate, embarrassed, they chattered on, eking out their stock of narrative, remembering to add that the thatch had been blown off the gate-house, that a roof-tile had been blown as far as the walnut tree.

The prioress sat by the hearth, turning the empty bowl in her hands. When at last she spoke it was to say: 'Where is Sir Ralph? Why is he not here? I must see him at once.'

When he came, entering the room with a wary animal composure, she began to discuss with him the arrangements for Dame Susanna's burial and the masses that must be said for the repose of her soul. Such arrangements were ordinary enough, a commonplace to both of them, and scarcely needed discussion; but she spoke as though she were a commander issuing directions in the heat of battle. For the last eighteen hours he had been sweating with anxiety as to how she would take the news that her spire was in ruins and her novice-mistress dead with every appearance of self-slaughter. He had allowed for fury, dejection, misery, weeping and wailing and gnashing of teeth, and even for fortitude and magnanimity – since he knew her to be capable of almost anything. The one thing he had not expected was what she presented: this front of trivial authority, like a plaster representation of a carving in stone. It threw him out, and he resented it, and felt for the first time in their mutual relations that she was a thoroughly disagreeable woman.

He was not alone in feeling so. If the prioress had shown a sociable grief her nuns would have been very willing to grieve with her; but she wrapped herself in a mood of cold sulks, and left them to turn their compassion on themselves – the victims of a calamity which her ambition had provoked. Not only had the spire fallen, and killed Dame Susanna; but it had fallen piecemeal, and so incompetently that it would be cheaper to rebuild than to pull down, which meant a further expense and all the dust and clamour of building to be endured over again. The masons were aggrieved at being fetched back, and a quarrel arose between the convent and the master-mason, for naturally the nuns blamed him for the fall of the spire. He for his part asserted that the fault lay with the convent; if the ladies had been able to make up their minds so that he could have gone ahead with the job the mortar would have dried out evenly, the weight of the stone-work would have settled. But ladies never can make up their minds.

Then one of his boys, clumsy with cold, tripped, fell off the scaffolding, and broke his thigh. The masons left the work and stood about saying that there was a curse on the spire and that it would be against God's will to finish it. The Oby people who worked with the builders, carting stone and loading and carrying the hods, now added their witness. Floods, pestilence, murrain, scarcity: there had been one misfortune on the heels of another since the spire was begun. If the nuns were so wealthy they should spend their money on succouring the poor, as Christ bid. Succouring the poor, indeed! – why, they had even turned away blind John Ragge, poor soul, and as a result no one in Oby could call his hen his own, for since the convent had turned him away he had fallen back on the tricks he had learned in the wars; even a blind man must live. Of course there was a curse on the spire. Who could wonder that God had toppled it over, for what right had nuns to be building spires? – keeping men from their work by extortion of cartage and labour dues, and wasting the manor in order to heap stone on stone and feed a pack of strangers. From abuse of the nuns they turned to abusing the masons. Young Scole swore that if he saw another mason perched in the scaffolding like a crow in a winter tree he'd send an arrow through him. That night the men of Oby mobbed the masons' settlement, kicking down their huts and scattering their gear. After that they marched round the convent singing at the tops of their voices, and in the midst of the procession was John Ragge, twanging an old viol and lovingly supported – for he was popular for the nonce. Next morning the masons took down the scaffolding. By that same evening they were gone, William Holly taking it on himself to arrange transport for them and their stuff as far as Dudham, where his cousin's homestead was soon the better for several repairs and innovations.

While the people of the neighbourhood were saying how chop-fallen the nuns must look, the nuns were warming themselves over the possibility of a law-suit. Oby had not had a law-suit since the stirring days of Prioress Isabella, but most of its ladies had hearsay experience of the law: family litigations about dues, dowries, maimings and slayings, neglect of flood-gates, encroachments on land, abduction of heiresses, poaching of deer, and contested legacies. Law, they all knew, is tricky and costly, and much depends on knowing the right people; but this was no sooner admitted than it appeared that a great number of the right people were known: a cousin, an uncle, a talented and rising nephew, a prodigiously hoary and crafty kinsman by bastardy, a step-niece at court; and both Dame Margaret and the novice Philippa came of legal families. 'And we must not forget the Stapledons,' put in Dame Salome, turning courteously to Dame Matilda, who acknowledged this tribute with an uneasy shifting of her bottom. It seemed to her that there was little hope of averting a popular form of ruin.

For the moment there was too much to say for anything to be agreed, for each nun had her own view as to what ground the action should lie on. Dame Margaret was for breach of contract. What could be plainer? There stood the unfinished spire to prove it. Dame Beatrix objected that Edmund Gurney might plead that the spire had been finished, and that the wind which threw it down was an act of God and no fault of the builders; surely it would be better to catch him on an accusation of scamped work; an honest piece of building would not have been overthrown by a mere winter's gale. Dame Helen was all for manslaughter. How else had Dame Susanna died? What a loss to the community! Something must be due to them for that, surely? They had never had such a novice-mistress, and who could tell what novices might not be lost to them by losing her. Her fame was spreading far and wide, such a good musician, such delicate manners, and such piety! In old days such a nun would have been canonised, if only for her piteous death. There she had knelt, her hands stretched to heaven as if to ward off the disaster, praying aloud that the convent might be preserved. And sure enough, a minute later the wind fell, the air was as still as midsummer. Dame

Johanna had remarked on it at the time. If they were to lose such a nun and not get exemplary damages, there was no justice in England. And another thing ... what about those repairs at Dudham, that new roof on the Hollys' granary? As plain a theft as ever finger pointed at! At times they even remembered to put in a word of regret for the spire, which had been so beautiful and their cherished ambition for the last twenty years. It was useless for Dame Matilda to remind them that they had constantly grumbled about the spire. It was useless for Dame Johanna to explain that she had never said or supposed that the wind fell because of Dame Susanna's prayers. They were united in longing for a law-suit, and only waited for the prioress to lead them to it.

But the prioress seemed to have lost all interest in life. She lay in bed, or sat in her chamber listlessly teaching her bullfinch to pipe the *de Profundis*. Loyal, though fraying with impatience, they maintained that she was stunned by the shock.

On Holy Thursday a pittance was distributed among the old people of the hamlet, and since John Ragge could not be kept out and might make trouble Dame Matilda had asked Sir Ralph to be present. Afterwards he and she stood for a while dawdling in the sun, before the gate-house. Spears of young grass were poking up through the winter mud-banks. The clump of wormwood that grew by the threshold had put out its sharp new green.

Feeling the sun warm on his back Sir Ralph remarked that it had been a wonderfully peaceful Lent.

'Peaceful?' said she, stopping short and staring at him.

'The peacefullest Lent I have ever experienced. I have never confessed such a sequence of untroubled consciences, souls so free from wrath and agitation.'

'It is the peace before the storm, then,' she said, 'for they are all set on a law-suit.'

'Ah, that accounts for it! I thought there must be some reason.

Lent is usually acrimonious. Ladies, I think, find it particularly trying. It really is extraordinary,' he continued, 'quite extraordinary, to reflect on the means employed by God's providence to . . .'

Tough and evasive as a snake, he was sliding away from any share in the convent's temporal concerns.

'I find man's improvidence quite as much as I can reflect on,' she said. 'What if we are all ruined by this law-suit?' Her voice, escaping from its usual control, was harsh and tremulous, like the chirp of a fledgeling bird.

He turned, and looked at her. She was almost as tall as he, and she looked back at him steadily, though her cheeks were flushed with resentment and angry tears brightened her small eyes.

'It will not happen,' he said. 'I assure you, it will not happen. The things which one dreads never come to pass.'

She had never heard him speak with such authority. It might have been a stranger who spoke. Abashed, and yet comforted, she hurried away, making off before this astonishing being should decompose into their familiar, shabby, bulky, running-to-seed Sir Ralph.

Left to himself he continued to walk about in the sun, feeling the gay air, admiring the sharp tint of the wormwood, and reflecting on the means employed by God's providence. Here, for instance, was another springtime. At any moment now he might hear the cuckoo. At any moment, too, he might hear some little rattle inside him, or some twang in his brain, and know that death was after him. As you are when you hear the first cuckoo, whether busy or idle, merry or sorrowful, so you will be the year through; so Magdalen Figg had said, standing mud-coloured under the apple trees in bloom. He asked no better from the first cuckoo than to be found here, walking and thinking before the gate-house at Oby. For life on every springtime confirmation of it was sweet, and would be sweeter still with Dame Matilda as prioress. Life was durably sweet, it improved like a keeping-apple. If he could live to be old, live tranquilly and keep his health, he might yet get such enjoyment out of life as would astonish the devils when they came to unpick him. He gathered a spray of wormwood and rubbed it between finger and thumb. It was an old acquaintance. These sproutings were the tenth generation that he had seen put forth since that morning when he first stood here so lean and fretful. Not damned then, and yet so fretful. Damnation had taught him tranquillity and resignation to God's will. Not damned then; and yet, God being timeless, as much damned before God then as now, damned before his birth, damned before his begetting, native to hell-fire as a salamander. What would Dame Matilda say, that sensible prudent woman, could she know that with the prioress-ship of Oby she would inherit the services of a damned man? And yet he had been within an inch of telling her.

Dame Matilda was so powerfully impressed by Sir Ralph's assurance that the things which one dreads do not come to pass that she preserved her equanimity even when Dame Johanna, speaking in chapter, said she wished to say a few words about the proposed law-suit.

It was plain that Dame Johanna had learned her few words by heart, and her hearers resigned themselves to a sermon. Pitching her voice too high she was checked by a coughing-fit before she finished with her views on submission tempered with zeal; then she had to clear her throat; then she went on to her *Imprimis*. *Imprimis* was that nuns should not go to law, it being their part to live in the world as though the world were not. *Distinguo*, the world may so press upon nuns that law-suits must be undertaken; but if so undertaken, the nuns must go to law in a spirit of charity – which some present yet lacked. *Secundo*, it is forbidden to covet. She had nevertheless overheard the nuns of Oby talking about the damages they hoped to gain. Such hopes were both wrong and fallacious, for at Dilworth it had been shown – then followed several anecdotes from Dilworth. *Tertio.*

The prioress had been sitting hunched up, listlessly turning her ring. Now she raised her hand as though to brush away a fly, and said, speaking in a faint voice, brittle with exasperation, that she for one was already convinced by Dame Johanna's eloquence, and begged there might be no more talk of the law-suit. There was a murmur, if not of agreement, at any rate of sympathy and understanding. Was it possible, Dame Matilda asked herself; could Sir Ralph have been right? But at that same moment Dame Johanna began to talk again. Now she was congratulating the prioress on so wise a decision.

'For as I was about to say, dear Mother, *tertio* . . .'

The prioress sunk her head in her hands.

'. . . *Tertio*, it is forbidden to bear false witness. Yet with my own ears, dear sisters, I have heard you say that we are certain of our suit because the stones fell and killed Dame Susanna, and no court of law can remain unmoved by a dead nun. But this is not true. I saw, and so did you all, how Dame Susanna sought her own death. If she had stayed quietly with the rest of us she would be alive now, as we are. Furthermore . . .'

A clamour of disagreement arose, most of it quite sincere, for by now Dame Susanna's exemplary death was canonical.

'Furthermore . . .'

The prioress leaped to her feet and boxed Dame Johanna's ears. Her first blow loosened Dame Johanna's coif, the second dislodged it. Fastening one hand in the short grizzled locks the prioress began to scratch Dame Johanna's face. Dame Johanna screamed, moaned, called on the saints, and choked. With no expression beyond a sort of sleepwalking attentiveness the prioress clawed on in silence. Her silence was more alarming than anything else; it was as though she had forgotten speech, or felt no need for it, and had become an animal, killing without malice and almost without thought. No one knew what to do. The hopeful confidence that Dame Matilda would deal with it died away. Dame Matilda sat biting her finger; her eyes were shut, her face was livid. They remembered that Dame Matilda always felt sick at the sight of blood, and at the regular blood-lettings was as regularly sick. It was Dame Alice, the other nun from Dilworth, who, with an 'Excuse me, dear Mother,' seized the prioress in her sturdy arms and carried her back to her seat. Dame Beatrix and Dame Helen approached to mop and tidy the victim. The prioress looked on approvingly, and advised them to carry her away, adding in a voice airily resigned: 'We shall never have any peace while she is with us.'

From that day onward the prioress, awakened from her trance, persecuted Dame Johanna with remorseless artistry, inventing one derision after another as gleefully as a stone-carver inventing a set of gargoyles. She decided to enforce the rule of a good book being read aloud during dinner, and appointed Dame Johanna to be reader because, she said, of her scholarship. Perched in the reading-desk Dame Johanna coughed and stifled, while her appetite – she had a punctual appetite – proclaimed itself in unseemly rumbles. Dame Johanna, too, was peculiarly unhandy, one of those women doomed to drop, fumble, tear, dishevel, crumple, and soil. But because of her piety, her particular piety, Dame Johanna, said the prioress, must have the post of sacrist. Candles fell from their sticks, vestments caught on nails, incense spluttered, stains spread on the altar linen. Worst of all, there were the altar breads to make. Sweating with anxiety and desperately praying, Dame Johanna thumped and rolled an intractable lump of greying dough, scattered flour everywhere, and burned herself on the oven-tray. Finally she was set to repair the Trinity Cope. The Trinity Cope was one of the few treasures of Oby, and the nuns plucked up courage to defend it from Dame Johanna's puckers and gobble-stitches.

'Look how she is ruining it! And it is so beautiful.'

The prioress looked at it. Indeed, it was very beautiful. All her life she had loved beauty. Her spire was broken; since Dame Susanna's death the singing had become screeching; her nuns were ugly; Adela, the de Retteville novice, was a half-wit. In everything she attempted she was mocked and frustrated, and she could make nothing out of her despair but an exhibition of spite and vulgar malice. Biting back her sobs she said:

'Very well. No one shall repair it. Since you wish, it can go to ruin, like everything else. I have been thinking about the law-suit, too, and I have come to the conclusion that it would be useless to go on with it. I cannot carry it through alone, I have neither the health nor the spirits for such an undertaking. And I know by experience that I cannot count on any of you to help me. We will get the spire botched up somehow – sufficiently to prevent the draughts blowing down on you, that is all that matters. And everything shall go on as usual.'

V

The Lay of Mamillion

(*June* 1360)

On Holy Thursday Sir Ralph had walked in the sun thinking of the peacefulness of Oby. By midsummer he wondered if he would ever know peace and quiet again. Just as when two dogs fight to the death all the dogs within earshot fly at each other, the affair between the prioress and Dame Johanna set everyone by the ears. Through the bland spring weather the nuns bickered, the servants fought, and his new hawk was unmanageable. He could not even find repose in Jesse Figg's orchard. Jesse and William had fallen out, too, about the repairs at Dudham. Though the quarrel had not parted them, for they were as inseparable as ever, they were now inseparably locked in reproaches and recriminations. Beyond bringing them out cider in a larger jug – for quarrelling is thirsty work – Magdalen Figg took no part in their wrangles. She flowed on like the Waxle Stream, slow, calm, impenetrably muddy, foretelling the weather as indifferently as a river reflects the sky. Sometimes Sir Ralph found himself thinking that carnal pleasure with Magdalen might be very pleasurable, and that one would come away from it feeling refreshed and suppled like a washed shirt. But the fancy remained fancy; he knew that he would not be thinking of her at all if he had not failed to make William Holly more attentive to his troubles with the hawk.

He would have to find another hawk unaided. Unaided, too, he must somehow fit the convent with a new prioress. Things could not go on like this: sooner or later the prioress would kill Dame Johanna; and that would be a great pity, for the prioress was an exceptional woman and Dame Johanna invincibly a nonentity. So he must procure a hawk, a prioress, and the bishop; for the three novices were clamouring to make their final vows, and though a bishop was not really necessary for this, parents prefer a bishop.

It was Brother Baltazar, one of a pair of friars who lodged for a night at Oby, who told him of the hawks at Brocton.

Sir Ralph knew Brocton by hearsay. It was a small manor lying westward of Lintoft. The Lord of Brocton, though a young man, was blind. He had inadvertently ridden into a Corpus Christi procession, and his horse, alarmed by the singing and the banners, had taken fright and trampled down the priest carrying the pyx. Thus involved in sacrilege and already head over ears in debt, the Lord of Brocton had despaired and hanged himself – as if, said Brother Baltazar, that would make things any better. His goods, of course, had been seized; but friends can always find a way round the law. Sir Ralph had only to ride to Brocton, offer his ghostly comfort to the widow, turn the conversation to falconry, and the hawk would be his. Brother Baltazar added that he should not delay. The widow, it seemed, was being difficult, and there was talk of an excommunication pending to bring her to reason.

A few days away from Oby was such a heavenly prospect that as Sir Ralph on the dun horse looked westward from Lintoft and saw before him the oak woods through which he would ride so pleasantly all day he almost forgot about the hawk. It was enough to be on a holiday. The smell of the fern, the squirrels, the hares leaping about the glades, the buzzing of flies, the screams of the woodpecker, everything delighted him. He seemed to himself to be a hundred miles away from Oby, and restored to the days of his youth. Nightfall found him still wandering in and out of woods. A woman in a forester's hut to whom he described his route assured him that he must twice have been within a stone's throw of Brocton. Now he was a good five miles away from it. But in the morning, she said, her little boy should sit on the saddlebow and guide him.

The next day's sunrise waxed into a day of burning heat. The little boy was not so good a guide as he had been promised to be, and the sun was high before they came to the manor house. Seeing himself reflected in the moat Sir Ralph realised how fat he had grown. He had often seen his image in the pools of the Waxle Stream but the Brocton moat, reflecting him among sharp details of architecture, was more revealing of his shapelessness than the Cow Pool or Kitt's Bend. *Here comes such a nun!* Among all the unpleasantness of that night when the prioress returned to her broken spire he had not failed to notice this mortifying exclamation; and watching the porter lead away the dun horse he could imagine the comments that would be made on its rider. The Dame of Brocton, the porter told him, would see neither priest nor friar. He wondered if this was a pretext to conceal that a sentence of excommunication was already in force; but having got so far he asked if he could see the hawks.

'I will not go beyond a sparrow-hawk.' He had been saying this to himself ever since the conversation with Brother Baltazar, but handling the birds, seeing the love-lorn way they tilted their heads and poked with their wings, he forgot all prudence. Come what might, cost what it might, he must have a tiercel. While he gazed at them he heard a quick step and a rustle of skirts behind him. The falconer bowed and fell silent. Sir Ralph had to hoist himself from his contemplations to salute the Dame of Brocton. Though he was dazzled by the beauty of the birds he saw that she was young, and very handsome, though her face was deformed by weeping and her lip swollen with the bites she had given it to stop her tears. She greeted him frankly and began to question him. Why she had changed her mind about seeing neither priest nor friar she did not explain, but it did not appear that she had sought him out for any religious reason. When she bade him come into the house and dine astonishment spread over the falconer's broad face. The house was furnished with great elegance, and so clean that he could not believe himself in England. It was no wonder these people were in debt. She led him into the solar where an elderly woman, some sort of aunt, made the third at table. A little while after they had begun to eat a fourth member of the party came in – a boy about thirteen, a brother to the Dame of Brocton. His countenance showed how beautiful hers would have been if grief had not marred it.

With the same arrogant directness as when she had questioned him about himself and his journey the Dame of Brocton now began to question him about poetry. Many of the poets she mentioned he had never heard of, and to defend himself, and also because it was truly his opinion, he replied that the poets of the present age were of little account in comparison with the great men of the past.

'That is because you do not know them,' she replied.

'That may be true. It is many years since I have been amongst poets.' The admission cost him something, but he hoped a hawk would come of it.

She continued:

'And why do you only mention such old poets? All poetry is not in Latin.'

'No. But it might be better if it were. Since God and man between them have given us the Latin tongue and the Latin mode for poetry, it is waste of time to turn aside and scribble in the vernacular. That sort of thing can be left to old nurses, and jugglers at wakes and fairs, and those who cannot think how to go on unless a rhyme prompts them to their next thought.'

'Do you call the great Dante an old nurse? He wrote in the vernacular, and used rhymes.'

There was a sauce flavoured with ginger that he would have liked to give his whole attention to; but he thought of the hawk. Italian, he said, French, too, for that matter, being dialects of the Latin tongue, were more musical and better suited for poetry. The fallacy of the vernacular was exposed as soon as the tutelage of Latin was lost. In Norway he had heard a man declaiming parts of an epic in the dialect of that country, and it had sounded like the snuffling and growling of bears.

At this the boy looked up, and laughed.

'Yet some poet wrote it,' she said. 'And perhaps he was as great as Virgil.'

'If he were – which I cannot believe, for language is a great part of poetry, where the language is imperfect the poem must be imperfect, too – if he were, none but his own countrymen will know it.'

The Dame of Brocton frowned and fell silent. His mind was returning to the sauce when the elder lady asked him if he were skilled in music. She had been told that the ladies of Oby were renowned for their singing of the plain-chant.

'There again!' he exclaimed. 'Another example of what I maintain. These vernacular tunes, sung and forgotten in the space of a lifetime, and these descanters with their flourishes – how trivial they are by comparison with the classical modes of the church!'

The aunt now enquired about the nuns' needlework. It seemed that she was trying to divert the conversation from the question of poetry in the vernacular. He replied that the nuns embroidered very prettily, and that the convent had also possessed a fine illuminator. Unfortunately the house was damp and much of her work was already impaired by mildew. She asked if there was a moat. A moat was the only hope for a dry house. He explained that Oby stood on a rise of ground where no moat was feasible.

Meanwhile the Dame of Brocton sat biting her lip. Presently she began again, constraining her voice into amiability.

'I cannot help thinking that you might change your mind about poetry in English if you heard more of it. My husband . . .'

The boy looked at the aunt and folded his hands as if to say: 'The same old story!' Sir Ralph found that he was to spend the afternoon listening to a reading of the dead man's verses. There was a long poem, the widow explained, long, but unfinished, which her husband had considered to be his finest work. He had brooded over it for many years, sometimes coming home with a score of stanzas, sometimes with a line or two: for he found his invention worked most freely when he was on horseback, and he would ride hour-long over the waste, a groom going with him to pull the horse away from the thickets or out of the quagmires. On his return he would repeat his day's work and she would write it down. Before their marriage he had used a secretary; but the secretary had thought himself a poet also, his copies were not reliable, and at other times he was drunk when he wrote and his script could not be deciphered.

'And is it all in English? – and all in rhyme?'

'Of course. It is an English epic.'

He resigned himself. A hawk might have been purchased elsewhere at a less exorbitant price. But he was at Brocton, his adventure had mastered him, and till it released him there was nothing for it but to submit.

Yet the afternoon was not entirely unpleasant, for his seat by the window was cushioned and he could look out and see the dragon-flies darting over the moat, or the aspen quiver of the reflected sunlight on the mossed wall, or a water-rat swimming across and dragging its wheat-ear pattern of ripples after it. It sharpened his appreciation to remember that all this was in the hands of the law, and that at any moment the summoner might ride across the drawbridge. His adventure had brought him here just in time. A few weeks later and there might be no hawks, no cup of wine, nothing but sunlight and water-rats and dragon-flies. As though no calamity had befallen or ever would befall she sat reading aloud, her voice persisting through the flies buzzing and the haymakers calling for drinks. Though the poem was unfinished there was a great deal of it, he could tell that from the bulk of the manuscript. Its chief character was someone called Mamillion, a giant, it seemed, or perhaps an enchanter; but a gentle giant, for his power was of small use to him and he did little but ride from one place to another, often pausing to hold long conversations with birds, or to wash his hair and beard in enchanted fountains. The poem was full of bird-songs and voices of water. No doubt the author's blindness had sharpened his other senses, so that the tweedle of a wren or the taste of a bilberry meant more to him than to the sighted.

'I wonder that your lord did not write a poem about Samson,' he remarked at the close of a section. She answered that Samson was a person with no attributes of chivalry and quite unsuited to be the subject of a poem. To the best of Sir Ralph's remembrance Samson was well-born, at any rate Samson's parents were people of substance, but not being sure of it he did not care to commit himself. He thought too that Samson, if not a good christian, was at any rate nearer to christianity and more deserving of an epic than Mamillion. Whoever Mamillion might be he was certainly a heathen. Though the Lord of Brocton's verses referred from time to time to the Virgin or the saints it was obvious that this was merely because the poet himself chose to do so. Even when Mamillion came on Christ in the depth of a yew forest, bewailing, and hiding his face in the bitter yew boughs, no conversion or judgement came of it; Mamillion only gazed, and pitied, and rode on.

The sunlight quitted the water, the reflected light danced no longer on the wall of the moat. A swarm of midges rose and fell, a minute chaff fanned by some mysterious breath of living. Somewhere overhead a thin wailing arose. After a while he realised that it was a baby crying. So there was a child in the house. This was natural enough, yet for some reason it surprised him. When next Mamillion fell asleep under a thorn tree, or came to a castle, or found a boat of stretched skins and paddled off in it among the reeds, so putting a colon to his unadventurous adventures, he would speak to the Dame of Brocton about her child. Possibly she would then go off and see to it, leaving him free to look again at the hawks. He had lost hope of getting away before nightfall.

Yet in such a house there would be a good bed. Though he itched to be gone he was also pleased to be staying. All his life he had wondered how it would feel to live as the rich do. Now he was in a way to find out. God in heaven, what happiness to be rich!

Mamillion's wanderings halted where they would for ever halt, on the brink of a blood-stained river and a blank page, but Sir Ralph remained at Brocton. By force of acquaintance he had come to like the poem and even to find pleasure in the sound of English rhymed verse. The sharp consonants, the rebellious false quantities, put him in mind of a wide mere bristling with reeds and flawed with a choppy wind. Taking the manuscript he began to read aloud to himself, experimenting with the scansion, trying to find some reason in it. One might as well try to scan the paces of a hare. Sometimes it loped, sometimes it ran: all one could say of it was that it had its own ways of moving.

'And what became of Mamillion? Did he find a kingdom, did he marry, was he slain?'

'It was to end with a piece of mistletoe,' she replied. 'He was to find the mistletoe growing on an oak tree and lop it off with a golden sword.'

'An imitation of the golden bough in Virgil, no doubt.'

'I do not know.'

Though she had a child (true, it was only a girl-child) all her maternal feeling seemed to be fastened upon this unfinished poem. Having compelled him to listen to it, having persuaded him into liking it, she led him on to her main purpose, which was to make the poem known. Would the fact that it was unfinished make the world reject it? He answered soothingly that there was a great deal of it already: an unfinished epic would have a better chance than a few lyrics. If it had been in Latin, he muttered to himself; but there was no object in going through all that again. He pointed out that thanks to her scholarship and her wifely devotion the story of Mamillion was already in writing, the first step towards being known. She said that being written down was not the same thing as being read. A happy thought struck him. Very earnestly he advised her to make a second copy. The boy and the aunt also asked him what he thought of the poem. The boy mocked gracefully, the aunt seemed to be consulting him as though he were a physician and the poem something he might prescribe a cure for. She thanked him too effusively for his interest and was sure that the Virgin had sent him to Brocton. It was evident that unless he were careful he would find himself saddled with the obligation of introducing Mamillion to the world of letters. In their different ways, the boy with his derision, the aunt with her hypocrisy, the widow with her sincerity, they were easing their burden on to his shoulders. It was very silly of them, for of course he could do nothing about it. How was he to go among the writers and poets saying: Here is an unfinished English epic which you must admire? Perhaps he had misled them, mentioning during that first meal the countries he had visited, the notabilities he had seen; yet even the nuns at Oby, those simple ladies, had known such talk to be the ordinary brag of the penniless travelling student, and took it for no more than it was worth. Brocton swallowed it whole. He marvelled at the unworldliness of these worldlings, till he remembered that far away in the past he had seen the same thing. Apparently if one were sufficiently rich and sufficiently well-born one need have no worldly cunning, it was enough to exist – in which case the lilies commended by Jesus were several degrees higher in the social scale than King Solomon. Even these Brocton people, and Brocton was not a great manor, were too sophisticated to distinguish between a poor priest on the lookout for a hawk and a fashionable scholar: all they knew of the world was that it could and would support them, as kings and dukes travel from one estate to another, eating up a year's food in a month and, when everything is eaten, travelling on. Yet the poem of Mamillion stayed in his mind, and he began to wonder about the character of the poet, that lord as attentive as any shepherd to wild berries and signs of rain, who had so haughtily and unpractically hanged himself. There was a parish priest, a red-faced sharp-eyed little Welshman to whom he had been introduced after mass on Sunday (the ban of the church had not fallen on Brocton after all), and Sir Ralph began to question him. Indeed, yes, it was very sad, a great pity, said the little man, his black eyes dancing in his red face. He was very sorry for them, the poor women, the poor servants who would so soon be trotting. His lamenting sing-song was belied by an undertone that it was no great loss after all. Presently he said that the Lord of Brocton was a bad young man: proud, harsh, luxurious, an unkind lord to his people.

'Yet the serfs look thriving,' said Sir Ralph, thinking of Oby.

'No wonder, indeed! He granted them whatever they asked. That is one reason why his debts were so many. He was a bad lord, and much hated. He had no consideration, and people like to be considered. It makes a serf feel silly to be given whatever he asks.'

He marched Sir Ralph off to the parsonage and showed him his geese, his pigs, his bees, his little cow. Everything told of neatness and management – the beds heaped with goosefeather pillows, the flitches drying in the chimney, the bee-skeps smoking among the bean-rows, the loom, taking up half the room, where Sir Jankin sat weaving blankets on rainy days. Learning that Sir Ralph was only a nun's priest, Sir Jankin condoled with him. No glebe, no goods of his own, no occupation: life on such terms must drag heavily.

Learning that Oby lay among reeds and osiers he urged Sir Ralph to take up basket-making.

As busy as the Georgics, thought Sir Ralph, walking back through the silent Sunday landscape, hushed with Sunday and dinner-time. One might be very happy in such a life, jostled through the sameness of the days by a hundred small thrifts and contrivances. In spring one sows, in autumn one garners, there are nuts to pick and little pigs to geld, and morning and evening one milks the cow and looks about for eggs. There is no time of year when one cannot bring home something profitable, and that is how nature would have one live, as attentive as a lover.

Sir Jankin proposed basket-making. The Dame of Brocton proposed Mamillion. Everyone had a plan for him, he only had no plan. 'What ails me?' he said, stopping under an oak tree as though the question must be answered there and then. 'What ails me that I can never have a plan for myself?' Was it lack of ambition, was it lack of desire? In his youth he had been ambitious. Desire had not failed him even now. Desire for a hawk had brought him to Brocton, and certainly his faculty of desire had not perished, for he was capable as ever of disgust, and disgust is the inversion of desire. He had as much ability as other men, as much endurance, more health and strength than many. If he could get rid of his fat he would be in excellent condition. But his life had been aimless as an idiot's, in his youth running from place to place with an idiot's delight in motion, and now, like an idiot, set down in the chimney-corner. He was a bastard and penniless? Other penniless bastards had done well enough for themselves, so why not he? But he was damned – and can a man who despairs of salvation in the next world frame desires in this? A bird hopped in the tree, and before it had settled, his mind had tossed away this answer as worthless. Long before he had come to Oby and damned himself he had lacked whatever it is that holds a man to his purpose.

What impulse, what little puff of wind, had sent him towards Oby? The thought of a breakfast. Clear as in a dream he saw the track rising to a knoll with trees on it and the colour of the moonlight as the dawn began to tarnish it, and felt once more the physical desolation which had preceded his vomiting. 'I am stricken,' he had thought. 'I shall die here, alone and unfriended. And nobody will know or care.'

Perhaps that was the answer: his stubborn lifelong loneliness, a celibacy costing no effort and earning no approbation, cold as the devil's loins when he genders with a witch. And suppose he were indeed begotten by Satanas, and came into the world inheriting damnation as all others inherit original sin? The devil might have come stamping into the brothel as the rest of them did, someone must have fathered him, so why not Satanas? Here was a thought to run mad with. He stood snorting under the tree, waiting to feel the blood climb into his neck and the hairs bristle on his scalp. A brilliant hope flashed before him. If he ran mad at Brocton as he had run mad at Oby he might wander away in his madness; and when his wits came back to him he would be far away with no one knowing who he was, far away and free to begin another life.

He wrung his hands in an agony of hope. But nothing happened. At last he began to walk on, for there was no sense in staying.

That same afternoon he saw that the days of his popularity at Brocton were over. Though his hostess continued to thank him for all he would do to make known the poem of Mamillion she thanked him without conviction, and though the aunt continued to heap his platter and fill his cup he saw her exchanging glances with the boy, and imagined her slow furry voice saying: 'One might as well fodder that great beast Leviathan.' But melancholy now made him as stupid as a baby; it took the news that the summoner and his officers were within a day's journey of Brocton to dislodge him. Nothing like damnation to disgrace a man, he thought, hearing himself say that his absence would now be more comfortable to them than his presence.

'You must not go without your hawk,' she answered. Stumbling over her long-tailed gown he followed her to the falconry, and while he was biting his knuckles she chose out a couple of falcons.

'Can you carry them both, or shall I send a man along with you?'

One such bird would cost a fortune, a pair of them was out of the question. He must avail himself of the excuse of priestly orders and get off with a sparrow-hawk. Then the thought of his inadequacy, his disgraceful departure, smote him, and he resolved not to flinch before any price she asked. The money must be raised somehow. He could sell his books. He could make baskets as the Welshman had advised.

Her voice cut through his expostulations. The falcons were a gift.

He rode away, a clumsy candelabra for the two birds. The dun horse neighed and looked back towards the manor of Brocton as though he were riding it out of Eden. The poor brute also had a taste for high living, for clean water and sweet hay. There was actually a gloss on its coat. I am riding like Mamillion, he thought, riding through woods and past little woodland meres. But it was not possible to conceive Mamillion riding to Oby, to that epitome of humdrum, a provincial nunnery. Topping the rise of ground between Lintoft and Oby he looked down on his bishopric. The corn was ten days yellower, the beans were ten days rustier. The Hollys' dwelling was being re-thatched, and bristled like a boy's head. There was the Waxle Stream, winding in its green sleeve. There was the convent, with the spire cased in scaffolding – so the masons must have come back. Within it were his ladies, all at sixes and sevens, no doubt, just as he had left them.

He spoke to his two falcons.

'Now you are going to live in a convent and become two holy nuns.'

Their demeanour was so composed, they were so gentle and dignified, that he was constrained to add: 'God forbid it!'

But something had resolved the sixes and sevens. Voices were low, brows were smooth, and the prioress had resigned. Seemingly this had been achieved without a struggle, for she told him the news with a satisfaction only triflingly enhanced by her natural art.

'You know how often I have said that my one wish was to be relieved of my office. Only the thought of the expense held me back. Now our good treasuress tells me we can perfectly well afford an election. You cannot imagine how thankful I feel! Saint Leonard has never freed a more delighted prisoner.'

What was more, she meant it. Her eyes were clear, she had the washed girlish look of a convalescent.

What had effected this miracle? There was a new cook, a good one. A good cook can do much, but surely this was beyond the mediation of cookery? Dame Salome had fallen and broken her leg, and at her age and with her bulk it was unlikely that she would survive it; but Dame Salome had never been a nun of any importance, the prospect of losing her could not have brought about this mysterious millennium. During his absence the convent had been served by the new priest at Lintoft, whose name was John Idburn. But there was nothing to suggest that John Idburn's ministrations had spoken peace to Oby. Questioned, the nuns reported that he was a very quiet young man, that he looked weakly, and stammered.

At Brocton Sir Ralph had congratulated himself on being out of earshot of his ghostly daughters. Now, racked with curiosity, he wooed them to converse with him, but wooed in vain. To Dame Matilda he remarked that it must be a relief to her to have the election fixed at last and that there could be no doubt as to the succession. She answered that whoever was chosen could at best only hope to be a poor copy of such a distinguished prioress. When he grinned she gave him a look so austere that he began to revise his cheerful anticipations of her term of office. When he condoled with Dame Margaret on the headaches which the renewal of work on the spire must be causing her she asked him if he had seen the revised design? – it had several notable improvements on the other. Nothing came of a visit to Dame Salome, who lay in the infirmary, mildly delirious, and mistaking him for Prior Thomas. Even Dame Johanna, with whom he cautiously strolled in the cloister, said no more than how much she was looking forward to meeting the bishop. They had some secret; but as she-cattle put the calves in their midst and confront the wolf with a ring of lowered horns and trampling hoofs, his nuns kept him at bay with primmed-up lips and lowered eyelids. He would never know.

He had never learned, either, how a game of Flying Saint Katharine had ended so awkwardly. So how was he to guess that Dame Salome, increasingly put about by the quarrels of the convent, quarrels in which she was quite unfitted to play a distinguished part, had been re-creating that incident in a shape more favourable to her self-esteem? She might be a fat old woman, and of no account. Yet if the truth were known, the truth which envy tried to conceal . . . The nuns were in chapter and only gave half an ear to Dame Salome's grumbles. They went on with their interchange of more topical accusations while Dame Salome worked herself up with complaints of how she had always been slighted, her opinions disregarded, her age unhonoured, her plate constantly heaped with bones when it was well known that she had not the teeth to deal with them. Then came some quotations from the Magnificat and an allusion to stones which the builders rejected, and developing from stones and builders a reminder that she had always said the spire was too tall to be safe. The prioress, who remained sensitive about the spire, bade her hold her tongue. Dame Salome then harked back to envy and conspiracy, saying that if a man should rise from the dead the nuns of Oby would not be convinced. No, they would declare that nothing had happened, that he had been mistaken and had better drink a little soup and forget about it. The nuns failed to see the import of this hypothetical man who rose from the dead and was given soup. It was not till Dame Salome cried out from the head of the steps that they should see for themselves whether or no there was a flying saint among them that they grasped her intention. By then it was too late. Flapping her arms and screaming, she launched herself off the topmost step, rolled to the bottom, and lay stunned, one leg projecting at an unnatural angle from her dusty petticoats.

This shocked them out of their quarrels. If they had been rooks they would have migrated. Being nuns, they revolted. After compline Dame Matilda, Dame Beatrix, Dame Helen, and Dame Margaret followed the prioress to her chamber and said, speaking one after another as if it were a liturgy: 'Dear Mother, we ask you to resign.' The prioress with a gasp of relief replied that that was exactly what she wished to do. Then and there the letters of resignation were written, one to the bishop, the other to Adam de Retteville, the secular patron of the house, and Sir John Idburn rode with them to Waxelby, whence they would be carried on by the friars.

VI

Prioress Johanna

(*July 1360–January 1368*)

To John Idburn who, like everyone of his generation, had heard countless stories of the indecorum and flightiness of nunneries Oby had seemed like something out of the age of faith. He was deeply touched. Being a young man and still inclined to literature he wrote a long account of his visits there to an Oxford friend. 'In such a house,' the letter concluded, 'so uncontaminated by strife and worldly cares, so peacefully set like Mary at the feet of Christ, one might even expect to see a miracle take place.' He wished that he could have served Oby rather than his parish of Lintoft; though he had not been six months at Lintoft he was already disheartened, afraid of his parishioners, and very lonely. Soon after Sir Ralph's return he invited him to dinner. He had seen the nuns' priest once or twice and had not been prepossessed by the fat old man balanced like a bag of soot on the dun horse; but he might after all find in him the friend that he craved for, and at any rate he came from Oby.

After the first interchange of professional conventionalities Sir John had the luck to ask the right question. His sexton had told him that the timbers in the Lintoft church roof had been taken from a Danish galley, and that the sea-salt could still be tasted on them. Could this be true? Sir Ralph discovered that all those boring disputes he had listened to in Figg's orchard were in truth the material for his own antiquarian researches. He was able to tell Sir John everything about the voyage up the Waxle Stream, where the galley grounded and why, how the old woman brought her poisoned cup, how most of the Danes succumbed, how the others, surviving but disheartened, remained to work for the inhabitants, ingratiated themselves by introducing a new kind of wolf-trap, intermarried with the natives, founded red-haired families and bequeathed a number of Danish words to the local speech. He had no hesitation in assuring Sir John that the timbers in his church roof had grown in some Scandinavian forest. On their second meeting Sir John began with another lucky opening. He spoke of hawking. But when that subject was exhausted his own plight came to his lips and he broke out into a complaint of his isolation at Lintoft.

'What else can you expect?' cried Sir Ralph briskly. 'A strong young man like you must do more than preach and say masses if he is to earn the esteem of his parishioners. You should work, young man, you should work! If you want to be a good priest you must have the best sow, the best beans, the sweetest honey, the cock that crows loudest. You will do nothing with books and prayers. Turn your mind to pigs.'

As though his words had summoned them a number of pigs just then rushed screaming and grunting into the parsonage cabbage-yard. Screaming and grunting the priest's house-keeper rushed out and drove them away by jabbing at their noses with an iron-shod staff.

'I hate pigs!'

'Very well, then!' – Sir Ralph's voice was injuriously tolerant – 'Why not take up basket-making? But in God's name, do something! It is better to work than to whine and grow costive. Most of your troubles are the common lot of man, if you will allow an old man to say so.'

They parted with civility, but each knew that civility would be the limit of their acquaintance. Riding home Sir Ralph trounced himself for his aspirations. He had actually looked forward to telling John Idburn about his travels, had prepared phrases and rehearsed anecdotes. Bah! What would his old stories mean to a young milksop, absorbed in his own troubles and thinking that there was nothing notable in the world until he had opened his eyes on it?

Smoking his hands over a wet fire Sir John exclaimed: '*Turn your mind to pigs!* You've done it to some purpose, haven't you, with your paunch and your greasy gown and the bristles starting from your skin. Turn your mind to pigs!' And when his housekeeper came in and idled into gossip about Oby he listened greedily, stuffing the wound in his heart by stories of how Sir Ralph was no priest at all but the paramour of an old nun called Dame Agnes who had smuggled him into the convent to stay her lechery, though she was thrice his age; and how another of the nuns, young, and very rich, was with child by him, but the old nun, frantic with jealousy, beat her so terribly that she died, spitting up blood by the pailful, and not even her own spells could save her, though she was a sorceress; and how a very honest woman, a widow, called Pernelle Bastable, had tried to lodge with the nuns but their gross behaviour had driven her away; and how the bishop had come and scourged all the nuns and ordered Sir Ralph to be gelded, which was why he was now so fat. Though he did not credit these stories he listened to them, drooping his head over the smoking brands and vaguely wondering when she would remember to clear the dinner-board.

Though Sir Ralph's main mind was given to his new falcons it tickled him to hear stories about the insufferable tediousness of the priest at Lintoft, who would follow his parishioners into the field to tell them of his poor health and his bad dreams. But after a little indulgence he would stop the stories, saying that whatever sort of fool the young man might be, he was a priest and should be respected as such: people who allowed themselves to mock at a priest were but half a step from beastly lollardry. This went down well. The hamlet was in a ferment of loyalty to the church, knowing that a bishop was imminent. Other bishops had come and gone and the hamlet of Oby had been none the better for it; nevertheless, the advent of a bishop aroused pleasurable expectations. If a bishop did nothing else he improved the quality of the broken meats served out at the wicket. Bishop William had been half a roast goose to old Granny Scole.

The permit to proceed to an election came in August, 1360, and in the convent, as in Jesse Figg's orchard, there was a cheerful certainty that Dame Matilda would be elected. In Dame Matilda's heart, too, there was a cheerful certainty. She had served the convent well as treasuress, she looked forward to serving it better as prioress. Above all, it pleased her to see the novices looking forward to the day which would make her a prioress and them her nuns. Lapsing from her usual realism she saw herself ruling an Oby from which all the elder nuns had conveniently disappeared, leaving her a household of the young, the open-countenanced, the practical.

Two nuns had been chosen as tellers, one was Dame Cecily and the other Dame Alice, the second of the Dilworth nuns. She it was who had intervened when the prioress was killing Dame Johanna, and from that hour Dame Matilda had conceived an esteem for her, and had tried to bring her forward as something more than a set of stout arms and sturdy legs coupled to a willing disposition. After prayers and a special mass for a good decision the tellers set out to collect the votes. Each nun spoke her choice in private. At the close of her round Dame Cecily looked flushed and uneasy. She scrutinised the countenance of the other teller but learned nothing from it. Together they went to the chapter-house where, having given their votes, the nuns had assembled to hear the result.

Dame Johanna was elected prioress with a majority of one vote.

Dame Cecily glanced from face to face, and her distress at the miscarriage was swallowed up in a more personal regret: that she could not at once use her sketch-book and her silver style. Such physiognomies would supply initials for the whole length of Jeremy's Lamentations. What had happened was one of those accidents that overtake the righteous in the midst of their prosperity. Feeling sure of Dame Matilda's election, grateful to be relieved of the old prioress whose temper had grown so disturbing, nun after nun had yielded to the thought: Why not vote for that poor Dame Johanna? – one vote can't upset the result, and it would please the poor wretch.

Speeches of congratulation and joy were made in the gloomiest tones, and the meeting broke up. In the general mortification no one appreciated how very suitably the prioress-elect was behaving, nor did anyone surmise that for many years Dame Johanna had contemplated exactly this happy event, and so walked into her new dignity with the calm and decorum that come from long practice in day-dreaming. Her humility, her courtesy, her affability – everything was irreproachable, and stale as a treatise.

Seeing her so bleak and so meek, every soul in and about the convent groaned at the thought of the future and of the revenges which Dame Johanna could be expected to take. Jesse Figg cursed and swore, William Holly was silent but prepared to move himself with all that was his, and a little over, to Dudham, and

Sir Ralph in his chamber over the gate lamented as feelingly as King Saul. The servants trembled. They foresaw that the new prioress would set Dame Alice over them, Dame Alice who would expect everyone to be as active as herself. 'That skinny one?' said the masons. Edmund Gurney said nothing but looked at the spire. It was again almost finished and now more beautiful than ever, at any rate to his mind, since in the rebuilding he had been able to go ahead with it, unhampered by his employer's second thoughts. Though it was beautiful and almost finished he looked at it with pursed lips. He knew the goings-on inside the convent as well as though he were (Heaven preserve him from it!) a nun of Oby himself. What more likely than that Dame Johanna would have it pulled down in revenge for the beatings and floutings she had endured? Even in the bishop's palace the news of the Oby election was heard with paternal grief. 'They have elected a Dilworth nun!' exclaimed the bishop. 'Am I never to be rid of those Dilworth nuns?'

Only the old prioress was serene, absorbed in designing a new cope. This had begun as a work of reparation, a copy of the Trinity Cope which her malice had handed over to Dame Johanna, so much to its detriment. But in the course of copying the original so many new interpretations of the design, and then so many variants and improvements, crowded into her mind that it became clear to her that no mere copy would do, and that what God willed of her was an original penitential tribute to his glory.

The Trinity is a boon to the designer. It gets over all those difficulties of antithesis – light and shade, man and woman, good and evil – which, however proper they may be in nature and philosophy, are monotonous in art. Dame Alicia, as she again heard herself called, often paused to give thanks to the Godhead for having, somehow or other, outwitted the dualism of the moralists and insinuated the idea of a threefold unity. Perhaps her thanks were not quite so explicitly theological as that. The best minds of Christendom had travailed, fathers of the church had fought, bishops had fallen into heresy, deacons had been martyred, saints had imperilled their sainthood, councils had taken to fisticuffs, all in order to arrive at this doctrine which she was now sketching in charcoal on six ells of the best linen; and whole sections of that seamless garment, the church of Christ, had been rent away by misunderstandings of what was now a commonplace to every novice at Oby. Dame Alicia by luck of time and place was nearer to the novice than to the fathers of the church. She accepted the doctrine of the Trinity and found it just what she needed.

'I hope you will work in some Herb Trinity,' said Dame Beatrix. 'I have been using it on our poor prioress, and really I believe her breathing is easier. At any rate she doesn't seem to me to snort quite as loudly as she did.'

Like many other artistic people, Dame Alicia did not know one flower from another. She asked what colour Herb Trinity was.

'Three colours, yellow, purple, and white . . . a little flower that grows in stony pastures. Some people call it Three Faces under One Hood.'

Of course, of course! Three faces under one hood, three faces in one glory, a right and a left profile developing from the full face instead of ears, four grey eyes, one crown, three beards. Purple, yellow, and white: the robe purple, the crown golden, the white beard of the First Person flanked by golden beards in profile; and the purple, yellow, and white of the little flower acknowledged in a surrounding garland. Whistling under her breath like a schoolboy she began to erase the centre of her design, which had followed the more ordinary crucifixion trinity of the old cope, and to sketch in the threefold countenance.

She had never been so happy in her life as now. Officially a retiring prioress returns to the standing of a simple nun, but civility softens this regulation, and Dame Johanna wished particularly to be magnanimous. Blithely accepting magnanimity, Dame Alicia had a room of her own, meals on trays whenever she wanted them, her bullfinch and her posset-cup, a stuffed mattress and a recorder; for when she tired of stitching, or waited for a problem of design to thaw out, a little music refreshed her. In summer the open window gave her a view of her spire. In winter she had the best brazier. Her ageing lap-dog snored at her feet, and Adela stroked the lap-dog.

Adela, poor child, was a disappointment. Released from her mother's biddings and beatings she proved to be noisy, arrogant, and unbiddable; even her sweet temper was like a kind of obstinacy. She was, however, very pretty; and when she was newly arrived and still regarded as an acquisition it had delighted the nuns to compare her little hooked nose with the profile of her ancestress Alianor, whose effigy had gazed towards the altar of Saint Leonard since the convent's foundation. Alianor was ugly and had no waist, the child complained. Her feet were big and rested on a cushion instead of on a dog. When she, Adela, was a nun she would have fifty dogs. Why could she not have a dog now? Please could she have a dog? Please would Dame Cecily draw her some dogs? There was one little dog too many in the convent already, said Dame Cecily snappishly, a little she-dog called Adela. They wanted no more. A noisy little dog with no tail, Dame Philippa added. If Oby was disappointed in Adela, Adela was no less disappointed in Oby. A house of nuns was a place where everyone was cross, where doors were closed against one, where skirts were twitched out of one's hands, where Our Lady was displeased. 'Look, Adela! She is frowning at you!' The child would whisk round and study the wooden countenance;

but it had always resumed its cold and rather threatening smile, and she grew to feel that a frown would be better. The only escape she could find was to creep off to the old prioress, where she could warm her chilblained hands, stroke Mouton, and pair the strands of bright embroidery silk. Even this was not reliably secure. Sometimes the sight of the de Retteville novice would recall to Dame Alicia the occasion of their first meeting: the sounds and the smells of the christening feast would recur, and all her suffering and melancholy amid the clashing of dishes, the laughter and belching, and elderly boasting. She would turn savagely on the child, and drive her away. But as the new cope came to life and was her only responsibility, Dame Alicia accepted the position of being fond of Adela: one of her failures, admittedly, but not a very painful one.

Adela's dowry, too, seemed like being a failure: the rents which had looked so well on paper were badly paid, and the promise of victual had resolved into a cartload of stinking venison. But these things which formerly would have roused her to an intensity of vexation passed over her like thistledown.

They did not much trouble the new prioress either. She was accustomed to insolvency: Dilworth had taught her that. Had Dame Matilda remained treasuress many items in Edmund Gurney's final bill would have been challenged. But in her pursuit of magnanimity the new prioress decided that it would be painful for Dame Matilda to retain a post which brought her so continually in contact with the person who had supplanted her: Dame Dorothy, a dull nun, was hoisted up into being treasuress and Dame Matilda, complying with a delicacy of feeling which she did not herself feel, became sacrist. If she had had a shred of saintliness in her character the mortification of this change of occupation might have burnished her into something quite remarkable. But no such outlet was possible, for she was incapable of religious feeling. She burnished the altar plate with energy, and spent her spare time unwieldily larking with the young nuns. Prioress Johanna frowned and sighed to see her sacrist rolling along the cloisters arm-in-arm with Lilias and Eleanor le Bailey like a Silenus among the nymphs. She could not forget that Dame Matilda had been married. The marriage had not been consummated, Dame Matilda was a virgin; but through no fault of her own, the prioress opined.

Perhaps the spectacle of Dame Matilda, so red in the face and so rowdy, encouraged the prioress to develop her scruples about four-footed beasts. Saint Benedict had forbidden his monastics to eat the flesh of four-footed beasts; yet beef, pork, and mutton were served as a matter of course in the refectory of Oby, just as they had been at Dilworth, and just as they were in any Benedictine house. At Dilworth there had been frequent outbursts of carnality. No doubt such outbursts would happen at Oby too. Dame Alice, the cellaress, was commanded to reform the dietary, at least to modify it by making more use of eels and dumplings. Dame Alice said that a dumpling is nothing without gravy, and that for a good gravy there must be meat. She appealed to Sir Ralph as an authority on gravy. The prioress appealed to him as an authority on discipline. To the cellaress he recommended a freer use of mushrooms, and confused the prioress by citing other prohibitions in the Rule. She was not entitled to pick and choose. Further, if Holy Church had learned from heaven that a reversal to the original rule was desired, Holy Church would have informed its children *ex cathedra*. Having wound her up in heresy he judged that he had done all that was needed, and went out with his falcons after some partridges; for he disliked mutton.

Presently the nuns were tapping on Dame Alicia's door with a new story. The prioress had turned her mind to another aspect of the Rule. Surely her nuns were very idle? Oby was commanded to delight in labour, and everyone was set to spin. Dame Cecily was taken from her illuminating, Dame Alice from her marzipan: only Dame Alicia was left in peace with the Trinity, for the prioress would do nothing that might seem vindictive. Though no one span very industriously a certain amount of yarn accumulated and was sent to the Dudham weavers. Back came a scanty quantity of bad cloth. But it was not too scanty for the prioress's ideas; for now her scruples had fastened on apparel. Gowns, she saw, were too wide, and far too long. Sleeves were too ample and frontlets not ample enough. A nun should be covered, but no more. As for Dame Lilias, who laced her kirtle on both sides in order to show off her long weasel waist, she must have a new and conforming gown made from the convent's homespun immediately.

Yet none of these vagaries provoked rebellion. It takes a strong character to create an opposition; and there was an inherent mediocrity in all the prioress's ordinances which made them tolerable, and almost welcome. She supplied her community with something to talk about, and beguiled the tedium of convent life as a jester beguiles the tedium of life at court. Besides, all this was an interlude. She could not possibly live beyond another six months. When she was dead it would be time to take life seriously.

She lived on for seven years, coughing and creaking: an extraordinary figure whose skeleton head and hands emerged from an apparent corpulence; for she was so thin that Dame Beatrix kept her wrapped in layers of raw wool, like a seven-month child. Dame Beatrix, who could love anything provided it was sickly and needed her help, used to come away from wadding the prioress weeping real tears and crossing herself as though she were returning from a visit to the sacrament. Then she would take

Dame Lilias on one side and describe to her the staring bones, the sores, the veins that showed through the yellow skin like illuminations faintly remaining on an old parchment. For the infirmaress had diagnosed her successor in Dame Lilias, and was now acclimatising her.

Even after the prioress's death they still heard her cough, or thought they did so. Dame Alicia remarked: 'What a noisy house this will be when I have died too. What with Dame Johanna's cough and my recorder you will not be able to hear yourselves think.'

'No matter. We are nuns, we don't think,' Dame Cecily answered.

Dame Cecily was nearing thirty now, and had grown ugly and shrewish. Her eyes troubled her. A discharge came from them, and none of Dame Beatrix's remedies helped her. To be properly cured, said the infirmaress, Dame Cecily should bathe her eyes at Saint Winifred's shrine. But that was a long way off, at Holywell in the marches of Wales; and however cheaply the journey was made, even if Dame Cecily and her companion were to go on foot across England, such a journey, and the thankoffering that must accompany the cure, would entail a considerable outlay. Besides, added the infirmaress, how could she have left the prioress, who needed her so badly? – for Dame Beatrix was determined that Dame Cecily's fellow-traveller should be herself. But when the prioress was dead, Dame Matilda would soon get her hands on to Isabel de Scottow's legacy: then there would be money enough for journeying to any shrine.

Dame Isabel de Scottow's bequest of the ten years' profit on her vineyard and the interest at ten per cent on that profit had fallen due in 1364, three summers before the death of Prioress Johanna. After a year's expectation the nuns began to urge their prioress to look into the matter. But nothing was done. A few months later Etchingdon sent in a claim for half the cost of repairing the church at Methley, which had been struck by lightning. Since Oby still received the Methley tithes this liability could not be shirked; and a letter was sent to John de Scottow, nephew to Dame Isabel and now the head of the family. After some time he replied to it, saying that the funeral expenses of his parents had cost a great deal, and that at present he could not part with the large sum of money involved in his aunt's legacy (how much that sum amounted to he was too wary to say). He begged the honoured house of Oby to be patient for a month or two longer. Six months later Oby sent a second application, and again John de Scottow wrote temporising. In due course Oby wrote once more. It seemed as though these letters would become part of the yearly routine, like the feasts of the church and the quarterly blood-lettings. Then Fulk de Scottow, Dame Isabel's brother, poked out his head from under a Cistercian hood, and wrote to the prioress austerely enquiring how she could make such a claim. Did she not understand that in becoming a nun his sister had renounced the goods of this world and was therefore incapable of bequeathing anything except her immortal soul? If, indeed, Dame Isabel had, in her infirmity, so far forgotten her vows as to sully her death-bed with thoughts of money, or if she had been regrettably influenced to do so, then at least christian charity demanded that the living should speak no more of it.

This was a difficult letter to answer. Custom winked at legacies by people in the religious life provided that the money was not alienated from the church; but custom was not canonical. Just what one would expect of a Cistercian, said the ladies of Oby. For what made Fulk de Scottow's interposition so particularly ill-natured was that he himself stood to make nothing by the diversion of the legacy. Malice, flat black Cistercian malice against a Benedictine foundation, must lie at the bottom of it! (Here, in fact, they were wrong: Fulk had compounded with his nephew for half of the disputed sum, as a price for getting him out of parting with the whole of it.) Things were at this pass when the prioress died.

This time at least there should be no mistake in the election. The votes were unanimous, except for the favourite's own vote, politely given to Dame Alicia, and Dame Matilda was prioress.

VII

Prioress Matilda

(February 1368–December 1373)

The installation took place in February, 1368, during a spell of bitterly cold weather. Treasuress Matilda's thrift had been proverbial. Prioress Matilda's installation was unprecedentedly magnificent. There were new clothes, new hangings, an abundance of candles, sweet rushes strewn on the floors so thickly that it was like walking through a meadow; and as she had had the prudence to work up to these splendours gradually the nuns had become accustomed to them before the guests arrived, and did not discredit the fine feathering by staring at it as though they had never seen its like before. For once, the house was tolerably warm, good fires having been kept up throughout the previous week, and on the day of the installation the prioress ordered a great bonfire to be lit at the convent gate so that all those who came to watch the show and wait for pickings should do so in comfort. At intervals servants came out with trays of hot mutton pies and roasted apples whose blackened hides were daubed with honey and poppy seeds: there was not a child in Oby who had not got a scorched mouth by midday. The old and the infirm were given clothing, and two girls belonging to the manor received marriage portions of bed-furniture to celebrate the spiritual espousals of the newly-made Dames Adela and Lovisa. There was a procession; and just after the bishop had given a general blessing a great thumping of drums introduced a party of professional entertainers from Waxelby with a performing bear. For one day at least the manor of Oby was devoted to its convent. The bishop remarked on it, and Sir John Idburn, thinking of his own surly parishioners, wished to God there were nuns in Lintoft rather than pigs. His horse had a sprain, he had walked the freezing miles from Lintoft to be present at the installation; but his cares were exorcised by the puffing incense and the smell of warm wax. On this festal day even Sir Ralph seemed to look at him with good-nature.

Sir Ralph was in a state to be good-natured. He was counting de Stapledons. During three days they had been arriving to witness the glorification of their kinswoman, and some more had arrived this morning. The air rang with greetings and family jokes, and Dame Matilda's short barking laugh seemed to echo from every corner of the building. Wherever one looked one's eye fell on the red faces, the large noses, the three badgers couped proper of the de Stapledon coat. The family was one of those everlasting families out of the North: litigious, tenacious, unprincipled with prudence, living in small houses on large manors. If they had lived rather further north they would have made a loyal livelihood by forays across the border; as it was, their position was very convenient for disposing of Scots cattle, for some they passed onward and some they kept and fattened, and all they handled at a profit. Even with one's eyes shut one could tell what manner of folk they were by the smells that came from their garments: an uncle's lined boots, a grandfather's hat, the velvet gown a great-great-grandmother had bequeathed. Looking round on the antique finery whose trusty material preserved the bulges of dead and gone wearers, Sir Ralph thought that it was just as though the de Stapledon effigies had come south from their freezing chapels; and at the end of the holiday my uncle's boots, my grandfather's hat, Lady Edith's gown faced with wild-cat, would have the dust of travel switched out of them and be put back in chests and presses, or hung in the wardrobes where the stink of healthy de Stapledon piss would keep the moths away.

Nowadays such families had grown rare. Nowadays one went to court and made one's way by a pleasing son or a handsome daughter, or turned, as the de Rettevilles were turning, to this new sort of parasitic trading, buying and selling of tolls, rights, and monopolies. He thought that the prioress's resort to the de Stapledons was a gamble: even if they continued to prosper it would be touch and go between family loyalty and family close-fistedness. But gamble or no, it was a policy; and after seven years of Prioress Johanna and eleven years of the old prioress, any policy was a refreshing change. His interest in how Prioress Matilda would tackle the legacy affair (it was certain to come up when the formalities were over) overcame the modesty he was wont to feel in the presence of bishops. Quite patently he hung about inviting the invitation to our good priest to join the party in the prioress's chamber.

She must have primed Hugh de Stapledon, for it was he who opened the matter.

'... And a sorry botch you seem to have made of it, knowing that you had the Scottows to deal with. Though I daresay you were not able to do much to guide it at the time; she was dying, I understand, and no doubt everybody was praying and screeching, death-beds are always the devil.'

The bishop sighed.

'Women should never be allowed to do business,' Hugh concluded. Hugh's wife Arbella, a hard-featured dame, settled her gold buckle and smiled.

'But something written is something written. I'd like to look at it, if you have it at hand.'

The prioress handed him the little scroll with a bloodstained corner.

'I can't make it out. Here, wife, this is more in your line.' Arbella's beady eyes whisked to and fro. She began to read aloud.

'"... The vineyard which by love of my good father had always been accounted mine; its revenues for the space of ten years and the usury at ten in the hundred thereon accumulating. And I beg my good father, or his true heir should he be no more living, to give freely to the house of Oby."'

'For a chantry, no doubt,' interposed Bishop Giles.

'"For love of Our Lady and of Saint Leonard, and of kindness to me, Isabel, now in my last agony and awaiting the deliverance of God ..." No. Nothing about a chantry.'

'Well, have they accepted it? It will hang on that,' said her spouse.

Now the bishop was reading Dame Isabel's document for himself. He was a handsome man in a sheeplike, saintlike way, and the attitude of study became him because it concealed the fact that he squinted. He read carefully and attentively, without a vestige of expression.

Arbella de Stapledon now spoke.

'I do not pretend to know anything about business, I know nothing of the law. But speaking as a simple christian it seems to me that Fulk de Scottow might be unwilling to enter on a law-suit. He is a monk, he has abjured the world's wealth. Would there not be something of a scandal if it were made known that he is contesting a legacy?'

The bishop raised his head and gave Arbella a thoughtful squint.

'But even if he withdrew his objection,' said the prioress, 'we should still have John de Scottow to deal with.'

'Make no account of him!' said her brother. 'I know him, he hasn't the stomach for a law-suit.'

'No, no, no!' cried the bishop. 'It must not come to that. No law-suits!'

'Why not? She would win it. You church folk always win your law-suits against us wretched laity.'

'Oh, no, indeed!'

Whether the bishop was repudiating the law-suit or denying that the church always won hers it was difficult to say.

'The house, I suppose, is in debt?'

Andrew de Stapledon asked this. The prioress nodded. Simultaneously Hugh said of course it was, all nunneries were in debt, though heaven knew why, for they were rich enough. The bishop looked pained.

'Dear son, do not say such things. They are not true, and they are exceedingly harmful. In the past, I do not deny it, the piety of our ancestors enriched many of these establishments. But then think of the commitments, the many outgoings, the alms, the decorations of the altar—'

He paused. Dame Alicia had moved out that he might have her chamber, but she had left the new Trinity Cope behind. Should he speak of it? If so, what should he say?

'—many of which are wrought by the nuns themselves with exemplary devotion. In this very house I have seen a cope which, considering the advanced age of the lady who made it, is most creditable. No one can say that our nunneries are places of idleness. But unfortunately there are some so envious, so impious, that they do say so.'

He looked around with the triumph of a rhetorist.

'And that, my dear prioress, is why I must beg you to proceed in this matter with circumspection. The world is full of wolves, all ready to rend the garment of Holy Church.

Lollards, Poor Men, and worse. Let us do nothing to provoke them.'

'Any Lollard,' said Hugh, 'who comes on my manor goes off it again with my dogs after him. For all that, there is something in what they say. No christian who leaves property to a religious house likes to think of it running to waste, and squandered by thriftless ladies or monks who sing all night and sleep all day and leave everything to bailiffs.'

'None of us is faultless,' said the bishop firmly. 'Meanwhile, my daughter, do not think that I will forget you. I will do what I can. I will consider. I should like to examine these letters. All the letters, if I may.'

She gave them over and he rolled them up with an air of relief, and remarked that the wind seemed to be rising. Breasting the ridge halfway to Lintoft John Idburn felt the tears freeze on his cheeks. He sat down in the lee of a furze-brake and stared through the whirling darkness towards Oby, seeing the embers of the bonfire flap into a blaze and sink again.

Jesse Figg had put two men of the manor to sit up with the fire till daybreak in case it should rear up out of its ashes. Fire, he remarked, is a good serf but a bad lord. At other times he would say the same thing about water and about wind. In his old age he repeated himself most tediously: everyone was weary of his proverbs, his anecdotes, his wife's gift of foretelling the weather. But though he was old and his wits sprawled he was still a sharp bailiff, shrewd as ever about earth and beasts and men. For instance, for this night's watch he had picked the two men of the manor who most hated each other, knowing that neither cold nor liquor would send them to sleep while they had each other to glare at. In the slaty dawn they were still wakeful, sitting on either side of the ashes like two beasts disputing a carcass. At the inquest each could testify that the other had borne him company all night and so could have had no hand in Figg's death. Some time between the first and second cockcrow, the widow said, Jesse had gone out to ease himself. She had heard him groan and cry out, but she had not thought anything of it as he was pained with a strangury. Then she had heard the thud of feet running hard over frozen ground. No one else had heard footsteps. Oby lay in a blissful drunken slumber, dreaming of bishops and sweet singing. Even Magdalen Figg's outcries (she had gone out with a lantern and found the old man lying wounded and past speech) had been heard as psalmody. So it was never established who had murdered the bailiff, only that the deed must have been the work of several men, for no one man could have stabbed him in so many places. It was a hard winter, such a season as brings wolves and outlaws from the forest. Probably the installation, with its press of visitors and abundance of pickings, had fetched some outlaws to Oby; and while they were dividing their spoil the old man tumbled into their midst.

Now there was a new bailiff, William Holly, to match the new prioress. She was sorry to lose old Jesse's counsel, but he could not have lasted much longer, and if the murder had to take place (and all things are in God's hand) at least it befell at the least inconvenient time of year, when there was nothing much to be done but threshing and mending up harness. William Holly's first concern was where to bestow the bailiff's widow. A woman with her gift for smelling rain must not be lost to the manor. 'Someone will carry her off within a month, do you don't seize hold on her!' he exclaimed. It was clear that he felt she should be taken as a heriot. Magdalen said she would marry no one on the manor. She wanted to be a nun. That was out of the question, but it was agreed that she should come as a corrodian. The prioress was in two minds about it, for though Magdalen brought a good portion she was under forty, and might well outlive it. Besides, corrodians are always a dubious speculation; they live in the convent, yet outside its discipline, and can't be got rid of. In the past there had been a terrible corrodian at Oby. She filled the house with gossips and nephews, she got drunk and played on a trumpet, and at the most unsuitable moments she would appear with no clothes on, declaring that she was the Patriarch Job.

Yet to refuse Magdalen Figg would be to alienate William Holly, which she could not afford to do. For similar reasons of policy she must relinquish all hopes of Dame Isabel's legacy. Bishop Giles had carried off the papers, saying he would consider them. She knew that his considerations would begin and end with the expediency of doing nothing, for to a scandal-fearing bishop a convent in debt, however irksome to itself, is less irksome than a convent claiming a nun's legacy.

Matilda de Stapledon soon discovered that a prioress of fifty feels very differently about economy from a treasuress of forty. It is the business of a treasuress to attend to the time being: a prioress must attend to the future. For herself, she thought she could carry both parts, and so, appointing Dame Dorothy to be sacrist, she chose for her treasuress the agreeable Dame Helen, who had a neat handwriting and no views of her own. Oby, she thought, would never become prosperous by mere saving; something bolder was needed; and as one must throw a sizable sprat to catch a whale she had spent lavishly on her installation. For the rest, she largely relied on family loyalty.

The first reaction came from one who was only by marriage a de Stapledon. Arbella was a hard woman of business, long-clawed and tight-fisted – even the de Stapledons said she was niggardly. She was half-way a Lollard, and in addition she had taken a vehement dislike to the bishop. Being more passionate than logical she expressed this by an Easter gift of three coverlets of fox-fur, a bale of the best wool, a parcel of spices, a dozen horn spoons, and six pieces of gold money. The two hard-featured serving-men who brought these gifts also brought a letter in which Arbella urged her sister-in-law to be firm with the de Scottows, and promised her a pair of novices: *Both girls are straight and sound and will do you more credit than that young rat with leprosy whom you were forced to put before the bishop*. The young rat with leprosy was the newly-made Dame Lovisa, a de Stapledon bastard; and it had to be admitted that she was a blot on the ceremonies at the installation, for she was undersized and crooked, and her face was scarred with scrofula. She looked the worse being paired with the newly-made Dame Adela – grown so beautiful a girl that her parents had tried to snatch her back into the world. She had been willing enough to go with them, chattering about how she would wear a dress of white satin and ride a horse with blue harness, and hunt with a pack of white hounds, each hound to be trimmed with bells and blue ribbons. Perhaps it was her chatter which in the end made her parents decide that God should keep her: too beautiful for the cloister, she was too silly to be safely invested in the world. She was, indeed, almost an idiot; but in the convent no one quite said so. At the most, it was said that Lovisa, poor little crooked thing, had wits enough for two. Only Lovisa loved Adela, loved her seriously and without delight. Only Lovisa was indignant when Dame Alicia suddenly turned against her pet and boxed Adela's small ears, crying out furiously: 'Zany, zany, zany! Would to God I had never set eyes on you!' This flash of former days ensued on a letter which brought the news that Marie de Blakeborn was dead, dying of dropsy. The old prioress stared at the letter, mouthing, and twisting her face. Then she burst into violent weeping. All her placid light-hearted senility was scattered like the leaves of a Saint Luke's summer. She wept as a young woman weeps, stamping, and clawing her bosom; and from that hour she either grieved or raged till a flux ended her. It seemed an unaccountable degree of mourning for Marie de Blakeborn.

This was in 1370. Dame Beatrix, who was dying of cancer, staggered from her own sick-bed to nurse the old prioress and lay her out 'You force me to do it,' she told the prioress. 'I can't lie still and think of anyone I loved being bungled by Dame Alice. If you had made my Dame Lilias infirmaress it would have been a different matter.'

In every community there must be someone who is odd man out. Now this position was shared by Dame Lilias and Dame Cecily. Both in their beginnings had been brilliant young nuns. Both had brought very good dowries and had advantageous relations in the world, both were virtuous and well-behaved. Blindness had snuffed out Dame Cecily. Quite naturally she had declined from being the most profitable member of the house to being a sad cipher: a mouth to be fed, a voice in quire, a patient countenance to be turned to the light and poulticed. The decline of Dame Lilias was harder to account for, and it was tenable to argue that she had not declined at all, that she had merely grown sulky and unsociable.

That was how the prioress argued when Dame Beatrix – who had suddenly become cantankerous, as though the arrogance of her cancer had infected her character – reiterated her complaint that Dame Lilias had been slighted in not being chosen to succeed her as infirmaress.

'But it is no slight to be made cellaress. Cellaress is a very responsible position.'

'I tell you this, she is breaking her heart.'

'Most nuns break their hearts between twenty-five and thirty. They lose their complexions, and a tooth or two, and break their hearts. Then they settle down and are no more trouble to themselves. Besides, Dame Lilias is not the only nun to be considered.

Dame Alice had been cellaress for ten years, it was time we hauled her away from the kitchen. And she is doing very well.'

'She can pat pillows and season purges just as she could pat pastries and season broths. Wait till there is another pestilence! Then you will see what Dame Alice is worth. I hate the sight of that Dilworth dumpling. How can I have any piety in my death while she is simpering at me as though I were a skinned eel?'

At this juncture the Dilworth dumpling came in, together with a strong odour of boiled fennel. In a manner modelled on Dame Beatrix's own she whisked off the lid of the bowl, saying: 'Now drink this while it is hot, and the virtue is still in it. It will ease you wonderfully.'

'I am a dying woman, not a baby with wind,' said Dame Beatrix.

The prioress broke into laughter.

'You are growing as cross as old Agnes! Do you remember . . .'

Waving away Dame Alice and the fennel she sat down by Dame Beatrix, and took her hand.

'How far away it seems! How badly we used to behave, and how light-hearted we were! The young are different nowadays, they are as melancholy as though they were living in the world. And do you know why? It is because we ourselves are not so strict with them as the old nuns were in our day. When I think how Roesia used to thump us, and how Dame Blanch starved us for the least little fault . . .'

She exerted herself to put out all her charm: to be quarrelled with by a dying woman afflicted her sense of propriety. Her charm, when she took pains over it, was considerable, and Dame Beatrix laughed and forgot Dame Lilias. Feeling more at ease the prioress became more natural, and began to talk of their indebtedness.

'But the spire has been paid off?'

'Yes, by raising the loan on our land at Tunwold. But there is still this wretched church at Methley. Now they have sent us a bill for glazing its windows. That is the worst of being tied to Etchingdon, they do everything as royally as though they were doing it for themselves. Glass windows for a parish church, whoever heard of such nonsense? And now there is this new levy. If only . . .'

She hesitated. An angry colour rose into her cheeks.

'All these years Sir Ralph has been with us, living at rack and manger. He has his horse and his falcons, two years ago we had to strengthen the stairway to his chamber with new wood, now he wants a hat. He might do something for us in return.'

'He has been very faithful to us.'

'You defend your nursling. There is another thing he owes us. If it had not been for your skill in curing him he would have been turned out on to the road as a madman twenty years ago. He might very well give us part of his savings as a thankoffering instead of buying books – and worse.'

'Yes, I cured him with a black cock. The cock is the bird of the resurrection, you see, and a melancholy madness is like the grave. But it must be a black one. Black overcomes the moon, whereas the moon at her full has dominion over lunatics. How black his hair was then! – as black as the cock's feathers.'

'There is no fool like an old fool. I wish we had never taken the Widow Figg. My corns can tell me when it is going to rain quite as well as she can. And Sir Ralph does not lust after my corns.'

'I don't believe half of it,' said Dame Beatrix.

'Nor do I. He is too fat to do more than fondle. But she will bleed him of his money, poor old man! Now if he would lend it to us . . .'

The bell began to ring for nones. Dame Beatrix crossed herself with a look of relief. How many uncomfortable conversations, boring confidences, protracted jokes, that blessed bell had cut short!

'And with thy spirit, dear Mother!'

Swish-swish, shuffle-shuffle, yap-yap-yap from Dame Adela's little dog. The bell ceased and the chanting began. It was loud and hearty, dominated by Dame Alice's oversweet soprano. Hearing it, Sir Ralph reflected that one could distinguish the changing moods of a convent by the way its nuns performed the unchanging chant of the office. In the days of the old prioress the singing had been elegant, reedy, almost insubstantial, like the notes of water-birds secluded in some distant mere. In the time of Prioress Johanna it had grown ragged and strident. Now the tone was full and saccharine, the cadences were reposed on as though they were cushions, and Dame Alice executed the ornaments exactly as she executed the marshmallow roses on her sweetmeats: a whisk, a twirl, a tapering, and there you were! He had looked forward to the reign of Dame Matilda. It had come; and he was satisfied, and yet he was not satisfied.

To his surprise, his pleasures with Magdalen Figg had awakened his spiritual man. From every possession of her he emerged with a rediscovered sensibility, a sensibility such as he had not known since he was a very young man. But now it was better. In his youth he had only a piecemeal enjoyment of his senses: ambition and necessity shouldered him on and away. Now he was old. His manner of life remitted him from hope and anxiety. He could live in the present, and be as poetical as he pleased. No one would suspect it, no one, not even himself, would mock him for being so; and there was no compulsion (ambition having released him) to turn away from the delight of feeling poetical to the distracting labour of constructing poetry. 'As free as a fish,' he repeated to himself, watching the willow-boughs moving so easily against the wet sky, waiting for the wren to burst into another flourish of song. Sometimes, remembering the manor of Brocton, he would alter the words and say to himself, 'As free as

Mamillion.' But on the whole, freer. Mamillion might seem to have the completer freedom; he had no obligations to a nunnery, he traversed a wider landscape and encountered more adventures; but Mamillion, however eludingly, was tethered to a quest, sooner or later he must remember the mistletoe and take the golden knife in hand and end the story. Ralph, happier than Mamillion, sought for nothing. He had only to make his mind a blank and some interesting speculation would enter it. He had only to turn his back on God to be flooded with appreciative gratitude to his maker. It was God the Maker he praised, not Magdalen Figg. She, like the water of baptism, was instrumental. At night, lying awake as the young do, for the pleasure of remaining conscious, he admired the discernment which had led him from the moment he first set eyes on her to think of this heavy uncomely woman in metaphors of water or of the creatures of the fourth element. She was smooth as an eel. She walked like a goose. She goggled like a carp. She was dumb as a fish. She smelt of stagnant water and the river mud-banks. She was the water of baptism. She was the source of joys as reliably as the convent's fish-pond was the source of dinners.

The pleasure he had felt at Brocton was a stammering prophecy of what he now enjoyed. At Brocton there had been much that was delightful, but he had been too far self-absorbed, and too gross of palate, to be more than outwardly delighted. Brocton with a delicate finger had stroked his skin. Now, in his dusty chamber or walking his accustomed rounds, a mere thinking could pierce his heart with pleasure. A boy riding down to the river, his thick tow tresses rising and falling with the movement of his beast; a yoke of oxen turning at the furrow's end and confronting the winter sun with mild faces; the mists wallowing inland at the day's end, towering with the reflected rose of sunset above the poor dusky heath; the intonation of a voice, some fragment of peasant speech, clumsy and true, like a coarse instrument skilfully played on, the enskied speaking of the plain-chant, the eloquence of gospel or collect, Saint Paul's transfigured faith suddenly bursting out amid his polished arguments as the face of the satyr looks out from the laurel bush: all these ordinary things were new and entrancing to him, and his alone. For privacy was a great part of his pleasure. If Magdalen Figg, that Eve made of cool clay, had enjoyed this paradise with him, it would not have been paradise.

But, though he was an unfallen Adam in paradise he was also nuns' priest at Oby, and where his awakened sensibility could not make him appreciative it made him critical. Thus he was both satisfied and not satisfied with Prioress Matilda. As the upholder of his world she could not be bettered. She carried every responsibility, her nuns were well-fed, well-clothed, contented, and in all his years at Oby he had not been so free from the trouble of troubled consciences. Her eye (except that it was blind to the Widow Figg) roved into every cranny, oversaw his dinners and noted his need for a new hat. All this was admirable. Everything would have been admirable if he had remained the same Ralph Kello. But now, just as meals became regular and dishes clean and consciences calm, he found that he did not live by bread alone, and in a house that was a model of sober carnality he began to worship the spirit. That was why he sometimes felt disappointed in Dame Matilda, and censured her in that among all her healthy, creditable virgins there was not one who could sing like Dame Susanna, or distinguish like Dame Isabel, or dream of beauty as the old prioress had dreamed.

Prioress Matilda, too, was shrewd enough to know that her performance was falling short of what she and others had anticipated. It was well enough; in time to come Oby would number her among the good prioresses; but it was not excelling, and she had meant to excel. More distinctly, she had meant to be popular. The long years during which she had seemed to be stuck for ever in an ungainly immaturity, her sojourn in the post of treasuress when she had so often to be disobliging in order to be esteemed, had bred in her an immense appetite for popularity. Now she was popular, just as she had intended to be, and in just such a way as she had intended: a pedestrian, unspectacular popularity with no nonsense about it. But in practice such a popularity seems slovenly, and she was beginning to resent being approved of as a matter of course by a household that increasingly struck her as lacking in discrimination.

Every death entails an audit. When Dame Beatrix died in 1371 the prioress contemplated a vista of very mediocre nuns. Dame Helen, Dame Margaret, Dame Dorothy, Dame Alice, the extinguished Dame Cecily – there was nothing of interest till one came to the three nuns who as novices had played at Flying Saint Katharine. Then, they had seemed of exceptional promise, as promising as that year's crop of walnuts. The walnuts had proved admirable; she could still remember them. Seven years of Prioress Johanna's blow-hot blow-cold climate must be held to account for a less perfect development of the nuns: for Dame Philippa's nonchalance, Dame Eleanor's obstinacy, Dame Lilias's exasperating detachment. Last came Dame Adela, who had no wits, and Dame Lovisa, who had wits enough for two, but was ugly enough, unfortunately, for seven. There, if it had not been for the prohibitive ugliness, one might look for the next prioress of Oby.

God willing, Oby would not need another prioress for many years to come. There is more to being a prioress than ruling a household of nuns; beings who are, in any case, much less interesting when seen from above than when studied sideways. There was, for instance, the rule of the manor. In the realm of crops and cattle such words as *satisfactory* and *thriving* possess their full weight, they do not have the heart eaten out of them by considerations of whether or no their objects lack distinction. The manor was doing very well; and as she was magnanimous it did not spoil her pleasure to know that the performance was more William Holly's than hers, and that William Holly very plainly said so. The prioress was seldom heard to praise her bailiff; but then she did not praise the sun either. She had found in him the sort of friend she had once hoped to find in Sir Ralph: a more trenchant and active version of herself, a Matilda not encumbered by vows and the female gender.

But most of all she enjoyed finance. Little by little, here by a cautious envelopment and here by a bold stroke, she was pulling Oby out of its insolvency. The work was so congenial that she was glad to think it would go on for a long while yet; for when your feet are once set on the right path you can guide them as you please, even a few steps backward is no more than a prudent measure for getting up your strength to go forward more advantageously a little later. Thus she had raised two loans; and the indebtedness was nothing because she secured them at a rate of interest which proved that usurers now considered the house of Our Lady and Saint Leonard a sound investment. Such loans are not debts: they are demonstrations of solvency, stairways to other loans on even easier terms, a stairway, in particular, to the loan which in 1373 she began to negotiate with Hugh de Stapledon. The family connection was already in good working order. It had transmitted encouragement, good advice, gifts in kind and promises of better gifts to come, with return of thanks, assurances that advice was followed, reciprocal gifts and promises of prayers (Arbella, oddly enough, was extremely susceptible to being prayed for). Now the moment she manoeuvred for had come. Hugh de Stapledon, sympathetically comprehending her dislike of raising money from strangers, had suggested lending her enough to pay off the other two loans and leave a little over for improvements, a loan which he would grant on terms no higher than she was paying already, and which would be all in the family.

Her first letter of acceptance was so incautiously eloquent that on second thoughts she did not send it. A more circumspect acceptance was composed and despatched. Sooner than she expected the hard-featured serving-man brought a letter from Hugh. It was almost as eloquent as the letter she had not sent. Hugh was engaged in a new law-suit, a law-suit of compelling intricacy and far-reachingness, against his brother Andrew and Andrew's son Nigel. He described it at length, and in the course of his description he made it clear that she need not expect the loan, or any other financial assistance beyond good counsel. This was calamitous, but it was not surprising. She had always foreseen that if it came to a choice between family litigation and family affection, litigation would have it. What she had not foreseen was that Hugh would ask her to contribute towards the expenses of the litigation.

She gave a loud brief laugh. It was a pity that she had no one to share this joke with. Presently she told herself that she was really no worse off than before. She must go on rather longer, that was all; and why should she regret the extension of what she found so congenial? Dame Cecily's expedition to Holywell must be postponed for a while longer. Saint Leonard must be patient for his new coat of paint. She turned to reckoning up possible small gains. The tenant of the saltings along the river Alde (part of Dame Lilias's dowry) could very well be asked to pay a higher rent. Lovisa's peace-loving father could generally be squeezed for the good of his soul; and then there was Sir Ralph's private purse, which must have something in it besides comfits for the Widow Figg.

VIII

Saint Leonard, Patron of Prisoners

(January 1374–June 1374)

Day by day, season after season, Dame Lilias, walking in the cloisters, looked at the spire, and her mind experienced the same train of thoughts. There was the spire, and here was she: the same day had ceremonialised them both into the fabric of Oby, and a long, a too-long novitiate had preceded that day. The spire had tried to get away. It had broken itself in the gale and fallen and killed Dame Susanna in its fall. But it had been rebuilt, and here it was, so much a part of Oby that now it was not even grudged at. No one remembered what a nuisance it had been, and with the death of the old prioress went the last thought of the time when it was still only a project and the dearest preoccupation of a mind. For that matter, the old prioress had lost interest in it long before she died. But she, Dame Lilias, had never tried to escape her destiny, and no gale had thrust such an idea upon her. She had been a novice, and now she was a nun; and in all her life she had known nothing more impassioned than what came to her from a narrow highly-specialised sensuality. She had an extreme sensibility to sweet smells and the warmth that nurses them, and to certain aspects of light, as when it lies trembling in a bowl of water. Underlying this, as the grim root underlies the flower, she had a less-explored sensibility to what was harsh, foul, and noisome. It was this latent sensibility that Dame Beatrix had discerned and exploited, ignoring everyone else's Lilias to elicit the five-year-old child who had trotted, attentive and forgotten, through a castle where the Black Death had usurped any other ownership. It was sickness and not the sick, death and not the dying, which drew Dame Lilias towards the infirmary: as the sick must have perceived, for when the post of infirmaress was given to Dame Alice there was a general outcry of relief.

Appointed instead to be cellaress, Dame Lilias sometimes asked herself why this veer in the wind should be so chilling. She had not lent more than half an ear and half a heart to Dame Beatrix's persuasions; and as appointments go, cellaress was the less disagreeable post, it is better to smell stale fish than sores. But from the hour that snapped off her rather indefinite intention she was overcome by a sense of coldness and stagnation. Little by little the sensuality which had quilted her wore thin and fell away. No one could have guessed it. She was still fastidious about her food, she dodged physical discomfort as dexterously as ever, and now that she had command of the spice cupboard she castled herself in sweet scents, was never without a couple of cloves or a bayleaf in her pocket, and rubbed powdered cinnamon into her veil. But scents must be nursed by warmth, and she was cold: cold to pleasure, cold to her own coldness even. When she lounged in, late as always, for the night office, yawning and shrugging her shoulders, no one could have guessed that she came – not from sleeping, but from a frigid and boring wakefulness.

Among her companions her languor was diagnosed as pride. She was too proud to speak, they said; and if one asked her a direct question she was too lazy to give back more than a bare Yes or No. It became a current pastime to address remarks to Dame Lilias – the sillier the better; when she replied, one exclaimed at the wit of her answer or thanked her for replying so graciously. Dame Adela put a great deal of energy into this sport, but she was not so skilful as Dame Lovisa. It was Dame Lovisa who hit on the device of consulting Dame Lilias on matters of beauty and the toilet, magnanimously exposing her own ugliness for the pleasure of the community by asking Dame Lilias how often she should wash her face, how best she could improve her complexion, what she must do to grow long eyelashes; or thrusting her ill-odoured face under Dame Lilias's nose she would enquire if her sores were not wonderfully mended by the rose-water.

If the sores had not been vizored by so much hatred and derision this particular sport might have mended Dame Lilias. The sensibility to what was foul and noisome had made a better resistance than the sensibility to light conversing with clear water or strawberry leaves trodden by the sun, and reacted to this young, pitiable, and intelligent little monster. Looking down on the sores and the pimples and the weak glaring eyes Dame Lilias felt as though she had turned from a painted landscape to a window giving on the whole real world, the world of our first parents as they walked away from Eden gate under trees whose fruits were unmystically wholesome or deadly, a world where serpents were sufficient in being mortal serpents, no more, no less. But an artificiality of malice and the routine amusement of the other nuns interposed between her and what she might have got from her tormentor, and presently she was insensible even to Dame Lovisa.

It was God's will, she supposed. God's will had taken away Dame Cecily's eyesight, God's will had taken away her sensuality, and with it the sins of the flesh which nourish the life of the spirit. She could feel neither pleasure nor disgust, neither rebellion nor contrition. For a while she tried if austerities and mortification would revive her. Nothing revived her: austerities and mortification fell on her like ashes on the dead.

At length, and almost inadvertently (for she did not doubt that her wretchedness would be quite as boring to others as it had become to herself) Dame Lilias in confession spoke of her state of mind. To her astonishment Sir Ralph roused up and seemed interested. It was accidie, he said; a malady of the soul that in its final intensification of wanhope is one of the seven deadly sins.

'Accidie,' she repeated. 'Dame Susanna spoke of it when she taught us our sins.'

'Dame Susanna!' he exclaimed. 'A lot she knew about it.'

The convention of the confessional seemed to have broken down, here was Sir Ralph talking to her as if she were a person. Recovering his manners he went on to say that accidie was not so very rare, though unusual among women; and with patience and God's help, curable. She rose from her knees with an impression of having pleased. It was momentary: as though, travelling through an endless cavern, a ray of sunlight had for an instant touched her cheek. A moment later the laconic voice of her intelligence was assuring her that since the majority of mankind will be found among the damned the addition of herself to that number could not be remarkable, and that if Sir Ralph were interested it could only be because wanhope was rather more of a rarity than sloth or anger. But to Sir Ralph it appeared as though his last prayer were about to be granted. In addition to the pleasures of the senses he enjoyed with Magdalen Figg and the pleasures of sensibility he enjoyed with himself, he was, it seemed, in a way to enjoy the pleasure of conversing with a spiritually-minded nun. She had touched his heart. The words, so inadequate and true, in which she had described her wasting misery were like a descant on his own revival. Her dreariness was the antipodes of his delight. Everything he had, she lacked;

and the antithesis drew him to her because it completed his self-realisation.

His first fear was that she might recover too quickly, and become as dull a penitent as the rest. Time went on, she made no step towards recovery. She was too wretched for eloquence. His sincere attention drew from her little more than a glum: 'It is no better. I can feel no hope.' But the few bare words seemed to him to have a classic grace. And so he continued to reason with her and admonish her, genuinely concerned for her state and at the same time snuffing up her odours of clove and saffron, the sweet scents that breathed from this barren fig tree.

As for what went on in the convent it was really no affair of his. But one day Magdalen Figg said to him that the nuns would murder Dame Lilias among them, and he plucked up his resolution and went to the prioress, telling her that Dame Lilias was in a state of perilous melancholy and should be handled with consideration. Immediately it sprang into her mind how abominable it was that Mary can always catch a man's ear while Martha grunts unheeded.

'Dame Lilias has always been singular. It is just what I should have expected of her – to choose this moment to doubt of her salvation while all the rest of us are worrying night and day how to pay off the convent's debts.'

He had happened to approach her on the day after she had received Hugh de Stapledon's repudiation of the loan. He could not know this, but he realised that he had chosen a bad hour. It struck him that the prioress was growing vulgar and uncongenial. If she would not listen to him about Dame Lilias he would not listen to her about debts. He ignored her hints about a little loan from a friend, some old friend who could be trusted, and she grew angrier than ever and more confirmed in her prejudice against the nun.

Christmas passed, the days grew lighter, colder, barer. It seemed to him that Dame Lilias and he were wading through some classical Styx, a cold corner of Hell that Christ had never harrowed and where the writ of christianity did not extend. When he said: 'Why do you not pray to Saint Leonard? He releases prisoners,' he thought how falsely the words rang and how her silence made mincemeat of them. For months she had been incapable of prayer, he might as sensibly have told a lame man to put on red shoes, and see what that would do for him. That same evening she knocked on his door.

'Saint Leonard has heard me. He has shown me the way out.'

Even now she was not eloquent. Her narrative was broken by long pauses during which she seemed to be falling asleep, but it was plain and coherent. She had done as he had bid, escaping from the afternoon recreation to go and pray before the statue of the saint. She had done her best, but no sense of devotion had come to her. Instead, she had been submerged by resentment against her companions, remembering all the pricks and gibes they had given her, until the last convention of charity was torn away from her mind. She had felt, she said, all of a sudden such a force of loathing that it was as though a headsman's axe had fallen on the nape of her neck, and she had tumbled face forward on the ground. Then she was aware of Dame Dorothy standing behind her and saying: 'What a pity to disturb such devotion! But the rest of us are such dull grovelling creatures that we have to live by the Rule; and it is time for me to light the candles.'

'And while she was still speaking,' she concluded, 'I heard another voice. And it said: 'Now see the reason of all this hating. Go, and become an anchoress.'

'An anchoress!' she repeated. 'Saint Leonard bade me become an anchoress.'

'You did not see the saint?'

'No, for I was lying on the ground when he spoke. But I felt him. It was he who struck me that blow. See if there is not a bruise.' The bruise was not large, but there was no doubt of it. Saint Leonard must have a small fist and a strong arm. Saint Leonard, or Dame Dorothy. It looked like woman's work, to him.

'And when you felt this blow . . . '

'I was free, suddenly free. It broke a chain.'

Even if the blow came from Dame Dorothy, one might say that Dame Dorothy must be accounted instrumental, a signet snatched up in a hurry while the wax was in perfection, as one seals with a groat or a dagger-hilt.

'There is a bruise, certainly. But do not speak of it.'

She gave an adjusting shrug of her shoulders, and winced at the real pain of the real bruise. Her veil fell, her spices flowed forth. He would miss her. But she must go to her anchoret cell, and he must help her departure.

After she had quitted him he remembered the dried plums in his cupboard, and began to munch them, grateful to be eating. He had always dreaded something like this, now it had happened. Dame Lilias had heard a voice from heaven, and the voice she had heard was now reverberating in him, and assuring him with the greatest distinctness that it takes a sacrament to make a priest. Learning, custom, the habit of years, all that is of no avail, tinting water does not make wine: here he was, reacting to Dame Lilias with as much simplicity as a ploughman. Dame Lilias had heard a voice from heaven and so little a priest was he that he thought none the worse of her, and even took her at her word. The bruise, he supposed, was Dame Dorothy's handiwork. She was a dull unnoticeable creature, in all the years he had known her she had been a nonentity. But every nonentity must have a moment when it flashes into something positive, the immortal soul is not housed in flesh for nothing, and very probably Dame Dorothy's soul had had its moment of necessity in striking that blow from behind. The blow was necessary if Dame Lilias was to be freed. Everything is planned by divine intelligence: a cipher is begotten and born and lives for thirty years in religion in order to deliver a blow on the neck; and after that, naturally, it lives on, according to the law of its kind. Whether or no Dame Dorothy's soul must suffer the penalty of nursing malice and giving way to anger was a fascinating speculation, but one to be deferred. Her part was played, a 'Here beginneth' to the voice of Saint Leonard, a supernatural voice released by the natural instrumentality of her blow, like the waters which sprang from the rock when Moses struck it. *Now see the reason of all this hating. Go, and become an anchoress.*

All in the imperative as usual. A model of conciseness, as well struck as Dame Dorothy's blow. But it is not enough for heaven to speak, the supernatural for its completion must be adequately accepted otherwise the work is not worked-out. Dame Lilias had matched her moment. She had heard and believed. As for himself, he really could do no less.

He had eaten two more plums before he recalled his own part in the affair, his advice to Dame Lilias that she should pray to Saint Leonard, patron of prisoners. He too had been instrumental, a figure balancing Dame Dorothy's. Everything is planned by divine intelligence.

But now came the formalities; and his heart sank as he contemplated the morass of tact and negotiations through which he must move. Dame Lilias could not become an anchoress with the bishop's permission. Her application must be made through the prioress, which meant that the voice of Saint Leonard would reach the bishop at third-hand. In theory his own voice, as the professional witness, should out-shout that of the prioress, but it was questionable whether this would be so in fact. Above all, the voice of Dame Lilias must be pitched very low.

As a first step he commanded her to say nothing about it. Then he set about the prioress, who pointed out that no letters could be sent from Oby till the floods went down, and added that it would be best if for the present Saint Leonard's speech remained a matter of confidence. 'For I am sure you don't want to have everyone chattering about it, and plaguing you for advice on how to hear voices. No doubt many of them would enjoy a word or two with a saint.'

'It is her own wish that nothing should be said of it,' he replied artfully.

'I am glad she is so sensible.'

Sir Ralph was glad that the prioress was so sensible. He had not expected her to take the news so indulgently.

It had been an exceptionally wet season. The watery skies were mirrored in acres of water, flocks of water-fowl cried and swooped across the floods, and in the hamlet people were laying bets as to what course the Waxle Stream would be found in when the floods withdrew. Pigs, poultry, and cattle, men, women, and children, all the livestock of Oby was gathered on the rise of ground. Lowings and gruntings, cock-crowing, shouting and chattering, the thump of the flails and the hymns of the nuns, all resounded together as in some jovial ark; for this winter there happened to be plenty of victual, so the prevailing mood was cheerful and rather childish.

Feeling that Dame Lilias might be the better with something to divert her mind after all she had been through, he lent her his copy of the Georgics. It was a cheap copy, the scribe had used his worst ink and saved space and time by employing all the recognised contractions and some others of his own invention; though Dame Lilias was a fair scholar he wondered how much she would be able to make out. He thought, too, that a book so appreciatively devoted to the active life would make odd reading for a woman who proposed to spend the rest of her days in a cell fastened, like a moth's coffin, to the side of some church. Yet her cell would have its window-slit, and she would see, as in the compass of a pentameter, oxen at plough, a tom-cat courting its female, the cloud retreating behind the rainbow. Meanwhile her mind was at rest. Her outer life too had become easier, so Magdalen reported, for the prioress had called off the tormentors.

The prioress had done so for a sound reason. She had not forgotten the affair of the old prioress and Dame Johanna, and she knew that only a thick universal plaster of good manners could save her from expressing a most impolitic annoyance. An anchoress, even more strictly than a nun, forswears worldly goods; but would Bishop Giles allow them to lose Dame Lilias and retain her dowry? He had behaved scurvily over the de Scottow legacy, ten to one he would behave as scurvily now, and rule that the revenues of those water-meadows and saltings should be diverted to some almshouse or some altar. First the failure of the loan, now the loss of a considerable revenue ... Fury shook the prioress as she saw her work jeopardised by this nonsense of Saint Leonard and a discontented nun. But if the situation were to be retrieved she must not show her fury. She must seem to believe, and she must seem to approve. Even in her letter to the bishop she must somehow combine disparagement of Dame Lilias with piety towards the saint and indifference to a possible reduction of income.

She made many drafts of the letter. Fortunately the floods gave her a breathing-space; and when they went down William Holly could not spare a man to carry letters. Regretting this to Sir Ralph she added that Etchingdon bursar would shortly come to collect the interest on the Methley tithe, and that the letters could be entrusted to him. He came, stayed a night, and went away. Only after he had gone was it discovered that in the turmoil of trying to persuade him to take part of the interest in kind the prioress had forgotten to give him the packet. But a week later when Brother Baltazar called for a meal she gave him the packet herself.

'The bishop?' said Brother Baltazar. 'But he has gone. He has been appointed to the see of Auch, a great advancement, and they say that Pope Gregory will soon make a cardinal of him.'

'What a loss to us!' she exclaimed. 'Has the new bishop been chosen?'

'Not that I know of. But many wish that it may be Sir Walter Dunford, the archdeacon. He is a poor man's son, and a very holy clerk, and much loved by the poor.'

It was a friar's answer. Friars ramble everywhere and are as slippery as coins rubbed smooth by all the hands that have transmitted them. She had no doubt that Brother Baltazar knew something of Walter Dunford which it pleased him to keep from her; and since it pleased him to withhold it, that something must be something which it would advantage her to know. At the same moment the companion friar, a great hulking youth with lips like sausages, cried out in a strong west-country accent: 'Oh, he's a lovely clerk! He will make a lovely bishop.'

So Walter Dunford was the man.

But even friars may be misinformed, and Oby continued to speculate until the eve of Palm Sunday. The nuns were out gathering willow-palm. It was a sudden hot day, as hot as summer; bees were lolling from one golden tuft to another, and followed the cut boughs into the chapel. Light-headed from the conjunction of lenten abstinence and this luxurious weather the nuns were frisking about and pretending to beat each other with the willow boughs when a messenger rode up amongst them. Where was the prioress? There was the prioress, trying to put a bee down Dame Philippa's neck. But she came up with her usual sturdy dignity to receive the letter. The new bishop was Walter Dunford, who greeted his beloved daughters and begged for their prayers.

In a fine springtime there is always a lot of coming and going; before long more was learned about the new bishop. Yes, it was true, he was a man of low birth: his father had been a candle-maker, his mother a midwife, and between them with great piety they had reared up a long family. The father's connections (he supplied candles to the great Abbey of Holy Cross in Middlesex as well as to the house of Our Lady at Barking) helped him in getting an education for his children, and he placed many of them either in religion or near by it. By the time Walter, the youngest son, entered the priesthood the Dunfords in their small way were a dynastic family. Yet he had much to contend with, for he was sickly, diffident, and unprepossessing: up to his fortieth year no one would have thought him the stuff of a bishop. Then came the Black Death, and cut a swathe for him. In that time when so many priests died and others hid themselves in routine, the sickly diffident Walter Dunford became known as a man almost angelical in energy. He ministered, he comforted, he organised. Respectable witnesses averred that he had been present, at one and the same time, beside a death-bed and at the altar. Some had felt healing flow from his fingers with the holy oil, others had seen him, whilst running to catch the confession of a dying outlaw, caught up by his zeal as if on wings, and wafted across the empty market-place like a bird. In the year 1351 many people were saying that Walter Dunford was a saint. Five years later twice that number were saying he was a man with a future. He became eminent enough to have slanderers, the retinue of eminence. He had the evil eye, it was said; he was leprous, he was crazy, he was a plotter, he was a sorcerer. Beyond doubt he was undersized, pious to eccentricity, ludicrously thrifty. His reputation spluttered, and hung fire. It did not seem likely that he would ever win more than a local fame. He was made an archdeacon, with every expectation that he would die of the office, but he did not die. All of a sudden, as startlingly as a grounded heron displays its wing-span, he was in every mouth as a man who should by every right be a bishop. There is only one statesmanly answer to this sort of challenge, and in 1374 he was given a mitre.

The reports that came to Oby by pedlars and palmers, people who carry rumours as naturally as they carry fleas, told a rousing tale of Bishop Dunford's austerity and industry. He drank only water and slept on a mat. He journeyed incessantly, dismounting to kneel at every wayside cross. He listened to the poor talking among themselves, he plucked young girls out of brothels, he visited leper-houses and poor parish priests. He asked rich ladies how much they paid an ell for velvet and how many ells it took to make a mantle. He had not changed his shirt since his ordination. He had an open sore on his left side but no one was allowed to look at it. His sister cooked all his food for him, for he feared to be poisoned.

Roger Salhouse, Dame Cecily's lawyer cousin, staying the night on his way to Bury Saint Edmunds, confirmed much of this, and added that Walter Dunford was a hard and shrewd man of business, and that so far no one had found a handle to him; but that he would probably wear himself out in a year or two. Meanwhile, he was extremely popular, with the wealthy praising him even louder than the poor, and thronging to hear his sermons against luxury and vanity.

Such a bishop, thought Dame Lilias, who kneels before the

Christs of the wayside, would understand my wish to become an anchoress; and such an industrious functionary will not fail to read that request. Her patience took heart. Patience is an easier merit under Taurus when cold does not drive one to the chattering fireside. Dame Cecily liked to hear the birds singing, and during recreation she and Dame Lilias sat in the orchard, the sighted nun winding silk off the blind nun's hands. Dame Cecily listened to the birds and Dame Lilias thought of her cell and wondered to which quarter its window would face. She still kept her word not to speak of her calling.

Such a bishop, thought Sir Ralph, will blow like an east wind through Oby. What with our debts and our dinners we shall certainly feel the admonitory end of his crozier. But such a bishop, rating austerity so high, will be more inclined to favour Dame Lilias, if only as a slap in the face to the remainder of the establishment.

The prioress also thought about the new bishop; and among weightier considerations she recalled her letter to Bishop Giles about Dame Lilias's vocation. The former bishop would have read it sympathetically, but this one might not be so responsive to her disparagement of the kind of nun who hears voices, especially if he believed himself to have been whisked over a market-place. But there had stood Brother Baltazar, eyeing the packet in her hand and ready to tell the world that the prioress of Oby wrote letters to a Bishop Giles which a Bishop Walter might not read, and so she had let him carry it off. How silly of her! – any woman with her wits about her would have said it contained a recipe for a febrifuge. But when Bishop Walter's answer came it was pretty much as though Bishop Giles, that prudent man, had written it. For a nun to quit her convent and become an anchoress, he wrote, demanded so clear a vocation and such special gifts of the spirit that he could not consider the application without further evidence and a personal interview. He would go into it when he visited the house of Our Lady and Saint Leonard, which he proposed to do, God willing, before the feast of Saint Michael and all Angels.

IX

The Fish-pond

(July 1374–September 1374)

Sooner or later, everyone has his turn. During that spring and summer the nuns of Oby noticed that the prioress was making a favourite of Dame Alice. Dame Alice noticed it herself: she had sharp eyes. There was a certain sharpness in her gratification too. She had been a nun of Oby since 1358, always cheerful, always obliging, and bringing in a tidy little profit by her marzipan: it seemed to her high time that her merits should be acknowledged. Perhaps the merits might have been acknowledged more flatteringly. However much one may boast oneself as being just practical and sensible, one would like (if only for a change) to be commended for something more celestial. But the prioress continued to express pleasure in Dame Alice's common sense, candour, and lack of imagination, so Dame Alice continued to manifest common sense and lack of imagination.

Dame Alice was the first nun to be told that the bishop had fixed on the second week in September for the date of his Visitation.

'Which gives us nine weeks to prepare in, dear Mother.'

'I think we will entertain him quite modestly. He is said to be very austere. If he seems vexed we can always explain that we are living in a poor way because of our debt.'

Dame Alice said concurringly: 'Goose?'

'Goose, I suppose. Goose with forcemeat. And some fish, something out of our own fish-pond. And some sweet eggs with whipped cream. And your marzipan, of course. If he says it is too much we can explain that it is only what the manor provides. In fact, we had better say at the start that it is all home-grown, no bought dainties. And the quire must concentrate on singing loudly and pronouncing the words plainly, for they say he is rather deaf.'

'And Sir Ralph?'

'Yes, he must be tidied up. But he looks more creditable now that his hair is so grey.'

After a pause Dame Alice said: 'And the Widow Figg?'

Though she kept her voice level, and said no more than any of the others might have said, a View-Halloo sounded through the words. The prioress coloured angrily, but she said with a laugh: 'The Widow Figg is a corrodian, so we can keep her in a cupboard till he's gone.'

She began to speak of their debts again – more philosophically than she was wont to do – saying that they were no worse than anyone else's, and that they had the spire to show for it, which was more than most houses could put forth in extenuation. They walked up and down in the sunshine, dashed by the shadows of the martins hawking round the spire, and nothing more was said of Sir Ralph and the Widow Figg. But as the bell sounded and they turned towards the quire door Dame Alice exclaimed: 'Do not say I have not warned you, dear Mother!'

It was plain enough what the woman meant. A new-broom bishop who slept on a mat would certainly take exception to a convent priest living in fornication with the convent's corrodian.

It would be a damaging disclosure. But who was intending to disclose it? She had not a nun who was not good and loyal – unless it were Dame Lilias? Wrath bounced her in her stall at the thought of Dame Lilias justifying her wish to leave Oby by tales against Sir Ralph. But Dame Lilias depended on Sir Ralph's testimony, she could not at once invoke his advocacy and denounce his incontinence. Might it be Dame Alice herself? Dame Alice was a Dilworth nun, and a woman of low breeding. Imported nuns are never reliable. The prioress recalled – and turned cold at the recollection – how surprisingly Dame Alice had risen up in chapter, laid hands on the old prioress and carried her off from beating Dame Johanna. But that was long ago; and since that day Dame Alice had never surprised anyone, knowing, if ever a nun did, on which side her bread was buttered, and avoiding unpleasantness as a cat avoids puddles. Was it not to avoid unpleasantness that she bore away the prioress?

Arguing herself in and out of confidence the prioress arrived at two certainties: that she must question Dame Alice, and that she dreaded doing so. The affront of the second certainty stung the old woman into action. Dame Alice was summoned.

'Shut the door, my daughter. On the day before yesterday you told me to remember that you had warned me. Against what?'

'We were speaking of the bishop's coming, dear Mother.'

'We were. We spoke about our debt, and of a goose stuffed with forcemeat. Were you perhaps warning me that a goose might be too rich for the bishop's stomach?'

'No,' said Dame Alice. 'I spoke of something fatter than a goose.'

The prioress swallowed.

'Of something fatter than a goose,' Dame Alice repeated, raising her voice, 'and more foul-feeding. I spoke of Sir Ralph and the Widow Figg.'

The prioress put her hands into her sleeves, for they were trembling. Hammering inside her was an unwonted girlish fear, such a fear as she had not known since those nights when she had been thrust into the same bed as a naked, hairy, and angry man. Then she had screamed and fought. Now she sat still, and said:

'We will speak no more of them. To anyone. Do you understand?'

'Speak of it? Not I! But do you suppose, dear Mother, that we, your poor loyal nuns, are the only people who can talk of it? If Bishop Walter has not heard of it already, he soon will. The nearer you are to earth, the quicker you hear these stories. And the bishop is only a candle-maker's son, you know. He is quite a low-bred gossiping sort of person – like me, dear Mother.'

She paused, watching this arrow sink in. Like an animal that runs wild as it smells the blood of its quarry she showed her teeth and cried out savagely: 'We are simple people, the bishop and I. We think like the common folk we are. We have no patience with fornicating priests and their strumpets! . . . They will bring down God's vengeance on the house,' she whispered. She crossed herself with a shaking hand. Her berry eyes stared bolting from her round face.

The prioress told her to sit down. For the moment that was all she could do. Her composure staggered under Dame Alice's assertion of her own and the bishop's kindred morality. But inside that great mass of heated and quaking flesh the habit of ruling persisted, calm as a compass in its binnacle. Under an appearance of dignified grief she collected herself and began to think.

She could afford to discount Dame Alice's moral indignation. Moral indignation at its most powerful, the indignation of a Bishop Walter, could not really inflict more than some hard words, a penitential contribution to the diocesan money-chest, and Sir Ralph being put away to muse on his indiscretions, as Prior Thomas had been, and then, like Prior Thomas, fished out again to be a credit to holy contrition. The teeth of the threat lay in Dame Alice's blackmail of God's vengeance. For now, in these bad days, it was not only the Pope who could impose an interdict: the people could do it themselves. First the cook goes, and then the scullions follow the cook; piously removing themselves from the neighbourhood of an avenging God the workers begin to leak away, the hind leaves the plough, the thatcher makes excuses not to come and mend the roof; the harvest is not gathered, sheep are not shorn, calves are not gelded; and presently dues are not paid, novices are diverted elsewhere, and the moneylenders demand their capital. Only an indubitably solvent establishment, a house built on a rock, can afford to disregard rumours of God's vengeance. And Oby was not solvent.

On the other hand, Oby was by no means so insolvent that an incontinent priest should bring the house down.

The flies buzzed, and Dame Alice panted. Her outburst had left her short of breath. She pants like a dog, thought the prioress: like a mad dog. Perhaps that was the explanation of her extraordinary behaviour, and the no less extraordinary perturbation felt by the prioress herself; for one is instinctively afraid of madness. The prioress peeped hopefully. One glance at Dame Alice was enough to do away with any such hoping. A leg of mutton could not look further from madness than Dame Alice did. What's more, she had seen the peep. The situation suddenly presented itself to the prioress in a new light. She saw it as comical. With this, her courage returned, and she felt sure of her next move. Since Dame Alice had become the mouthpiece of the common people, who are the mouthpiece of God, she should be treated as such. Mouths, thought the prioress, can be shut.

She looked up, and sighed suitably.

'H'm, h'm. It's a sad business, my daughter. If it comes to his knowledge we cannot expect the bishop to overlook it.'

'I do not expect God to overlook it.'

'No, indeed. That would be impiety. God sees all and judges all. A bishop's position is a little different.'

Dame Alice made no reply.

'In many ways I should be sorry to lose Sir Ralph.'

'Would you be sorry to lose the Widow Figg?' enquired Dame Alice in a voice of tremulous insolence; and burst into tears.

A parleying castle and a listening woman are both ready to give in. The prioress knew this saying, and had often proved its truth. Disregarding the sobs and the snuffles she launched into an account of the convent's finances and why at this juncture it would be inconvenient to dismiss Magdalen and part with the remainder of her money.

'If she were a healthy woman it would be different. But she has a swollen neck, she faints, she goggles like a sleep-walker. Anything may finish her.'

Dame Alice had undoubtedly begun to listen.

'People like yourself and Bishop Walter may despise these considerations. I'm sure I should be very glad to despise them myself and give over my mind to considering heaven and hell and so forth. But we cannot all be saints. Some of us have to be stewards. Where do you suppose Oby would be if I were to fall on my knees every time something happens that calls for God's vengeance?'

Dame Alice had left off crying, and was thoughtfully licking the salt off her upper lip.

'I am like a man pursued by a bear,' said the prioress, 'and who carries twelve small children on his back, and a horsefly settles on his face. He might like to knock off the horsefly, but how can he? – for with both his hands he supports the children, and if he stops to put the children down the bear will catch up with him. Do you suppose that I like to have this scandal in my house? Do you suppose that I am so devoted to Sir Ralph that I keep on the Widow Figg to pleasure him? Do you suppose that I would not prefer a new clean priest instead of this greasy gobbler? But who's to pay for it, eh?'

The listening woman listened harder.

'So the horsefly sucks and I trudge on. And let me tell you, the Widow Figg is not the only sting that Sir Ralph has given me. He won't lend us a penny, though I have told him how things are with us, and promised him good interest. And now he stings me in a new place, and plans to steal away my nuns.'

Carried away by her own eloquence the prioress had told everything about Saint Leonard, Dame Lilias, and the dowry before she remembered that this was a secret. But the castle had yielded; Dame Alice was once more her usual unimaginative self. She caulked up the disclosure with a command of silence, and sent off the mouthpiece of God with an affable: 'Now, remember! One of our secrets, my daughter.'

'One of our secrets, dear Mother.'

Left alone the prioress wondered why at the onset this interview should have seemed so portentous. Really she had worked herself up for nothing. Too long taken for granted, too suddenly favoured. Dame Alice was suffering from nothing more than an indigestion of self-importance. Better now than two months later, when all this might have been poured out to the bishop.

Two months to go, thought Dame Alice: there is no need to hurry. I will not do anything yet, while her memory is still raw. If I leave it a little longer she will forget that I threatened her, and only remember what a blessed thing it would be to lose the Widow Figg. Then, when the Widow Figg goes, she will thank God for it, and ask no questions. For that matter, she as good as urged me to it herself. Did she not call her a horsefly, and talk about her dying? Two months ... anyone might die in two months. She might die suddenly, and in all her sins, and yet not get further than purgatory, if at the last moment she remembers to invoke God's mother. I mean no harm to her soul. And then the bishop will come and go and harm nobody, all will go on quietly. Not, O God, as at Dilworth, that hell on earth!

Only exceptional characters, or very imprudent ones, murder for a pure motive. Dame Alice had a retinue of motives for wishing to help on Magdalen's death – the word, murder, she did not admit. There was the motive of being spiritually inconvenienced – how could she not fall into unchaste speculations while this example of unchastity was for ever under her nose? There was the motive of averting scandal – for it was quite true, she really had overheard a great deal of kitchen comment, and though so far it had been indulgent, it might change at any moment to condemnation. There was the motive of the new bishop. Above all, there was the motive of preserving Oby from becoming like Dilworth. But with all these motives for wishing Magdalen out of the way, Dame Alice would not have gone beyond wishing if the prioress had not armed her with those words: 'anything may finish her.' And what could be easier for an infirmaress than just to hasten the parting between Sir Ralph and his whore? The woman was sickly, always pleased to take a medicine. Dame Alice let time wag, the warm days falling one after another like wild raspberries, dropping from their own ripeness, confused in a rotting unregarded sweetness underfoot. Every day someone, prompted or unprompted, would speak of Bishop Walter's coming; and Dame Alice would glance at the prioress, and the prioress would remark that they must put their best foot foremost. In August Dame Alice felt secure enough for her first attempt. First attempts are often failures. So was this one. So was a second, and a third. It was as though Magdalen Figg, mysteriously weatherwise, had a similar power for nosing out death in a drink.

William Holly now came every day to consult his oracle, and followed her advice, though it strained his faith to do so. In spite of the intense brooding heat, the dewless nights and the dull stars and clouds that boiled up every afternoon Magdalen continued to assure him that it would not rain yet. Many of the strips in the great field were cleared already, for in spite of Magdalen's reputation the harvesters could not believe her. But the manor corn had been left to ripen to the uttermost, and the shocks were still standing in the field, bold as castles.

Dame Lilias was the only nun who did not complain of the heat. The weather that was like a trance, the enormous unstirring noontides that lay on the face of the earth as a snake lies basking in a cart-track, the hot breath of wheat that filled the air at dusk as though it came out of a baker's oven had brought her to a speechless acquiescence. She had ceased to hope, to fret, to pray. She waited. The pother about the Visitation had no more relevance to the bishop's coming than the smell of hot women that was constantly in her nostrils had anything to do with the sun's journey overhead. This placid pregnant state she had fallen into was a relief to Sir Ralph, who felt the heat acutely, and would have found it hard to support any troubled soul just then. His gate-house chamber, in winter as cold as a cage, was hot as a furnace. He skulked out of doors, lying under the willows of the Long Pool, trailing his hand in the tepid water. The midges would have driven him away, but he carried his brazier with him and a faggot of lavender stems. Being this year's stems they burned slowly and gave a strong odour. A fat man sweltering under Leo and carrying a smoking brazier: he must look like the emblem of Fatuity, he told himself; but for many years now it had not mattered what he looked like, he was as familiar as a waymark. Sometimes Magdalen would sidle through the willows and sit down beside him, with a pretext of looking for a strayed hen, or gathering the wild watermint whose smell keeps flies away from the larder. She dangled her feet in the water to wash off the dust and the chaff which sweat had plastered on them, and sometimes she carried a cluster of the little corn-bindweed which is like a pink star and smells of almonds. Though it was too hot for desire he liked to have her beside him, talking slowly of commonplace things; for life in a convent had taught her to speak, though in Jesse's orchard she had been dumb as a fish. Like all the rest of them she was besotted with the bishop's coming. She was to help with this and to oversee that. Dame Lilias had asked her to rub down the dried fleabane which was to be scattered in the bishop's bed. Tomorrow morning she and Dame Alice would carry water to refresh the fish-pond: already they were throwing bread to the carp twice a day, so that they might be well-flavoured when they came to table. There was to be a dish of carp as well as the stuffed goose and the sweet eggs, and she would have a taste of all these, and a good view of the bishop, wearing her black hood. Next to a virgin a widow has the approval of heaven, she had heard this in her wedding sermon at Wivelham.

'A virtuous widow,' he put in mechanically.

'I shall wear my black hood,' she repeated, gazing at him with mud-coloured eyes. There was no more reproach in them than in the water that went so gently by, and suddenly his heart smote him, not for the offence he had done her, for indeed she seemed unwrongable as water, but because of her simplicity. In his hours with her he had come to be able to speak without fear or supervision of his words, and now he heard himself asking her to pray for him. She promised that she would do so. She spoke in her usual placid voice, and he might have been asking her to sew on a button. Yet he could see pleasure moving under her muddy skin like a sun through a mist.

After she had gone he sat looking at the squashed grass where she had sat, and enjoying the sensation she had left with him: the sensation of being a philosopher and his own man. A reed-warbler's nest came twirling down the river. It was so dry that it floated like a coracle and as it twirled on out of sight he wondered if it would sail as far as Waxelby, and how long the journey would take it, and if it would get there before the bishop made his portentous arrival at Oby. But he did not dread Bishop Walter. When a dog has slept in the same corner for so many years no one is likely to enquire into its pedigree. The nest went out of sight and Sir Ralph fell asleep. When he woke he had the impression that something fortunate had happened, and presently he traced this to the fact that Magdalen would be praying for him. On his way back he met her. She was looking rather perturbed and walking hurriedly, like a goose that had snuffed a fox behind the hedge.

'I feel water rising,' she said, 'I must go and tell William.'

Neither of the two Frampton novices (Arbella's sending) had set eyes on a bishop. Destined from their cradles for the religious life they had stayed at home at the tail of a long family while their elder sisters were taken to solemn masses and banquets. Now they pestered Dame Philippa with their expectations. Would he come riding, or in a litter? Would he have a jewel on his shoe? Would he bring his best crozier? Was he going to be a saint? Did he sleep in his gloves? Would he make them nuns? No, indeed! No bishop would give the veil to girls who slopped their soup and forgot half the saints in the calendar, she answered admonishingly. Unabashed the younger one asked if the bishop would poke with his crozier in the pork-barrel as Saint Nicholas had done. Nothing likelier, she said, turning aside to smile. For the younger nuns saw with amusement the fuss their prioress was in about this Visitation, and laughed among themselves at Dame Alice lugging buckets of water to refresh the fish-pond and Dame Dorothy blowing dust off the images and Dame Helen and Dame Margaret hurrying with pursed lips to unburden themselves to Dame Cecily. Tormented with an incessant face-ache Dame Cecily now spent most of her time in the infirmary. But her curiosity flickered on. Though she was subject to the usual calamity of the bedridden, to be visited only by bores, she liked to hear what was happening, and anything that could make a picture roused her into asking question after question. Now she asked how Dame Alice carried the water. Did she carry it on a yoke? They answered that the Widow Figg went with her, carrying the second bucket.

'I see. And so they stand on the rim, emptying the buckets at arms' length in order not to get splashed. And do the fish put up their heads in gratitude?'

'I don't suppose so. Dame Alice has said nothing about that.'

'She is joking, Dame Helen. I must say this seems to me great waste of water, for they do it twice a day. But when I suggested this to our prioress she flew into a huff and said that Dame Alice knew what she was about. I thought of saying, Then why has she never done it before? – for we have had other droughts, you know. But now it seems that Dame Alice can do no wrong.'

'Do you know what I think it is? I think it is a plan, and that the prioress herself invented it, a plan to keep the Widow Figg out of our priest's way, so that he may be preserved from falling into sin until the bishop has come and gone. They say that this bishop is remarkably acute. Which of the saints was it, Dame Cecily, who was so chaste that he could smell unchastity just like cheese? Was it Saint Thomas Becket? We don't want that to happen here.'

'And does the Widow Figg wear her russet kirtle?'

'Oh no, it is too hot for that. She is wearing a kirtle of grey canvas and going about barefoot. It grows sultrier every day. When the storm comes it will be a terrible storm.'

Dame Cecily saw in her mind's eye the barefoot walking of those who are accustomed to walk unshod; the widespread toes, powerful as fingers, taking hold of the ground, scattering the burned gold of the camomile, twitching aside from a thistle. Meanwhile Dame Helen was remarking in her most oracular voice:

'Sometimes I think the storm will not break until we have received the bishop.'

They could tell Dame Cecily nothing about the weather that her own senses could not tell her more lucidly, and her imagination returned to Magdalen Figg's bare feet and the ground they trod, to the spurts of dust, the litter of broken snail-shells round the thrush's stone, and the conversing shadows of the two water-carriers. Suddenly their talk gave her a new picture.

'I have never seen anyone in such fear.'

'She is afraid of thunder.'

They were talking of Dame Adela. Dame Adela's countenance was one of the last things Dame Cecily's eyesight had pulled out of the dull broth into which her world was dissolving. When the girl was at a loss she drooped her lower jaw, and this gave her flowerlike face the additional vacancy of a flower, of a rose so fully expanded that in a moment a petal will fall.

'There she sat with her mouth open, gasping. And when I took hold of her to give her a shake, she was cold with fear. Cold in this weather! I told her to pray to Saint Barbara, to ask Saint Barbara to take our spire under her protection. I shan't be in the least surprised if the lightning brings it down.'

'Is Dame Adela as pretty as ever?' the blind nun asked.

'Yes, I think so,' said Dame Helen, and at the same moment Dame Margaret said: 'No, no! Nothing like so pretty. Her teeth are beginning to decay.'

'Well, to my eyes, she is still pretty. Though she spoils herself by walking in the sun and getting freckled.'

'Yes, and now she is growing thin.'

Finally they agreed that Dame Adela was by no means the beauty she had been, and that by her twenty-fifth year she would be positively haggard. Dame Margaret added that no one could expect to keep her beauty in the climate of Oby; the most one could hope for was to maintain a pleasant expression.

After they had taken themselves away Dame Cecily began to despise herself for the entertainment she had found in them. While she still had her sight she had preferred beyond anything else to draw caricatures and grotesques; and perhaps it was for this that God had blinded her. She tried to hold in her mind's eye the beauty her bodily eye had slighted, but it was not much use: the recollection of Adela's novice loveliness wavered out before the image of Dame Margaret maintaining a pleasant expression. She lay gasping for breath, sometimes waving a branch of elder to drive away the flies. Guiltily – for there is no more abject sense of guilt than that which is born from recurrent bouts of pain – she felt another spell of her face-ache coming upon her. If they had been able to find any alleviation she would not have felt so guilty; but nothing overcame it, neither draughts nor plasters nor pulling out her teeth nor change of season. It persisted like an original sin, and the kindest thing they could do was to overlook it.

She waved her branch towards the sound of the flies and tried to direct her thoughts elsewhere. Poor Dame Adela! – so lovely, so stupid, and so much afraid of thunder. For days now she must have been dragging herself about in an agony of apprehension:

straining her ears for the first growl of thunder, starting in terror if the sunlight should happen to flash back from some reflecting surface, a bowl of water or a dangled key. Of course she expected the lightning to strike the spire, and talk of Saint Barbara would increase the apprehension to a certainty – just as the thought of Saint Lucy's eyes on a platter wrenched Dame Cecily's own eye-sockets.

The air was stifling as ever, yet something told her of a diminution of light. Clouds must be covering the sun. She heard the men in the field shouting to each other, dogs barking, the creaking of axles. The sounds were like pictures in a psalter, brilliant and minute. Excitement heightened them like gold-leaf. Below the window she heard the Widow Figg's slow mumbling tones, and Dame Alice's sharper note replying: 'No, no! Not yet. It will threaten and go past, just as it did yesterday. I won't have my poor fish defrauded.'

She heard them come back from the well with their clattering buckets and go towards the fish-pond. Far away, so far away that it seemed to be something sighing in the room, there was a long puff of sound. It might be thunder, it might be a gust of wind. A door banged.

Though she was blind she saw the first lightning-flash. It had traversed her senses and left her gasping before she heard it confirmed by Dame Adela's wailing cry, and the bellow of thunder overhead. The house began to resound with footsteps, questions, orders, exclamations. There was another terrific thunder-clap, and the rain fell in torrents. A voice somewhere outside the building called out: 'Help! Help! Here – at the fish-pond.'

They've fallen in, thought Dame Cecily. Apparently she was the only person to hear Dame Alice's outcries. An obligation of compassion overcame her amusement, she went to the door and said to someone going by that Dame Alice seemed to be in the fish-pond, and needing help. The footsteps were stayed. There was a pause, a breath drawn in, and the prioress exclaimed in a loud sharp voice: 'What's that you say?'

'Dame Alice, dear Mother. I heard her calling for help. I think she must have fallen into the fish-pond.'

Without answering the prioress walked slowly away. Dame Cecily supposed, but without much surprise, that she had said the wrong thing: such mishaps had been frequent since her blindness. She stood about hoping that someone else would come by, for her face-ache was less acute, and she would have liked to discuss the storm. But there was only a gabble of voices, calling for cloths and basins for the rain was coming through the dormitory ceiling, and Dame Margaret saying: 'The prioress! Where is the prioress? We should ask her what to do.'

The prioress had gone out by the side door and into the hedged walk leading to the fish-pond. She walked slowly, setting her feet with deliberation on the puddled path. She was so fat and the hedges so overgrown that she had to fold her veil and her skirts around her in order to pass.

'Help! Help!'

Dame Alice crouched by the fish-pond, bending forward as though she were landing some enormous fish. But it was Magdalen's feet that she was clasping to her bosom, and the rest of Magdalen lay face downward under water. Clasping Magdalen's feet as though in a frenzy of prayer she looked at the prioress and continued to scream. Sir Ralph, sheltering under the walnut tree, had heard the screams, saying to himself that Dame Alice screamed just as she sang – with hearty efficiency and without a trace of sensibility.

For a minute or two the prioress looked at Dame Alice. She wanted to go away and leave the woman to get on with it; but she could not afford to retreat a second time. She drew a deep breath, stooped down, and unclasped Dame Alice's hands. It was as if she were pulling open the lock of a fetter. Magdalen's legs dropped into the water, their descent propelled her body a little further from the rim of the pond. The ripples spread and subsided, the raindrops speckled them. Dame Alice's hands settled heavily on the wet grass. The prioress became aware that she had left off screaming. In silence they looked at Magdalen's body that lay, unnaturally large, unnaturally still, under about a foot of water.

The prioress said with profound conviction: 'Fool!' Her face puckered up into the grimace of a thwarted baby, and became scarlet. Without another word she turned and stumped back into the house.

Dame Cecily supposed that a fresh outburst of scurrying and exclamations was caused by another leak. Even when the door of the infirmary opened and let in shuffling footsteps and heavy breathings, the noise of dripping water that came in with them only bore out this supposition.

'I don't know why we bring her in here,' said Dame Eleanor's voice. 'She is certainly dead. Lord, what a weight she is!'

'Lay her face downward, so, and help me to rock her. No, not so hard. Gently, like a cradle.' This was Dame Lilias. 'Where are the hot cloths?'

'They are bringing them.'

Water splashed on the floor. From her corner Dame Cecily asked: 'Who is dead?'

For a long time Dame Eleanor and Dame Lilias laboured over the dead woman. The monotonous creaking of boards and rustling of garments, the rhythm of their breathing, the smell of hot linen and hot wine, became soothing as a lullaby. Away to the eastward, over the ocean now, the thunder growled softly. From time to time the nuns spoke of Sir Ralph, wondering when he would come to do his part for the dead. The situation embarrassed them, they were careful to speak of him only in terms of his office. Only Dame Dorothy, coming in to report that he was still being searched for, spoke out what they all were thinking, saying that no doubt he would now run mad again, an awkward thing to get over when the bishop was so imminent.

The storm broke the drought. But on the morrow it was as hot as ever – a steaming, oppressive heat. Everything began to go wrong. The cream soured. The food in the larder spoiled. Doors stuck. Patches of mildew came out on the walls. The house was invaded by hordes of ants. Feeling as though she had been hit over the head by a pole-axe the prioress drove on through these various calamities, hearing of each new disaster with the grinning patience of despair. She was even patient with Dame Dorothy, who pursued her everywhere, saying that as the Widow Figg had drowned in the fish-pond it would be impossible to serve the bishop with carp.

Every report of something gone wrong, every demand, every enquiry, ended with a comment on how unfortunate it was that Dame Alice should choose this juncture to go to pieces. For Dame Alice, prostrated by shock, had become as worthless as Adela. She did nothing but weep, pick quarrels, do all over again what someone else had done already, and complain of Dame Lilias – who had usurped, she said, her function in the infirmary and so mismanaged the Widow Figg that she had died. For how could anyone drown in the fish-pond? It was not deep enough to drown a dog in. Again and again she told her story of how the Widow Figg, dazzled by the first flash of lightning, had uttered a great shriek, declaring that the fiend was upon her; and had slipped, and fallen into the fish-pond, where she lay wallowing, too frightened to help herself, and too heavy to be pulled out, though Dame Alice had strained her arms trying to lift her. Then

Dame Alice would roll back her sleeves and show her swollen arms.

Her story and her big arms were disgustingly exuberant in such hot weather. Though as a rule a person with a story is popular, Dame Alice aroused nothing but dislike and avoidance; and because she expressed a strong desire to have an interview with the prioress, only the prioress could understand her feelings and soothe them, Dame Margaret and Dame Helen took special pains to thwart this desire. Dame Alice, feeling their ill-will, and seeing them so constantly called to consult with their Superior, could draw only one conclusion: that they had been told the true story of Magdalen's death.

For the first time in her term of office the prioress was finding it natural to turn to her two senior nuns for support. Their sympathies were no wider than a coffin – but wide enough to lie down in. Being themselves old and stiff and pained by any departure from the normal they could understand something – not all – of what it had cost her to tell Sir Ralph of Magdalen's death. Breathless, and red in the face, she had blurted it out to him – like an order. 'Drowned,' he had said, drawing out the word as though he would never come to the end of it, as though the word were itself some dark pool in the Waxle Stream which he would never plumb to the bottom. 'Drowned.' She hastened on to talk about the burial and requiem masses. 'Drowned,' he said again; and it was almost as though he spoke with some kind of assent and approval.

It is an old observation that the drowning never drown alone: they take something along with them, if possible the would-be rescuer, if not him, then a reed, a handful of turf, a handful of ice. Magdalen Figg had taken away the prioress's only sentimentality: her sense of kinship with the young. Completely old, she stood on the threshold of Oby to welcome Bishop Walter.

But at her age it takes more than a shock and a few days of self-reproaching to alter the long habit of the body. Saying to himself: 'So you are the Prioress Matilda!' Bishop Walter saw what he was prepared to see: a burly old woman whose air, at once imperious and jovial, made her seem better fitted to rule a brothel than a nunnery. Meanwhile to the Frampton novices it seemed that Saint Nicholas himself had come to Oby. Dame Cecily, present with the rest, was soon able to put together a mind's eye picture from such whispered exclamations as: 'A bishop out of the Golden Legend!' – 'What dignity for such a small man!' – 'Oh dear, they should not allow him to get wet!' Snuffing Dame Lilias beside her she asked in an undertone: 'What is he like?' 'White as thistledown,' was the answer. The bishop's voice, however, was unexpectedly resonant. It was a golden, rather syrupy voice with a chanting intonation. It puzzled her to find it sound so familiar until she recognised that it had much in common with Dame Alice's singing. During the *Te Deum* she was able to make sure of this, for Dame Alice sang loud and sweet. Too loud, indeed, and too sweet – but if it betokened that she had recovered from her tempest of nerves they could be glad of it. Through all the hubbub of the final preparations there had run an undeclared dread that Dame Alice would make some sort of scene before the bishop; but with his coming she became useful and cheerful, just as usual.

The dinner, thought Dame Lilias, went off very well – except that there was rather too much of it. The bishop had arrived with an unexpectedly small retinue: two secretaries, his chaplain, and a body-servant. But the surplus food went to the poor so it could not be called wasted. Immediately after dinner the bishop hoisted himself nimbly into the chapter-house and got to work.

Outside fell the rain, a persistent small rain. Inside, the bishop asked questions in a voice of persistent sweetness. His two secretaries sat beside him, writing steadily, and in addition he took notes himself. His questions went into the minutest detail, and covered everything: the number of vestments, their age, and state of repair; the number of cows, and how many were in milk; the number of household servants, their wages and perquisites; the state of the quire books and of the brewing-tubs; what became of the nuns' old clothes, how often the nuns were let blood, how often their heads were shorn; how many fires were lit during the year, how many doles given at the wicket, who mended the casks, what precautions were taken against fire. Coming to the subject of revenues and expenditure the questions ramified and became yet more searching. The account-books and all the more recent business papers had been put out in readiness for him; but from time to time there were others he wished to examine. While these were being fetched he sat with his head in his hands, his fine white hair stirring in the draughts that scourged the chapter-house; but the moment the new document was before him he came out of his abstraction with a smile and began gently, politely, patiently, to ask questions again. Such an interrogation was impressive but not intimidating. He was so lucid, so methodical, that each obedientiary came out of her examination with the sense that she had given a good account of her ministry, while the listeners felt that they were assisting at a very fine sort of performance. Only when the sitting was broken off did the nuns realise how exceedingly tired they were and how their limbs ached, as though they had been taking some violent and unaccustomed exercise.

Supper had been made ready in the prioress's chamber, a suitable supper – light but reviving – for a frail old man. But he excused himself with childish simplicity, saying that he was sleepy, and went to his bed with some bread and milk. Rosy and refreshed as a child he reappeared to attend the night office, wrapped in a white woollen gown.

His chaplain and his two secretaries spoke of him almost with adoration. They had more time to bestow such confidences the next day, for after a morning with the account-books he sat alone in the chapter-house receiving each nun in turn for her private interview.

When Dame Lilias went in it seemed to her that she carried with her all the fluster of housewifery and would be unable to speak except of geese and brewing-tubs and the price of almonds. He held out his cold ring for her kiss. When she gave her name he recalled that she was cellaress, and made her somewhat of a lecture about the responsibility of such a post; only after this did he begin to poke about among his papers for the letters dealing with her application to become an anchoress. She repeated the tale of her long melancholy, of how Sir Ralph had bade her pray to Saint Leonard, of how poorly she had done so; and how the saint had felled her to the ground and then spoken to her. It was disconcerting to see the bishop make a note of his words. But the words of a saint, however memorable to the hearer, may be less striking at second-hand; besides, he was an old man, and made notes of everything. He manifested neither surprise nor disbelief. Saints often speak, he said – more often than they are attended to. He told her of his sister, a nun at Barking, who had twice been addressed by heavenly voices. On the first occasion the voice warned her that the tap of a wine-cask had not been properly turned off, so that the wine was wasting. On the second occasion, when his sister had cracked a nut and found nothing inside it but dust and a fat white grub, a voice had rebuked her disappointment by exclaiming: 'You should thank God for this picture of a good nun!'

Without a change in his tone of voice he began to question

her about Oby. She admitted that there was often talking at meals and after compline, that sometimes the nuns ate sweets in the dormitory, and gossiped, and took the name of God in vain, and kept pets. As she answered these enquiries the triviality of the offences overwhelmed her with boredom and melancholy; and when he asked her if there were no graver offences, no fornications or abortions, her voice was almost apologetic as she replied that no such things had happened within her memory.

At intervals the bishop sniffed. Perhaps he had caught a cold. Bishops visiting Oby usually caught colds. He had the abstracted look of one who feels an ailment gathering within him. He sat sideways to her, his mantle shrugged round him, his eyes averted.

'And you wish to become an anchoress. Why? What gave you this idea?'

She could only say over again and with less confidence what she had said before. Would he once more make a note of the saint's words? But instead he turned on her suddenly and fixed on her a long rigid stare. It struck her that she had seen exactly such a look from King Matt, an old lunatic beggar whom she had served at the wicket. It was part of his madness to believe himself a monarch, and while his hand clutched at the dole he would stare angrily out of his red-rimmed eyes as if to enforce his delusion of might and majesty. But then the bishop smiled, and lost all resemblance to King Matt. In a murmuring voice he said: 'When God gives me leave, I, too, shall look for some hermitage,' and dismissed her.

When Dame Philippa entered after Dame Lilias the bishop was still abstractedly smiling, so much lost in contemplation that he did not appear to notice her. Dame Philippa, a nun of considerable shrewdness, immediately said to herself: No one looks like that for nothing. I must not be led away into criticising anything.

Says all is well, noted the bishop. *Obstinate and a liar*. His handwriting grew neater as his mistrust and indignation grew. Even before that worthy honest nun, Dame Alice, gave him her report he had suspected that he was in the midst of a conspiracy to pull wool over his eyes. No nunnery could be so pleased to welcome a bishop on a Visitation as this nunnery had pretended to be. That dinner; those too evident regrets that he had not brought a pack of young clerks with him; that red-faced prioress, with her recollections of all the other bishops who had held the see before him; those undisciplined little novices, staring at him as though he were a monkey or a unicorn, even peeping round the door of his chamber ... Where was virgin trepidation, where was the mortified life? Where was the oil? It was a house of Foolish Virgins, lacking prudence, propriety, solvency. The book-keeping was scandalous, and the priest – though more to be pitied than deplored – really ought to be replaced by a younger man. For in her determination to cover her tracks Dame Alice had represented Sir Ralph as a good simple man, worn out by his unavailing struggle to correct the levity of his flock. Being so simple he had been completely hoodwinked by Dame Lilias who, repudiating even the featherweight discipline of Oby, had invented a vocation to become an anchoress. But did she look like an anchoress? Even the prioress (Dame Alice continued) was shocked and incredulous at first; but Dame Lilias had talked her round, promising that her water-meadows and saltings along the river Alde should remain in the convent revenues. Burdened with debts, the prioress had given way. But was it not outrageous that Dame Lilias could talk of *her* water-meadows, *her* saltings, as if she had never forsworn the world's goods? She was always like that, however, in great things and in small. There was a little comb she used (the bishop noted the comb), and once when Dame

Alice had also made use of it Dame Lilias picked it up, turned as red as a soul in hell-fire, and cried out: Whose hairs are these in my comb?

'Oh, I am as wretched among them as a pelican on the house-tops!' exclaimed Dame Alice. The bishop only responded with a slight frown; but no doubt he disliked learned nuns. She glided on to how the nuns despised her for her lack of learning, and thought her only fit to work in the kitchen. 'To labour is to pray,' replied the bishop, but only as one says an Amen; there was no malice in the words.

This plain, honest good woman made a most congenial impression on the bishop, and he noted and underlined her desire to leave Oby for some simple God-fearing nunnery where she could live as inconspicuously as possible.

On the third day he went away. Talking him over they decided that he was not so remarkable as rumour had made him out to be, neither so saintly nor so eccentric – certainly not the kind of man to fly over a market-place. A few hours after his departure the wind changed, the low roof of cloud broke into towering masses of vapour. It was a pity that he had not seen the place at its best, with the clouds sailing through the intense blue of the sky and seeming to set their course by Dame Alicia's spire. It was a pity, too, that the second key of the convent chest should not have turned up till after he had gone, for he had been rather pettish about it being mislaid. But things always fall out that way, and the Visitation was over and might well have been worse.

Sir Ralph walked out and stood in the sun, sighing, and hearing his gown flap about him. He supposed he was thinking of Magdalen until he discovered that it was Mamillion he was thinking of. On such a day, the first day of autumn, Mamillion would have set out on another of his wanderings. On such a day the blind Lord of Brocton would have mounted his horse and ridden past the blackberry thickets and the sodden bean-stacks, knowing the one by the smell of hot wine and the other by the stink of decay. Magdalen was lost, and little remained. Yet he could re-read the poem of Mamillion. The Lady of Brocton had sent him a copy some time since. It was beautifully written, he had no excuse not to have read it. Well, he would read it now. This coming winter he would read it, spinning it out. Then he remembered that he must get back his copy of the Georgics from Dame Lilias. Poor woman, her affair was scotched, no doubt of it. Observation of Bishop Dunford had fitted Sir Ralph with forebodings – a religious cockatrice, a man with neither meat nor mercy in him.

William Holly came by, slackened his pace, and remarked that Sir Ralph might do worse than think of getting himself another saddle.

'Too stiff,' said Sir Ralph. 'It's a cushion I need. If your wife has any feathers to spare she can remember me.'

William Holly's glance roved over the spire, the gate-house, the yellowing tufts of wormwood, the rain-plumped islands of moss on the thatch, as if to see whether the bishop had made any difference in them. Then he looked along the track towards the point on the horizon where the bishop's party had disappeared from sight some hours before, and said: 'Well! Now we've got Martinmas to think of.'

Having thus expressed his condolence on the loss of Magdalen Figg and his mistrust, tempered by scorn of all bishops, of this particular bishop, he walked on. So he, too, smelled something in the wind.

For his next sermon Sir Ralph took as a text: *For the foundations shall be cast down. And what hath the righteous done?* To him the implication seemed so clear that there was no need to labour it, accordingly the bulk of the sermon was devoted to classical examples of calamity, such as Job, Tobit's father slumbering, Caesar on the Ides of March, Roncesvaux, and the Gadarene swine, which got in by accident and had to be driven out again. Dame Helen recalled her uneasiness about the spire. Dame Lilias tried not to recall that King Matt stare from the bishop. Of the two Frampton novices the elder thought with detestation of Brutus and the younger wondered if fish gall would cure Dame Cecily. Only Dame Lovisa snuffed out an application, and sat flicking her eye from the preacher to the prioress. But she kept her own counsel – and as a warning the sermon fell flat. It was not even given credit for being a portent or a coincidence, for when the bishop's letter came it caused a stir in which no one had time to remember a sermon.

Before reading the letter aloud in chapter the prioress studied it by herself and digested her feelings enough to have a certain anticipation of amusement. At any rate, she would show them that she was not so much run to seed as they might suppose.

Greeting his dear sisters, Bishop Walter informed them that he had earnestly considered the plight of their house, which was like a house builded upon sand. As a house builded upon sand is liable to be inhabited by imps, apes, and serpents, the house of Oby was full of pride, sloth, greed, falsehoods, worldliness, pet animals and private property. His grieving eyes had beheld spiced meats, soft cushions, perfumed and flowing mantles, better befitting harlots than the brides of Christ, whose joy it should be to feed on roots and wear narrow garments. Instead of the silence of the tomb, which to the ear of religion is music, his hearing had been tormented by the yelpings of little dogs and the clattering of egg-whisks. Even more had it been wounded by overhearing such words as: Where is my brooch? or: Who has taken my spoon? Yet among all this care for worldly things he had discerned no care for convent property. Keys were mislaid and could not be found. Windows did not fasten securely. Account-books were deformed by such entries as *sundries*, *one shilling and one penny*, or *things bought at Waxelby*: entries shocking and inarticulated as the young of bears. Furthermore, he had noted an entry for October eleventh, in the year of Our Lord thirteen hundred and seventy, saying only: *Rabbit*. No mention of the cost nor the purpose of the rabbit, no record even of whether the rabbit had been bought or sold.

The prioress drew breath and read on.

As Mary was preferred before Martha for having chosen the better part, a household of nuns might be forgiven their careless stewardship (the more so since women are ordained the weaker vessel and have no business sense), if those same nuns neglected the goods of the world by reason of their devotion to heaven. But at Oby he found no such excuse. The office was performed with worldly glibness, the song was too loud, the words were not fully pronounced. He had seen no traces of true piety, no fear, no trepidation. All was blighted by complacency, and an old incense-boat bad been sold without permission. Also he had seen in the poultry yard a peacock without a peahen, reprehensible both as wastefulness and thwarting the purpose of God, who framed the animal creation to multiply the food of christians. With even greater concern he had noted the unfitness of the prioress to hold her office. Supine, and weak of purpose, gullible, and a groveller (the prioress remitted this passage with particular elegance of diction), she was a toy in the hands of her nuns, and cheated by her servants. Her incompetent stewardship was reflected in the state of her house: burdened with debt, failing to call in its rents and dues, selling sacred vessels, and not keeping up a sufficient intake of novices. The bishop, therefore, grieving paternally, would apply remedies. First, he would nominate three additional nuns; second, he would commission two psalters, which he would pay for at a just and reasonable price when they were completed and in his hands; third, to restore the finances of the house and yet avoid the scandal of a prioress deposed for mismanagement and levity, he would appoint a custos, to oversee the temporal affairs of the house of Our Lady and Saint Leonard till all its debts had been paid off.

Raising her voice above an outburst of horror and indignation the prioress read the bishop's final assurances of the prayers and personal austerities he would offer up on behalf of her establishment. There seemed no reason to doubt their sincerity.

'The crocodile!' groaned Dame Margaret 'This, after all our trouble to please him!'

'That rabbit! – if only he had asked me about the rabbit I would have explained about it, for I remember it perfectly. It was a rabbit . . . '

No one ever hesitated to interrupt Dame Helen, and Dame Eleanor exclaimed: 'If a bishop were Antichrist he would have to assert himself in his first Visitation. Let him say what he pleases! But these nominated nuns!'

'But the bursar!' said Dame Dorothy. 'Surely that is the worst of all. Such a slight to you, Dame Helen! Such a slight to our dear Mother!'

'As if convents never had a debt! All convents have debts.'

'Yes, and three nominees arriving with no dowries and enormous appetites. That will better it!'

'Three new novices for you, Dame Philippa!'

'Three bishop's pets, ready to grow into tattletales. I'll novice them!' The colour rushed into her long face, mild as a sheep's.

'I wish we had roasted the peacock,' said Dame Cecily; adding: 'The perfumes must be you, Dame Lilias.'

'I'm afraid so.'

It was the first time she had spoken. Dame Alice looked at her searchingly and said: 'I wonder who told him all this. Someone must have given him a bad report of the house. Very unfortunate!'

'There's worse to come,' remarked the prioress amiably. 'Do you know what I have been thinking, all this while? That I shall have to tell William Holly about the custos.'

Dame Adela's wild-flower countenance was shaken with a thought. 'Why should not William Holly be our custos?'

The nuns laughed and clapped their hands. Not for years, thought the prioress, have they been in such good humour. Holy Bishop Walter had been catnip to them – and to herself: she had not felt so alert for years.

Meanwhile, Dame Lovisa was saying that she would undertake a psalter.

'But who is to put in the pictures and the decorations?'

'There will be the text, he must put up with that. After all, a book is for reading, not for admiring.'

She spoke with such decision that no one felt inclined to contradict the statement, though no one agreed with it. Dame Helen whispered to Dame Lilias: 'Another de Stapledon prioress.'

Another de Stapledon prioress, thought Dame Lilias, looking at her persecutor. And I shall be here to endure her. In five years, in ten, in twenty: as plain as the voice of Saint Leonard another voice now spoke in her bosom, saying: You won't get away.

X

Triste Loysir

(*October* 1374–*May* 1377)

Quare fremuerunt gentes, wrote Dame Lovisa in her heavy, undistinguished script. The first psalm was behind her, and already the distaste for David which became so marked in her later years had begun to form itself. The man talked like Dame Helen: he said what he had to say, often silly enough, and then immediately said it all over again in rather different words. As something to sing it might be well enough, but as a statement from one rational being to another – and God is the sum of rational being – it was poor. The sunlight fell on the page and lit her scarred face and the few light eyelashes stuck in her swollen eyelids. Her hand, moving in the sunlight, displayed all its defects, the toad-skin, the misshapen nails, the look of being ingrained with dirt which overlies unwholesome blood. Her attitude and expression showed a slow-burning thrifty happiness, and she resembled a virtuous wolf. Wolfishly, she had got her teeth into the psalter, she was at last doing something positive and profitable. Thus Dame Lovisa, unwittingly, was a confirmation of what Bishop Walter was writing on that same morning in the peroration which closed the first book of his treatise *De Cantu*.

> The song of David tempers the clarion of the victor; accords the inharmonious cries of the oppressed; awakens the slothful; mollifies the furious; rebukes the luxurious; exalts the despairing; purges the glutton; abashes the proud; confutes the envious. It instructs the ignorant and refreshes the scholar. And as the psaltery is made of reeds of differing lengths, varying from the most treble to the most grave and yet all by the lips of the player breathe forth a melody, even so doth the Psalter conform itself to every mood of man and melodiously control and express them.

He leaned back and shivered. In spite of the warmth of the day and the sound of the two wasps buzzing over a dish of pears which lay on the window-sill he was cold with the effort of expressing his thoughts and controlling that metaphor of the psaltery. Now he looked at the two wasps, and smiled vaguely. Wasps, he thought, are the laity of bees. It was remarkable, he had noticed it before, how one metaphor puts you in train for another. He began to think of how the wasps and the bees could find their place in the second book of his treatise. Both make a noise, and that would bring them into the fold of the title. The bees are the religious, no doubt of that, leading chaste lives, obedient, constantly industrious, storing honey in such abundance that they can feed both themselves and the laity with sweetness: the wasps on the other hand ... The wasps had been the laity of the bees in the first conception of the metaphor, but two laities would be troublesome and lead to confusion. The wasps should be ... The door opened. His chaplain showed in a short man with a snub nose and green eyes that were staring and sorrowful like those of a hungry cat. He was Henry Yellowlees, a clerk in lesser orders. He had been recommended to the bishop by the abbot of Revesby (whose distant relation he was) as being honest and mathematical and the sort of man the bishop would find useful. The bishop disliked recommended men and so far had not found a use for him. But now on the report of his chaplain he thought Henry Yellowlees might do very well for Oby, and no doubt his mathematics would make him a sharp accountant.

Opening with a reference to the valued opinion of the abbot of Revesby the bishop went on to his Visitation of Oby and its shortcomings. Henry Yellowlees interrupted him to say that he was sorry to hear it. The establishment had a good name in the locality as a nunnery that went along quietly and had no scandals. He had a soft diffident voice – a voice that the bishop, if he had been more attentive to humankind, would have recognised as the kind of voice that goes with an obstinate character. But while noting that Henry Yellowlees had implied better knowledge of his diocese than he had himself, the bishop exclaimed: 'A whited sepulchre! And the buildings are in very bad repair. That must be one of the first things you look into.'

Henry Yellowlees said that he remembered hearing that the spire had fallen shortly after its building but that he understood it had been replaced by a much finer spire. Why the chaplain should have put forward this fellow, thought the bishop, qualifying the fellow as an upstart fellow, he would subsequently enquire into; but he went on to explain, with great smoothness and clarity of diction, all that Henry Yellowlees must do as custos: which amounted to discovering all that was or was not done at Oby and reporting it to Bishop Walter. He then rang for the secretary and told him to bring the documents relating to Oby, and spent some time reading them aloud with comments. Then he handed them over, saying that he could spare no more time and that Henry Yellowlees must study and digest them at leisure, and bring any doubts or queries to him.

Henry Yellowlees went away with a mind divided between

loathing the bishop and looking forward to Oby. The appointment was not congenial: he knew nothing of domestic administration and hated fiddle-faddle; yet it was an appointment. He was tired of hanging about, waiting for his cousin's recommendation to take effect, and being jostled by secretaries. He was in debt, too. Though this appointment carried no salary with it his expenses would be paid, one can always make a little out of that; and an unpaid appointment may lead to a paid one, and the prospect of being led to a paid appointment improves one's credit. His spirits, sharpened by disliking the bishop as an appetite is sharpened by pickles, took an upward turn. He began to think well of a future in which he would clear up the usual nuns' tangle at Oby and become Oby's champion against that sanctimonious old gadfly.

Henry Yellowlees was too poor to have a lodging of his own. He slept in a hostel for poor travellers and spent wet days in the nave of the cathedral, fine days among the stumps of masonry and grassy hummocks which had once been a Roman temple and now was the city's rubbish-tip. Today was fine; but a wind was blowing which would toss the papers about so he turned into a tavern, ordered some beer, and sat down to read about herrings and vestments and rents of meadows and repairs of roofs and bequests for masses. He read with such concentration that he was scarcely aware of the lad who came in and sat down beside him, except that he continually scratched himself. Only when a louse crawled across the details of the Methley tithe did Henry Yellowlees move himself a little away: he had picked over his shirt the day before and did not want to be at that trouble again before the week's end. Other lice, however, had already established themselves; and that though he did not know it, was why he presently sickened with typhus, and had to squeeze through an interminable thicket where every thorn that pricked him struck at the same time a loud iron bell and every bell-stroke must be counted – instead of riding across the cheerful October landscape to Oby.

It was not till Saint Stephen's Day that he was well enough to set out, riding a horse provided by the bishop, a very poor beast. He was to lodge with the priest at Lintoft: 'to spare the house of Oby any temptation to distraction and needless expense,' was Bishop Walter's message; but to Henry Yellowlees, his temper worn threadbare by sickness, it was patent that he would lodge at Lintoft in order not to be bribed by the nuns.

For his part Sir John Idburn was very ready to welcome a visitor. Sixteen years at Lintoft had exhausted his sensibility, he had settled down, come to terms with his parishioners and even with their pigs. Nothing remained of the earlier Sir John except a liking for company, the scar on his thigh where a boar-pig had ripped him, and the scar on his memory where Sir Ralph had snubbed him. He told Henry Yellowlees that the Oby nuns were proud, heartless, and cared for nothing but eating and drinking. He also recounted the old tales that had so much disgusted him when he first heard them from his housekeeper: the sorceries of Dame Isabel, the babies strangled at birth, etc. Time had mellowed them into being good stories, and he told them with every intention of pleasing, but they fell on drowsy ears, for Henry Yellowlees was overcome with a day's hard riding and a supper of raw onions. By the morning he remembered little beyond an impression that Oby was a very unpleasant establishment and that only such malice as Bishop Walter's could have made him its custos.

Expecting a cold welcome, he got it. As it had not occurred to Oby that anyone sent by the bishop could be less ill-intentioned than the bishop himself, there had been an unanimous agreement among the ladies to cold-shoulder him. Accordingly, a very ill-favoured nun who introduced herself as Dame Lovisa met him at the door, enquired after the bishop's health, excused the prioress from attending on the grounds of sickness, and suggested that he should begin by going round the outbuildings. With this he was handed over to William Holly.

Through the chinks in the window-screens the nuns watched this peregrination. Nothing could have been better, they agreed, than Dame Lovisa's reception. Even her singular ugliness was recognised as providential, a putting of Oby's worst face forward. First Dame Lovisa; next William Holly: the new custos would spend a nasty forenoon. Plastering Dame Adela's mouth to stifle any indiscreet cries of pleasure they moved round the inside of the house as the two men walked round its outside.

The custos stared upward so intently that Dame Margaret said he must be looking at them. He was looking at the spire. As the web of low-lying cloud scurried under the wind it seemed to breathe like a living thing. Sometimes it inhaled the light of day, and then its pallor enriched to the colour of a primrose; a moment later it waned, and pulled the misty air over it like a veil; and whether it brightened or waned it seemed to be flying towards him against the scudding sky, so that he felt that in a moment it would bend down to his embrace. The bailiff stood beside him drawing his attention to a faulty piece of guttering, a wet wing of thatch that beat against the rafters, the damaged coign on the brewhouse, the crack that ran down the granary wall, the great puddle that lay stinking and soaking outside the kitchen door and ought to be filled up, the tattered reed fencing, the well-head which had been nothing but a trouble since the men who came about the spire started mucking it about, the rot in the beams, the doors off their hinges, the scandalous condition of the barns. He looked where he was bid; but the spire, or the thought of the spire, distracted his attention, and at every lightening in the atmosphere he turned to stare after it, to see it breathe in the daylight and come to life.

Now they came to some pigsties. Pigs, he had learned from the priest of Lintoft, meant a great deal in this locality: he must assert himself and say something about the pigs. Remembering that three hours earlier he had ridden past droves of Lintoft pigs snorting among the oaken scrub, Henry Yellowlees remarked on these pigs still being in their sty. William Holly, his bark brightening at a prospect of contradiction, replied that he had always given his pigs a long lie, and would continue to do so. Henry Yellowlees recalled that sloth was one of the accusations against Oby. He said that the pigs must be half-starving. William Holly said that a long lie in the morning fattens a pig. Henry Yellowlees remarked that this was mere legend and against nature. The pig by nature is a foraging animal.

'Not my pigs!' exclaimed the bailiff. 'My pigs don't need to go round poking their noses in where they have no call to! My pigs aren't clerks and custoses!'

Up to the knees in mud the two men glared at each other, then they waddled stiffly off in different directions.

When Henry turned to enjoy the spire in solitude it wrapped itself in vapour. A tooth began to ache in his upper jaw and immediately a confederate tooth in his lower jaw ached in sympathy. The pain shuttled from one to another. In the barn they were threshing. The noise of the flails resounded, clouds of chaff blew by. It was starvingly cold, lifeless and lightless. It was as though the sun held such a day so cheap that it would scarcely trouble to light it. An Egyptian Day, thought Henry Yellowlees, a day blasted in the calendar. See into everything yourself the bishop had told him. Now, with nothing to rely on but the bishop whom he hated, he obeyed the instructions, wandering about the outbuildings, peering into sheds, and finding the wind round every corner. The inventory rattled in his hand. Sometimes a woman hurried by him, or a child, muddy to the thighs, blear-eyed and snivelling. 'Good woman, can you tell me ...' – 'My child, where shall I find ...' It was no use. They ran past him as though deaf and blind. Already the news that the bailiff had quarrelled with the custos had flown through the manor, and with the loyalty of fear no one would be seen speaking to the man whom William Holly had quarrelled with.

Presently he found his horse. It had been moved from a clean stall to a dirty one. His hand on the bridle-rein shook with rage as he led it out. He would stay no longer, to be blown around with the chaff. He would ride off, and make a formal complaint to the bishop.

'Surely you're not going away without eating something? It's a cold ride from here to Lintoft.'

The voice came from overhead, from a fat old man who leaned from a window above the gate-house.

Henry Yellowlees dismounted, and hitched his horse on the lee-side of the gate-house, and went unwillingly up the crazy stairs. He did not wish to stay, but he did not wish to be seen riding away defeated either. The priest's lodging was as small as a nutshell. Its walls were hung with faded red canvas that rippled as the wind blew through the chinks. A bed took up half the floor-space. His host poured out some beer and cut some hunches of bread and fetched a handful of raisins from a cupboard. The two men sat down side by side on the bed. The thump of the flails seemed to fill the room.

'You've come on a busy day. How do you find things?'

Henry Yellowlees shook his head. He was trying to remember what the bishop's chaplain had told him about the Oby priest. But he could only remember that whatever it was it had prejudiced him against the man.

'What? You don't think much of the corn? The heads were well-ripened, at any rate. I have never known a hotter harvest.'

Ashamed to say that fear of William Holly had kept him from the threshing floor, Henry Yellowlees remarked that they were late in threshing.

'Two of the best men are sick.'

'This is a time of year when one buries strong men. In summer one buries children. Children die under Leo.'

'Children die at all times of the year. The curate at Wivelham buried two of his a little before Christmas. Of course, one might say he should not have had them. But he grieved, like any other sinner.'

'Indeed.'

This cat-headed fellow, thought Sir Ralph, is no great acquisition. Can he do nothing but munch and drum with his heels on the bedstead?

'Oby seems an unhealthy place. I understand that the prioress and the treasuress are also unwell.'

'Ah, yes, poor ladies!' Sir Ralph answered imperturbably.

Henry Yellowlees half-rose from the bed. The room had been growing colder and darker, now a storm hit the house. Hailstones pattered against the window-screen, the red hangings fluttered. He had to sit down again. To depart at this moment would look petulant; and though he disliked the fat man beside him, he still hoped to find in him – being a man – an ally against this household of invisible women.

Sir Ralph got up and creaked over to the brazier and put on more charcoal.

'There is one thing,' he said, 'that I hope you will see to now you are our custos. We are wretchedly off for firewood. And the wood-reeve sells it off the manor to anyone who'll pay him a good price for it.'

'Poor people must have fires, I suppose. They can't be left to die of cold.'

'If anyone is left to die of cold it will be the nuns of Oby. They can't go about from manor to manor, wherever an extra penny whistles them.'

'If landowners did not offer more than the statutory wage the labourers would not wander,' said Henry Yellowlees.

'Young man, that is very true,' said Sir Ralph. 'Nevertheless, and as I was saying, labourers now move about and live on the country, just as kings do. For if your house has no roof you can leave it without regret. And if you have no land, you do not have to stay on it. How perspicaciously the scriptures say: The poor ye have always with you. Whoever else is ruined and undone, the poor will always scramble out with something they have managed to snatch from the wreck.'

His guest remarked that he did not believe the text about the poor was intended in that sense.

Just what the bishop would send us, thought Sir Ralph. He went on to be as annoying as possible.

'Consider another thing. The poor, being loved by God, are miraculously enabled to love one another. In themselves they are as full of rancour and mistrust as the rest of us, but the grace of God teaches them to be mutually loving and helpful even while their own hearts persuade them to act with malice. And when a poor man rises in the world, it is his own kind who hoist him up. Consider our bishop, for instance. He would be nowhere if he had not started as a nobody. But being a nobody . . .'

It took him aback to hear Henry Yellowlees chuckle. They turned to face each other. Intelligence flashed from one to the other, and then they began to look rather sheepish, embarrassed at the sudden discovery of a common bond.

'H'm,' sighed Sir Ralph, the first to recover. 'He's a good man of business, they tell me. That's what's needed in a churchman, nowadays.'

Having found a mutual dislike they settled down to be affable. They talked of food, pestilence, women, weather, the likelihood of a papal schism and the date of a Last Judgement. Sir Ralph did not consider that a plurality of popes would accelerate the coming of Christ.

'But on the other hand, the Last Judgement may have happened already,' he said in an obliging tone. 'In any case, it would be a mistake to expect too much from it. What's done can't be undone, you know.'

It began to dawn on Henry Yellowlees that the priest of Oby might be a little crazy. Smoothing his vast belly, the old man continued: 'Take, for instance, the position of the Holy Innocents. As far as they were anything, they were Jews. As such they died in a state of damnation. Are they in hell? I do not see where else they can be. Yet we invoke them and celebrate their martyrdom.'

Henry Yellowlees blinked. Sir Ralph looked at him kindly, and went on: 'That's what you say. But I am convinced they are both blessed and in hell. Such a state is quite possible, and an intelligent man like you should realise it. Hell, you know, must have its saints as well as heaven.'

Holding on to the bedstead Henry Yellowlees asked if Sir Ralph would advance the converse proposition.

'God save us, yes! Paradise is full of the damned. It is their doom and their torment to be in the presence of God. Where else could they feel such infelicity?'

Henry Yellowlees said that damnation was more than infelicity. Infelicity was the common lot of man, and the expectation of continuing to exist in eternity as he had existed in mortality would give man a quite insufficient motive for repentance. Sir Ralph said that on the contrary it would be amply sufficient: if mankind could be brought to believe that the state of damnation would be merely a continuation of life in this world mankind would be forced to take steps to improve its present living conditions. Why else should God give man the art of logic?

There could be no doubt but that the priest of Oby was mad, riddled with heresies and speculation and quite unfit to be holding his post; but reporting on dilapidated priests was no part of a custos's duty, and he would say nothing to the bishop.

His horse was stamping, the brief January day was closing. He made his farewells to Sir Ralph, and found that he did so with regret.

'By the way – the bishop wished me to enquire how his three nominees are settling down, and if you are satisfied with their spiritual estate. Though really it is none of my business.'

Presumably habit imposed some kind of sanity, for Sir Ralph's answer was quite ordinary and correct.

Of the bishop's three nominees two had yet to make their profession. But there could be no hope that they would not make it, they were delighted at the good fortune which had transplanted them to the religious life. It was a step up in the world for both of them. Joan Cossey was the daughter of a small tradesman, Amy Hodds a bastard. To be called Dame and live in a cloister was a better prospect than their natural future of scrubbing trenchers, clacking at a loom, and bearing great hordes of hungry children. Dame Sibilla, the third nominee, was a Dunford. To look at she was the image of her great-uncle, with the same slight build, small prim mouth, receding chin and vehement eyes. Unlike him, she had a loud discordant voice. She was twenty-one and had been for nine years a nun in a small house called Allestree. Pestilence and a cattle plague had brought the house to the brink of ruin, and to readjust its finances two of its nuns had to be farmed out elsewhere.

Joan Cossey and Amy Hodds came with only the minimum of dowry. Their thrifty nominator had seen to that. Dame Sibilla, being a transferred nun, brought no dowry at all. Bishop's kin, and foisted upon them, she did not seem likely to make many friends at Oby. Yet in a little while she was popular; for she brought what to the bulk of the convent was almost as good as a dowry: a narrative. Oby was enlivened by the misfortunes of Allestree: first came the portents which had foreshadowed the pestilence, the spots on the milk, the horde of invisible swine which flew over during a storm, the mysterious beggar, superhumanly tall and with blue teeth; and then the starving spring, when the nuns wandered about gathering nettles in fields strewn with rotting sheep and oxen, and the two friars who helped them get in the rye harvest, two friars who had seemed rough simple men, full of ordinary jokes, yet when they went on their way a light from heaven trailed from their dusty heels. Whether one believed her stories or no, such stories were pleasant to listen to; and as well as stories Dame Sibilla had a stock of practical wisdom, and could darn and mend and was full of expedients and contrivances.

Being friendly to everyone she was friendly to Dame Lilias also.

'Have you noticed,' said Dame Alice, 'that our Dame Lilias has become quite talkative – to Dame Sibilla?'

There was no need for Dame Alice to insinuate the obvious. Everyone could put two and two together and perceive what part Dame Lilias had played in the catastrophe of the Visitation. Everyone had noticed that for some months previously she had been bland and abstracted, like one who ripens a revenge. Everyone had observed that her interview with Bishop Walter had lasted nearly half an hour and that she had come out looking like a cat coming away from the dairy. When the bishop's letter came it was easy to guess whose malice had subjected them to insults and the ignominy of a custos. Who would have thought Dame Lilias capable of such treachery? It appeared that many would have thought it.

So now more than ever they were banded together to cold-shoulder her. No one wished to sit by her, to pass her the bread at dinner, to tie the fillet on her arm after the blood-lettings. It was remarkable how many elbows jostled her, how many spits happened to land on her back and bosom. Her short sight was nobody's concern. Dame Margaret, seeing her about to stumble over a brazier, said no word of warning, said no word of condolence when Dame Lilias and the brazier together pitched down stairs; said nothing at all until a few days later when during the chanting of the day's psalms she was heard to sing with particular clearness: 'What portion shall be given unto thee, thou lying tongue? Even hot burning coals.'

The prioress thought it very likely that Dame Lilias had complained (others, no doubt, had also complained); but as Dame Alice had blown up this fresh persecution she took no part in it. Excellent as it might be to dwell together in unity, she could not see herself being pleasurably united with Dame Alice in anything. But it is one of the inconveniencies of convent life that though you may suspect your fellow-nun of being a murderess you are obliged to live cheek by jowl with her for the rest of your days, and make the best of it as best you may. The best the prioress could do was to turn her attention elsewhere.

Fortunately there are always practical considerations, and Bishop Walter had supplied her with several new ones. His three nominees stretched the accommodation of the house, the Visitation had somehow cost more than she had meant it to, and though he had inflicted a custos on them the custos had no silver lining, the Oby finances were just as they had been before, the only difference was that now she was hampered in any attempts to set things to rights. A further consideration hung over the future – the question of Sir Ralph. The loss of Magdalen Figg had certainly shaken him, and she thought he was going mad again, though not with such a madness as can be cured by a black cock. This was a different affair, a kind of misty eccentricity into which he might altogether vanish. Against all this she could set nothing but the profits of Dame Lovisa's unappetising psalters, and the money owing from Esselby. Esselby was a small property lying inland, bequeathed to Oby a hundred years before. It had been profitable then, but the Black Death had almost unpeopled it. The land was not tilled, the mill, since no one brought corn there, paid no dues and fell into ruin. During the prioress-ship of Dame Johanna the convent was glad to rent the old manor house to a family of iron-workers. Being so far away their payments were never reliable and for the last three years they had paid no rent at all.

One day she spoke of this in chapter.

'Sue them,' said Dame Margaret.

'It would cost almost as much. Yet if we do not recover it soon we shall never recover it. These little properties, here, there, and everywhere, are more trouble than they are worth.'

Dame Lovisa looked up.

'Should we not ask our new custos to collect the Esselby rent for us?'

'Never!' exclaimed Dame Margaret, while at the same moment the prioress laughed and said she might think of it.

This was in February, after Henry Yellowlees' first visit (he had said nothing injurious about Oby, only reporting that the bailiff neglected the pigs, whereon the bishop, knowing more about pigs, told him he was a fool); but it was some time before Dame Lovisa's suggestion was put into effect, for on the first day of

April Henry Yellowlees appeared once more, bringing a letter which created such a stir that the Esselby rent slipped everyone's memory until after he had ridden away with Dame Alice behind him. For Bishop Walter informed his dear sister in God that he wished to remove Dame Alice to another house, where her simple piety would be better placed than among the broils and superbities of Oby. Since the Visitation, he said, her plea to be removed had echoed in his ears like the plaint of a turtle-dove; and as she was healthy and active he supposed she could quite well make the journey riding behind Henry Yellowlees.

So she had pleaded to be removed, had she? It was a movement of conscience the prioress had not expected, supposing that murder would lie as quietly under Dame Alice's self-assurance as a dead rat at the bottom of a cream-bowl. She accepted the current indignation with a grave countenance, though she wished that it were possible to have someone to whom she could confide her relief, and her amusement at finding herself obliged to this sweeping and scouring bishop.

Meanwhile, Dame Alice was performing a very creditable *Nunc Dimittis*, tripping to and fro with farewells and parting solicitudes, and at the same time making up a considerable bundle to carry with her to the new house whose austerities would render it so much more congenial to her than Oby. Her parting with the prioress, her kneeling for a last blessing, was exemplary. Both women played their parts with relish, each tendering her performance to the other like a final testimonial of mutual hatred and self-control.

So departed the second Dilworth nun.

In the course of her farewells Dame Alice deposited one parting gift. Breathing on Dame Lilias's cheek she had whispered: 'Two women grinding at the mill, the one shall be taken and the other be left.' And with a final kiss of peace she added: 'Who would have supposed that the bishop would have favoured my request and not yours?' Thus it became clear to Dame Lilias that the prioress had betrayed her secret. She saw Dame Alice ride off with the same bleak vision as she now saw everything. Everything was visible and everything was lost. Even her melancholy had forsaken her. She was a quite ordinary nun, who would lead an ordinary nun's life, no better than the others and no worse, and dying would suffer the ordinary pains of purgatory, no sharper and no lighter.

About this time Dame Helen began to fail; and this became another reason to defer mentioning the Esselby rent, for as her wits – scattered at all times – weakened she was preyed on by doubts and frets about her account-books; though she would not hand them over to anyone else, saying that there was just one thing she must be sure of, one column she must add up again. While they prayed round her death-bed they heard her wandering through income and outgoing, and anxiously explaining to the bishop about that unaccounted-for rabbit. Coming out of her distraction she looked at them gathered round her and reckoned them up with a shaking finger.

'One less; and Dame Alice gone, that's two less. It will be more manageable now,' she said hopefully.

By dint of coming regularly once a quarter; praising their singing and taking their medicines; bringing them news of the world and stories of the bishopric; doing little errands and commissions; showing the novices geometrical puzzles, and interfering as little as possible in the convent's management, Henry Yellowlees had become acceptable and was on his way to becoming dear. Sir Ralph was always brisker after his visits, too; and that was another reason for welcoming Master Yellowlees, for no one wanted to admit that Sir Ralph was past his usefulness. For his part the custos of Oby also enjoyed his inspections, though as time went on he asked himself what good came of them. Though the day-to-day management was good enough, the long-term muddle was as bad as ever, and worse, and he did not see how it could ever be remedied. If he could get the bishop to attend ... but the bishop now avoided any mention of Oby, even in his dislikes he was fickle; and as Henry Yellowlees disliked the bishop as steadfastly as ever, he could not bring himself to a degree of intimate conversation which might make the bishop attend. He had been reporting the Esselby debt since 1375, nine times in all, as his reports were quarterly. He supposed it would go on like this for ever, that is to say, it would last out his time.

Receiving the bishop's order to go to Esselby, Henry Yellowlees felt wings break from his shoulders. To travel into a new county, to see strange towns and the unwinding of strange roads and the glitter of unforeseen rivers, to hear people talking in a different dialect about things he had no concern with, to be overtaken by dusk in an unfamiliar place: all this made his blood quicken. Yet routine and its slow mildewing of the mind had so far decayed him that to break with his work even for a week or so seemed like a break in the earth's surface, and a minute later he was asking what would become of his scholars – for he now taught in a school for pious poor boys which had been founded by Bishop Walter; and an uncommonly dull set they were, being chosen on merits of piety and poverty without regard to intellectual promise.

That, and everything else, had been arranged for. His route was planned, his expenses reckoned: so much for lodgings, so much for stabling, so much for tolls, and a small sum for gratuities and incidental expenses.

'Please count it,' said the treasurer's clerk, pouring out small money from a bag, 'and sign the receipt. You will start on the day after the feast of Saint Pancras. We shall recover the money, of course, from the convent of Oby.'

The convent of Oby had been lightly taxed. Everything was planned with the greatest economy. For the first night he must lodge with the chaplain of a leper-house, and on the morrow he must ride several miles out of his direct route in order to avail himself of a midday dole at Killdew Priory.

'You will need to ride hard on the last day in order to reach Esselby by nightfall. See that they give your horse a good feed and a good rub down, he will need it. And as these debtors are blacksmiths, they might very well re-shoe the beast.'

'What sort of place is Esselby?'

The clerk shrugged his shoulders.

The weather turned wet. All through Saint Pancras' day the rain dripped through the schoolroom roof. The patter of raindrops mixed with the clatter of his pupils' abacuses, and random peals of thunder rumbled in the cold air. But he did not think so much of what a detestable journey lay before him as of the certainty that the school's warden was too much devoted to Bishop Walter to ask for the roof to be mended.

When he set out the sky was still a heavy slate grey, darkening to purple where the sun slashed through the clouds. The night's rain still dripped from the house-eaves, young leaves and immature fruits floated in puddles. Before he had left the bounds of the city he was splashed to the thighs.

Once beyond the gate, riding became easier. He could choose his path, and by keeping to the outer edge of the track he escaped being more muddied than he was muddied already. The sun was now above the horizon, the air was growing warmer, the thatch of the suburb hovels and the dung-heaps before their doors were steaming. This was the brothel quarter. Vice had lately been put out of the city and had settled down philosophically just beyond the gate, waiting till the alarm died away and it could go in again. He remembered hearing a whore in a tavern declaiming at the injustice of this. Within the city walls, she said, clients came and went quickly, as easy as a Hail Mary; but once a poor whore was put outside the wall a client who outstayed the shutting of the gates at nightfall would make it an excuse to stay till morning. How could a whore make a living that way? – she asked; and for all the young men, thwarted by this ordinance, what was there but to turn to sodomy? – which was grievous, the more so since many of them had given their lives to God. It would distress the bishop if he knew how hardly his virtuous intentions bore on poor girls. He was so kind a man, and loving to all the poor. Sure enough, as Henry Yellowlees rode by one steaming hovel a young clerk came out from it, yawning and stretching.

Everywhere the cuckoos were screaming. It was a senseless noise, and turned his thoughts to how Francis of Assisi had preached to the birds. Did he number many cuckoos among his devotees? 'Would to God I had made you a holy friar and got you off my hands!' his mother had said to him as she lay dying. Afterwards he had thought pretty seriously of becoming a friar. Black, though, not grey. He could forgive Francis his cuckoos, preaching so cheerfully from other birds' pulpits, opening their jaws so deedily in the bosom of Mother Church. What, after all, had the saint of Umbria done but lay a new egg in an old nest? No wonder that the laity, seeing the friar begging so hard, staggering under the weight of his bag, streaming with sweat, whisking from door to door, and comparing him with the monk in his cloister, should think the friar the honester of the two. He could forgive Francis his friars. But not his nonsense: not those birds, that wolf, that jackass brotherhood with grass and thistles, sun and moon.

At the summit of a long rise he drew rein and stared out over the landscape. The clouds were gone, only a few shadows were left, hastening to the northward. Brilliant, senseless, irresponsible, the landscape stretched before him. What soul was there, what trace of praise to its Maker? What trace of reason, what trace of purpose, except where man's sad hand had etched it? Alongside the river water-scars like old burns showed where the winter floods had run. Now it was spring. Everything was new, was remade. The night's rain glittered in every runnel, flashed from bush and bramble, lay pearled in the clasp of daisies and liverwort leaves. Rain had washed the face of the earth like the waters of baptism. And the young leaves on the oak tree were not more bright than those which the storm had torn off and cast on the ground, and in the furrows the weeds were growing up with the corn. How can this praise God? he said sternly to the ghost beside him; all this beauty and promise is barely a month old, and already it is full of ruin and has not the sense to know good from evil.

His horse tossed its head, jerking away the flies. Having despatched Francis he rode on till he found an elder bush, and broke off a handful of twigs and fastened them in the headband. He was beginning to feel pleasure in his journey. It was pleasant to sit with his back against a thorn tree eating cold bacon while the horse cropped the young grass. Though a cuckoo sat in the branches it did not irk him. Before vespers, he said to himself, I shall be in country I have never seen before. So it was; though he could not be certain where the familiar changed to the unknown, the change had taken place. Presently he began to meet groups of labourers, their tired legs moving in time to the gait of their oxen, and when he asked them if he were going right for the leper-house their accents were strange to him.

The chaplain of the leper-house, a burly man with tow-coloured hair and a mincing manner of speech quite out of keeping with his looks, welcomed him warmly enough: that is to say, he continued to repeat that he was delighted, though at the same time he yawned and stared at the horse as if it resembled something he knew of by hearsay. Supper was scarcely on the table before he asked if his guest could read music at sight.

'What sort of music? I can read church-note, of course.'

'No, no! Music in measure. Do you understand the prolations? Well, I can soon teach you.'

He laid out a music-book among the mutton bones and the breadcrumbs, and began to explain.

'See, these red notes are to be sung in the triple prolation. And these red minims, following the black breve, show that the breve is imperfect. Bear that in mind, and the rest will be simple. You have only to get the knack of it. Let us begin with an easy one. This is charming: *Triste loysir*. Suppose I just run through your part to give you an idea of it? When it comes to *mors de moy* the longs are perfect, and you will be enraptured.'

His voice was slender as a reed, but accomplished. As he sang he thumped the measure on Henry's shoulder. Though written out with such complications, the music itself seemed simple, almost like a ballad-tune, and before long Henry interrupted, and rather scornfully at that, saying that he was ready to take his part.

He began loudly and steadily; but after half a dozen notes it seemed to him that he must have gone wrong, and he broke off.

'Go on, go on! You were doing excellently.'

'But surely there was something wrong? It sounded very odd.'

'No, there was nothing wrong. Perhaps the interval unsettled you. You expected a fourth, no doubt. This is composed in the style of the *Ars nova*, it is disconcerting at times. Let us begin again. And hold on: you will soon become accustomed to it.'

This time he held on, though he felt himself astray, bewildered by the unexpected progressions, concords so sweet that they seemed to melt the flesh off his bones. Coming to *mors de moy*, where the chaplain's voice twittered in floriations high above his tolling longs, he could hardly contain himself for excitement.

'But this is astonishing,' he said. 'Are there others like this?' He began to turn the pages of the book.

'Yes, most of the things in this book are in *Ars nova* style. This Kyrie by Machault, for instance . . . Unfortunately, it is for three voices. Of course, we could sing it without the middle voice, but you would not get a true idea of it. The bishop's message did not tell me to expect a musician.'

Henry Yellowlees realised with certainty how strongly Bishop Walter would dislike *Ars nova*; and if anything could deepen his dislike of the bishop, this did.

'Out here, one has so few chances of meeting a competent musician. It is a stroke of good fortune for me that you should come. That is why I wish you could hear the Machault. Of course . . . ' The chaplain paused, staring at his hand as it lay on the music-book. 'One of my lepers here has an extremely fine voice and is a skilled singer. He used to be in the Duke of Burgundy's chapel. I don't know if you would object – he is not an advanced case of leprosy. He and I often sing together. To him, too, a third voice would be a godsend.'

Not knowing whether he turned hot or cold Henry Yellowlees answered: 'No, of course not. I should like to hear the Kyrie.'

The chaplain slid back a panel in the wall and called: 'John! Will you come and sing?'

Shuffling footsteps approached. The leper came in. In the dusk of the doorway he seemed to glimmer like bad fish. He stank, too. He stationed himself at the further end of the room; it was clear that he knew his place as a dog does. There he stood, rubbing his scaly hands together, drawing preparatory breaths. His expression was professionally calm.

'Now, John! The Machault Kyrie.'

The three voices sprang into the air.

If *Triste loysir* had seemed a foretaste of paradise, the Kyrie was paradise itself. This was how the blessed might sing, singing in a duple measure that ran as nimbly on its four feet as a weasel running through a meadow, with each voice in turn enkindling the others, so that the music flowed on and was continually renewed. And as paradise is made for man, this music seemed made for man's singing; not for edification, or the working-out of an argument, or the display of skill, but only for ease and pleasure, as in paradise where the abolition of sin begets a pagan carelessness, where the certainty of Christ's countenance frees men's souls from the obligations of christian behaviour, the creaking counterpoint of God's law and man's obedience.

It ended. Henry Yellowlees raised his eyes from the music-book. The rays of the levelling sun had shifted while they sang and now shone full on the leper. His face, his high bald head, were scarlet. He seemed to be on fire.

'Again! Let us sing it again!'

'I told you so,' said the chaplain. 'I tell you, there has never been such music in the world before.'

All through the evening they sang, the leper standing apart and singing by rote. And Henry thought how many an hour these two must have spent together, the leper at one end of the room, the chaplain at the other; or perhaps they bent over the same music-book, their love of music overcoming the barrier between life and death-in-life. What did the other lepers think of it, those who could not sing, sitting in their straw, mumbling their sour bread (for if the food given to a guest were so bad the food given to the lepers must be worse), and hearing the music go on and on? Most of the night Henry lay awake, recalling the music, humming it over again to the burden of the chaplain's snores, with half of his mind in a rapture and the other half wishing that there were not so many and such ferocious bugs. It struck him that every bug in the place must have heard the good news and forsaken the lepers for flesh that was a novelty.

'You will come again?'

'Yes, indeed. In a week's time, perhaps.'

'I hope you slept well?'

'Excellently, thank you.'

The morning mist was just floating off the meadows. It would be a hot day, and he had started late. But the heat of the day was as yet only a theory, and he huddled his cloak round him, chilled by lack of sleep even when the mist had cleared and the sun filled the long narrow valley. Singing and whistling he rode on, and presently came to the valley's head and a hillside where the track showed out clearly in the poorer grass.

A mile or so further on he met two of those happier travellers he had been considering (for still occupied by the music of overnight he had been thinking that in this world, where all lives are subject to so much discommodity, and death muddies the bottom of every cup, golliards and wanderers probably make out the best). A man was leading a chained fox and a woman staggered after him with a bundle on her back and a harp slung across it. He asked them the way to Killdew Priory, while saying to himself that it was waste of time, he could leave it to the horse: any horse from Bishop Walter's stables would know by instinct the detour that led to a free meal. The man directed him, dragging the fox this way and that as he swung his arms explaining the way to be taken, the way to be avoided, while the woman looked on with a satirical expression on her sweaty face; no doubt she was thinking of the dole for travellers, and perhaps with experience of it, for her look conveyed that he was going a long way for very little.

It might be better to have some settled habitation, and to live, like the chaplain at the leper-house, with enough routine to ward one from the reflection that a man's fate is no one's concern but his own. The chaplain might sometimes regret the lack of a bass, but otherwise he had not much to sigh for; and though in the end he might catch leprosy the shock would not fall on him with such astonishment as on other men. I could be happy living like that, thought Henry: nursing the music-book among the mutton bones, having forsaken this world to live in the fifth element of sound ... Ah, that Kyrie, and the rondeau they had sung after it, and the song with the bass part descending with iron tread at *mors de moy*! Such music, and such squalor! ... never had he seen a house so dirty, or slept in a more tattered bed. But out came the music as the kingfisher flashes from its nest of stinking fishbones.

From the brow of the hill he looked down on Killdew Priory, a modern building, ostentatiously symmetrical, and at the priory church, cluttered with scaffolding where the nave was being built higher. They'll run into debt for it, he said pleasurably, and be colder into the bargain. He passed the vineyards and the fish-ponds without envy and asked for his free dinner without humiliation. It was just such a meal as a flourishing community provides, clean, adequate, and disagreeable, with a strong flavour of fennel to mask the mustiness of the dried fish. He told the serving brother he would be back in a few days' time. He reckoned without his host. Wild hyacinths and wild garlic had taken the place of windflowers in the copses before he saw Killdew again.

For at Esselby the worst of a visitor's misfortunes overtook him: he became indispensable.

At first sight the house seemed calm enough, a house fit for the end of a journey, sheltered under a little craggy hill. There was a well-head and some sheds near by, and a smithy, and in the dusk he saw great hammers leaning against the anvil. It should not be difficult to get the money from such a thriving concern. He entered the house and explained his errand. There was a handsome child crawling on the floor, and feeling that some civilities should garnish the rent-collecting he complimented the young woman on its sturdy looks.

'It's no brat of mine,' she cried out, furiously.

Absorbed in its own life the child pulled up its smock and began to make water. The young woman began to whimper, an old woman chimed in. He discovered they were telling him a story. What it was about, and why they should be telling him, he could not make out, for they had told it so often that they mislaid the tale in the telling, going off at a tangent to argue whether something or other had happened on a Tuesday or a Wednesday, in one or another Lent. Meanwhile, he seated himself at the board hoping his attitude would suggest a supper. No food came, and the man of the house went out, talking about bedding down the horse.

Presently two nuns appeared in the story. They came seeking something, but while they were still parleying at the door a mastiff burst into the narrative, and mauled the older nun so savagely that if some workmen had not run to her rescue she might have died. Then came a long wrangle as to whether it was before or after this affair that the lightning struck the great oak at the foot of the pightle. This they could not determine, but harking back to the nuns and the mastiff they explained how a sentence of excommunication falling on a household that traded in ironwork, and specialised in church furniture – here again was an excursion to a neighbouring chantry whose screen had not been paid for – was reason enough, as Master Yellowlees must see, for an inability to pay one's rent.

'So this house is under the ban of the church?' asked Henry

hopefully; for if it were, it would give him an excuse to go elsewhere to a better likelihood of a supper.

God forbid, they cried out: no such thing. And after a long account of how the mastiff was hanged for sacrilege they quieted down to explain that the ban of the church had fallen upon Roger Longdock, the old woman's husband, and on their daughter, the mother of the child there. She was a nun. But when she appeared one day with the child in her belly Roger had harboured her, and it was after barring the door against the nuns who arrived to reclaim her that the mastiff had been let loose.

Appalled by the sentence of excommunication the nun had craved to submit herself and go back to her convent, but the old man had kept her and the child under lock and key for almost a year. At last she escaped, and fled to the parish priest. Finding her gone, Roger walked out of the house and ever since had been living as a wild man in the woods; and now, old as he was, he had a woman with him.

By the time all this was told and the daughter-in-law had remembered that their guest must be hungry, the fire had gone out. Long past hunger, his head throbbing, his eyes smarting with sleeplessness, Henry wanted nothing but to lie down and sleep. But the two women had now persuaded themselves that he would get them out of all their troubles and not be exigent about the rent, and this being so it followed that they had to keep him waiting for another couple of hours while they poked up the brands into a smoke and roasted some eggs for his supper.

In the morning the household was reinforced by other members of the family: a married daughter, two swaggering cousins, and the old woman's brother who somewhere or other had picked up some tags of law Latin, and bowed incessantly. With one accord they thanked God for his arrival; with one accord they were ready to accompany him to the woods, where he would talk Roger Longdock out of his contumacy. By then Henry Yellowlees had taken a look at the son of the house: a young man with the frame of an ox and the bolting eyes of a fanatic. He remembered that he had come to collect a debt, not to call sinners to repentance, and said he was ready to be taken round the buildings in order to make an inventory.

What overnight had seemed so thriving was only a husk of prosperity. Walls and roofs needed mending, the wood-stack was overgrown by moss and ferns, thick curtains of cobwebs hung on the anvil, the tools were rusted. No one, young Longdock bewailed, would commission as much as a poker from them now, because of the ban of the church. But the church, said Henry, had discriminated between the guilty and the guiltless, and surely the parish priest had only to make this clear for trade to return? All the Longdocks began with one voice to say how kind, how good, how considerate the village priest had been. While they expatiated a little old man, wrinkled and very thin, began to appear and disappear at the back of the workshop, flitting about like a lizard.

'Now I come to think of it,' said Henry Yellowlees, 'my horse needs re-shoeing,' – the old man at the back of the shop showed his broken teeth in a grin – 'though it is a small matter to kindle up your forge for.'

The old man darted forward and began to pull out the embers of a long-cold fire.

'Yet one piece of work may bring another. The sight of your smoke will tell your neighbours that you are ready to work.'

The old man gave an exploratory pull at the bellows. They wheezed with disuse and quantities of dead flies fell out of their foldings. Henry continued to talk of industry and the value of a family business and secrets of handicraft passing from one generation to another.

At last the fire was going, the ingot melted and laid on the anvil. Mouthing woefully, young Longdock picked up a hammer, sighed, swung it and let it fall. It fell awry.

'You seem to be out of practice. But it will soon come,' Henry observed.

At the same moment the old man, speaking for the first time, cried: 'Spit on your hands, master! Spit on your hands!'

'So you tried to get Sim to work,' was old Longdock's greeting on the following morning. Accompanied by troops of Longdocks Henry had looked for him in vain the day before. This time he had gone to the woods alone, and found him quite easily. 'You'll get no work out of my son Sim, I can tell you, unless you thrash him.' He was an alarming old man with quantities of shaggy hair and one eye. He lolled under a tree, eating the leg of a goose and childishly dabbling his enormous bare feet on a cushion of moss. 'Seeing as you've come so far, I'll tell you this much. There are two ways to get the rent for your good ladies. One is, put me right with the church, so I can finish that screen for the Congres chantry. 'Tother is, to squeeze my wife's brother for it.'

Henry felt no love for the brother-in-law, but it seemed to be his duty to press the first expedient. He did his best to reason the old man into submission, but unavailingly. Perhaps the thought of the mastiff tied his tongue. The wood was a frowning place, full of old quarry holes, and looked as if it might contain any number of fierce dogs. When he had finished old Longdock remarked: 'Best thing you can do is turn them all out. Let them go to my good brother.'

Hatred of his brother-in-law seemed to be his fixed star. For the rest he rambled on about the gates and shrines and fetters he had made in the old days. In his snarling way he was hospitable, probably he enjoyed having a stranger to talk to. When his woman came out of the bushes driving a couple of nanny goats he told her to make a meal for the visitor.

The parish priest, who did not appear till the fourth day, for he had been away looking after a law-suit, was no help. All his thoughts were given to the child, whom he had snatched away, he said, from under the ban. Now the boy would grow up a good christian and if things went well become a friar – priest he could not be, being a bastard – and so be serviceable to God and atone in some measure for the sins of his family. Henry remarked that the younger Longdocks seemed pious enough. Pious, oh yes, certainly; but troublesome parishioners and exceedingly covetous. Covet, indeed, was the root of the whole trouble. Settling down to a story (for it was a wet afternoon and he was pleased with a new listener), he related how, many years before, a friar had passed through Esselby, pausing to preach a sermon on the heinous sin of taking usury. Quite uncanonical, Henry commented. The friar must have been old-fashioned. Aye, but so was Esselby, replied Sir Robin. Most of Esselby had borrowed money at some time or other from Cuthbert Ledwidge, old Longdock's brother-in-law, whose terms were extortionate, so the sermon had been heard with enthusiasm. Half-way through the sermon, continued the priest, Ledwidge had thought it best to steal away. But what he had heard had wrung his conscience, and when a couple of his debtors defaulted and his house was set on fire he surmised that God's wrath would not wait till eternity but was snuffing round him already. So he arranged for his younger niece to become a nun, paying down a good dowry with her. With a niece in a nunnery, it seemed to him, he would stand better before God, and with any luck she would make such a virtuous nun that her merits and mortifications might help to shorten his years in purgatory. But instead, she fell in love, was got with child, ran home to her father, and became the cause of all this trouble. Ledwidge would have been better advised to lay out his money on masses, said Henry, and Sir Robin warmly agreed; but these people were as wrong-headed as strayed pigs; they had no conception of God's will.

'As for the upshot, you have seen it for yourself. Roger Longdock will not submit, the church cannot give way. Sim Longdock, between ourselves, will never do a stroke of work, your rent will never be paid. The water will not quench the fire, the fire will not burn the stick, the stick will not beat the dog. Now tell me about Bishop Walter. I hear he is a very holy man, and in his youth even did miracles.'

That Bishop Walter should wing his way hither and collect the rent would be a timely miracle. But Henry Yellowlees' obstinacy was now engaged. The rumour spread that a man had come to Esselby who could get money out of the Longdocks, and presently he found himself charged with half a dozen hopeful furious creditors. The tangle yielded where the knot had seemed toughest: Roger Longdock suddenly declared himself ready to submit to the church. Henry haled him off then and there to repeat this good news to Sir Robin. The stick would beat the dog, after all. His work was done, and he told the Longdocks that he would start on the morrow. They were profuse in praising God, though he observed that Sim Longdock's praises had a pensive note in them, as though he already foresaw his father back and the cudgel lifted. This supposition must be his reward for a most unpleasant sojourn; expensive, too, for they whined him into paying more than above for his lodging and his horse's stabling. Not even a pair of horseshoes, he said to himself; but here he was wrong, for he found that the goblin old man who haunted the smithy had made and fitted them.

When the morning mass was over he waited to say goodbye to Sir Robin. Holy Church would thank him, piped the old man, wrinkling his eyelids in the pure sunlight. Thanks to him, another soul would be safely cupboarded in religion.

'In religion?'

'Aye. In religion. Roger came to me last night. He is set on it, nothing will appease him but to spend the rest of his days in a religious order.'

'A religious order?'

'Yes, indeed! Nothing else will serve. He swears that he cannot go back to his old life, for if he were to do so he would only damn himself over again by murdering Sim and Cuthbert. So he will flee from temptation.'

'And the rent?'

Sir Robin began to cackle. Willy-nilly, Henry Yellowlees had to laugh too. They laughed and dug each other in the ribs, till Sir Robin became so weak that he had to be propped against a buttress.

'God bless you, my son. God be with you on your journey, and for evermore. I shall always thank God that you came to Esselby.'

A good story to tell the bishop, Henry said to himself; though not so good a story to tell at Oby. In a little while rents and bishops were forgotten, for now he was riding towards the leper-house and *Ars nova*. At last, early in the afternoon of his second day's travelling, he looked down from the ridge where he had met the musicians and their fox into the valley where now the buttercups had come fully into bloom. They were blooming so richly, their colour was so burnished and intense, that by contrast the green of the meadow-grass seemed almost blue. Riding through them he felt himself growing dazzled and giddy, as though he might fall into this whispering golden sea and drown there. At every turn of the valley he stared ahead, searching for the shabby building which encased such music. Bishop or no, errand or no, he would stay two nights, perhaps three. He saw a building. But it was not the one he looked for. It was roofless: some ruin, some old cattle-shed which he had not noticed when he rode by before because of the mist. Then through the hot pollen-scented air came a whiff of burned thatch. It was heavy and fulsome, the stink of a recent burning. The mare put back her ears, and snorted and made to turn away; but he drove in his spurs and set her onward. Riding nearer he saw that the elder bushes and the young nettles growing around the ruined building were newly blackened. And while he was still staring, and not believing, a figure sprang up from the threshold and came uncertainly towards him, crying out: 'Pity! In the name of the Virgin, have pity!' Then he saw that this was the leper who had sung in the Duke of Burgundy's chapel. The mare reared, and the leper stopped, shielding his race with a shapeless hand. 'Have pity!' he said again. Peeping out from behind his hand he recognised the rider. 'I am John of the Chapel. We sang together. Do not forsake me, do not slay me! I swear before God I had no part in it.'

There was stale blood on his clothes and flies swarmed about him. Still warding his face, and turning his head to listen this way and that, he came a step nearer.

'They set on us while we were singing. We were singing, we did not hear them come. They had armed themselves, some with sticks, some with bones. They struck him down and beat him, and one of them thrust a bone into his mouth and down his gullet, and worked it to and fro till his gullet split and the blood ran out. Then the others set fire to the roof, and they all went away.

'The lepers that could not walk they put in a cart, and the rest went alongside with clappers and bells, saying that now they would beg and be well-filled,' he said, his eyes staring down the valley as though he were watching still. 'But the men went that way.' He turned, and pointed up the hillside.

'What men were they?'

'I do not know. They had carts, and booty, and some had blackened their faces.'

'They were robbers?'

'They called themselves the Twelve Apostles, they said they were going about to right the poor. One of them had been here before, and had heard the lepers complain, I suppose. They were always complaining and saying that he spent all on music-books that should have been spent on them. And it is true, there was often nothing to eat. It was the lepers who killed him, they had hated him for a long time. The others only shouted and destroyed.'

'And when was this?' The question was partly answered by the stink of decay that now seemed the only smell in all the rich valley. The brook chattered to itself, and presently he rode off towards it with an indistinct purpose of cleansing himself, and dismounted and rinsed his mouth and wiped the sweat off his face with a handful of water-cresses. He had no sooner done so than he was again sweating with fear and feeling sick, for it seemed to him beyond any doubt that just here was where the leper had lapped the water and pulled the cresses which, so he said, had been all his nourishment for three days. The leper – what was to be done with him? He looked back and saw the man standing in the same place, staring after him in a desolate doubt. He thinks I shall ride on and leave him, thought Henry; and so I might, and not cause him much more distress, since already in his mind I have forsaken him.

He beckoned, and the man came on, at first in a flurry of relief, then more slowly as his doubts gained on him; and stopped within hailing distance.

'What became of the music-books?'

'They poked them into the thatch to burn.'

He threw to the leper what food he had. Then he asked him how well he could walk. The leper's assurances that he could walk as well as a sound man Henry discounted by half. But as there was nothing else to be done he mounted again, jerking his disbelieving beast back into the way they had come, and rode slowly on towards the head of the valley, telling the leper they would be at Killdew before nightfall, and that at Killdew he would be well cared for. Killdew would not be best pleased, he thought; but the news of the Twelve Apostles being abroad might quicken their loving-kindness. At intervals he paused and looked back. The leper was still following, dragging his shadow over the buttercups. The hillside would have been too much for his strength if Henry had not remembered the length of cord that fastened his wallet to the saddle. Throwing one end to the leper and fastening the other to the saddle-bow he hauled the man after him as the musician had hauled the fox. So at last they came to the brow of the hill and looked down on the Priory, and heard the bell ringing for compline. Its reiterated notes rose up straight and slender as a row of poplars. The leper hawked, and crossed himself, and began to sing *Te lucis ante terminum* and as Henry took it up he deserted the plain-chant and sang a descant. The horse wandered about cropping the hill-top turf, and Henry and the leper sat on the grass, the leper sitting a dozen paces away, but near enough to prompt Henry in the bass part of *Triste loysir* until he could sing it steadily enough for the tenor to be added. They sang it three times through, and if in the beginning Henry remembered the chaplain, from whose stinking body the chill of evening had now swept off the flies, by the third repetition nothing remained but the delight of the two voices answering and according, and a regret that they could not sit singing all night through. But they could not delay; as it was they would arrive after the hour of the great silence, the porter would be grumpy and might stand on the rules. As they went downward past the vineyards and the silvered fish-ponds John of the Chapel talked with excitement of hearing the singing at Killdew. To him music was something which could be found here or there indifferently, like a mass.

They reached the Priory. The porter came out, protesting, but also boasting that late comers were nothing to such an establishment as Killdew. The leper was disposed of, a sub-infirmarian conveying him away as efficiently as a river swallows a pebble. As for the news of the Twelve Apostles, it was stale news.

'They are not likely to trouble us,' said the guest-master. 'If they do, we have made our preparations and no doubt God will defend his servants. It is only small establishments that need fear them – like that unfortunate Hospital of Saint Sepulchre, which in any case was scandalously mismanaged. Still, as our cellarer is riding to Ingham Fair tomorrow I suggest you make one of his party. In any case, to ride in company is pleasanter than to ride alone.'

The cellarer's party was so stately and so well-mounted that Henry Yellowlees riding the bishop's provision of a horse and depending on the very small residue of the bishop's provision for gratuities wished at first that he had said he would travel alone. The cellarer's clerk, however, a Lombard, was an easy talker, a man with so large an acquaintance with religious establishments that he seemed to find all of them about equally criticisable. To such a man, Henry realised, the shifts of poverty were so far removed as to be entertaining. So he recounted the story of the Esselby rent. The cellarer's clerk was delighted with it, and at dinner Henry was called on to tell it all over again, and again it gave much pleasure. Then the cellarer remarked that it was just what one would expect of Oby, he feared Henry Yellowlees must have nothing but annoyance in the custos-ship of such an ill-managed house. The bishop had succeeded in blackening Oby as far as the exalted ears of Killdew, had he? Henry at once launched into an eulogium of Prioress Matilda, her nuns, so discreet and well-connected, and the good old priest who had served them so long and devotedly and who was despite his years a most discriminating theologian.

'I heard he was out of his wits,' said the cellarer's clerk.

'I seem to have heard he was no priest,' said another. The cellarer remarked that if one believed all that one heard one would despair of the providence of God. Fortunately one need not take such rumours seriously. He had heard some odd things about Bishop Walter, too, for that matter. The librarian, who was also of the party, travelling to the fair to buy oak-galls and vellum, said more seriously that the most damaging rumours about Bishop Walter were those telling of his poverty and abstinence. Such talk suggested to the poor and ignorant that the majority of churchmen lived inordinately richly. Personal austerities were all very well no doubt, but to obtrude them was disloyal to the tonsure. He added that if Bishop Walter ate two dishes at dinner instead of one, in all likelihood the unfortunate chaplain at Saint Sepulchre would not have been clubbed to death.

The next day they separated. Riding on by himself and nearing his journey's end Henry Yellowlees began to think of his errand and of what he should report. His fruitless errand, which had been to the monks of Killdew a story for dinner, and to himself a nut to crack, like a problem in mathematics, would be to the ladies of Oby a matter of bread and bacon. For each one of us lives in his microcosm, the solidity of this world is a mere game of mirrors, there can be no absolute existence for what is apprehended differently by all. And if he could have brought back the music-books his fruitless errand would have been as rich for him as a return from the lands of Saba.

The fruitless errand had lasted much too long: this was the first comment of the bishop's secretary, who went on to say that during his absence his class had mislaid the large compasses while roasting larks on them. Tell the bishop that money is the root of all evil, he replied. Some new element, perhaps *Ars nova*, perhaps the conversation of that sophisticated Lombard, had made a new man of Henry Yellowlees, and the secretary reported to the bishop that Master Yellowlees had been away for so long because he had been consorting with the Lollards.

XI

A Sacrifice to Woden

(*June 1377–January 1380*)

Riding out to Oby, Henry Yellowlees looked over the landscape with sunlike benevolence. The hay was newly cut and lay in swathes on the meadows as orderly as a mackerel sky, the spire laid its delicate shadow across the green ground, the willows drew their silvery foliage across the enamelled red of their bark. In returning to Oby he was returning to something he might love; and the thought that he might love it and the thought that he had no hold upon it swept over him together, so that he saw it as imperative that he should at once apply for priest's orders and be ready to succeed Sir Ralph as convent priest. The old man could not last for ever; indeed, would he last long enough to fill those comfortable shoes until Henry was ready to step into them? Yet how foolish and impetuous to plight himself to Oby because it was enjoying a moment of midsummer beauty! – for the rest of the year what was it but mire and mist, boredom, loneliness, a worthless soil, and the wind ruffling the winter floods?

Sir Ralph rose out of the Waxle Stream to greet him, splashing and snorting through the reeds like a cow or a river-god. He had been poking about with a net for perch, his gown was bunched up round his thighs and his face with its deep wrinkles and tufted eyebrows and features shaped for wrath wore an expression of silvery innocence like the full moon. Full of pleasure at seeing Henry again he questioned him about his journey. Soon his attention slid away. He began throwing grasses into the river and drawing designs on the mud bank with his toes.

'Since Whitsun,' he said abruptly, 'I have been thinking about the sacrament of baptism.'

Henry Yellowlees resigned himself. Sir Ralph's thoughts on baptism had led him to conclude that the rite did not go far enough, what was squirting a baby? Well enough for a beginning, but for the full-grown man there should be a full immersion, for such was the baptism of John. For the sake of conversation Henry Yellowlees represented that there is no evidence in the scriptures that John had immersed Jesus, and that the tradition of the church, as expressed in art, was that John had scooped up the water of Jordan, perhaps with some vessel, perhaps with his hand, and had poured it on Jesus's head. Meanwhile Sir Ralph was beating the Waxle with his net, and fidgeting. Suddenly he threw off his gown and waded back into the stream. 'Let me baptise you,' he begged. 'You look very warm, a good sousing is just what you need. Come, off with your clothes! The nuns will not see you, they are all asleep.'

Moving a little further up the bank Henry asked if the prioress were in good health, if Dame Philippa were still coughing. But he asked in vain. The old man waded to and fro, happy as a cow, and rambled on in praise of water, water, he said, which was the innocent element. Why was the Redeemer of mankind for ever faultless and incapable of sin? Because he was a fish and for ever immersed in the flood. He swam for eternity in the waters which are above the earth. And in those waters, Sir Ralph continued, wading and splashing, in those waters there swim with Christ the souls of all his blessed; for heaven is a great fish-pond, and there you can see the Bishops and the Confessors nosing about like carp, and the Martyrs with bright bloody spots are trout, and the Virgins in their silver mail of chastity are dace. Whoever loves holiness must love water by natural inclination, he shouted, and whoever dies by drowning goes straight to God, filled to human bursting with the innocence and absolution of water. Scooping up a handful of water and pouring it on his head he threw himself under with a splash and displacement which sent the ripples over Henry's feet.

With such a madman the only way was to humour his fancies. When he came up again Henry called out: 'And what are the eels?'

'The Doctors, the learned Doctors!' cried Sir Ralph. 'Are they not full of small bones and fatness? Wade in, young man, and receive the baptism of John!'

He showed no ill-feeling when Henry Yellowlees excused himself. His madness was akin to childishness: he was so perfectly convinced by his nonsense that he felt no need to proselytise.

Yet what if he should begin to throw the nuns into the Waxle Stream? If he did so, and a nun died, her death would be upon Henry's soul. I am a custos, he said to himself, riding along the track between the willows; my only concern is with their temporalities, and if I say to the prioress that in my opinion her priest is mad she may ask me what my opinion has to do with it, and if I speak of it to the bishop he will have Sir Ralph out and a new man in; and what then will become of my plan of being priested myself and following Sir Ralph, and growing, I daresay, after ten winters as mad as he? It was clear to him that he would say nothing either to prioress or bishop. He also had a pretty strong impression that Sir Ralph was totally uninterested in the souls of his nuns.

By the time he reached the convent the picture of Sir Ralph

tossing nuns into the Cow Pool seemed very unlifelike. It lost all validity when Dame Lovisa's face looked out of the wicket. She raised – not her eyebrows, she had no eyebrows – but the roughened tracts of skin above her eyes, and remarked that he was quite a stranger. Though women arouse the lusts of the flesh they atone for it by quelling any vagaries of the imagination.

He made his report to the prioress. It struck him that he would not make her many more reports. In spite of her massive bulk and her straight back she seemed hollowed by some inward decay. She would drop suddenly, as the limb of an elm tree drops. She heard the news from Esselby with imperturbability, laughed, and turned the conversation to ask about the management of the vineyards at Killdew. Her gruff good manners made him realise for the first time how completely he had disgraced himself in his errand. But *Ars nova* had waylaid him: the man who arrived at Esselby was not the man who had set out on the morrow of Saint Pancras day. Like those who fall in with fairies, he had been conveyed under the green hill; and *Triste loysir* was the tune of that place. He would never be his own man again. *Ars nova* had worked its will on him only a little less commandingly than on the chaplain of the leper-house. One man it had killed and the other despatched without death into another world. If he seemed to come back, and be the same custos of Oby, who had miscarried of a business errand, it was only by force of habit, and with such inattentive freedom of mind that he was now asking himself whether Sir Ralph's madness or the materialism of the nuns was furthest from real life. Yet what was real life? Not his own life, assuredly. He felt no pavement of reality under his feet, wandering among a chance assemblage of geometry, hunger, sickness, loaned horses, debts and shifts and other people's intentions. Whose life was real? – old Longdock's in the wildwood, the chaplain's at the leper-house, the suave Killdew clerk's? Each of them in his way knew what he wanted and sought it with self-will, and for that matter, with self-denial; for no doubt the Killdew clerk must have denied himself something in order to live with such a rotundity of worldliness, he must have trampled down some artless predisposition such as wishing to recite his own poems.

On the morrow there was William Holly waiting to go round with him, and the usual litany of this needing doing and that ill-done. William Holly was one of those small, tight men like a knot of wood, his cross-grainedness seemed a warrant of longevity; while there was a young man to snub, a new opinion to confute, a youthful hope to disparage, one would expect William Holly to be at his post. But today he had scarcely a contradiction in him, and in a manner quite unusual to him he stopped and pointed out the grave of the elder Frampton novice, who had died of measles, and Henry saw with amazement that tears were standing in his eyes. They finished their round and were looking at a spotted ox which had recently come in as a heriot when William Holly suddenly remarked that something in his inwards was gnawing and biting him, which he opined to be a toad, swallowed small in a salad; for nothing less malicious than a toad would have withstood the purges he had been taking. Henry Yellowlees foolishly allowed himself to say that he did not think a toad could live within a man. William Holly replied that every fool knew that a toad can live inside a stone for a hundred years if it pleased to.

The crab, the archer, the man with the water-pot – there is not a sign in the zodiac which has not its patronised malady, there is death, thought Henry, staring up past the spire, death in the firmament. Prioress, priest, bailiff, they were all growing old in this midsummer air. Another prioress would follow, another priest would be found; it would be harder to replace the bailiff; for William Holly was one of those yew-tree characters which do not allow younger yew trees to grow up in their shade. He rode away thinking of the pretty child who had outgrown them all in her dying, and that she would not have to suffer another winter's chilblains, or a new-broom priest imposed by Bishop Walter. And as for the Esselby rent, let the bishop deal with it, he said to himself.

Any such hope was wiped out when he next saw the bishop. Here was another old age under sentence from a sign in the zodiac – in Bishop Walter's case perhaps the sign of the scales, for his eyes were netted in wrinkles of calculation, and the word *judgement* continually recurred in his talk.

'It is a judgement!' he exclaimed of the non-payment of the Esselby rent. 'Why should I intervene when God has judged? Oby is judged, I assure you. We can do nothing. It is taken out of our hands.'

His chaplain signed to Henry to say no more of it, and primmed up his lips as if to contain something unspeakable. No sense could ever be got out of that chaplain. Henry Yellowlees went to Humphrey Flagg, the bishop's doctor. Humphrey Flagg was also devoted to Bishop Walter, but his love had more secularity in it. Besides, he was a Yorkshireman, a fellow-countryman of Henry's.

'It is no use. And I beg you not to vex him with any more talk of your nunnery. It only upsets him. And after all, what is one nunnery?'

'But what has he got against it? What maggot is all this? What has anyone got against it? I suppose it is the most respectable nunnery in all his bishopric.'

'I can only say that it made a bad impression on him. I have felt his pulse jump like a ram when someone has mentioned Oby.'

'But why? The ladies of Oby don't skip like lambs when someone mentions the bishop.'

Evading this, Humphrey Flagg continued: 'The bishop is not like other men. His will is stronger than other men's, his sensibilities are much more acute. His body is at the mercy of his soul, and the soul is a hard master. For some reason or other his soul flogs him with Oby, that is all I can tell you.'

'Some prejudice,' Henry grumbled. 'Well, he sent his Dame Sibilla to Oby, anyhow. Why did he do that if Oby is such an offence to him?'

When Bishop Walter asked himself that same question, though he found many answers he could not hit on one that silenced it. At first the question had been no more than any other question, an exercise of a conscience which fed on scruples; for the bishop was a man who constantly asked himself questions and as constantly resolved them to his own satisfaction. But the Dame Sibilla question came back and back, and grew more urgent and more mysterious. Correspondingly, his first dislike of Oby, the dislike he had so naturally and properly conceived on discovering that the Oby nuns supposed they could throw dust in his eyes, had deepened into an apprehension of something quite unusually baleful, a wickedness beyond all the faults he had been able to catalogue and rebuke, a wickedness so wicked that it transcended his diagnosis, and only God could put his finger on it. That, of course, was why his first dislike had been so much sharper and more quivering than an intention to deceive a bishop might warrant. Oby was not singular in hoping to deceive a bishop, any more than in being luxurious, frivolous, worldly, and insolvent. Under these everyday offences a deeper abomination lay in wait.

Having got thus far in his surmising, the bishop naturally went on to seek out more information, keeping his ear to the ground; and naturally, he heard a good deal. Though everything he heard could be construed to Oby's disadvantage he really heard nothing at all telling until just before Henry Yellowlees came back from Esselby. Then, in the course of conversation with a newly appointed summoner whose uncle had been clerk of the works at Etchingdon, he learned the true story of the Methley tithes: which was, that Thomas de Foley had given them to Oby as a price for the carnal pleasures he had enjoyed with his cousin, the Prioress Alicia. Hard on the heels of this enlightenment the bishop made a Visitation to the convent to which he had transferred Dame Alice. In many ways the Visitation was grievous, he noted for instance a shocking degree of gluttony, and the nuns were bristling with quarrels and slanders; but amidst all this Dame Alice's simple homely pleasure at seeing him warmed his heart. In the course of their private interview she told him how she and Dame Johanna had always believed that the spire had fallen, and Dame Susanna had thrown herself under it, as a plain manifestation of the wrath of God. She also recounted the deaths of the boy who fell off the scaffolding, Ursula who fell down the stairs, the corrodian, Magdalen Figg, who fell into the fish-pond, and Magdalen's husband, the old bailiff. Did it not seem as though God would scarcely allow a christian death-bed at Oby? How could she express her gratitude to the bishop for having delivered her from such a place?

And how, she added, was Dame Sibilla? – that sweet lady, the pattern of what a nun should be.

He stared at her, not daring to turn aside the question he dreaded to hear.

'I have often asked myself why you sent Dame Sibilla to Oby.' Her eyelids closed down, as though the sight of his distress were something that must be eaten in private. Sighing appreciatively, and gently wagging her head, she murmured: 'I should not be so presumptuous. But it seemed to me you were sending a lamb among the wolves.'

'Yes, yes!' he answered, and hastily blessed the understanding creature.

Dame Alice was perfectly satisfied with this interview, and lived on in peace of mind. It was not in any case likely that the prioress of Oby would denounce her; but if she did Bishop Walter would not now be inclined to listen with any favour. That goose was cooked. The bishop's satisfaction did not last so long. By the evening the answer supplied by Dame Alice to the inexorcisable question had shrivelled into no answer at all. It is a function of lambs to be sent among wolves; such a sending would have been pious and meritorious, and God might have been expected to bless it. But this was no such thing. He had placed his great-niece at Oby in order to chasten an extravagant house by compelling it to take in three unprofitable newcomers. Dame Sibilla had not been so much sent as a lamb as applied as a leech.

Yet God had permitted it. Perhaps God had even designed it. It was in God's hands, and there he must leave it. He had repeatedly tried this answer, and whenever he tried it, it led to Abraham and Jephtha. Abraham had been ready to sacrifice Isaac, Jephtha had not been ready to offer up his daughter but had done so nevertheless. Of the two, it seemed to Bishop Walter that Jephtha's case was nearest his own. With Abraham, God proceeded directly and with the authority of a father, but in his dealings with Jephtha he availed himself of a stratagem, at the last moment substituting Jephtha's daughter for what Jephtha very likely expected to be a ram. Preaching on the duty of obedience the bishop perplexed his hearers, for it was unlike him to enter so feelingly into the emotions of pre-christian characters. Yet the lesson was clear, and several fathers went home to beat their children with renewed zeal and confidence.

Why had he sent Dame Sibilla to Oby?

In his crannies of spare time and in his wakeful nights the

bishop brooded over the girl and over his kinship with Jephtha and over the curse accumulating about the house of Oby. Suppose that the spire, bought by incest and profanation, should fall again, and Dame Sibilla be underneath it? . . . but the death of the body is of no importance, he could not consider withdrawing her for such a light reason. Suppose the miracle of the Esselby rent (it could hardly be less than a miracle that a hardened excommunicate should be melted by the exhortations of Henry Yellowlees) should be repeated and repeated till Oby became insolvent? . . . why then, of course, the nuns would have to be dispersed, Dame Sibilla among them. But suppose that while remaining at Oby Dame Sibilla fell under the power of whatever mysterious evil accumulated there, and by some mischance or the dire deliberation of God's will were damned? . . . would it not be his doing, and would not God require her soul at his hands?

He thrust the thought away. It was a sleight of Satan's, who also tempted Job. But after a while the speculation would creep back again, hooded in the guise of an omen, or lurking in the pages of a book, or dancing in a candleflame. Throughout his life Walter Dunford had availed himself of his naturally strong sense of the supernatural, and had been constantly assisted by visions and by voices, sometimes almost believing, and never quite disbelieving, and always convinced that even if he did a trifle enhance and exploit these adjuncts from another world it was by God's will and for God's purpose that he did so, just as he allowed his authentic mortifications to play their useful part in the world's eye. Now he was nearing threescore, and the visions and the mortifications had done their work on him. The Dame Sibilla question, which had entered his mind as no more than a whet to his prejudice against the house of Oby, had become his meat and drink, his scourge and hair-shirt, his prayer and his sentence. In reality, he might have been hard put to it to recognise her among his other nieces and great-nieces in religion; but she was the sole grand-child of his dead brother Thomas, whom once he had loved; and now the remembrance of this, jangling his rusty affections, enforced her on his imagination, and made her seem dear, and terrible, and like a vow.

Meanwhile, Oby was due for a Visitation. A date was fixed. He became accustomed to hearing Oby spoken of: it took its place with other commonplaces, it assumed a covering of other people's fears, his doctor's fears of ague and unsuitable diet, his secretary's fears of finding a great deal that would be troublesome. It eased him to hear such talk of Oby, and to reply that the Visitation was a painful duty which he must at all costs fulfil. The day before he was due to set out an attack of fever and vomiting prostrated him, and Henry Yellowlees was sent off to tell Oby that the Visitation must be postponed.

He did not recover till after the equinox. By then the weather made going to Oby impossible, so Humphrey Flagg said, and the secretary remarked that a few months more or less could not make much difference to an establishment like Oby. Their fears muffled Oby no longer, and the bishop was left to contemplate his own, until the November evening when his brother's voice spoke in his ear, louder than the north wind and the sleet that rattled on the windows of the lady chapel, saying: 'Deliver my darling from the power of the dog!' It was a plain command. But he could not obey it, because of the terror it roused up in him, and because he failed to obey he feared the more.

'You think too much of Oby,' his secretary said, when on the morrow he was told to make arrangements for Oby to be visited by a proxy.

A few nights later another gale got up. This night he was in bed. He rose, saying he must pray, and dismissed his attendants.

Presently they heard him shuffle out of his chamber and along the gallery from which stairs led down into the cathedral. At the head of the stairs he saw that they were following him, and turned on them so furiously that they stayed where they were, eyeing each other uneasily, and saying that one must not intervene in such manifestations of piety. The wind was shouting in the north porch like the sea struggling in a cavern, and it seemed to him that he was walking on the cold pavement of ocean. There, like the bones of a wreck, was his tall throne: he paused for a moment and looked at it. Then he went on into the lady chapel, and threw himself on the ground as a dog casts himself down in his kennel. The gale gathered up more strength, the first handful of sleet struck against the windows, and Thomas's voice spoke in the wind; using the words indeed of David, that same David whom the bishop had praised so handsomely in the last paragraph of the first book of his treatise *De Cantu*, but uttering them in the voice of a character much less venerable and amenable than the son of Jesse, a character dark, frightful, and unknown, some god of the ancient Britons, perhaps, whom Walter Dunford's ancestors had appeased with living sacrifices.

The gale died down a little before dawn, and it was then that the sleepy group in the gallery heard their bishop's footsteps on the stairs. They took him up in their arms, and he looked at them, but could say nothing for his teeth were chattering with cold. Whatever it was that Walter Dunford had heard in the north wind it had wholly delivered him over to the supernatural on which he had so long and so confidently relied. His faculties of piety and imagination were at work with him as they had never been at work before, and the people about him began to say that he had fallen suddenly into dotage. What else could they say, seeing him sit groaning, with his hands wandering through his white hair?

After this he allowed himself to be treated as a sick man, to be kept warm in a little room, and fed on wine-whey, and to have his feet washed in warm water. Christmas went by, and Epiphany, and Candlemas, he grew no better and no worse. Then Humphrey Flagg remembered the only weakness that Walter Dunford had ever indulged himself with: an affection for other Dunfords.

'Would you not allow one of your nieces to come and nurse you?'

The old man looked up with a sudden watery brilliance like a dash of November sunlight.

'My great-niece Sibilla. Let her come.'

The doctor suggested that one of the intermediate generation of Dunford nuns might be more comfortable, and have more leech-craft.

'No, no! Let it be Dame Sibilla. She is the nearest, she would travel at the least charge. I will have no unnecessary expense.'

Humphrey Flagg congratulated himself on finding the right stimulant for the poor old man. It was extraordinary how at the thought of seeing another Dunford he roused up and became almost his former self. He even remembered that the custos of Oby could combine fetching Dame Sibilla with his customary visit of inspection. However, Henry Yellowlees was not troubled with this errand. The occasion called for something more ceremonious, and a litter and a discreet escort set out for Oby to bring Dame Sibilla away.

Still clasping her bundle of remedies and delicacies she fell on her knees beside the great chair where the bishop sat, huddled in a white woollen gown. All through the darkening afternoon he had sat before the fire, seeing her image among the flames which were alternately the flames of hell-fire and the flames of the seraphim. Sometimes a log fell to bits, sometimes the missel-thrush in the pear tree set up its song against the gusty rain-pelts. At intervals his doctor or his chaplain came to his side and glanced at him.

Now he turned and looked into her very face. It seemed to him that he had never seen such a worldly countenance. Her cheeks were flushed with the sudden change from the cold journey to the heated room, her eyes flashed and twinkled, her teeth, protruding under her short upper-lip, gave her smile an expression of carnal alacrity – and she smiled a great deal. The world, which he thought he had foresworn, gazed up in his face, patted his arm, fingered his ring, as confidently as though he had never slighted it.

Still on her knees she began to rummage in her bundle, pulling out one thing after another, misnaming and mislaying them, and littering the floor with waddings and wrappings. Here was some honey, broom honey which never fails to allay a cough. Here was some of Oby's marzipan, specially made on purpose. Here was a bottle of mead. Here was a little pillow. Here was a most remarkable salve for stiff joints, and here was an ointment for chilblains, and here was a plaster to be laid over the heart. Here were some comfits, and here was a distillation of mugwort, and here was another psalter from Dame Lovisa, and here were some candied stems of angelica, and here was a towel embroidered by the novices, and here was some damson jam. Everything had a recommendation or a message or had been specially made or had a history of healing. And in the confusion of giving she displayed and explained at random, so that the pillow was to be laid over the heart and honey was sovereign for stiff knees.

The doctor came forward and whispered that the bishop was extremely weak and must not be tired with talking.

'Of course, of course, I quite understand,' she replied; and out came more damson jam, and a long story of how the tree had been pruned by a passing friar, and had responded with a wonderful crop, but after all not so many had been gathered because the magpies came and pillaged it; but next year they would throw a net over it, a fishing-net which had been bought at Waxelby at much below the usual price because the vendor was a fisherman's widow who had been thankful to close with Dame Lovisa's offer of half the price in money and the rest to be made up in prayers for the fisherman's soul. For Dame Lovisa managed such things cleverly, and would make an excellent prioress.

'What? Another de Stapledon prioress?' enquired the dying man.

'Yes, indeed! We have quite made up our minds, she is certainly what God wishes. And Dame Eleanor will still be treasuress, and Dame Philippa will stay with the novices, and Dame Dorothy will be cellaress, and . . . '

'And you, my child?'

'Sacrist, perhaps. Unworthily, but you see there are so few of us.' But the first two words had sufficiently proclaimed a violent spiritual ambition socketed in complacence. In due course, a Dunford prioress.

'A solemn charge,' he said.

The flask of mead, set working by its journey, had been placed injudiciously near the fire, and now it blew its stopper out. The bishop started and crossed himself. While Dame Sibilla mopped and talked, and mingled the goodness of the mead and the privilege of being sacrist and how much mead was lost and yet how much was spared, all with a kind of tranquil flurry, he stared at the flask with his jaw trembling and his thin hands fidgeting. The doctor rose from his bench in the corner and began mixing something in a little bowl. He was too late. The bishop staggered up from his chair, and fell on his knees, howling. The doctor ran with his bowl, the chaplain snatched up a crucifix, exclaiming:

'These accursed women!' and held it before the bishop's eyes. But he eluded them both, dragging himself about the room on his knees, howling, and knocking on his breast. It was Dame Sibilla, getting in front of the chaplain, who stayed him. Kneeling herself, and clasping him round the waist, she wrestled with him until she had him down on the floor with his head in her lap.

'How you frightened us!' she said. 'You mustn't pray so loud, nor so suddenly. You must tell us when you wish to pray, then we will all pray together, like Abraham and his household.'

'Not Abraham, not Abraham! Jephtha!'

'Who was it? Did you see a vision?' she asked.

'An omen!' he said, gasping and whistling. 'God's wrath!'

'Tuba mirum spargens sonum
Per sepulcra regionum,'

intoned the chaplain.

'I saw a vision,' said Dame Sibilla. 'Just when the cork flew out and I was blaming myself for my carelessness in putting the flask so near the fire and wasting all that good mead that Dame Margaret showed us how to make, just then I saw Saint Magdalen spilling the ointment from a vase and smiling, as much as to say one need not worry about a little waste.'

'*Quid Mariam absolvisti*,' said the chaplain, glaring at Dame Sibilla but following her lead.

'But it is not the first time I have seen one of the saints,' Dame Sibilla continued soothingly. 'At Allestree I saw Saint Jerome several times. He used to sit in the cloisters with a book on his knee. The Allestree priest was unable to believe it, and told me that nuns had no business to see visions. But how can one help it, if heaven sends them? However, I do not talk about it. How do you feel now? Perhaps you might eat a little angelica. It is the best kind, the kind that is prepared with vine-leaves.'

The chaplain laid down the crucifix and said in an undertone to Humphrey Flagg that they would have to get rid of her somehow. The doctor replied that she seemed to be doing him good. Shrugging his shoulders the chaplain remarked that it was no sort of death-bed for a bishop to lie with his head in a nun's lap mumbling angelica, and that he would not have expected a doctor, a professional man, to be so tolerant of convent quackeries, little pillows and what not, to which the doctor retorted that speaking as a professional man he did not look to see the bishop die for several days to come. They were still wrangling in their corner when Dame Sibilla announced to them that her great-uncle was now in a peaceful sleep and that she thought he should be carried to his bed.

The way she oversaw this operation and particularly the ineffable little pats she gave to the pillows drove Humphrey Flagg to the chaplain's way of thinking. With single-hearted courtesy they conducted her to her lodging, where a respectable widow was in readiness to wait on her. But a couple of hours later they were compelled to call her back, for the bishop had started up in bed declaring that he had seen her carried away by a piebald dog as large as a horse, that she was lost and God would require his soul for it. Now for more visions, the chaplain observed sombrely. This time Dame Sibilla quieted the bishop with a long account of the finances of Oby. But the chaplain was no better pleased. He had taken a prejudice against her.

Meanwhile, all the poor in the city knew that Bishop Walter was dying, and with the irrational hopefulness of the poor were praying fervently for his recovery. They trooped in processions to the cathedral, they knelt in prayer at the palace gate, they clamoured for relics to be brought from all parts of the kingdom immediately. Children were beaten to make them pray more fervently, for the prayer of a child has more power than any grown person's prayer, women vowed the babe in the womb to God's use provided God would spare them the bishop, and hunchbacks, who are known to be luck-givers, were seized on by the crowd and rubbed against the palace walls. For he was the poor man's bishop, he had considered the poor, he was their father, their treasure, their only warm garment, their champion before God and man, their only flatterer. The crowd wept and swayed, telling each other how even now, at death's door, he would not lie in a bed but lay on the ground with nothing but straw beneath him. None was more fervent than the harlots whom he had cast out of the city, and who now came in a procession, combed and clean and wearing their best clothes, to pray for the man who had taken them seriously. Walking among these crowds Henry Yellowlees felt himself someone apart, a ghost perhaps, or more truly a figure in geometry, a stalking displeased triangle among these swelling curves of emotion. The death of Walter Dunford, whom all these people were so passionately and so pleasurably lamenting, and whom he had for so long so violently hated, roused in him nothing but a kind of quiet despising astonishment at having hated so violently. In the same way, a stink which has half-choked one, when run to earth becomes no more than the shrivelled body of some wretched rat.

Since his scholars were constantly being called off to sing litanies he had time on his hands, and spent it wandering in and out of the crowd as one wanders in and out of a forest. It amused him to hear all the talk about the nun who was in constant attendance on the dying man. She was a nun of extraordinary saintliness, and in a vision of the Virgin she had been commanded to go to him. She was a doctoress of renowned skill and was keeping him alive by a secret remedy. She was a witch, and killing him as fast as might be. Who would believe him if he had said that he knew all these remarkable ladies and had discussed the price of salt fish with them? He noted that it was quite untrue to suppose that men will fight for their beliefs. All three schools of thought about the bishop's nun heard each other's heresies without the slightest movement of ill-will. Mankind untutored and savage will fight for bread or a bedfellow, but must be schooled by theologians before it will fight for a faith.

He had tired of watching the crowds (which anyhow had grown less as the bishop's dying delayed) and was sitting in his old haunt among the scattered masonry of Jupiter's temple when the note of the passing bell clashed out. It was evening. The dew was falling, the scent of the gone blossom hung on the chilling air like the ghost of the day, the birds had left off singing and were settling themselves for the night with occasional screeches of alarm. A little while before, a party of vagrants had come into the enclosure where they pulled up some gorse stakes and kindled a fire. He had watched the first twine of smoke stain the pure dark blue of the sky and listened to their quiet grunting voices as they sat unbinding their feet before the blaze. The smoke veered aside, and where it had been he saw the first star, and a moment later the first stroke of the bell expanded in the air and died trembling.

Walter Dunford was dead. But every other consideration was lost in a transport of gratitude for his part in the elegy, for the death which had set the bell tolling in the innocent solemn dusk with notes as apt and compelling as the longs in *Triste loysir*. If he knelt to pray for the bishop's soul it was because his pleasure was so intensely physical that he must buttress it by some constraint of asceticism, and the discomfort of his knees on the cold turf would substantiate his delight.

Closer within the circumference of the bell's vibration the

news was heard with rather different ears. The clerics hurrying to take their part in the prayers glanced at each other with a flash of eye, admitted man's poor mortality with small shrugs. 'At last!' said the glances, and the shrugs replied: 'We are well out of it.'

For Bishop Walter's last days on earth had been painful and unedifying, and his vitality was so obstinate that no one could feel assured that he would not contrive to exert himself in some irreparable dying scandal. Twice he had broken out of his chamber, saying that he must go out and repent in the face of the poor (for he was acutely aware of that vast audience waiting outside); and only the deftness of that nun had turned him back. Repentance is proper. But Bishop Walter repented beyond all decorum, raving with fear of death and fear of hell and with a self-hatred that slashed out to include all mankind. What it was all about no one had leisure to surmise, any more than when a house is burning the men fighting the fire have time to speculate what caused it. He raved like a madman, they agreed; but the madman was a madman in full possession of his wits, able to rip up the sophistries of would-be comforters, able to recall in their utmost niceties the intrigues of half a century before. Theological acumen had never been attributed to him, even by his backers. He had made his name by simple piety, personal austerities, industry, saintly eccentricity, and a marvellous head for business. But now in the process of demonstrating himself damned no schoolman could have bettered him. He argued like an eel; and the force of all his arguments and of his natural acerbity was directed against the consolations they offered him. Nothing would persuade him to lie down and die in quiet, trusting to the church to manage his affair for him. The devils they exorcised were no sooner disposed of than they came back reinforced with more devils. The relics they brought him he greeted with computations of how much they had cost, how much they had earned, how much they would be worth in ten years' time at that rate of earning. They brought in strangers (against better judgement, but his misery was so authentic that they were ready to try any remedy), summoning friars, anchorites, pious children, even an old woman of the locality who had been whipped for declaring that the Virgin was so familiar with her as to have picked the lice out of her head. But these were no more effective than the people of his household. For a minute or two he welcomed them with craving submission, clasped their hands, whispered in their ears; but the welcome would turn into satire, confutation, abusive home-truths, and mockery. They had waited till he seemed past speech before giving him the holy oils. Half an hour later he began to writhe, and muttered that the oil was burning him, was eating his flesh away; and to their horror they saw his dry skin redden and rise up.

After his death the marks were as plain as if branded with a hot iron. The chaplain, exhausted beyond endurance and beyond tact, pointed them out to Dame Sibilla, saying: 'There they are. What do you make of it?' She replied that to her they looked like roses. The doctor, who had really loved Walter Dunford, and was half-dead from watching him die, turned aside with a groan at such silliness.

Yet when he was an old man, and the death of the bishop had taken its place in his memory as one of many deaths, he often quoted Dame Sibilla as an example of the medicinal virtues of virginity. For the bodily heat of a virgin, he said, is at once purer and more vehement than the heat of a deflowered creature, and when the physicians put Abishag into King David's bed they were applying this knowledge, and put her there with no carnal intention but exactly as they would have poured virgin honey into a wound or bound virgin wool about an inflamed joint. And the brain of an old man, he continued, is vexed with cold humours, and chafes and maddens like a river impeded with ice, so that meekness itself becomes irascible and breaks out in furies and contentions. In such cases a virgin, the more simple-witted the better, can do more than any other medicine. She need not be put into the sick man's bed; her mere presence is enough.

That was how, twenty years after, Humphrey Flagg accounted for the behaviour of Dame Sibilla. Of all those taking part in the bishop's last days she alone remained confident and serene. As his fits grew worse, as he raved more savagely and feared more abjectly, she seemed to be in her element like a water-spaniel in the flood. She was clumsy, she was obtuse, she was insufferably trivial in the remedies she suggested and the consolations she offered. But her devotion to the dying man was unquestionable and in the face of his agony her obtuseness took on a quality of intrepidity. Nothing daunted her competence. Did the bishop see devils? She saw them too, in gross and in detail. Naturally, at the death-bed of a bishop the powers of hell would make the most of their opportunity of such a catch. Repentance? But of course! The greater the saint, the greater the repentance. Reproaches and revilings? Again of course. What could be more distressing to the eyes of a dying man than the sight of the world's wickedness, and how could a bishop spend his last breath more valiantly than in rebuking sin and confounding the vain-glorious? Doubts, self-damnings, despair? Yes, yes, that was how the dying must feel, but it was all quite natural and nothing to be alarmed at. Besides, think of God's mercy, and of all the poor folk outside, all praying for his soul. The crowd was larger than ever, she said, stepping back from the window with her eyes enlarged as if they had spread to contain the sight of such a multitude. So she flattered and consoled, and belittled this and magnified the other, holding her conjuror's mirror before his eyes. And in the intervals of peace that she won for him he lay with his head in her bosom, clutching at her veil to cover him and sometimes murmuring that he could die in peace for he had saved her from the power of the dog, and at other times listening with a drowsy satisfaction to her chatter about Oby. After he was dead she began to weep, and shook as if an ague shook her; but almost in the next breath she was supping hot wine and patronising Humphrey Flagg, her tears splashing into the cup as she assured him how interested the ladies of Oby would be when she told them of his prescriptions.

By the time the funeral had taken place (naturally she stayed for the funeral) reports of the bishop's manner of dying had got out; and this was spread about as the doing of the nun who had bewitched him, calling up devils to torment him and prolonging his agony by knots tied in the fringe of the counterpane. Such a person should be got rid of expeditiously and with as little show as possible. But when the steward sent for Henry Yellowlees and told him that he must take Dame Sibilla back to Oby, Henry expostulated that if she were to ride openly through the streets she would be stoned: let her stay a while longer, he urged, while he himself rode to Oby and arranged for an escort of some of her own community with whom she could travel back, a nun among nuns. But no one at the palace cared what became of Dame Sibilla, all they cared for was to be rid of her and rid of the last Dunford. Fortunately the old widow who had been told off to wait on her admired her profoundly; by her arrangements and connivance Dame Sibilla slipped out before dawn, dressed like a serving-woman in short petticoats and a hat with a flapping brim. By the time the sun rose they were well away from the city, riding over the green turf speckled with primroses. It embarrassed him to see her dressed like a secular person, but she took it very lightly and enjoyed the hat. He was relieved when later in the day she went into a thicket and came out in her nun's clothing.

When they got to Oby all the nuns were standing in front of

the house to receive her. Looking for the spire to prick the horizon Henry had wondered how she would be feeling, returning after those weeks of violent emotion to a future flat as the landscape that lay before them. Such a life was comfortable, creditable, happier, probably, than the lives of most other women; and of course in accordance with God's wishes; but after her part in the drama of Walter Dunford's death-bed it must seem tame. She jumped nimbly to the ground and dived in among the others and disappeared.

During Dame Sibilla's absence a new voice had been added to the familiar voices. There had always been plenty of owls round Oby, but this spring an owl established somewhere near by had taken to hooting by day. It was astonishing to hear its *tu-whoo* come floating out from amidst the pink and white of the apple-blossom or tranquilly joining in the midday office. Because this is the kind of thing that frightens servants and excites novices, the ladies of the convent took the line that such behaviour on the part of an owl showed a wrong-headed playfulness; and Dame Philippa's comment that the poor creature must be kept awake by the thought of its sins was often repeated. Possibly Dame Lovisa, so coolly attentive to every hint of a prioress-ship hastening towards her, may have thought otherwise of the owl. But she was quite as discreet as Dame Matilda had been towards the old prioress thirty years earlier, and when Dame Adela (as usual voicing everyone's silliest thought with an added personal tactlessness) said that it was a good thing that Dame Margaret was too deaf to hear the owl hooting for her, Dame Lovisa left it to Dame Eleanor to retort that deafness saved people from hearing a great deal of silliness besides owls, and only remarked that living in a damp climate often renders people hard of hearing.

The convent was full of old women. There was the prioress, Dame Margaret, Dame Dorothy, Dame Cecily – true, she was not really old, but she was blind and sickly: the owl had plenty to choose from before it hooted its *Come-away!* for Adela; but death, even the death that takes someone else, is frightening, and Adela feared the owl. Her fear expressed itself in bravado. Perhaps because the de Retteville blood ran in her veins, and from Brian onwards the Rettevilles lived for hunting and were more in sympathy with the beasts they slew than with their own kind, Dame Adela was what in later days came to be called a nature-lover. Birds perched on her hand, lizards ran up her wide sleeves, she had pet toads and spiders as well as her troops of pet dogs; though she had never learned her plain-chant she could bark like a fox, whistle like a blackbird, and imitate perfectly every noise in nature. Now when the owl hooted she answered it; and if it did not hoot she would hoot herself, and provoke it to reply. No one troubled to check her. Perhaps even they inclined to encourage her. If there was anything alarming about an owl hooting in broad daylight there was nothing alarming about Dame Adela, so the one was approximated to the other. And when Sir Ralph, poking out from under his abstraction as a tortoise pokes out its head from under its shell, remarked in his Whitsunday sermon that there seemed to be a great quantity of owls about this season and that no doubt owls had their own language as much as the Parthians, and Medes, and Elamites and the dwellers in Mesopotamia, but that as there was no record that the Apostles began to understand owls Christians must wait till the second coming of the Paraclete before they tried to do so, his hearers paid no special attention to this observation.

Then one noontide, to make conversation, Dame Sibilla asked when the daylight owl had begun to hoot: she had not noticed it before she left Oby. One remembered one thing and one another, the date was hunted through remembrances, it was when Dame Amy had a whitlow, it was just before the pear tree blossomed, it was round about the time when the refectory was whitewashed. Then Dame Cecily recalled that it was on Saint Bennet's eve.

Dame Sibilla changed colour, and presently asked another question about something else. She need not have troubled. Conversation flowed on, Bishop Walter was dead and gone from their minds, the fact that the midday owl had begun hooting on the day he died struck no one, nor would anything have been made of it, had it been otherwise. If the midday owl hooted for any purpose it hooted for Oby.

Seeing that no one put the owl and the bishop together she felt relieved. Not to anyone, not to herself even, would she quite admit that there had been anything unseemly in the bishop's manner of dying; but though in the main she was zealously self-deceiving she had filaments of shrewdness floating from her, and it was with one of these that she sensed that other people were willing enough to be scandalised, and that there was plenty to scandalise them. What had been the likeness of roses to her, for instance, the chaplain had seen with impurer eyes. So hearing the owl – or Dame Adela – she was grateful that no one at Oby was so ill-natured as to suppose that these untimely cries voiced the uneasy estate of her great-uncle's soul. Why should they, why should they? Unfortunately, by combating the idea that anyone should think so, she began to think so herself. To admit such a thought was disloyal to a man of saintly character and unjust to herself: what would become of the shining part (she knew it had been shining) she had played at the vexed death-bed of a saint if in reality that death-bed had been the death-bed of a reprobate? One must flee from temptation. Becoming convinced that this was a temptation Dame Sibilla fled from it to the best of her considerable abilities, smothering it in prayers, industry and sociability. For all that, it was soon remarked on that Dame Sibilla could infallibly distinguish between the real owl and Dame Adela – she had such a fine ear.

It was about this time that Dame Lilias plucked up enough resolution to follow Dame Sibilla into a corner and go through with what she wanted to ask.

'While you were attending Bishop Walter I suppose you and he sometimes talked of Oby.'

'Yes, indeed! He asked me many questions, and even when he was too weak to question me he liked to hear me talk about it. It is astonishing how much he remembered about us, what an interest he took in us. Truly, a father to his poor nuns!'

'Did he happen to say anything about me?'

'Oh yes, I told him how you made the salve and the distilled betony water.'

After a bitter swallow Dame Lilias brought herself to ask if that were all. Umbraged, Dame Sibilla replied in the tone of voice most commonly used towards Dame Lilias, a brisk rallying tone of voice: 'I think that was all. He was very weak, and suffering much, and he had a great deal to think of besides us and our little affairs.'

Dame Lilias straightened herself out of her habitual drooping posture and looked fixedly at Dame Sibilla.

'When your great-uncle made his Visitation here I asked him for permission to become an anchoress. He then said he would think of it and send me word. That was five years ago. I wondered if, in his last hours, he had time to remember this.'

Out in the orchard Dame Adela hooted.

'But perhaps he had too many things on his mind to give a thought to me.'

The owl replied to Dame Adela. Dame Sibilla said warmly: 'An anchoress! I never knew that you wished to be an anchoress.

How did it happen, how did you come to wish it? An anchoress! How well I understand such a wish!'

When Dame Sibilla wished to please she could put a great deal of skill and determination into it. Willy-nilly, Dame Lilias had to tell the whole story. Willy-nilly, she received from Bishop Walter's great-niece the sympathy she had hoped for in vain from Bishop Walter. Everything in the story, the long desolation, the voice of the saint, the bruised neck, assailed Dame Sibilla in her core of romantic and real piety. Overlooking the implied disparagement of the bishop, she exclaimed:

'You really heard his voice? How wonderful, how satisfying! I have sometimes seen saints myself but I have never heard one.' (For it was also wonderful and satisfying that these supernatural experiences should be thus diversely distributed.)

'Bishop Walter did not think so well of it, you see,' said Dame Lilias.

'He had so many things to think of, he had so much on his mind,' reiterated Dame Sibilla, but in a graver voice.

Sometimes God sends a death-bed, sometimes a martyrdom, sometimes, as at Allestree, a pestilence. Now God had sent a mission. In a flash Dame Sibilla realised that she and she only could put through this affair of an anchoress and carry out the spoken command of a patronal saint. The notion of making an anchoress glowed in her imagination; perhaps, later on, she would become an anchoress too. Meanwhile, she would give an anchoress to God and the church.

'If only I had known in time,' she sighed, 'I would have spoken to my dear uncle. He would have listened favourably, he would certainly have found time to give his blessing and order the preliminaries. Well, we must do what we can without him! I shall always feel that it has his approval, that we are carrying out his wish.'

It was not so much a moral scruple as personal fastidiousness that made Dame Lilias say:

'I cannot feel sure that he wished it. He did not give me such an impression. And during five years he did nothing about it.'

'It slipped his memory. He was so desperately busy. He never slept more than four hours, he snatched his meals, his whole time was given to God and the church. Or perhaps he did remember it, and gave directions to a secretary, and it was the secretary, not he, who forgot. That seems much likelier. It took four secretaries to keep up with him, and anything may be mislaid among four secretaries. No doubt that was it. My uncle would not have forgotten anything to do with Oby.'

'He was not very well pleased with Oby when he came here.'

'Oh, but all that was quite changed, you know.'

Dame Sibilla knew that this was not exactly true. But then there are two truths, perhaps three truths, perhaps a dozen. In any case there is the exact and mortal truth which marches with the living and there is the other truth whose dominion opens out with death, a more insighted truth which enables the survivors to give a tranquillising variant, to anoint the waves with oil. It was the mortal truth that when Bishop Walter gave his attention to Dame Sibilla's talk about Oby he usually did so with an appearance of reservation and mistrust. But then all she had told him must have combated his prejudice and led him to change his mind. And as his features up to the moment of death had been vexed and furious and after his laying-out were the image of an austere repose, so his suspicions of Oby, she felt sure, must have changed to a discerning benevolence. Thus her statement to Dame Lilias which neither of them could mortally and exactly credit was true nevertheless, and not to have spoken it would be impiety and injury to the dead. Surely the souls blessedly afflicted in purgatory need not endure the further pang of hearing themselves misrepresented by truths merely mortal and occasional. In the same way the owl, more often than not, was only Dame Adela. She could not really believe that some little mishap like slighting Dame Lilias's vocation could compel her great-uncle's soul to hang hooting round Oby: but in the light of the post-mortal truth now shining so clearly on Walter Dunford it was plain that he would wish poor Dame Lilias to achieve her ambition, and so one must endeavour, if only as a simple piety to the dead, to bring it about.

It was a thousand pities that the first movers in the business were now so ineffective. The bishop was dead, the prioress heavy with age, and it was impossible to get any sense out of Sir Ralph. Though he remembered everything to do with Dame Lilias and was full of good will, nothing developed from the good will but more good will, and speculations as to the view Dame Lilias would have from her slot window and if the angels, which in a marish country are winged like herons, might not be winged like pigeons in a more comfortable type of landscape. There remained Dame Lilias and Saint Leonard. Dame Lilias was almost as ineffective as the others. The long decline of hope deferred, hope disillusioned, hope slighted and put away, had left her in a state of apathy. She was so apathetic that she did not even oppose Dame Sibilla's intentions. She was like a weed in the water. As for Saint Leonard, another word from him would have put everything in train. But he did not speak it. And the image of Our Lady gazed at the crucifixion of her son, intent as a child at a fair with her blue eyes and pink cheeks, and could think of no sorrow like unto his sorrow.

All this was very discouraging. If Dame Sibilla had not possessed her full share of the Dunford suppleness and resolution she might have abandoned her project. But she persisted, with here a step and there a tweak, praying intemperately and hinting discreetly until she actually contrived to fan up a sort of community pique that Oby, possessing a nun called by heaven to adopt the mortified career of anchoress, could not have been better attended to. Yes, really, it was a great slight! Not every convent can make such an offer, not every convent wants to; yet for five years Oby had been offering its Dame Lilias and was offering her still.

In order to establish this frame of mind Dame Sibilla had had to yield a little ground in the matter of Bishop Walter. A new truth was made plain: that saintliness and episcopacy cannot abide under the same hood, and that a bishop as saintly as Bishop Walter left too much to his secretaries, and was flouted by his underlings, who disregarded his intentions and hoodwinked a good old man with stories of: 'Yea, immediately, it shall be seen to tomorrow.' Witness the case of Dame Lilias's vocation, trampled and forgotten under the feet of these officials.

'They should have left him in peace among his poor,' she grieved. 'They should not have compelled him to become a bishop. He was not meant for a bishop. If they had not bishoped him, I daresay he would be alive and with us to this day.'

She was about to add, 'And making Dame Lilias an anchoress,' but she remembered that the presentation of anchoresses is an appurtenance of bishops.

XII

The Candlemas Cuckoo

(*February* 1380)

A wolf dead is half-way to being a lamb. Bishop Walter Dunford dead was emerging as the mild admirer of Oby, the more easily since a new bishop had taken his place, a complete novelty, and so to be dreaded. The new bishop was Perkin de Craye, a Fleming of a great moneylending family, who was said to be a fat, smooth, proud man with a stammer, caring only for Our Lady, works of art, ritual, and foreign cheeses. Such a bishop would look with little favour on Dame Lovisa's magpie psalters. He would be more efficaciously wooed with an embroidery. When next Henry Yellowlees came on a custodianly visit he was questioned about Bishop de Craye's views on gold thread and *opus anglicum*. As for Bishop de Craye's views on anchoresses, that subject was put by for more immediate considerations.

In a convent any long-term strategy is at the mercy of the present. In the excitement of blue satin, white sarsenet, silks and fine needles, gold thread and spangles, Dame Sibilla forgot to hear the owl, and Dame Lilias, who was always admitted to have very good taste whatever her failings might be, was suddenly gathered into the life of the community to animate the party which favoured a design of white ostrich plumes, naturalistically treated, rather than the gold and white lilies advocated by the traditionalists. It was many years since the convent had undertaken a large needlework. The prioress possessed no skill as a needlewoman, Dame Lovisa's broken nails made it out of the question that she should handle an embroidery: needlework had become involved in the politics of the community, and its laying-by was a sign of the de Stapledon ascendancy. Now the enthusiasm for the proposed altar-hanging nursed up an opposition party, brought Dame Lilias into popularity, and kindled a revival of admiration for the Trinity Cope embroidered by the old prioress, Dame Alicia de Foley the spire-builder.

Unnoticed for years, this was now brought out and studied in all its details. One stitch used by Dame Alicia baffled every needlewoman of the current generation; there was some trick in it, some manipulation of the thread, which they could not reproduce; and then came a dramatic turn when Dame Adela paused by the group of nuns puzzling over this stitch and said that she knew just how it was done, for she had often watched the old prioress doing it. Give her a needle, she said. Unbelievingly they gave her a scrap of canvas and some cheap green thread; and before their eyes she performed the old prioress's stitch, so exactly that only by the materials could you tell the new from the old. Dame Adela being a de Retteville this discovery strengthened the anti-de Stapledon party. It was agreed that the way Dame Adela was neglected and allowed to wander hooting about the grounds was part and parcel of the de Stapledon usurpation of power, and Dame Adela was made miserable by finding herself kept at needlework instead of being left to her own out-of-door devices.

When William Holly took to his bed only the prioress was sufficiently detached from the politics of the altar-hanging to think that Oby might lose an invaluable servant. The peril of her contemporary roused up her faculties, she wept and fretted and lay awake at night fingering her beads and reckoning incomings and outgoings much as she had used to do in her treasuress days and often confusing the calculations of those days with the calculations of the present. But now she saw all with the despondency of the aged: the interest on the Methley tithe, the debt on the Methley repairs and the interest on the loan which had been raised to pay part of that debt, the rise in the cost of living, the expenses of the next Visitation (God be thanked Bishop de Craye made no move so far to come to them but sooner or later come he must), the expenses of her own funeral and the cost of installing Dame Lovisa as her successor (but who could say? – there might yet be a schism, an Eleanor prioress debating with a Lovisa prioress, elections and counter elections), the repairs needed at Tunwold, the deadlock over the Esselby rent, the diminishing returns from the river-dues at Scurleham, caused by the silting up of the estuary and the lessening value of the water-borne trade, the burden of Henry Yellowlees (he was not so bad as he might have been, but every custos is economically bad, for he authorises expenditures too easily and corrupts the community he is put in charge of by lifting the sense of responsibility from the nuns in chapter themselves, this or that is granted, agreed, neglected, because the custos wills it or because the custos will see to it), the burden (another legacy laid on them by Bishop Walter, might he burn in hellfire, God rest his soul!) of those two healthy eating gawks, Amy Hodds and Joan Cossey (who both had lived through the measles which had killed Lucy Frampton) and an undowered Dame Sibilla, the fact that these three nominees took up room that might otherwise be given to advantageous novices, the difficulty, though, of getting a good novice nowadays, the alarming increase in convent servants, nuns and servants alike now grew so luxurious that more servants were needed to wait on the nuns, and more servants to serve the servants, the cost of a new priest, for Sir Ralph was so senile that really he was a scandal and something must be done about him and in any case he would die, the blindness of Dame Cecily and the cost of the opiates that must be given her for mere pity's sake – and now all this expenditure on blue satin. And nothing to put against it but William Holly's heriot if William Holly died. And a new bailiff to choose and train who would never be a patch on William Holly.

So the old woman lay awake, grunting and grieving. There was another thing on her mind too, though she managed to keep it from getting into the inventory. Dame Alice had drowned Magdalen Figg in the fish-pond. It was all long ago, Magdalen had drowned in water and now was decaying in earth, and Sir Ralph was out of his wits and remembered nothing; but earth and water are but two elements, there are also fire and air to reckon with, and air can body a story and fire can burn the soul. The nuns heard their prioress grunting and sighing, and the bedstead creaking and the dry rattle of the beads, and since they heard such sounds every night thought nothing of them.

Having twice been anointed for death William Holly recovered. Soon he was snapping round the manor again, boasting of how he had squelched his toad with a great blow he had given himself in the belly. His sickness had left no mark on him except that he was rather thinner and considerably more fault-finding. Everything had gone to rack and ruin, he said, during his illness; the prioress herself could not persuade him to admit that many of the deficiencies he complained of were long standing and had been complained of by him for years. The vivacity of his complaints compelled them to face the fact that nowadays a manor was not what it used to be, and little more than a rather tiresome way of supplying oneself with milk and poultry, bread and firing.

More tiresomely, a manor in these days was a camp of malcontents, and one must be on good terms with one's people, and not press them too much, lest they should take part in the rebellions which were jumping up, here, there, and everywhere, like a fire in the stubble. Anything is better than being burned out or murdered in one's bed.

'But should we not aim,' said Dame Lovisa, 'to do something more than please William Holly? That will soothe no one, since they all detest him for his prosperity and his extortions. We should find some means of seeming to serve them all.'

'Then we must first make a fortune,' answered Dame Eleanor. 'Food, clothing, new thatching, the gleaning bell rung an hour earlier, a remission of dues – there is no way of pleasing people that is not costly.'

'There is one way. We can teach their children. That would cost very little except time and trouble. People like you to make a fuss of their children, nothing pleases them so surely.'

'Teach them? Teach them what?'

'Really, as little as you wish. A few hymn tunes, the names of the patriarchs, a little hearsay Latin, how to wipe their noses . . . it is the attention that pleases, the learning is no matter.'

She could read a *non-placet* in their looks even before they began to make objections. 'Where should the children be put? – in the nave? Their fleas won't stay in the nave, Dame Lovisa, their fleas will come leaping into the quire.' – 'And who is to teach them, are the novices to be neglected on their behalf when heaven sends us novices?' – 'And if we have them here, how are we to get rid of them? They will stay all day, we shall never be free of them.' – 'And if we teach them they will all go off the manor to become friars and clerks, nuns and jugglers, they will never stay at work once they begin to think themselves scholars. Besides, how are we to teach children when our hands are full of the altar-hanging?' Such were the answers, and Dame Margaret lifted up her ancient croak and recalled how Oby had once educated a boy, who had gone off with their best horse and a quantity of spices.

Dame Lovisa's project got no further. Thinking of her own project Dame Sibilla sighed with relief. The anchoressing of Dame Lilias, the appeasing of the owl (it was still there, for owls are constant in their haunts, and in the dusky vapours of a November forenoon its tranquil disembodied note was quite as sinister as in high summer) were not proceeding as fast as she had hoped, and another distraction might be ruinous. It was now almost two years since Walter Dunford's death. But the great needlework would soon be completed: then would come a pause, an idle interim when she could command their attention.

And then everything was overturned by the affair of Dame Adela. Twenty years before it had been axiomatic that Adela would need to be watched; and her profession had been postponed for some time, since a seduced novice is less scandalous than a seduced nun. But a short watchfulness sufficed. Her apple-blossom beauty had not been substantiated by the slightest carnal intellect, she was as chaste as a parsnip; and now, nearing thirty, she was faded, awkward, gap-toothed. It was strange to reflect that the wonderful de Retteville novice, procured with such triumph by the old prioress and fought for as briskly as though she were Helen of Troy, should have turned into this harmless incubus, rather greedy, terrified of thunderstorms, who tamed mice and could hoot like an owl. Nobody reflected on it, however, for nobody gave Dame Adela a thought – except Dame Lovisa, who had never lost the protectiveness which she, the ugly novice, had so oddly displayed for her lovely contemporary. Her concern showed itself by harshness where the unconcern of the others was indulgent. She scolded her, tidied her, hunted her out of the kitchen court, discouraged the fellowship with toads, kites, and spiders. When it came to light that Dame Adela remembered the old prioress's trick stitch Dame Lovisa rejoiced in this opportunity to put Dame Adela on a level with the other nuns, though, as she knew, every stitch copied from the second Trinity Cope strengthened the de Retteville faction and injured her own prospects of becoming the next prioress.

In carefulness, in anxiety, in unpopularity, she was already almost a prioress, and it was strange that having so real a foretaste of the wormwood of office she should be so determined to drink it out of the official cup. Throughout that second winter the work on the altar-hanging was carried forward, and everyone who could thread a needle was engaged on some part of it. Since needlework cannot be done with cold hands all available fuel went to keep up a good fire in the parlour. The prioress sat there, and Dame Cecily was led in, to enjoy the warmth and the conversation and the sense of something in the making. Though Dame Lovisa could not take part in the embroidering because of her broken nails and her chilblains there was no reason why she should not sit there with the rest and be warm and sociable, and to do so would have been politic. But she was no sooner settled among them than an uneasy austerity drove her out. There was always a pretext to leave them: a message to the kitchen, a beggar to be relieved, a traveller to be interviewed. There was always a reason to go and never a voice to bid her stay. There was not even an open antagonism to challenge by remaining. Hers was a cold unpopularity. So she left the fireside: sometimes to stand at the wicket handing out food and drink, listening to the stamp or shuffle of feet, gulpings and whisperings and fragmentary news of another world; sometimes to hear long-winded complaints and give good advice which would never be heeded; sometimes to check account-books, sometimes to roll pills, sometimes to pray in the chapel – where she would no sooner be settled on her knees than she would notice something amiss and get up to right it. Coming and going she would hear the voices flowing from the parlour, or the thump of the flails from the granary, or from Sir Ralph's chamber a sudden gusty bellow as the old man, lying a-bed for warmth, would recall a tavern song of his student days, or from the kitchen a clatter of dishes and a steady rattle of narrative. Everyone had a voice and a will to use it except her. She could only think, unconversational as a snake.

And yet it was Dame Lilias who wished to become an anchoress and Dame Lovisa who willed to become a prioress.

Peering out through a crack in the window screen she stared at the thin-lipped landscape, foggy with long frost and sought in herself the reason. In her heart were two wishes: to become prioress and to make another psalter. The copying of those psalters had been the only pleasure she had known; to be prioress was the only ambition she could conceive.

Among the voices in the parlour she could hear Dame Adela's – a querulous note, interrupted by a yawn. Adela might weary of the needlework, but she must be kept to it. Every stitch she dragged through the blue satin fastened her a little more into the life of the community, and buttressed Dame Lovisa's fantastic resolve that when she became prioress Adela should be treated with more respect, should even be given some office. But what office? – since she had neither discretion, demeanour, industry, nor common wit. Nunneries, unfortunately, have no call for a verderer. The voices grew louder, someone had opened the parlour door; and at the same moment a figure came into her narrow view of the world, and by its coming, its dark shuffling approach, made that world twice as cold, twice as sombre. Man or woman she could not say; but certainly a beggar. Today it was Dame Eleanor's turn at the wicket, but she was a poor hand with beggars, alternately scorning and scornfully indulging them; besides, she would not wish to leave the fireside. Dame Lovisa went to the wicket herself and waited for the beggar to knock. She heard the footsteps pause, and the sound of a spit. The beggar knocked.

Disconcerted by being so instantly opened to, the woman stared at the nun with a look of antagonism. Then she began her complaint. She was penniless, she said, and hungry, she had been poisoned by eating bad fish, and was seven months gone with child. In the austere air her stink was almost intolerable.

But hungry she certainly was not, thought Dame Lovisa, watching her inattentive mouthing. More likely she had come to the wicket from loneliness. Loneliness is often the beggar's worst affliction, and thinking of this Dame Lovisa now opened the door to her. Sprawling on a bench with her hands over the brazier the woman began to tell of her rambles from shrine to shrine, misfortune to misfortune. It was at the shrine of Saint Cuthbert, at Durham in the north, that she had been got with the child she carried, a cruel thing to befall a virtuous woman, and certainly it must have grieved the saint. But if it proved a boy she would name it Cuthbert. As ill luck would have it Dame Adela now joined them, yawning and stretching and complaining of the fatigue of needlework; and took upon her to remark that it was a pity the child could not be born a monkey, for a monkey would be diversion and better able to fend for itself. The virtuous pilgrim gave her a displeased look. Dame Lovisa said hastily that she knew something of the north country, since she had been born there.

'Ah well, you're out of it now,' said the woman, 'and snug in the Virgin's lap. You convent ladies do not know how lucky you are.'

Dame Adela exclaimed that a nun's life was not so easy. There was the night office, the lenten fast, all day you were kept at needlework and the gold thread was sharp and cut the fingers. The woman replied that there was nothing she loved better than to see holy needleworks, whether on the priest's back or on the altar it did you good to see so much richness in a poor world, and every stitch of it put in by pure virgins, she daresayed. She began to describe copes and hangings she had seen, the white and the gold and the scarlet, the bullion standing out in lumps as big as your fist, the pearls like drops of mutton fat. Meanwhile her lice, enlivened by the warmth, crawled out over her neck and forehead and at intervals she caught one with a practised hand and inattentively bit it.

This altar-hanging now, she asked, what colour was it? Was it crimson? Blue, said Dame Adela. Our dear Lady's own colour, said the woman knowledgeably. Instantly Dame Adela offered to fetch it.

'Don't be a fool!' exclaimed Dame Lovisa. Dame Adela giggled and moved towards the door. Dame Lovisa boxed her ears, and Dame Adela began to weep.

The woman put on a discreet expression and busied herself with her lice.

A box on the ears is not much in a convent, yet Dame Lovisa sickened with a feeling of guilt. Alone at Oby she was conscious of Dame Adela as an immortal soul, a thing in which God's intention, however hooded by imbecility, stirred and chirped and was refreshed by the sacraments. Because of this she was harsh and irritable while the rest were tolerant. Now Dame Adela wept with her uncontrollable half-wit's weeping. Her laments would be heard, and some hearer would say: 'Listen to the poor wretch! Really, it's a shame,' and the shrieks of a pig-killing would not mean less to them.

Pulling herself together she turned to the woman, who met

her glance with a grimace of understanding and tapped lightly on her forehead. With so much knowledge of the world and of needlework, thought Dame Lovisa, this unpleasant pilgrim must be some cast-off bower-woman.

'And to what shrine are you travelling now?' she asked.

'We are going to Waxelby.'

There was no shrine at Waxelby, but she went on smoothly to say that she was in hopes that from Waxelby some ship's captain would be charitable enough to give her a passage southward, so that she could visit the shrine of Saint Osyth.

'Then you do not make this pilgrimage alone?'

The thought of other pilgrims straying about the hen-roosts, plunging their hands into corn-bins, made Dame Lovisa's voice sharp.

'How dare one travel alone in these bad days?' said the woman defensively. 'The others have already gone on. It was my sickness that kept me lagging behind.'

'You had better make haste after them.'

Seating herself more squarely on the bench the woman said that among the pilgrims there was one brought up in these parts – nearer home, may be, than it would be convenient to say. After pausing aggressively, she added: 'His mother was a nun in this very house.'

Dame Adela looked up, all eyes, and said roundly that it could not be true.

'Ah, my poor lady!' said the woman with condescension. 'You sit embroidering, you do not know all that passes.'

'As if I should not know if a child were born! No such thing, I tell you. It is true our priest used to fondle Magdalen Figg, for I have seen him at it. But she was no nun, and had no baby, she was too old for that.'

'I know who you mean,' Dame Lovisa said. 'He was called

Jackie or some such name. He went off on a stolen horse with other goods he had stolen. I have heard the older ladies talk of it. He is well advised to go on towards Waxelby. I do not wonder he made such haste.'

She stood over the woman, willing her to depart. The woman rose. In her bosom, tucked into her dirty wrappings, was the bowl from which she had eaten.

'I have a message for that same priest,' said the woman, rolling her eyes, 'whom some say is no priest at all. Jackie bid me say . . .'

'And our bowl?' Dame Lovisa enquired.

The woman handed it over with a kind of dignity. Then loyalty to her Jackie (from Pernelle Bastable onward many women had been too loyal to Jackie for their own profit) overcame her. She began to rant and scream, saying that such hospitality would choke her, and that the nuns of Oby were no better than their priest, shams all of them, cheats, wantons, greedy-guts, oppressors of the poor. The noise brought Dame Eleanor. Instead of being grateful that another should have borne the stress of entertaining this visitor she turned on Dame Lovisa and reproached her for usurping everybody's business: 'Though why you should be so anxious to poke your face out of the wicket, I do not know. Unless it be to scare people from our door. That would be thrifty, of course. That would appeal to you.'

'More thrifty still to leave them knocking with never an answer! But you were gabbling by the fire, forgetful of everything except your own ease. If I had not heard her and gone at last to receive her she would be knocking still.'

'And a pretty piece of work you seem to have let in.'

While the two nuns quarrelled in an undertone the woman had worked herself into a frenzy – the worse since she could get no attention but Adela's – and now she was beating on the walls and crying to be let out of this place, worse than a prison, worse than a brothel, worse than hell itself since every soul in it was black-damned. What else but damned could they be? – idle, devouring caterpillars listening to a mass that was no mass since a priest that was no priest performed it.

'How much longer do you propose to entertain this trull?' enquired Dame Eleanor.

'Now that you are here I will not trespass on your office. I am waiting for you to turn her away,' replied Dame Lovisa.

Dame Eleanor advanced on the woman, who instantly turned on her.

'Trull, do you say? True enough, true enough, I am no lady, so any word is good enough for me. I do not sit all day by a fire embroidering in gold thread upon satin. Yes, and deny the very sight of it to a poor woman,' she added, turning upon Dame Lovisa. 'You will stir your white fingers for God's altar, but when did you ever prick your fingers for God's poor? We go in rags. And you waste on one yard of your fancywork as much gold as would clothe and feed ten of us for a year's length. Where are the words of Christ, when he said, Clothe the naked? When do you sit down and spin for us? Spin! You cannot as much as spin for yourselves, you are not worth as much as spiders.

'But you won't laugh for ever,' she continued, having noticed Dame Adela's countenance brighten at the mention of spiders. 'You may laugh now, but you will weep sooner than you look for. You will have a fine fire to warm yourselves by one night, the red hen will scrabble in your thatch. Mark my words! I know what I know, I know what I've heard, and I tell you, it won't be long before they come to smoke you out. We have been eaten up long enough with lewd monks and idle nuns, we have lost patience with you. You have worn out the patience of the poor!'

On the threshold she turned back for a last look. By now half the convent had gathered, flustering, questioning, threatening.

She spat, and marched away holding forth her belly as if it were a shield.

The substance of her words was really nothing new. For many years the nuns had been accustomed to the hearsay of such talk, and could refer to themselves as 'we idlers,' and 'us worthless nuns.' Threats of destruction were no novelty either; the more romantically minded would sometimes discuss where they would go, what they would do, when the Lollards came and set fire to the convent. None of them had any distinct ideas as to their plans, and certainly their relations would not welcome them home; but that did not spoil the conversation. The more sophisticated among them, such as Dame Philippa and Dame Cecily, at times contemplated a more gradual kind of destruction, a day – beyond their own day, of course, but within reach of speculation – when well-dowered novices would be so few and expenses so heavy that convents would perish for lack of means. But there is a difference between hearsay and hearing with one's own ears; the woman's fury and insolence had genuinely fluttered those who heard her, so very naturally they fell into a violent squabble among themselves, some blaming Dame Lovisa for letting the woman in, others blaming Dame Eleanor for not being there to keep her out. Thanks to one or other of them the nuns of Oby might well find themselves murdered in their beds. Fortunately the prioress, asleep in her chair, knew nothing of it.

As they broke off their altercation to go in to vespers Dame Eleanor paired with her adversary and said in a low voice:

'Why did she say that about Sir Ralph?'

Dame Lovisa shrugged. 'It is one of the things they say – I suppose because when he first came here he was a stranger and spoke with an accent; and then there was that business with Figg's widow, and heaven only knows what he may have said himself, for he is quite irresponsible in what he says.'

'But do you suppose there is any truth in it?'

'No, no!'

'But it would be fearful. He has been here since the great pestilence.'

'Yes, he is older than the prioress. I wonder which of them will go first. Sir Ralph, I imagine. He is failing fast.'

Even so Dame Eleanor said: 'I think we ought to look into it.' She meant what she said. For one thing, she was a proud woman; and at the thought that for years she had been fooled with a spurious sacrament all her pride was up in arms; for another, she was aware that as the router-out of so frightful an imposture she would become a leading figure, the only nun at Oby acceptable as prioress – unless, of course, they chose to jump in someone from elsewhere: that very real danger must be borne in mind.

'We must talk this over, you and I,' she said, 'I thank my saints that I have you to consult with, one responsible person among this pack of feather-pates.'

Full of dejection and foreboding Dame Lovisa temperately agreed.

But all this was blown away when it was discovered that Dame Adela was gone, and the altar-hanging gone with her. Then it was remembered that Dame Adela had excused herself half-way through supper, had been absent from compline, absent from the midnight office. No one had noticed it, and the dormitory was so ill-lit by its one rushlight that her unoccupied pallet was not noticed either. Then, too, it was remembered that in their flurry over the quarrel at the wicket they had forgotten to put away the needlework.

Not till midday did they dare tell the prioress. They feared that the shock might be the last blow to her faculties. She flared up into her old competence, genial and cold-hearted, wasting little time in reproaches and none in lamentations, and at once sent out searchers and messengers and had the house protected against thieves.

Thieves seemed the likeliest hypothesis. The woman was the spy for the gang and after she had made sure that the altar-hanging was worth stealing (had she not fished to see it?) her companions had broken in under cover of the winter darkness and stolen it. How and why they had also stolen Dame Adela was less apparent; but possibly she, alone absent from quire, had found them breaking in, and they had gagged her and carried her away before she could raise an alarm. Why they should carry rather than kill seemed unaccountable; but no one could find her body, or any bloodstains or signs of a struggle.

Much was said of the ingratitude of Ursula's Jackie, plundering for the second time the house which had reared him – for he, no doubt, was at the bottom of this theft. Dame Margaret, crackling like a holly fire, recalled what a dirty, spoiling, impudent, thievish, froward and ugly child he had been. Sir Ralph, peering into the past, remembered him as a sullen and unimprovable pupil. Dame Cecily dwelt on him as a distasteful hobbledehoy who used to draw obscene pictures on the walls and torment Dame Salome. The prioress said less, but nursed a deeper resentment. Four days later, when news came that a vagrant man called Jack Nonesuch, also Jack the Latiner, also Jackie Pad, had been seized in Waxelby and cast into jail, her satisfaction was terrible to witness. She guffawed, she cracked jokes, she scratched herself, she suggested having a *Te Deum* sung for the occasion: it was as if all her de Stapledon forebears, so pious over property, so ruthless over flesh and blood, had come wassailing into the convent. That night at supper she ate and drank inordinately, and went to bed singing. A few hours later she was stricken by an apoplexy. Too tough to die, she lay motionless, a vast senseless ruin, a sounding-board for her stertorous groans.

But questioned and threatened and eventually maimed of his right hand as a known thief, Ursula's Jackie vouchsafed nothing about Dame Adela and the altar-hanging – only that in Waxelby he had met his leman who had a woman with her whom he had taken to be such another as she, and that he had quarrelled with her and had not seen her or heard of her since. As it would have been to his advantage to help towards the finding of a strayed nun there seemed no reason to disbelieve him.

All this had come about because Dame Lovisa in her self-importance must needs run to the wicket when it was no business of hers. Cowed by so much calamity she agreed with the common sentence. It was all her doing, her wretched doing. Her misery was so abject that she did not even forecast the consequences of the event, the loss in money, the loss in reputation with its contingent loss of more money, the death of the prioress, the impossibility that she should now succeed her. Among all these losses she brooded over yet another loss, in the common estimation the loss of least account, the lost Adela. The wind had changed, it blew from the south-west, and brought a rainy thaw. A white mist like steam from a cauldron billowed round the house. Out of this uncertain daylight the daylight owl hooted: hearing it she was transfixed with a hope as agonising as if a sword had been thrust between her ribs. Adela had come back! But it was only the owl. Adela was gone, in her last hours cuffed and abused and overlooked. Reduced to foolishness by her grief Dame Lovisa told herself that Adela had run away because of wounded feelings.

The fears of the half-witted drive them towards what they dread. As the rabbit runs towards the weasel, and the mouse presses itself to the cat's flank, Dame Adela's first impulse had been to follow the beggar-woman and hear again and again those threats of a burning roof and the angered poor. But she had not spent her life in a convent for nothing, some shreds of policy had been compelled into her mind; and while the nuns were quarrelling she sat down in her corner to think how best to purloin the altar-hanging. If she took it along with her the woman would receive her with more favour; and then it could be sold and with the money ten of those dreadful poor could be clothed and fed, and so for a whole year (the woman had said ten could be clothed and fed for a year) the roof of Oby would not burn, the poor would go elsewhere, Sir Ralph would be the same Sir Ralph as ever and no blood start from the wafer as he handled it.

She went into supper with the rest, and made her excuse halfway through it. But instead of going to the necessary house she went to the parlour and collected the gold thread, the silks, the pearls, and parcelled them in the altar-hanging, and wrapped it all in a towel. There was an old furred cloak, it had belonged to Dame Alicia de Foley, which had long lain as an extra wadding under the cushions of the present prioress. She pulled it out; and out with it came a complicated smell, compounded of wildcat, old spices, and fleabane. As she put on the cloak it seemed to her that she was creeping for warmth and shelter into the skirts of the old prioress as she had done when she was a child. She saw the old woman's hand, dry and waxen-white, with the ring that fitted so loosely that it was always slipping round, the light of its jewel shining inward on the palm, and felt herself dutifully turning it right way about again. It was there, it was gone. A brand broke on the hearth, the shadows of the room were re-made with a new shape, peaked and wolfish. It was her own hooded shadow she saw but she did not stay to recognise it. While the voices sounded and the spoons clattered beyond the partition she pulled the cloak over her bundle and went lightly to the little side-door and out across the orchard to the gap in the reed fence. Beyond was a stretch of marshy meadow. The cat-iced puddles glittered in the moonlight, and crackled under her tread. Beyond the meadow was the Hog Trail, the causeway to Waxelby.

She began to run.

The bundle was heavy, it slipped and sidled under her arm. Her running settled into a dog-trot.

Two horses were standing at the side of the causeway, nose to tail, pressed together for warmth. As she ran by one of them pricked its ears and neighed, and a moment later they both came trotting after her. For a quarter-mile or so they kept up with her. Then they stopped, their curiosity at an end, and she ran on alone. The moonlit sky seemed to be made of blue ice. Ice glittered in the crotches of the old willow trees that grew on the banks of the causeway. Their shadows laced the ground before her. She had no fear of the night and no sense that she was doing anything surprising. To be running along the Waxelby causeway was natural, the only thing she could be doing. The bundle under her arm was a nuisance, that was all. But her trot had fallen into a walk and the shadows of the willow boughs had lengthened with the dropping moon before she saw a figure going along the causeway ahead of her. She began to run again. The figure also began to run.

The quarry was heavy with child, it would not be hard for Adela to outstrip her. But some obscure hunting inheritance set her differently to work. She left the causeway, pulled off her sandals, and ran on under the cover of the willows till her ears told her she had drawn level with the woman. Then she steadied her breath and cried: '*Cuckoo!*'

She heard the woman stop and say bewilderedly: 'The Saints have mercy!'

'*Cuckoo!*' repeated Adela.

'You fool, Annis,' the woman remonstrated with herself. 'Whenever was there a Candlemas cuckoo?'

It was certainly the beggar-woman's voice. Adela scrambled up the bank and came out on the causeway beside her. Now all her sureness and invention left her, and all she could do was to hold out the bundle and look at Annis with a smile.

Annis stared her up and down, from the round simpering face to the bare feet. The feet were so white, white beyond any bleach of moonlight, the face was so wild and vacant . . . Annis crossed herself and said softly: 'Is it you in your flesh and blood?'

Adela nodded, and smiled wider than before.

'And your feet as bare as meadow saffron,' Annis continued, feeling her way between flesh and ghost. 'It's pitiful! But why are you here?'

'I've brought it,' said Adela. 'I've brought it for you, and all the silks, and the pearls. It's nearly finished, you know. We can soon finish it between us. I'll teach you the stitch.'

The woman did not answer.

'Aren't you glad? Look!'

Before Annis could stop her she unrolled the bundle and the altar-hanging was spread on the ground. Annis recoiled, crossing herself. Loosened by the journey the little bag holding the pearls gaped open. Some pearls rolled out. Annis threw herself down with a hoarse cry, and began to scoop them up. Still on her knees she held one up in the moonlight, scanned it closely, put it to her lips.

'They are not real pearls,' she said.

The shapes of the hungry and naked poor started up threateningly on every side. Once more the familiar sensation of having made a fool of herself descended on Adela, and she reacted with fear and fury.

'May your teeth drop out, ungrateful beast! How dare you say my pearls are not real pearls? I brought it because you are poor and I was sorry for you. I ran all this way. after you, and now you say they are not real pearls. I'll take it all back!'

She crumpled up the altar-hanging. With a cry of compassion Annis thrust her aside and began to smooth the ill-used satin.

'What a way to treat it! I marvel you don't dance on it. There, so – that's better. What a way to use you!'

The consolations addressed to the altar-hanging had their effect on Adela. She picked up a few pearls and handed them to Annis. The two women crawled about on their hands and knees peering into the ruts and hoof-prints. Annis was still half under the spell of this dreamlike encounter. A Candlemas cuckoo had turned into a ghost, the ghost into a half-wit, the half-wit into a furious child; and lying at the side of the track was the Oby needlework, which might mean a great sum of money and equally might mean a hanging. If this were not enough for her wits to contend with, there was also this mad nun.

The lesser risk would be to take them both back where they belonged. But after her outburst the nuns would not be likely to receive her with much favour, at the best she would come off with some old rags, a clipped shilling, and some more of that soup. And once more the causeway to Waxelby would stretch before her and at Waxelby Jackie would be growing tired of waiting as he was growing tired of her – for he tired easily. Some other woman might get him, or he might give her the slip, for a man can always get himself on to a boat whereas only a very drunken captain will welcome a woman far gone with child. Yet if she went forward to Jackie taking the altar-hanging, she must needs take the nun too.

In the end she decided to go on, with the hope of getting rid of her companion between now and daybreak. Let her get tired out, thought the hopeful Annis. Let her fall asleep, nicely tucked up in her cloak a little aside from the causeway, and leave her. Nuns would rather sleep than walk.

But the virgin capered along beside her, singing and showing off her bird-calls. It was Annis who flagged, it was Annis who could go no further, it was Annis who fell into a heavy slumber, lying with Adela under Dame Alicia de Foley's cloak. When she woke it was broad daylight and Adela was tickling her nose with a rush. And there, little more than a mile away, was the town of Waxelby, with the great Friar's Church standing up like a ship above the reeds and the waterways and the round tower of Waxelby Old Church seeming no more than a net-stake beside it.

After one glance Annis lay down again and shut her eyes. The daylight reality of the night's crazy dream appalled her. She wanted to scream, to scratch out those blue eyes, to scream again and again. She prayed with intensity that the pains of her labour might take hold of her here and now, and by their majestic anguish release her from having to think about anything else.

The prayer was vain. She sat up and began to comb her hair with her fingers and to smarten up her garments. Then she pulled a little pot out of her wallet, and reddened her cheeks and her lips. Adela watched with interest

'You must trim yourself up a little,' said Annis. 'We cannot go into Waxelby looking like scarecrows.'

But Adela had nothing to trim herself up with. By degrees, by lending a kerchief, by stripping off her petticoat and her ornaments and putting them on the nun, and by reddening her cheeks, she made Adela into a passable imitation of a whore. By adapting some of Adela's clothes to her own use she made of herself a more convincing representation of a bawd. All this touch-and-go exchange she carried through with admirable tact and wariness, though she was dizzy with exhaustion. But when it was done, even as she was congratulating herself on having done it so well, the thought of what would happen next almost broke her courage. There would be so many nexts! – to get Adela into

Waxelby, to hear a mass, to find a breakfast, to find Jackie, to put him into a good humour and yet not into too good a humour – for dressed as a whore the mad nun had developed a sort of mad beauty, a tattered faded crumpled beauty as if beauty were a garment that had been left hanging for years on a hedge and now were put on again. But Jackie would relieve her of the altar-hanging, and that would be one care off her mind. There should be no difficulty there, for the nun still prated about how it was to be sold for the relief of the poor.

Annis's thoughts considered the poor as they walked on to Waxelby. Her overnight's rant was nothing but beggar's rhetoric, as she knew well, the noise one hears in every alehouse, every jail, every ditch. It is not hunger and nakedness that worst afflict the poor, for a very little thieving or a small alms can remedy that. No, the wretchedness of the poor lies below hunger and nakedness. It consists in their incessant incertitude and fear, the drudging succession of shift and scheme and subterfuge, the labouring in the quicksand where every step that takes hold of the firm ground is also a step into the danger of condemnation. Not cold and hunger but Law and Justice are the bitterest affliction of the poor.

Entering Waxelby she hurried her companion to the Friary Church, and fell on her knees, thankful for the sense of respite that came with the rows of pillars so strong and upright, the reiteration of mouldings in triforium and clerestory, the echo that sanctified every common sound. Adela knelt beside her, staring about her, but momentarily quiet. Then she rose and began to walk up the nave. When Annis went after her she said placidly that she was going to take her place in quire. Hearing this astonishing statement an old woman looked round, and was the more astonished when she saw the tattered appearance of the owner of that imperious voice.

'Do you think yourself a friar, then?' she asked.

'I am a nun,' Adela replied. While Annis sickened, some obscure whim of grandeur impelled Adela to continue: 'We are both nuns.'

'Friar's nuns, I daresay,' said the old woman, 'the pair of you. Whipping's what you need.'

The echo could not do much for this. Abashed at having injured the friars in their own church the old woman turned around and addressed herself to Saint Blaize. Before Adela could get into any more mischief a mass began. Her readiness with the responses made more heads turn towards them, and Annis could think of no better expedient than to exaggerate her own devotion and hope they might be taken for pilgrims. But as they left the church some stones were thrown and the phrase of 'Friar's nuns' was hooted after them.

Adela's dread of the terrible poor returned. She clung to Annis. Annis was in no mood to be clung to. Her short cross answers completed Adela's dejection, and though the ships at the quayside interposed themselves between her and her alarm she was not allowed to gape at them but found herself shoved through a doorway into a narrow room full of men and men's loud voices.

A few looked up, one or two spoke; no one moved to make room for her. Here were the poor again, more and poorer and more intimidating. But the woman who kept the alehouse had already exchanged glances with Annis and now without a word she pushed the two women into a sort of lean-to chamber beyond. It had a couple of trestles in it, some cobwebbed fishing-gear and rags in bunches hung on the walls, it smelt fusty and sleepy; and indeed there was someone sleeping in it even now, an old man with a bald head covered with warts and scabs, who slept fretfully, grunting, and burrowing in his straw for the warmth that had left his limbs. Annis pulled away some of his straw and sat down composedly with the straw round her feet. Then she pointed to her mouth and rubbed her stomach. The alehouse woman nodded and went off, and came back with some bread and beer and two hunks of black-pudding. The beer was stale and the bread sour, but the black-pudding, violently flavoured, seemed to Adela the most delicious and appetising food she had ever tasted. After her first impetuous gulps she set herself to make it last out as long as possible. Absorbed in this she did not observe all the dumbshow proceeding between the other two (which was as well for her vanity, for it began with Annis making it plain that her companion was a half-wit, and negligible). But she looked up in time to see the dumb woman straddle her legs and set her arms akimbo. Annis nodded delightedly, and fetched her arm about in a wide gathering gesture and finally pointed to her bosom; and the woman, falling back into herself, hurried away.

They were in Waxelby, they had heard a mass and had breakfast; and Jackie was still in the town. Feeling that matters were not so bad after all, Annis turned to Adela and said they would undo the bundle and look at the embroidery by daylight. There was not much daylight in the room, only what came in through cracks in the walls and by the chinks of an outer door, which seemed to open into a yard or garden since no footsteps went by it; and the space was so limited that they could only unroll part of the altar-hanging at one time. But neither at Oby where it began nor in any of its later wanderings was the needlework so truly admired. Dame Lovisa had guessed too high: Annis was never in such comfortable circumstances as to be a bower-woman; but she had a natural bent for works of art which she had cultivated during a long course of visiting churches – sometimes for pleasure and devotion, at other times for more practical reasons of sanctuary. The Oby hanging was beyond all she had ever set eyes on. It was new. No incense smoke had tarnished it, no sacristans had torn it, no candle-grease had spotted it. The blue of the satin was as pure as the blue of heaven, the ostrich feathers were so freshly stitched that they seemed to wave and billow upon the ground-colour, the gold was unfrayed, the tinsel was bright as dew. And she could see it intimately, she could stare into every detail of its workmanship. When they unrolled the corner that was still unfinished she groaned and looked at Adela as though she would strike her.

There was a needle quilted into the stuff and Adela as a matter of course re-threaded it and wiped the grime off her hands and went on embroidering. Annis watched sharply, having a suspicion that she might begin to gobble-stitch some nonsense of her own devising. But the nun worked as dutifully as though she were in her cloister, and yawned and complained as though a task-mistress were over her.

More than an hour went by. When Annis pulled the needle from her hand and parcelled up the hanging it seemed to Adela that it must now be time to go into quire. Instead, the dumb woman reappeared, pushed in a man, and went out again. Annis scrambled to her feet.

'Jackie, my good Jackie! How have things been with you, Jackie?' Her voice was the voice she had used when she first spoke to Adela on the causeway. He stood with his legs apart in the centre of the floor, so bulky that he seemed to fill the room, and surveyed them with a broad dull grin. There was no doubt that this was the man the dumb woman had mimicked. The mimicry had frightened Adela, the original was worse. She shrank into the corner where the old man lay drowsing and clutching at his straw.

Annis was half-way through her story before Jackie troubled

himself to speak, and then it was only to ask her where in the devil's name she had been and why she had not come to Waxelby till now. She began her story over again, and this time she got it as far as the meeting on the Hog Trail, and the stranger who had started up before her like a ghost and given her the altar-hanging from Oby for pity of God's poor.

'Aha! And where is it now?' he asked scornfully.

'Here!' said Annis. 'Here!' echoed Adela.

Then the hanging was again spread out. He looked at it hard and appraisingly. His face showed no animation till the unfinished corner was displayed, and then he rounded on Annis and said that only a fool would steal a half-licked piece of work. Did she think she could finish it?

'No, but here is one who can and will. This ... this damsel here. We have the silks and the pearls and all we need, and she can work as fast as a spider. And while she works, Jackie, you must think how best we can sell it, and where. I have heard say that this sort of work fetches a high price among the French and the Flemings. If we all went to France together she could sit at her work while the ship carried it to market. But you must decide, Jackie, you must decide.'

Groping around for more straw the old man took hold of Adela's hand, and feeling its warmth he pulled it savagely towards him and held it on his breast. But she did not struggle, for all the sense she had was concentrated on this conversation between Annis and Jackie. After a glance at her, Jackie turned back to Annis and asked her what he would do in foreign parts with two women tagged to his heels and neither of them worth a penny-piece; and by that token there would be a brat too by then. Yet it seemed as though he were making objections more for the pleasure of making them and to keep himself in practice than for any real purpose; for it was plain that the altar-hanging pleased him and was accepted in his mind as a thing he could dispose of. Annis said they could sell the needlework in England, anywhere out of earshot of the bell of Oby would do. Yes, and be hanged for it, he replied thoughtfully. Annis went on to say that a fair might not serve their turn, for what you sell at a fair is every fair-goer's business; but wherever there is a prosperous shrine you can find a dealer in the neighbourhood who will buy anything he can sell again as an offering, and not bargain too much over it either, since he can be sure of making his price from some customer newly healed or full of a recent gratitude for a grace or a miracle. There was Walsingham, Bromholm, the great shrine of Saint Edmund; going further south there was Waltham Holy Cross in the forest or the shrine of Saint Thomas Beckett itself, and by taking a passage in a boat going to London ... She was rambling on, her mean worn face lighting up with a gadabout's pleasure, when he interrupted her with the same animation as he had shown when he found the embroidery was not complete.

'And what is to warrant me that she can finish the work? I do not see her working, all she does is to sit fondling that old carcass in the corner there. Let me see you work!' he said, addressing Adela for the first time.

'Yes, dear, show Jackie how cleverly you do it,' said Annis.

Once more Adela wiped her hands and took up the needlework. But she was flustered and the silk slipped from the needle.

'She an embroideress, she finish it! She will be a year at it and make a bungle of it when all's told. She knows no more of embroidery than you do.'

'That's all you know about it!' exclaimed Adela, nettled. 'I was the only one among us who knew the secret of this stitch. They all had to learn it from me, Dame Lilias and Dame Eleanor and Dame Philippa and Dame Sibilla and ... '

'Dame Meg and Dame Peg,' he said scornfully. 'And where did all you fine dames sit stitching?'

'In the parlour at Oby of course.'

He stared at her, at her foolish face and her smooth white hands. Satisfied that she had put him down Adela smiled primly and went on embroidering. Annis sidled up to him and began to stroke his cheek and whisper.

'I wouldn't hide it from you, Jackie. How could I? You're so clever, you nose out everything. But I dressed her up pretty well, don't you think? No one but you would guess it.'

'I'll have nothing to do with her. Since you brought her, you can take her away.'

'But I had to bring her, she was bent on coming with me. Besides, she can finish the embroidery, you see, something I could never learn.'

'I'll have no nuns,' he said.

'No, no! But just let her finish the work. I'll keep her at it, she'll be no trouble to you. The poor creature, she's as harmless as a sheep.'

Pulling at his lower lip he turned for another look. His swagger had evaporated, a mottle of fear overspread his face. He crossed himself.

Annis chuckled.

'I thought it would be another game with you, Jackie. You to be afraid of a nun? – I was looking for something different.'

'I'll touch no nun!' he burst out, so loudly that the old man sat up and stared at them, and the clash of voices in the next room seemed to be stayed.

'Hush, hush!'

There was no need for Annis to hush him. That exemplary sentiment if overheard might be construed very differently and to his disadvantage. He leaned trembling against the wall, and his eyes rolled dismally in their sockets as he looked from the embroidery to Adela, from Adela to the embroidery.

'Cold, cold,' said the old man, lying down again. Adela, pleased to assert herself further after having quelled this rough man of Annis's, took an armful of the altar-hanging and lapped it round him. Annis and Jackie cried out together that she was to do no such thing.

'I'll do what I please,' she replied. 'It's mine, it's my work. I brought it away to clothe Christ's poor. This old man is poor and needs a garment. When he's asleep perhaps I'll take it away again, but while he's cold he shall have it, poor old man!'

She spoke with the simple arrogance inherited from her forebears, and Annis turned to Jackie with more confidence and said: 'She's quite crazy, you see. Just listen to her!'

'She's none the better for being crazy,' he answered. 'If a woman's in her senses you can beat her. But that one—'

'And who's to know she's a nun unless you go shouting it? Once we're at sea—'

'No, no!' He crossed himself vehemently, and began to sweat. 'Nuns bring ill luck, nuns out of their cloister. I won't set foot on a ship with her for company.'

'Well, what are we to do? Stay here?'

'Yes, that's it! You stay here, you and she, and you keep her at it till the work's done. And then send Mum Margaret after me as you did this morning.'

'And where will she find you?'

He hesitated.

'No, that's not so good. Wait! I tell you, when it's finished, have Margaret put a fresh bough in the sign, a bough of yew. I'll watch for that.'

'And the three of us stay here in Waxelby, where every man will be looking for us? Because you are afraid to go to sea with a nun? What is there to fear, what is a nun when all's said? What was your mother but a nun?'

'The devil flay her!' he said. 'She reared me in a kitchen to be everyone's kick and flout. Do you wonder I sicken at nuns?'

'If you sicken at nuns the devil will flay you,' remarked Adela tranquilly.

'Once we're done with her we'll rub her off,' whispered Annis.

Jackie saw the problem otherwise: he would rub them both off if he could. Yet to do so with any satisfaction he must keep the altar-hanging, and to have it at its best it must be finished by the one and the other must be kept as his overseer. And every hour in Waxelby was dangerous. And yet he did not want to go to sea, and least of all with a nun. Any fool of a woman can stitch, he supposed. And if he could rid himself of these two, and find a third . . .

He sat chewing and sweating in a cage of considerations. At last he said he would go and see what could be done about a passage for the three of them. But the captain would need a sweetener, Annis must hand over her crown-piece, and he would take a few of those pearls.

'And take the hanging off that old dotard,' he said, 'and roll it up in the towel. For if we can get on the *Barbara*, there will be no time to waste. She's loaded already.'

'Don't tell the others,' said Annis. He put a good deal of feeling into the exasperated kick he delivered in reply, and as Annis picked herself up she admitted to herself that the advice had been foolish and uncalled-for.

The old man cursed and grumbled when they removed the altar-hanging, and Adela protested that she wanted to go on embroidering. Annis spent no words on either. She made up the bundle and sat down on it. They waited for a long time. The shafts of light shifted from midday to afternoon and sloped in by the door which gave into the yard. A thrush was singing there very sweetly. At intervals Adela complained of being bored and demanded to have the bundle undone so that she could go on with her embroidery. A day with no offices to break it seemed interminably tedious. She began to say some Hail Maries, and fell asleep. The old man rustled in his straw, the thrush sang. Annis sat in a prick-eared anxiety, feeling the child lumber against her backbone, biting her lip as she went over the things she had said to Jackie and saw how she could have mended them.

She started up when the door flew open. Jackie was on the threshold.

'They're after me! And the *Barbara* is weighing anchor. But if you slip out by the yard . . .'

'And leave her?'

'You think of nothing but your nun! No, bring her too.'

She shook Adela and got her to her feet. Then she stooped for the bundle.

'I'll see to that. Get along with your nun. Turn to the left, then by the alley towards the quay. On the quay you'll see a sailor with one ear. Follow him, and when you are on board, go straight below and stay there and speak to no one till I come.'

'But you will come, Jackie? You will come?'

'Will I stay here to be hanged? But I must wait till I know they have gone past.'

It was not easy to get Adela to stir, she seemed unable to comprehend the notion of danger and she had none of the uncloistered woman's instinct to obey the male. It took all of Annis's powers to move her and keep her moving.

Jackie followed them to the foot of the yard, cursing and encouraging. When he had watched them out of sight he relaxed, leant against a paling, and began very quietly to whistle. The thrush answered him, or seemed to. He answered the thrush back. For now, with both women off his hands, he had time for a little fancy and poetry. It was one of those February dusks that seem to leap forward into spring, that melt and are complaisant and full of promise and even have a few midges.

Meanwhile, the old man had come nimbly out of his corner. He undid the bundle and took the altar-hanging and buried it under his straw. Then he collected all the rags that were hanging on the walls and made up the bundle again, reproducing its shape and knotting with great accuracy. Then he returned to his corner. After a while Jackie strolled in, picked up the bundle, laughed, spat, strewed a curse or two on the sleeper, and went away. The straw rustled as the old man shook with senile laughter. Not all his difficulties were over, of course. There was still his hostess to overcome, whose eyes were all the sharper because she had not the use of her tongue. But the altar-hanging lay safe beneath him, and he reckoned – rightly, as it turned out – to be able to make a pretty penny by it.

Below decks in the *Barbara* Adela was experiencing her first qualms of sea-sickness and Annis, listening to her moans and groans, began to know herself made a fool of, with a child kicking in her belly, a mad nun on her hands and a sea voyage before her. As one puffs a green fire her invention patiently breathed on the circumstances before her, and she wondered to whom and for how much or how little she could dispose of this foolish virgin who was now her only asset in a harsh world, and her only friend.

XIII

A Green Staff

(*March 1380–June 1381*)

The people on the manor heard considerably more of Dame Adela's fate than the convent did; as was natural, since they enjoyed all the tale-bearing resources of cousins at Waxelby, aunts in Wivelham, and Brother Bartlemy dropping in so comfortably with talk of this world and the next. They knew, for instance, how Dame Adela had attempted to enter the quire of the Friary Church by force and had only been prevented by the resolution of old Emme Sampson, who was born a Holly of Dudham. They knew that Katharine Trump, one of the Waxelby whores, had a pearl bracelet which was not honestly come by. They knew that the *Barbara* had left port with a cargo of virgins, all destined for the King of Hungary. They knew that within an hour of the *Barbara* leaving port Jack the Latiner had tried to strangle the dumb woman who kept the alehouse and that in the fight which ensued five men had been injured and a whole cask of beer wasted because no one had time to turn the tap off. They knew that Dame Adela had spent most of the day shut up in an inner room at the alehouse where she had sung as sweetly as a captive bird and eaten inordinately of black-pudding. They knew that when she was dragged on board a vessel which was not the

Barbara at all but the *Boy of Whitby*, she was speechless with exhaustion and had three dogs with her. They knew that Annis was wearing the altar-hanging as a petticoat. They also knew that it was hidden in a dry well somewhere beyond Wivelham, that Jackie had given it to Katharine Trump, and that it had never left Oby where the nuns, in one of their quarrels, had torn it to shreds among them. Finally they knew, on the assurance of the old night-watchman who lodged by day at the alehouse, that Annis, contrary to appearances, was no woman but a short thick-set man with a red beard; but this was known rather later, and by the report of Sir John Idburn, who had encountered the old fellow crutching himself along to Walsingham in pursuance of a vow.

Meanwhile, the prioress, palsied and senseless, lived on. Her mere survival was a kind of support to her nuns; for while she lived they could defer the problem of an election and as she might die at any moment it was not worthwhile to choose a deputy. Throughout Lent the choice of the next prioress was endlessly and languidly canvassed, and by twos and threes they made up and unmade their minds. Dame Lovisa, long accepted as inevitable, was out of the question, since it was she who had let the enemy in among them, and Dame Eleanor, her natural rival, was now felt to be out of the question also; for if you choose the lesser of two rivals you create a schism, and though under some circumstances a schism can be enlivening it is a fair-weather luxury; one cannot afford it in times of misfortune. Dame Margaret was too old. Dame Dorothy was in her middle forties and healthy, but she was totally without initiative, she would be no better than an image carted about by one party and then another. Dame Philippa was neutral, discreet, and well-connected; but she flatly refused to have anything to do with it and said that if they elected her she would certainly resign. This left Dame Cecily who was blind, Dame Lilias who was unwanted, and Dame Sibilla. Dame Sibilla was too young, and she was not an Oby nun, and she was a busybody and her piety was like no one else's piety, and a house ruled by anyone so nearly related to Bishop Walter would not know an easy moment; besides, all her relations were in religion, which would make her an unprofitable prioress, since everyone throws his herring-guts to his own dog. Yet from the variety of reasons alleged why Dame Sibilla would not do it was obvious that she was generally and seriously considered. If one did not consult expense, the best plan would be to elect Dame Margaret, endure her ill-humour like a Lent and when she died choose – who? – Dame Lovisa with her talent for business, or Dame Eleanor who was the senior of the two and extremely personable. They were back where they had started from.

Never had an election been contemplated with so little spirit. Never had Dame Cecily heard so many sentences left unfinished, so many dubious sighs, so many desolate yawns, and such a general consent that it was too much for them, that it must be left for God to decide. She knew just what they must be looking like: sallow, sluttish, dispirited. Who would have thought a mere apple should undo the world? Who would have supposed that Dame Adela, that negligible being, should have created this cavernous absence? But that was because she had taken the altar-hanging with her – at any rate their disappearances had coincided. The loss of the altar-hanging was beyond the loss of money expended to no purpose, beyond the frustration of their hope of making a good impression on the new bishop. During the months they had worked on it together the nuns of Oby had become a community. Though in its early stages the needlework had been an instrument in the usual convent factions, a de Retteville banner waved against de Stapledons, as time went on it had become everyone's interest and everyone's purpose; and the satisfaction which Dame Lovisa had found in her lonely black and white psalters, and which the old prioress had felt with the second Trinity Cope, and which she herself (but how long ago!) had known with her paint-brushes, her cobalt and vermilion, had been felt by all, whether they worked or watched the workers. Something was being made, they had a reason for living together, the blue satin roofed them like a tabernacle.

It was gone. They were at sixes and sevens again, idle, dejected, and afraid; and years would pass before they would entertain such another project, for they had been bubbled, and once bit is twice shy.

Prioress Matilda lasted out for another twelvemonth. The permit to elect came on Shrove Tuesday, and the election gave the prioress-ship to Dame Margaret by a majority of three voices. Even those who had voted for her felt considerable qualms when they heard the result, and pitying glances were turned towards Dame Lilias, who would now have the liveliest reasons to wish she had got safely away into her anchoress's cell before this turn of events. Yet though the election chilled most hearts it expressed the general mind. Dame Margaret, so old, so cut and dried, with nothing to offer but her formalism, her shallow-moulded perspective of convention, was the only co-ordinating element in the community. They could believe in her because she was so incapable of suggesting anything they did not know already.

On his springtime visit to Oby Henry Yellowlees hurried up the stairs to Sir Ralph's chamber, and bemoaned himself to his friend.

'It is ruin! It is lunacy! Whatever possessed them to choose that withered thistle? And then to let her appoint that blockhead Dame Dorothy as treasuress! They neither of them know a rent from the grace of God, and the books are in such a state already – I shall tell the bishop that I cannot go on.'

For Henry Yellowlees was now a very different person from the hungry clerk whom Bishop Walter had made custos of Oby.

Bishop de Craye had come to his see resolved not to be scrambled over by a troop of disorderly English clerics, and resolved, above all, to winnow away the retinue of his predecessor. Among his earliest discards were the secretaries, the chaplain, and the doctor. When he had cleared his immediate surrounding he had a list drawn up of all the late bishop's nominations. In it he found the name of Master Henry Yellowlees, custos of Oby and teacher of mathematics at the school of the Holy Innocents. With his winnowing-fan in his hand Perkin de Craye came in due course to this particular threshing-floor, where he found Henry Yellowlees in one of his worst tempers, damning all bishops and in especial this new bishop who had dismissed his crony Humphrey Flagg. Being confident that his own dismissal would follow, Henry Yellowlees began to criticise the cathedral music in a very liberated spirit. As it happened, Perkin de Craye was a considerable musician; and though the two men almost immediately fell into a violent wrangle about Machault (whom Perkin de Craye thought to be too mellifluous and lacking in technical ambition), his opponent disagreed with him so intelligently that Perkin de Craye found himself saying that what Master Yellowlees needed was to hear some of the compositions of Landini, and promising in the next sentence that he should hear them as soon as he could get the parts copied and the quire thrashed into performance. As this could not be unless the winnowing were postponed, Henry Yellowlees remained in his post at the Holy Innocents until the bishop decided that it would be better if he were fanned into a personal secretaryship.

'Tell the bishop? – Oh, yes, this bishop. H'm, certainly! Yes, I should tell him if I were you.'

Sir Ralph was lying on his bed with a rug over him. Though the spring air puffed into the room he looked wintry, he looked like the snow-banks which lie on the north side of a baulk and will not melt.

'This is my seventh year as custos of Oby,' said Henry, beginning to excuse himself. 'It's a long time. At least it is a long time in which to have got nothing done. Really, I have no talents for management.'

'The patriarch Jacob served seven years for Leah and another seven years for Rachael. And I don't know that he got much out of it,' remarked Sir Ralph.

'I suppose seven years seems no time at all to you?'

'No time at all,' said the old man airily. 'Some deaths, of course. Some births. Lambs, and so forth.'

Though prosperity had set him up Henry was not altogether ruined by it. There was concern as well as patronage in his heart when he suggested that Sir Ralph himself might well think of retiring, that a word to the bishop, who appreciated scholarship, would translate him to some pleasant sinecure. Without affectation he added that he thought Sir Ralph would like the bishop.

Sir Ralph looked at him with affectionate inattention, and said: 'So you'll be leaving us? Well, I'm thinking of going away myself.'

Reflecting that the new prioress must be even worse than he supposed if she had loosened Sir Ralph from his red-arrased nutshell, Henry asked where he thought of going.

'To London, to London,' replied Sir Ralph as though it were the most natural reply in the world.

'To London? But that is a long journey.'

'The only place for my purpose. I want to make sure of finding intelligent men, men of culture. I should only waste my time if I trudged about to the lesser places, Oxford and Cambridge and what not. And I can't afford to waste time. I have let too much time go by as it is.'

Whatever he was raving about, he raved in a new manner. Henry had never heard him speak with such decision nor in such a magistral tone of voice.

'Now in London they understand such matters.'

What matters, Henry enquired, and Sir Ralph replied, poetry. He raised himself on his bed, took a manuscript, and began to read aloud. His reading voice was strong and pompous, he read with old-fashioned gusto, twanging off the words like a jongleur. Who or what he was reading about was hard to say, except that there was a yew tree and a weeping man whose tears dripped through its dark boughs. It was a poem in English, and apparently it was intended to rhyme, though the rhymes observed no obvious pattern. Henry's attention soon slid away from the reading and fastened upon this surprising new aspect of the reader, roaring like a schoolmaster, with his black eyebrows sitting astonished among his dishevelled white locks. What had changed him? Was it the approach of death which had kindled this vigour of mind in the old man? If only he had known him when he was young! The young Ralph Kello must surely have been like this, thought Henry Yellowlees, for the first time realising that Sir Ralph had once and authentically been a young man.

'What do you think of that, Henry?'

'I – I'm not quite sure. I should have to hear more of it before I could form an opinion.'

'Exactly! That is why I am going to London.'

Henry said meekly that if Sir Ralph would read on, or if he could borrow the manuscript and study it ... His meekness was of no avail. Sir Ralph replaced the manuscript under his bolster and dismissed him as though he were a schoolboy – a dull one at that.

Riding into Lintoft that same evening, his mind still occupied with Sir Ralph, Henry Yellowlees heard the same words: *To London*. It might have been his fancy repeating Sir Ralph's words; but the voice was nothing like Sir Ralph's, and the words had come from beyond his thoughts, as though they had been thrown like a stone and hit him. A moment later he heard another voice reply to the first voice: 'Aye, to London. That's where we must go.'

A group of labourers was standing under an ash tree. His horse carried him on and he could hear no more of what they were saying.

That night at supper the rector of Lintoft was full of stories about Oby, the extortions of the bailiff, the meanness displayed at the funeral of the late prioress and the haughtiness of the new one. Another thing which was causing a lot of talk, continued Sir John, was the fact that the two novices sent to Oby eight years before were still waiting to be given their veils. No fault of theirs; but they were both of mean birth and the Oby nuns were too proud to admit them. Such behaviour alienated the common people, and no wonder. Henry Yellowlees replied that both novices had been nuns for the past four years. He marvelled that Sir John's parishioners, who were so well-informed, did not know of it. Sir John muttered that there had been no feast for them, at any rate. He hastened on to suppose that there was no news of that unfortunate imbecile nun who had been kidnapped by the red-bearded man who had been seen by old Eustace the watchman; and before Henry Yellowlees could answer he went on to say that there could be little doubt as to what had become of her: people could stand so much and no more, and the new poll-tax had broken their patience. Kings should pay for their own wars, it was too much to ask the poor man both to fight in the king's armies and pay for them. What a war, too! Why must the English war again with the French for no purpose but to be beaten by them when our fathers had beaten them once for all thirty years before? Henry Yellowlees was unable to see what the French war had to do with the disappearance of Dame Adela, for surely not even the rector of Lintoft could suppose that she had been carried off to fight for the king? Raising his voice – John Idburn had grown somewhat hard of hearing – he asked if the woman who turned into a red-bearded man had been by any chance a soldier.

No, of course not, why should he be? – replied Sir John wonderingly. If a soldier wanted a nun and an altar-hanging he could find them in France. No doubt who he was: one of a band, and the band one of the many bands of the workless and dispossessed who were going through the country to sack and pillage. No doubt either that they had intended more that night than God had allowed them to do; but on the afternoon before Dame Adela was kidnapped a woman, a pious pilgrim, had forced her way into the nunnery and warned the nuns that they would be burned in their beds. Simon Maggs's daughter, who worked in the Oby kitchen, had heard her warning them. So they were prepared and had their doors and windows barred, and all the kidnappers could find when they came was Dame Adela coming from the necessary house. Henry Yellowlees asked how it was that Dame Adela should have the altar-hanging with her at such a time, but he omitted to raise his voice, and Sir John had rushed on to say that he, for one, did not wonder at this state of things. Look at Lintoft, for instance. It was twelve years since the Dambers had visited their manor house, for twelve years he had not preached to an educated hearer: they lived at court, they fought in the wars, they skinned the place and put nothing back into it; now they were felling their woods for sale, and soon there would not be as much as an acorn left for the swine to fatten on. Then on top of all this, the taxes, and on top of the taxes, this last poll-tax. He did not wonder that his parishioners were full of resentment. Starve a dog and it will grow wolf's teeth, was an old saying and a true one. He, for one, would wish them Godspeed when they set out for London.

'God's bones! Is everyone going to London?' cried Henry.

'No, not everyone. Some are not strong enough, and some must stay behind for the beans and the hay and to look after the cattle. You cannot expect they should all go. But the stoutest are going.'

'But why? What are they going to London for?'

'To tell the king. Why else should they go?'

'But what will they tell the king?'

'That nobody else will listen to them,' replied Sir John.

If it had not been for those men under the tree Henry would have discounted this as another piece of the Lintoft priest's nonsense. As it was, he thought enough of it to send a letter to Sir Ralph begging him not to set off for London until he could arrange to go with him. *I would fain go to London where I have never been, yet I fear to go to so great a city alone and untutored lest I be cozened there*, he wrote artfully. It alarmed him to think that the old man might really set out with his manuscript and fall into the hands of such travellers as he had seen scowling under the ash tree. If Sir Ralph persisted in going he would milk the bishop for a conveyance and a couple of men for an escort. Possibly the bishop on his next journey south . . . but on second thoughts Henry had to admit that his old friend and his new friend would have little in common; though Perkin de Craye would make nothing of taking an old nun's priest along with him, for his highly intellectual form of christianity regarded no social distinction save the distinction between the church and the world.

Sir Ralph put the letter carefully away in his Aquinas – a handsome volume which he used mainly as a repository. He need not answer it. There would not be time for that. Lately he had been subject to singular lapses of memory: not just ordinary forgetfulness, for in recollecting names, verses, dates, his memory served him as well as ever – indeed, it even seemed to be improving, for it was quite surprising how sharply he could remember every detail of events happening forty and fifty years ago. But with an odd inconsistency this good willing serviceable memory constantly failed him over things of the present. He had quite forgotten, for instance, till Henry's letter came to remind him, that he must go to London with the poem of Mamillion. Yes, Mamillion must set out on a new series of wanderings, taking the track to Lintoft and westward till it crossed King Street, there turning southward and on through Peterborough and Cambridge and Saint Albans – a long journey; but no longer than pilgrims go, or troops of jugglers and tumblers; and no doubt he would fall in with many lifts in carts and waggons, for people are kind to an old man, an old priest travelling on a good errand. He would meet scholars too, going fastidiously from place to place in search of newer teaching, as he had done in his day; and to them he could speak of the poem of Mamillion, and of his obligation, so long ago incurred, to make it known among the poets and scholars of the world. It had taken him a long time to come to a full appreciation of the poem: a course of time during which the poem's poet, that unfortunate Lord of Brocton, had almost faded from his mind. But while the poet waned the poem waxed, and now he knew it for what it was – one of the great epic poems of mankind, a poem that would wander through one generation to another, sometimes pausing, like Mamillion himself, in a deep wood or at some welcoming castle, but never abiding there, for its destiny was to wander everlastingly through the hearts of men. Yet the delay was not such a bad thing, after all. By so many desultory readings he knew it through and through. There was, for instance, that passage about the wild man, who capered up to Mamillion and smote him with a flowering branch, filling his nose and eyes with pollen-dust; and before Mamillion could clear his eyes and leave off sneezing the wild man had capered away again, uttering a loud booming Halloo. How many times he must have sauntered through it without seeing its quality! – and at last came a reading which became a first reading, and he had been as much astounded as if he too had been smitten over the nose with a flowering branch.

He took up the manuscript and found the wild man once more. The poets and scholars in London would be quick to admire such imagination. He looked out of his window: the screen was down, the sweet air and the light came fully in. Why should he not start tomorrow? Yes, and make sure of his purpose! Otherwise, his memory might play him another trick; and he could not expect to have a second letter from Henry Yellowlees to remind him that he meant to go to London. It was very obliging of Henry Yellowlees: an excellent, kind-hearted fellow, if for the moment rather too much taken up with his bishop.

If he started tomorrow, what must be done first? He must of course explain to Dame Margaret that he was obliged to go to London. There was always a Wivelham curate whom she could call on. Dame Margaret was so deaf that it would be fatiguing to explain for any length of explanation. He would have to bellow in her ear; and without being a voluptuary he very much disliked Dame Margaret's ear from which the short coarse hairs bristled out so hungrily. Why should he not explain to her by means of an intermediary? He would send her a message by one of the nuns: by Dame Lilias, who was always very kind to him. There was something about Dame Lilias, too, which he knew he ought to remember, but just now it slipped his memory. One cannot remember everything and at present he must concentrate on carrying Mamillion to London. What else? A good staff was essential, and he would see about it at once.

He thrust the manuscript into the pocket of his gown and left his chamber. As the door closed behind him a brimstone butterfly fluttered in at the open window.

An ash-plant was best. He set off for the copse in the eastern corner of the common field, there were ash-stools there, and there in the old days he had often cut himself a staff. As good fortune would have it Thomas Scole was at work in the copse. They searched together, trampling the bluebells, until the right ash-plant was found, and the staff cut there and then and its handle shaped and smoothed. Young Scole was an excellent workman. It was a pleasure to watch him, though as the last slow touches were given to the staff Sir Ralph could barely contain his impatience. At length it was in his hands, and with thanks and a blessing he turned away.

If they were all as civil as he, thought Thomas Scole, there would be less to complain of. He watched the old man walking over the furrows and getting along very nimbly considering his age and his bulk. A rabbit ran out of its burrow. Turning his attention to the rabbit, which is meat and clothing both, Thomas Scole failed to notice that Sir Ralph had turned westward along the track to Lintoft. Even had he noticed it, it would not have made any particular impression on him. An old man with a green staff likes to ramble about with it.

For a long time Dame Amy had been summoning up her courage. Seeing the priest's luncheon of bread and beer on the buttery shelf it seemed to her that this was the moment the Virgin had sent. So she said she would carry it up to his chamber. At the head of the stairs she knocked and waited. At last she pulled the latch and looked in. The chamber was empty. She set down the meal on the stool, and was turning away when a light sound caught her hearing, and she saw a yellow butterfly struggling in a cobweb. She freed it, and watched it fly out of the window, and was about to go when it struck her that there were a great many cobwebs about the room, and since she was alone in it and no one needed her she might pull some of them away. So she wandered about the room collecting cobwebs in her hand till she came to the opened cupboard where Sir Ralph kept his books. Here temptation overcame her. She took one down and opened it at random, mouthing the Latin which she could pronounce but could not understand. It was this which had brought her here. She longed to read the Latin authors, and she had brought up the bread and beer meaning to ask Sir Ralph if it were wrong for a nun to learn Latin. For some nuns it was certainly permissible. Dame Lilias could read Latin as easily as she could read French or English, Dame Philippa also, and the elder Frampton novice had been writing Latin exercises before she sickened with measles and died. But these were all nuns of good family, who had had books put into their hands as early as she herself had been taught to hold a distaff or the thumper of a churn. She was afraid to speak of her desire to Dame Lilias, whom everyone said was proud; still less could she speak of it to Dame Philippa, who could with such good reason raise her fine eyebrows and say: 'You should have thought of this while you were a novice.' Through her novitiate Amy had been idle and inattentive, for at first she could think of nothing but the pleasure of eating such delicate food and the discomfort of always feeling hungry, and afterwards she was so constantly sickly and sleepy that even with a new will to learn she could not profit by her lessons. Dame Philippa had said that it was useless to waste any more time on such a dunce, she knew enough to scrape through the office with the lead of the others, and that must suffice. Yet it was just in that last year when she was dismissed to run errands and be useful that she began to know herself clear-witted and to long for learning, and at the same time to be overcome with shyness.

She waited, but Sir Ralph did not come. At last, still clutching the cobwebs in her hot young hand and with the Latin murmuring in her head like a charm of bees, she went away.

At that time Sir Ralph was mounting the ridge whence he had so often looked back to admire the spire. But now he walked with his eyes to the ground, warily; for he had all but stepped upon an adder. This had frightened him, his heart still felt bruised by the leap of blood which had assaulted it, and when he poked the ground with his staff the staff wavered with his wavering hand. Turning at last for his look at the spire he found that it was already out of sight, sunk below the watershed. No matter! What was one spire more or less to a man who was going to see so many, and at his journey's end, among the ships and spires of London, the spire of Saint Paul's?

Most old women are somnolent, but the new prioress of Oby was as wakeful as an aspen. On this hot afternoon when the common wish was to sit still and be shaded she had been taken with a desire for exercise. Accordingly, the nuns were playing at battledore and shuttlecock. It was years since anyone at Oby had played this game, and it seemed that they might yet be saved by Dame Philippa's statement that it was so long since any of her novices had played at it that she fancied the bats and the cocks had been mislaid.

'Mislaid? I suppose you mean thrown away? And who gave you leave to throw away our property? Mislaid, indeed. There is no such thing as mislaying. Either they are here or they are not here. I suppose I must look for myself.'

Before anyone could intervene she had looked for herself and found – an easy matter, since they were lying where they had lain for the last ten years. Remarking that it was bad enough to have Dame Cecily cumbering the establishment, but that was nothing, every nun in her house was blind as a bat, and none so blind as those who wouldn't see, the prioress added that they would now spend a pleasant recreation together.

In her youth when battledore and shuttlecock had been fashionable the prioress had excelled in it. Even now she played with grisly agility; the more grisly because her style of playing preserved all the bygone graces of the early century – the upright carriage with the head a little on one side, the arched wrist and the alert expression. She pranced to and fro like a shuttlecock impelled by some invisible bat. Dame Eleanor incautiously remarked to Dame Lovisa that the prioress looked like an old shuttlecock herself. Dame Lovisa incautiously smiled. Immediately they were bidden to play a match. As Dame Eleanor was tall and stout and Dame Lovisa short, crooked, and narrow-chested, their match gave opportunities for a great deal of mortifying comment. Like many deaf people the prioress spoke her thoughts aloud, and scattered disparagement and insult with no intention to be wounding. As the air grew hotter, and even she began to be jaded and dizzy from so much exercise, she quite genuinely felt that she was suffering to forward the general good, and that they were all having a pleasant recreation together, or should be; and if they disliked it, it was no fault of hers. Speaking her thoughts aloud she remarked that it was a pity that nowadays no one enjoyed simple pleasures or knew how to move gracefully; really there was nothing to choose between the clumsiness of Dame Philippa and the clumsiness of Dame Amy, whose build and breeding would make her clumsy anyhow.

'Now then, now then!' she cried out 'Why do you all stand puffing and sweating, my daughters? This is the hour of recreation. We must play.'

In the latest re-shuffle of posts Dame Lilias had been appointed infirmaress. Nailing herself to her office she now came forward and bellowed politely that doubtless their dear Mother remembered that the spring blood-letting had recently taken place. Many of the nuns were still feeling its effect and found it painful to play games.

'We do not come into nunneries to pamper the flesh,' said the old woman, drawing herself up. Raising her voice she said that they must do without Dame Lilias, who rather than play at battledore and shuttlecock preferred to sit in the shade and await another message from Saint Leonard.

Sir Ralph had told himself that when he got to Lintoft he would stop at the priest's house and rest for an hour or so. Then it would be pleasant to walk on through the cooling evening. Though at the moment he could not remember the priest's name he remembered the man well enough – a lanky young man, fretful and impulsive, who was inclined to pity himself and to think he was the only scholar set down among the barbarians since Ovid. But as Sir Ralph approached the parsonage he saw a strange priest in the garden engaged in taking a swarm of bees: a middle-aged man with pursed lips and a waddling gait, a man who was a stranger to him and yet somehow called up the recollection of some distant mishap. So avoiding him and the bees, Sir Ralph went on till he met a boy herding a flock of geese, and asked him where he could buy a drink. The boy said that his mother sold cider, and directed him to a hut near by. It was a tumbledown dwelling, and so stinking that Sir Ralph preferred to sit on a bench outside. Bringing him the cider the woman of the house greeted him by name and asked him where he was going.

'To London,' he told her.

'To London?' she said. Her voice was heavy with stupidity and stupid surprise. Presently she called to another woman and said: 'Look, he's going to London. But what would take him thither?'

'There are some priests of our way of thinking,' the second woman answered. 'And what a great staff he has! – if he's strong enough to use it.' Together they came over and stared at him, and the second woman asked him why he had not set out before – with the others, she said. But the westering sun shone full in his face and the cider was heavy, so he blessed them and hoped they would go away; and presently they did so.

He woke with a start, feeling bemused and stiff. But his staff was to hand and the track lay before him. After he had walked for a while he began to recollect the talk in the alehouse. It had been about Death. Death was travelling through England, faster than those who travelled to escape it. Whichever road you took, said one man, Death went by you on that road and sat grinning to await you at your journey's end. There was no outwitting such a Death. This Death, said another, was an old woman; for it killed more men than women, and more men in their strength than children or the aged: only an old woman would have such a degree of malice. A third said that Death had come into England by a port in the south called Mamillion Regis, and travelled by the old grass-roads, the roads which had been before the time of the Romans. 'You frighten yourselves with this nonsense,' he had said, striking his hand on the board. 'Do you suppose Death wears boots?' Yet this much was true, the Black Death had come; and that was why they were all going to London. He too was going to London; and yet it seemed to him he had another errand.

This much he certainly knew: that he had been this way before. Presently he would cross a small brook and after that he would be sick. Then he would be lightened of the pain in his head, a pain that beat against his temples and hung an obstacle of darkness between him and the growing light in the east. He had only to traverse this last belt of woodland where the flies buzzed among the trampled fern; then he would come to the brook; then he would see the sun.

He saw it: a scarlet disk in a black sky. He tried to lift it from the paten but somehow it eluded his grasp and sank below the horizon. Uttering a heavy sigh he pitched forward and lay still.

Sir John was in his first sleep and taking swarms of mild gigantic bees when he was disturbed by blockings and shoutings which presently turned into a voice bidding him to come at once to the Oby priest, who was dying. 'Saddle my beast!' he shouted; but the voice replied that he would get there as quickly on foot for the dying man was at Mary Kettle's house. Another voice chimed in, saying that they could carry the man no further because of his great weight. The voices were unknown to him though they were voices of the locality and when he hurried from the chancel door carrying the oil and the holy elements his first question (for he was a man of methodical curiosity) was, who were they? Thomas Scole from Oby and his cousin Sylvester Scole, they replied. They had found the priest lying across the trackway a matter of a mile beyond Lintoft. He lay like a dead man, and a weasel was sporting around him, but as they turned him over and stared at his round pale face in the moonlight he had begun to groan. They had dashed him with water from the brook to revive him, but he only groaned the more, and so terribly that they decided he was beyond all ministrations save those of a woman and a priest. Staggering under the load of his bulk they had carried him back as far as Mary Kettle's house, and there he lay.

'I wonder how he came to be going that way,' mused Sir John. 'For that matter, how did you come to be there, and after sundown, since you are both Oby men?'

'He must have had some journey in mind,' said one of them evasively, 'for I cut him a staff this very forenoon.' The other man added that many were travelling at this time, both young and old.

'But some started later than others,' Sir John replied meaningfully. Though neither answered he could feel their confidence warming the silence, and he went on to speak of the Lintoft men who had already set out for London, and of the common distress and the common hope that the king might take pity on the plight of poor labourers.

'If it were not for William Holly we might have gone along with the Lintoft men,' said the one called Sylvester. 'One thinks twice and thrice of leaving wife and children behind at the mercy of that old extortioner.'

'That's as may be,' said the one called Thomas. 'To speak for myself, it's the thought of William Holly that brings me here. To hear the way he overrules all in the court of the manor you'd think he was judge and accuser, king and council, god and the devil. That's not justice!'

'They say he cheats the nuns beyond all measure,' said Sir John.

'He cheats us worse,' Thomas said, and his cousin added that they were skinned by both alike. Thus talking cheerfully of the wrongs of the poor they came to Mary Kettle's house.

Though it was so mean a hovel she welcomed them with composure. The homes which are too poor for any other entertainment are always prepared to give hospitality to death. Mary Kettle had brought out her stumps of candle, her Palm Sunday cross, her cup of holy water and the sprig of box to sprinkle with. There was a sheaf of clean straw under Sir Ralph's head. As the priest entered she fell on her knees with as much air of leisured dignity as if she had been a countess in her castle.

Something of the same grand manner had fallen on the dying

man. It was as though Mary Kettle's conviction that everything was taking place exactly as it must and should take place had extended itself to him. He was the wax which she had modelled into its final form before it cooled and set. The mad priest of Oby was dying as decorously as a prince of the church, giving a tenuous assenting consciousness to the ceremonies of his departure. He made only one request and that was really more a suggestion than anything else. There was a nun of Oby, he said, to whom he wished to say something; what, he could not remember; but if he could see her, her presence might prompt him.

Mary Kettle's neighbour had come in to bear a hand, and after Sir John had finished and gone the two women sat down to watch out the night. They talked of deaths gone by and deaths to come, of storms and snowfalls, miraculous cures, charms to aid cows and children, which woods to burn green and which to burn dry, taxes and tithes and the cost of living, the signs of a hard winter, and how to foretell the sex of the unborn child. They remembered old times, and the people who had gone from the manor either by death or departure, they unravelled cousinships and marriages and traced the long story of the blue cloak which Anne Hamlet who had been Sir John's first housekeeper, had won by a wager from the miller's wife. They talked of the men who had gone from Lintoft to join in the peasants' march, and of John Ball, the poor man's priest and of the wickedness of London and the wickedness of Waxelby. Sometimes a groan or a mumble from the man they watched would intervene in their conversation and they broke off, and said a Hail Mary. Then their talk began again, and they laughed from time to time, not because what they spoke of was particularly merry, but because of the oddness of the world and the surprisingness of mankind.

The room lightened, the lark began to sing, then the wood-dove, then all the birds together. Where one had seen a star through a hole in the roof one now saw the blue of day. Mary Kettle bent over Sir Ralph, and smoothed his hair and considered him. He would last many hours yet, she said, perhaps even to another morning. Her neighbour said that however long he lasted she would stay within call to give a hand at the last. She had noticed it before, said Mary Kettle: just as a child will be born and then be a long time before it will take the nipple, there are dying folk who are in a manner of speaking already dead and yet it is a long time before the soul knows what it wants and leaves them. Looking more attentively at Sir Ralph she exclaimed: 'Why, it is the same man who drank the cider and gave us his blessing!'

'Well, of course it is. Who else should he be?'

'I never thought to ask. It was dark, he was dying . . . that's all I thought of. What a numskull I am!' And she laughed at her own oddity.

XIV

Prioress Margaret

(*July 1381–March 1382*)

When the messenger came in the first purity of the morning to say that Sir Ralph was dying at Lintoft and had asked for her, Dame Lilias grieved to think that the rambling mind which had once been so near hers and then had rambled off again should be troubled in its last moments by any compunction at having forsaken or failed her. How should she speak? It would be easy to say that she had outgrown her wish to be an anchoress, and that to be a nun at Oby now contented her. It would be easy to say and easy to see through. He had treated her too well in the past to be lied to now. She must tell him that between them they had failed, that heaven had put some fault in both of them which had prevented the design and which they must forgive each other. Not for a moment had she foreseen that the prioress would refuse her permission to go to the dying man.

In the shock of this refusal she remained unaware of the turmoil that ensued. Dame Sibilla had been the first to expostulate with the prioress. That might well be expected. But when she came away, hoarse with upbraiding and shaking with temper like a wren in song, who would have supposed that Dame Amy, the young, the dull, the negligible dumpling, should be the next to take up battle? Dame Cecily followed on Dame Amy, and was perhaps the most menacing of the three, for her blindness was like an armour to her, and she threw herself into the fight with the added passion and resentment of her personal deprivation. By this time Dame Sibilla had recovered enough to be inflaming the others, and while Dame Cecily was still inveighing against the formalism and malice of the old, who might come to know, sooner than they reckoned, the sensations of the dying, and the prioress was still quoting the bull *Periculoso*, and asserting that this was yet another example of Dame Lilias's anxiety to gad, all the nuns gathered in a body to protest, and even compelled Dame Dorothy to go along with them and to give her valuable opinion that the wish of a dying man merits some attention since it is in all probability the last wish he will ever conceive.

They harassed the old woman with the less mercy because she herself showed no weakness. She had the frank and infuriating obstinacy of a young child or an animal. They were quite surprised when all of a sudden she broke down and began to weep and wail and declare herself worn out by their attacks. This it was, she said, tears leaping off her old nose with youthful vehemence – this it was to uphold discipline and good report among the young. And was it for this that they had elected her, only to make her a target for their scorn and satire? God pity the old in a world that had no pity for them! She wept and panted so violently, and trembled so much and grew so red in the face, that Dame Lilias was called for. Dame Lilias had been at her prayers, and her eyes were sunken with bitter weeping. But she dealt skilfully and gently with the old woman, putting hot cloths to her feet and cold cloths to her head, and gave her a sedative, disguising the bitter taste of the poppy seeds with honey and spices. She was long past any thoughts of returning good for evil. Someone was sick, and must be dealt with, that was all she knew.

The others watched her with curiosity and unwilling admiration. Afterwards they attempted to express their partisanship. She answered them without knowing what they said, and supposed that these were further expressions of the old dislike, but wrapped in a new weed. Undoubtedly she is proud, thought Dame Amy. She looks meek but she is proud at heart. But she herself would be proud, she reflected, if she were so learned a nun that a dying priest called for her to help him in dying.

When a messenger came on the following day with the news that Sir Ralph was dead they began to think of other things. The prioress was re-clothed with considerations of what was proper to do: the provision of a new priest, the funeral of the old. She looked forward to these interesting opportunities of doing things correctly and with decorum. Dame Lovisa, who for a whole day had ceased to think about Dame Adela and was much revived by the change, gave her mind to Sir Ralph's will: Dame Matilda, she knew, had expected a legacy to the convent. Dame Joan thought how delightful it would be if her cousin Oswald could be appointed as the new priest. She was painfully lonely in this place, where now even Dame Amy was turning away from her; if a Sir Oswald were to replace a Sir Ralph she could at least be sure of a familiar countenance to watch during the sermon, not to speak of the consideration which must accrue to the convent priest's cousin-germane. Dame Dorothy also meditated on the empty post. There was her nephew: a good quiet man of exemplary conduct and full of sound sense, but unfortunately without the flashiness which procures a man advancement. He had such a loud, clear voice, too; just what the prioress would enjoy. Dame Sibilla with so many living relations in the church thought with concentration of a dead one. She had no doubt that Sir Ralph had some last counsel to give Dame Lilias about becoming an anchoress. Now he was dead, dead as Walter Dunford; and though for some time she had not heard the owl, her mind was not at ease.

In spite of all their planning Sir Ralph was buried at Lintoft. Lintoft had no men to spare for bringing his body across the heath, and William Holly refused to send men from Oby to fetch it. This was no time, he bellowed to the prioress, for rambling to and fro with corpses, Sir Ralph could lie at Lintoft and thank his stars that he lay securely, and that he would not wake up and hear the sods crackling over his head. The living had no such assurance.

The prioress blinked and sniffed and bridled her stiff neck.

'I see no insurrection unless it is yours,' she said crossly. 'I have never heard such nonsense in my life. What? Set fire to the monasteries? Pillage the religious houses? Let them try that here, and they shall soon learn whether or no holy church is above them. Go away, I don't wish to hear another word about it.'

Dame Matilda, Dame Helen ... William Holly sighed for the good reliable treasuresses of former days. He knew that it would be waste of breath to carry his troubles to Dame Dorothy, for though he could soon frighten her into fits the prioress would frighten her out again. He waited for an opportunity to talk to Dame Sibilla. He had always found her a sensible body. The difficulty would be to get her to himself; but seeing her walking in the orchard with Dame Philippa he decided, since time pressed, to tackle the pair of them. As he approached he heard Dame Philippa say: 'If only I could pack off my novices! But where could we send them?'

'They will be in God's hands like the rest of us – if it really comes to the worst.'

Dame Philippa shrugged her shoulders.

'Of course they will. But it is easy enough to expect the worst. What I expect is something far more troublesome: half a dozen louts with their faces blacked, everyone screaming and bawling, a cold kitchen, no proper meals, everything in a hurly-burly and my little girls running wild through it all. If I had no responsibility I daresay I could look forward to having my throat cut as piously as you do.'

Meanwhile Dame Sibilla had beckoned him to come forward.

'We were saying how sad it is, good William, that Sir Ralph had to be buried at Lintoft. However bad the times, surely people would respect the corpse of a priest and give it safe conduct.'

'I can't say what they do for the dead, Madam Sibilla. I've got to concern myself with the living. Do they come this way we shall need every man on the place, not that I say that more than half of them will be either leal or willing. I'd as soon trust a toad as any Scole, and Noots no better. But how did you hear these stories, ladies both? The prioress, she make no account of them.'

'It was the Wivelham curate.'

'What's he? I'd never believe a word from Wivelham, the only true tongue ever came from Wivelham were Jesse Figg's Magdalen. The Wivelham curate! I daresay his knees were knocking under him. What did he say?'

'Pack of lies!' he ejaculated, when she had finished her recital of the curate's report. But his lip twitched and the fixed red colour on his cheekbones stared out of a yellowing face. The curate's story bore out in detail what he had heard himself.

'And the prioress, she won't hear of it? Well, I'll tell you what I've done. I've sent to Dudham for two of my nephews to come over here, either one of them would be worth a dozen of Oby fellows. But what about the gold and silver, the altar-ware and so forth? That's what they'll be after, they'll think of that before they think of driving away the cows or cutting your throats. Do you take my advice, you'll hide it. Burying would be best. Leave no more than the old pewter stuff for the Wivelham curate.

Good enough for him. He make out with nothing better at Wivelham.'

'I think they will be more likely to cut our throats if they find nothing worth stealing,' said Dame Philippa.

'They'll never do that, not they! Where they find no riches they do no harm. It's the rich houses they set on. By the mass, I'd like to see the Prior of Etchingdon this day. He sing small, I'll be bound.'

He cackled with abrupt laughter, and Dame Philippa smiled. Dame Sibilla crossed herself, saying correctly that sacrilege was no laughing matter. When William left them she repeated this more earnestly. By some means or other, she said, the altar vessels must be preserved from falling into unhallowed hands. If on a pretext of cleaning them ... Dame Philippa gave an unconvinced assent. True, they had suffered loss enough with the altar-hanging, they did not want to lose more. But what could be done while the prioress refused to stir?

That night Dame Lovisa helped Dame Sibilla to carry out the chest to William Holly. One of his renowned nephews was with him, and the burying-place, William explained, would be known to him and the nephew alone, for the hen that cackles least rears most chicks. The night was warm and so still that they could hear the Waxle Stream gurgling among the rushes, and the desultory cry of a water-bird. Then a bright light twitched on the southward horizon. They all started with terror, not realising till it flashed on them again that it was only summer lightning. Dame Lovisa said conversationally that it was early in the season for thunder-storms, but that the tuft of seaweed (by which they now guessed at the weather since Magdalen Figg could no longer foretell it to them) had been moistening for a coming rain.

'That rain may quench some hot ashes,' said the nephew from Dudham, speaking for the first time.

The two nuns crept back to the dormitory, but no one was asleep. Dame Joan had seen the flash of lightning and was sure, silly creature, that it was some roof that burned. She lay face downward, bewailing, and Dame Eleanor knelt beside her, trying to stifle her cries by pressing her face into the bolster; for Dame Philippa had come in to say that the noise could be heard in the novices' chamber and that they would all awake and scream in sympathy unless Dame Joan could be hushed.

'Amy, I want Amy,' lamented the poor wretch. 'O Amy, why did we ever let ourselves be made nuns of? We would be alive now, if we had been left in the world.'

Dame Lovisa went across to the window, where Dame Amy's snub profile was silhouetted, and pulled at her arm. 'Since for once you are wanted, I think you might bestir yourself,' she said. But Dame Amy continued to kneel by the window, shaking her head and muttering the prayers for the dying. They might talk of lightning, but she knew better.

The demeanour of these two nuns gave a dreadful sanction to the forebodings of the others. Nothing could dislodge them from a conviction that if the insurgents came to Oby they would be merciless in vengeance; and it was hard to refute an inner voice which reasoned that if anyone were likely to know how the peasants would behave Dame Amy and Dame Joan were the likeliest. 'Well, well, I'm afraid you will have to suffer with the rest of us,' was Dame Lovisa's ill-judged taunt. Dame Joan burst into renewed howling and when Dame Lovisa glanced round for approval she saw only pale and noncommittal looks.

Meanwhile, though everyone spoke of precautions, none was taken. Dame Dorothy, being both the prioress's crony and treasuress seemed the natural go-between. But nothing could be done with her. Self-importance stiffened her as frost stiffens a rotten board, and to no more effect. She would neither listen nor act. Though she was as much afraid as any of them her fears evaporated in vanity and fluster. Her only contribution to the common concern was to be meticulously accurate about the stories which now came in day after day, each louder and nearer than the last. 'They did not kill five at Blyberwick. They killed three,' she would say, or remind them that a house was not set on fire on the Eve of a Saint but on the Saint's Day itself, since the flames were not kindled till after midnight.

Rumour is a poison that carries its own medicine. After the alarms of the first few days it became as animating as a fever to hear stories, to compare one version with another, to reckon up ravages and calculate where the insurgents would strike next. It was remarkable that everyone now spoke of the labourers as though they were some unknown kind of beings, people from under the earth or over the sea. No one remembered what a few weeks before everyone had known and feared: that the revolt had sprung up from the soil as naturally as nettles, and that from every manor men had gone out in hope and desperation who were now coming back in despair. Perhaps this was natural. It went against the grain to identify such familiar useful shapes, figures at the plough's tail or at sheep-shearing, with the actors in these stories of wild and efficient vengeance, and to think of those wind-bitten red hands as reddened with blood. It was easier to listen to the stories from the other side: stories of reprisals, executions by scores, miraculous escapes, and the immense popularity of the young king, whom one and the same breath reported as loved for his clemency and dreaded for his ruthlessness. On the whole the most comforting rumour, and the most pervading, was that the rebels were powerless because no one supported them, that they were riven by internal jealousies, had neither weapons nor leadership, and were dying in thousands from hunger, thirst, and exposure.

Oby, though possibly no sillier than any other threatened community, became so drunk with rumour that quite a small impact with reality sent them reeling. Sunday brought the Wivelham curate. Absorbed in his personal preoccupations of fear and hay-fever he went through the mass without noticing any change in the altar vessels. The prioress was better disciplined, and had more elevation of mind. When the Canon began she noticed the substitution of pewter for silver, and as soon as the mass ended she sent for Dame Sibilla to learn the reason for this. Dame Sibilla lost her head and replied that the better vessels were being cleaned. The prioress demanded to see them. Dame Sibilla had to change her tune to a more heroic note. As sacrist, she said, she had commissioned William Holly to bury them. She had made an inventory, and here it was. Dame Lovisa, looking as sour as a sloe, then came forward and added her witness. The two offenders were immediately locked into the infirmary, to remain without their dinners and meditate on their effronteries while the prioress carried out a thorough investigation.

As Dame Sibilla and Dame Lovisa had been unusually skilful in keeping their own counsel the investigation, though as discursive and acrimonious as investigations commonly are, and extending till long after the normal dinner-hour, yielded no result except a general hardening of opinion against the prioress for not having safeguarded the treasure herself. Dame Dorothy said at intervals that if William Holly had buried the chest he was likely to know where it was, but had no reward for her pains except to be told by the prioress to hold her tongue, since in times like these – the first admission the prioress had made that these times were not like other times – it was essential to keep any lapses from cloistered serenity private from the outer world, lest some scandalous advantage be taken of the scandal. Thus it was not till early in the afternoon (by which time Dame Philippa had also been despatched to the infirmary for unseasonably demanding that her novices should no longer be kept without their dinner) that a messenger was sent to call the bailiff. The messenger came back saying that Master Holly had ridden to Dudham for a christening feast and was not expected back till nightfall. Clear as day it was revealed to the prioress that he had absconded and taken the altar plate with him. Her dinnerless rage soared to new heights and descended on Dame Amy, who selected this moment to wander into modernistic speculations and to ask why the rite of the mass could not be as efficaciously celebrated with pewter vessels as with gold or silver ones. She was still trying to beat Dame Amy, the nuns still at liberty were whisking to and fro in order to thwart her, the nuns in confinement were banging and kicking against the infirmary door, and the three little novices, having plundered the kitchen, were wandering up and down outside the building in pursuit of an escaped goldfinch, when Henry Yellowlees arrived in his capacity of custos.

He had been in London with Perkin de Craye. Though they had travelled back unharmed he had seen enough to make him uneasy for Oby, and where the track through Lintoft turned off from King Street he had parted company and ridden eastward. At Lintoft he learned of Sir Ralph's death.

Yet the news did not really become true to him till he halted before the gate-house and looked up at the old man's window, where the shutter knocked in the easy summer wind. He looked away from the window to the spire, which seemed to nestle against the blue sky. Unforeseen tears rushed to his eyes and blinded him. He was still weeping when the novices came up and began to tell him their news. Naturally they did not say a word of Sir Ralph – they were taken up with more recent events; but their forgetfulness reproached him like a comment on his own forgetfulness. That vague project for getting Sir Ralph to London in the bishop's retinue ... he had considered it and rejected it and had gone to London himself with never a further thought of the old man. Now he might consider it as much as he pleased, it would all be in vain, it was all and for ever too late.

Remembering what he had come for he dismounted and hitched up his horse and knocked on the door. When he had knocked for some time he tried it. It was not barred, and he walked in.

To the prioress his arrival was susceptible of only one explanation: he had come to ask about the altar plate. Wasting no time on formalities she swept into her account of what had happened. Rage had so much renewed her faculties that he could hardly reconcile her with the Dame Margaret of the past, she was not even very hard of hearing till he, beginning to understand what it was all about, remarked that Dame Sibilla and Dame Lovisa had taken a very sensible precaution.

'Aye, indeed, I am glad you agree with me. Who knows what else they might have chosen to purloin away? I have a great mind to keep them shut up till the vessels are found again.'

Finding that he could not force any sense into her he thought he would try what fear might do. He began to roar out news of the rebellion, describing the ruined houses he had seen, and saying that they took it very seriously in London. But all she would hear was such words as *riot* and *rebellion*, and these she applied to the state of things in her own household, assuring him with tossings of the head that she would soon put an end to it, for with the ringleaders shut up she could master the other malcontents, and adding that it would be better for the people in London to mind their own business; what happened at Oby was no concern of theirs. Dame Dorothy plucked at her sleeve, and screamed about fire-raising and murder, but was briefly bidden not to make mountains out of molehills, a household of insubordinate nuns was bad enough without rushing on to suppose they would begin killing and burning.

He looked round for someone who might hear reason, and began to speak to Dame Lilias. But Dame Eleanor shouldered her aside and began to give him her account of the quarrel; Dame Cecily, ejected from the infirmary, clung to his arm and poured out her indignation because the prioress had prevented Dame Lilias from going to see Sir Ralph on his death-bed; Dame Amy demanded the release of the prisoners; Dame Joan implored to be taken away immediately in order to safeguard her virginity. Dame Lilias, too, was telling him something, but what she said was lost in the uproar, worse now because the prioress was again assuring him that she needed no assistance to restore order and that he was wasting his time in listening to her nuns: listening to them only made them worse. At length he lost patience and walked out, thinking he would find William Holly. Learning that William Holly was at Dudham he rode back to Lintoft. He had meant to ask for a night's lodging at Oby, but now the thought of an evening with Sir John seemed as soothing as an evening with Seneca.

And after all if he had been there that night his presence would not have made much difference. It would have taken more than he to prevent Dame Joan from being raped, her fears were so implacably bent on that catastrophe; nothing he could have said to the prioress would have shaken her conviction that these men were in a conspiracy to release the three imprisoned nuns, so that as long as she could keep them away from the infirmary it was immaterial where else they ransacked; this being so it was inevitable that Dame Lovisa, the hastiest of the prisoners, should have wrenched her stomach trying to squirm out through the window-slit; and as for the fire, the rain quenched it before it had done any substantial damage. So he told himself, having ridden with Sir John to offer what help and consolation they might. They had been listening, deploring, inspecting, reassuring, advising for some hours before anyone remembered to tell them that William Holly had been killed. He and the nephews and some of the older men on the manor had run to the defence of the convent: to begin with, a battle of words, for the raiders had been placable enough, saying that they were only in search of food, and intended the nuns no harm; that every dog has his day and this was the day of the drovers' dogs against the lap-dogs – a sentiment in which most of the defenders concurred. But William Holly, finding his authority made a joke of by both his opponents and his followers, flew into a rage and attacked the ring-leader, who hit back with a mortal blow. It was after this that the fighting began, in which the defenders soon had the worst of it and gave way, leaving the raiders to have their will of the place.

These calamities, which had put the prioress to bed, brought Dame Sibilla very much to the fore. She looked uncommonly like her great uncle as she tripped to and fro ordering this and commending that and speaking to all and sundry with a particular trustfulness and simplicity. If she were not actually in two places at once she got very near it; and she was Bishop Walter to the life when she turned to Henry saying how thankful she was to whichever of the saints had put it into her mind to hide away the altar vessels, and what a cordial it would be to the poor prioress to think that they were preserved from falling into unsanctified hands. The protection of the altar, the safety of the novices: those were the essentials, and both, she thanked God, had been granted. As for poor Dame Joan, one must thank God who had preserved her senses from any soil of complicity: such was her fear, she had not known what was happening to her until it had happened.

'And what have you to say about my stomach?' interposed Dame Lovisa, looking uglier than ever because she was in such pain.

'That you should be lying down with hot cloths on it, as Dame Lilias prescribed,' replied the Dunford with ready sweetness.

But a portion of Dame Sibilla's gratitude was premature. William Holly was dead and the Dudham nephew who had helped him bury the chest could not identify the place. They had carried it a long way, so much he could remember, and that he had said to his uncle that it would be daybreak before they had disposed of it. But William Holly, full of obstinacy, had held on till they had come circuitously to the field lying fallow, and there, on its northern edge, the chest was put down while William Holly turned around and around like a dog searching. At last he had chosen a place to his mind. The chest was buried, the tussocks replaced, any loose earth scraped up and scattered about. The nephew had said at the time that it would be hard to find the place again, but the old stiffneck had answered there was no need of any mark, he had not lived so many years at Oby to be at a loss in finding what he had hidden.

Such was the nephew's story. Whether or no one believed it, one could not disprove it. Next year's ploughing, he added consolingly, would uncover the chest. It must have been buried deep, beneath the reach of a plough-share. It was never found.

This was a serious loss to the community. It was also a setback to Dame Sibilla. Though she retained her post of sacrist (the prioress remarking that since there was nothing valuable left Dame Sibilla might safely be left in charge of it) her chances of rising further were small indeed. Dame Lovisa was also in disgrace for her part in the misadventure. But no one put much heart into these recriminations, and the discrediting of Dame Sibilla and Dame Lovisa seemed only part of the general melancholy and loss of lustre. Oby had not even a distinction of ill-fortune to support its self-esteem. The loss of their altar plate, three tubs of butter, two sides of bacon, part of a roof, and one virginity was a small item in the general tale of outrage and spoliation.

By common consent this was no time to make outlays or take on new responsibilities. Sir Ralph's chamber remained empty and its red hangings were taken down to replace the scorched hangings in the infirmary. The Wivelham curate, or Sir John, or a friar from Waxelby, shared out the duties of his post amongst them – to the disappointment of Dame Joan, who had wistfully appointed cousin Oswald not only priest to the convent but godfather to the child she would bear in the new year. As for the bailiffship, it fell by default of a better to William Holly's son: a bad appointment, for Adam Holly was the usual dynastic heir, inheriting all his father's unpopularity and none of his ability. The harvest, however, was no worse than usual, the Martinmas cattle no thinner, and Henry Yellowlees made several attempts to convince the nuns that they were really no worse off than they had been before; for the loss of their plate, he explained, made no difference to their income, and they certainly had not thought of selling it. These sophistries consoled no one. Every time they looked towards their shabby altar they felt themselves poor and knew themselves come down in the world, and the words of Jeremy, *How is the fine gold become dim*, wailed through their minds.

A little before Epiphany he forced himself to pay them another visit. It was just such a day, cold and foggy, as the day he first came to Oby, quarrelled with William Holly and all but quarrelled with Sir Ralph. Eight years had gone by since then, years in which his circumstances had bettered almost beyond belief. Then he had felt this post of custos an advancement. Now he only continued in it out of complaisance. Then he had been a nondescript poor clerk with nothing to back him but a cousinly recommendation, which was only a politer form of the recommender washing his hands of him. Now he was secretary to the bishop, and a bosom-secretary at that, he helped young scholars and wore leather boots. But today his own rise in the world presented itself to him in inversion, telling him that everyone else had gone down, and was either dead or impoverished and dwindling. Adam Holly walked beside him and instead of William's sturdy grumbles he heard a vague and complacent talk of what was going well and no complaints at all.

Indoors they were subdued as ever, and Dame Cecily was dying. The house was cold. It smelled of dejection and incompetence. Partly from compassion, partly to be quit of a sense of responsibility, he told himself that they must be fitted out with another priest, and on an impulse he told the prioress that the bishop intended to appoint one. She flushed, and said sharply that she was in treaty for one herself. This was plainly a lie. But it would serve; for having told her lie to keep the bishop from interfering in her domain the proud old woman would feel obliged to substantiate it, a priest would be got from somewhere and with the stimulus of a newcomer Oby would creak into life again. He was not surprised when, a couple of weeks later, Perkin de Craye handed him a letter with the words: 'Here is a cackle from your henhouse.' The letter, after a great deal of preamble about decorum and necessity and the will of God and obeying the Rule and making exceptions, came to the point of asking the bishop's permission for two nuns to solicit alms in the cathedral city, because of the poverty of the house and especially to buy new altar vessels to replace those which had been lost. It was clear the prioress could not brook that a new priest should find nothing but pewter.

What a deal of discussion, he thought, must have gone to the framing of that letter, what a shaking of heads and pulling down of upper-lips, how much sighing and summing and sideways peeping! – and he wondered which of the nuns would be chosen to go begging.

That was soon settled. Having haled herself to the ignominy of begging, the prioress found a cordial consolation in ordaining that Dame Sibilla who had lost them their plate should stand soliciting for alms to buy new. As for Dame Sibilla's companion, Dame Dorothy soon settled that. 'Let it be Dame Lilias. She is the one we can most easily spare.' Dame Eleanor bestowed a commiserating grimace on her cousin. All this, she meditated, was the height of silliness, and they might beg till their feet were too swollen to carry them before they would ogle the cost of a chalice from the faithful. When she was prioress she would set about it properly, and a fine new set should be presented by her gratified relations or the anxious parents of some socially half-baked novice. Meanwhile, let it run as badly as they pleased. It would be all the more glory to her when she took over and guided things in her way. She had lived under four prioresses, each one of them a bungler of opportunities: it would be a strange thing if she had not learned how to do better.

Tossed between pride and panic the prioress could not for some time decide whether her expeditionary nuns should travel creditably or economically. Economy won. During Lent the Waxelby fish-merchants sent a string of waggons inland. By dint of riding to Waxelby along the Hog Trail the nuns could take their place with the fish in Master Bilby's waggon, and make their journey without further trouble to anyone. As for their lodging . . . Dame Sibilla here intervened to recall the widow she had lodged with at the time of her great-uncle's death. Such a good woman; so pious; so well-thought of: without actually saying so Dame Sibilla managed to make it plain that the widow's piety was so exemplary that she might even put them up for nothing. If Dame Sibilla compared this impending departure with the splendour of her journey to Bishop Walter's death-bed she was too discreet to mention it. She seemed wholly occupied with practical preparations for their journey and with asking the prayers of those remaining at home for the success of the mission.

The convent had bought its herring and haberdine from Master Bilby for many years, and during that time no one had suspected that Master Bilby had any special devotion to the house of Our Lady and Saint Leonard. But when Dame Sibilla and Dame Lilias dismounted in the freezing early morning (they had set out soon after mattins in order to reach Waxelby in good time) they found themselves caught hold of, greeted in loud voices, supported on their staggering frozen feet to a warm room, their backs slapped, hot drinks poured down their throats, and an enormous breakfast laid before them. Dame Sibilla took it easily enough. Dame Lilias was almost overset by gratitude. Since the death of Dame Beatrix, and that was now twelve years ago, she had not felt physical kindness. Her indifference to opinion and her susceptibility to strong smells simultaneously tumbled off her. These rough Bilbys seemed like angels, and their red faces, glowing in the firelight, like the faces of seraphs incarnadined with love. She became speechless as a child, obediently swallowing whatever they gave her, and leaving the expression of thanks to Dame Sibilla. Yet oddly enough it was she whom the company afterwards chose to praise; and to his life's end young Edmund Bilby remembered the nun who had come in the early morning, and who had looked so careworn and spoken so gently that she might have been the Mother of God in the midst of her sorrows.

When the convoy started they found that after all they would not have to travel among the fish. Master Bilby showed them to their place in a waggon which was carrying a load of Spanish wool recently landed at the port; here, he said, they would journey both warm and soft. Then for a long time the carters shouted one to another, the horses stamped and snorted, jingling their bells. At last they set out.

The sun was now rising. Dame Sibilla pulled back the curtain of the waggon-tilt, and called to her companion to admire the great bulk of the Friar's Church, slowly assuming its real stature above the housetops. Kites, daws and seagulls were wheeling and screaming around it. A few minutes later the convoy slowed down. They had come to the bridge over the Waxle Stream, and there were tolls to be paid. Dignified with a bridge the familiar river looked quite different, its current more determined, its waters more brilliant. The two nuns said a prayer for the soul of the bridge-builder. After crossing the bridge the going became easier, for the waggons now travelled over the turf beside the sprawling rutted track; and Dame Sibilla hollowed herself a bed among the bales and settled down to sleep.

Dame Lilias continued to stare out on the strangeness of the world, noticing the purpled leaves that hung on the bramble-clumps, the mild white face of the foremost horse drawing the waggon that followed theirs, the slow whirl of the horizon where a windmill was now taking predominance over the Friar's Church. Her mind was full of contending impressions: excitement at beholding novelties, gratitude to the kind Bilbys, awkwardness and trepidation at the prospect before her. She shrank from the thought of begging. For many nights her dreams had been vexed with throngs of faces all regarding her with contempt and ill-will. She held out her begging-dish and they heaped it, not with alms but with pebbles, dying crows, and poached eggs. Somehow the dish would be cleared of these, and again she proffered it, and now a hand poured in gold pieces, more and more of them, till the dish tilted in her hand and amid cries of: *Clumsy! Look what you are doing!* the gold pieces spilled off and rolled away down a gutter and dissolved. But in reality, she said to herself, it will not be anything like that, for I shall stand as befits a nun, with my eyes cast down, and so however scornfully they look at me I shall not see them, I shall only see their feet. Yet feet too can express abhorrence. They can pause for the malevolent survey, they can trample past in anger. Caught back into her dreams, she had indeed lowered her gaze and was conscious of nothing but the wheeltracks leaving dark bruises on the frosty turf. At last with a sigh she wrenched herself out of her preoccupation and looked round for something which might speak to her of comfort, or at least of resignation. She looked; and it was as if new eyes had been put into her head.

The rough ground stretched for a little way and there broke off in a line of stiffened tussocks, heath bushes, and close gorse-clumps. Beyond this, half the world was hung with a blue mantle criss-crossed with an infinity of delicate creases, and the whole outspread mantle stirred as though a separate life were beneath it. Coming to her senses she knew that this must be the sea.

But nothing that she had seen in pictures or read in books or heard in sermons was true to what she saw. Their sea was dark, turbulent, vexed with storms, a metaphor of sin, and exiled from heaven. This was calm. It lay as blissfully asleep as though it still lay in the trance of its first creation. Its colour was like an unflawed virtue; it lay there and knew of nothing but the God who had made it. Remembering how she had heard a preacher declare that in heaven there would be no more sea she broke into spontaneous laughter.

Dame Sibilla, waking with a sense of something unprecedented, sat up and enquired: 'What was that? Who was laughing?'

'Me,' said Dame Lilias.

'Why? How extraordinary! I mean, you don't laugh very often, do you? Why were you laughing?'

'For joy. Look! That is the sea.'

'So it is! Heaven save us, how close it is! And what a long way up the sky it goes! It is certainly a very pretty colour. And this smell . . . I suppose that comes from the sea too. It's like the smell of fish.'

'Doesn't it make you feel very happy?'

'Yes. Yes, in a way it does. Look, that must be a ship. Do you see? But it is so calm I don't suppose any mischief will happen to them. I wonder where it goes to – this sea, I mean. Do you suppose it goes to France?'

The line of land began to dip and fall away. Now they saw a beach, with long waves running towards it and breaking there in solitude. They fell lightly, twirling like a skipping-rope, and the ripples ran scalloping up the beach and sank into the brown sand. The nuns continued to hang out of the waggon, staring and exclaiming. A sharp wind blew on their faces, but the sea did not look cold. Its pure colour, its air of nakedness, its leisured movement, all spoke of summer, and the foam scattering so gently from the folded blue of the waves looked no colder than cherry-blossom.

Even when the track bore inland and the last snatch of blue was lost the sea remained in their minds, and on their faces, too, for they continued to look somehow cleaned and quieted. Then they found that they were extremely hungry and Dame Sibilla undid the bundle that held the food for their journey. Seeing how scanty it was they were at first dismayed, and then began to laugh.

'I wish we could always travel, and never beg!' cried Dame Lilias, and added: 'Unless we begged for food.'

'When we are there we will do more than beg,' Dame Sibilla answered, speaking primly and yet cunningly.

'Why? What else?'

'What else, Dame Lilias? Why, with God's blessing and the help of Our Lady and Saint Leonard, we will manage your affair. What, did you think I had forgotten that you are to become an anchoress?'

'I? No . . . It is not to be.'

'Not to be? What nonsense! Just because there has been a little delay and because we have an old stick for our prioress? Surely you are not so faint-hearted?'

'I know I shall never be an anchoress. Let us talk of something else.'

'Never be an anchoress? But what is there to prevent it? The letters are there, we know that they reached my uncle. He spoke of it to me. He wished it, I know he wished it. You must not turn back now, it would distress him, even in heaven. And here we have this chance sent us by God, all that is needed is a little poke, we have only to make friends with some proper person who will set it all going. Why, if needs be I myself will speak to the bishop about it. Perhaps that would be the best plan. I will say to Master Yellowlees that I wish to . . .'

'No!'

'No? But your vocation, your vision? Can you disobey that? Yes, yes! I know it was not a vision. But you heard the saint speak, you felt his hand strike you – why, there was even a bruise! You cannot doubt such a token as that.'

Dame Lilias's hands rose like birds fluttering in a net. 'Listen,' she said. 'I hoped I need never speak of this, but I see I must. You remember how when Sir Ralph was dying he sent for me? And how the prioress forbade me to go?'

'Of course I remember it. It was shameful! I told the prioress so myself, and she has borne me a grudge ever since. Not that I mind. I did it gladly, doing it for your sake, and knowing that Sir

Ralph must have wished to say something more to you about your anchoressing.'

'It was very kind of you. I am very grateful. But when I went to the prioress Dame Dorothy was there too. She did not speak till the prioress had dismissed me and I was coming away. Then she called me back.'

'Well? What had she to say that you need take to heart? You must be used to her taunts by now.'

'Yes. So I thought. But she had something to say after all. It was not the saint who struck me. It was she, Dame Dorothy. I was in her way when she came to light the candles. She had always despised me, and finding me in her way her hatred overcame her and she hit me with all her strength. She confessed this before the prioress, holding a crucifix in her hand. I can have no reason to doubt she was telling the truth. After her confession she begged my pardon for having yielded to her hate of me, and then for misleading me, for allowing me to go on imagining that it was the saint who struck me. She knew of all that, you see. She knew I hoped to become an anchoress.'

'I swear I never told her!'

'Dame Alice told her.'

'Dame Alice? How did she know?'

'She heard it from the Prioress Matilda.'

It was Dame Sibilla who was overcome and wept, Dame Lilias who comforted; though not very well, for those experienced in despair are seldom good comforters, though the world prefers to believe otherwise. Indeed, with the levity of the wretched, Dame Lilias regretted that this confidence should have been drawn from her just at a time when the sea had given her something new to think about. Dame Sibilla was incapable of any such calculating considerations. She was absorbed in a perfectly straightforward turmoil of regret, indignation, and uneasiness of conscience – for how was she to avoid the thought that if only she had exercised a more reckless zeal to forward Dame Lilias's anchoressing Dame Lilias might by now be safely in her cell and Dame Dorothy's confession of no account to alter anything? The more she reflected, the more she became convinced that Dame Dorothy's interposition could and should be disregarded. If one looked at things in their true light, it really could have no bearing at all on the fact of Dame Lilias's vocation. Because an angry woman had dealt a blow, could the words of a saint be invalidated?

'But the Saint's very words! You heard them!'

'Yes, I heard them.'

'Well?'

'It was I who spoke them. They came from me, from my heart, not from anywhere beyond me.'

'But your feeling of relief, of heavenly consolation?'

'Very much what Dame Dorothy felt after she had hit me.'

Dame Sibilla cried out that she could only call this blasphemy. Dame Lilias said mildly that she was sorry.

'But Sir Ralph believed it?'

'He saw the bruise, and did not know how else to account for it. We were both misled through not knowing all the facts.'

After a pause Dame Sibilla said: 'Do you know what I think? I am convinced that Dame Dorothy has made up all this story. She pretends out of malice that it was she who hit you – having heard it all, you see, from that shameless Dame Alice. What could be more probable? – she has always persecuted you, and now she is doting. Very likely it is the devil speaking through her, to shake you in your vocation.'

'I heard her, you know. She had the very voice of truth.'

'You are so simple, so candid. You would believe anything. You always believe the last person who speaks to you.'

Dame Lilias looked at Dame Sibilla.

'Not always.'

Her angel told Dame Sibilla that it would be fruitless to continue the discussion just now. Just now she would do better to pray, and having prayed, to be kind to her unfortunate companion, and to pick up some wayside crumbs from the distractions of their journey. She prayed fervently while Dame Lilias continued to look at the world. Mixed in with her prayers were skirmishing cogitations as to how best – by persuasion, by bargaining, by holy intimidation? – Dame Lilias could be conjured into taking up the vocation she had relinquished. It was so particularly perverse of her to lose her faith at this juncture when everything had suddenly become so propitious and when the hand of God was so notably evident; for hearing of the begging expedition, and that she was to be made chief beggar, the heavenly intention had instantly been manifest to Dame Sibilla, delivered to her, as it were, in a little bundle; and she had seen exactly why she should have been called on to endure so much unmerited reproach because of the altar plate. By no other means – at any rate by no other means so satisfactory – could she and Dame Lilias have found themselves so well placed to approach the private ear of the bishop. There they would be, herself, and the bishop, and Dame Lilias; and the speech would be made introducing Dame Lilias's vocation and her own resolution – really only one degree short of a vocation in itself – to carry it to fulfilment. To end the speech her uncle would be introduced giving his blessing – though one would not stress this unduly, since no shepherd likes to hear too much made of his predecessor's skill with the crook and tar-box. Then some secretary would be sent off to rummage, and the papers would be brought in, confirming all she had said. Thereafter it would be as good as done, with nothing more needed than to find some vacant anchorage and install Dame

Lilias. Perhaps this might even be done forthwith, so that she would return alone to Oby to recount the story, thus gloriously receiving on her own shoulders all the thumps which would otherwise have been Dame Lilias's portion.

All this was jeopardised by Dame Lilias's refusal to proceed. It was difficult indeed to be perfectly in charity with her companion. She had to tell herself repeatedly that Dame Lilias, puffed up by her doubts and scruples, could not appreciate all the planning and good intentions which had been devoted to her cause, nor guess how much Dame Sibilla had counted on its success as a countercharm against the painful recollections which must burst on her as she saw once more the scene of Bishop Walter's death.

How very painful these recollections might prove Dame Sibilla did not like to assess. The comforter of Walter Dunford's vexed death-bed was by no means confident that she could sail through the shadow as easily as she had sailed over the substance. Shadows can be much, much worse – as much worse as is an owl's hoot in broad daylight. A dead man decaying under a flagstone can lay a much more alarming hand on one than that same man when alive. So she prayed harder and harder, hearing the axles creak, the whips crack, the wheels rumbling over the frozen ground.

That night's bustle at the inn, the satisfaction of shielding Dame Lilias, the mass heard in a strange church, all helped to raise her spirits. As they neared the end of their journey she very much enjoyed pointing out the features on the skyline: the cathedral, the palace, the lesser churches, the hospital of the Holy Innocents where Henry Yellowlees set his foot on the first rung of the ladder. The widow, too, was extremely sustaining: most warm in her welcome and skilfully building a bridge between the bishop's dearest niece of 1377 and the begging nun of 1382. Alas! was not everything changed for the worse? – here, too, as elsewhere. For her, at any rate, there could never be such another bishop as Bishop Walter. A little later Henry Yellowlees looked in on them, bringing a box of sweetmeats and enquiring if they were comfortable. On the morrow he would call for them and show them their begging-station.

'And so, unless the wind blows from this quarter, I think you should be fairly comfortable here,' he said, having settled them in the south porch of the cathedral. 'The mats will keep your feet warm, and if you want anything or are molested Lambert the sacristan will be within call. He still talks of your uncle, Dame Sibilla, and disapproves of everything we have done since by way of improvements. He is a most excellent trustworthy old man, and the bishop delights in his sour sayings.'

So that is what he is like on his own perch, thought Dame Lilias, gazing at the custos of Oby. Well, it is very considerate of him to veil his glory when he comes among us. Catching her glance he smiled, and she thought better of him. After all, every man will climb if he can, and not many of them continue so kind to old acquaintances.

He turned back to say that on Thursday they should make a particularly good collection. A band of pilgrims from the north would hear their mass in the cathedral that morning, and as they had not been long on their pilgrimage they should be in a state to give generous alms. Dame Sibilla asked where the pilgrims were going, and he replied, to Jerusalem, taking ship at Venice.

Taking ship at Venice . . . All day Dame Lilias's thoughts sailed to Jerusalem over a blue transparent sea, blue as a flower and wide as a sky. And though in spite of Henry Yellowlees' assurances and the mats it was very cold in the south porch, and though old Lambert pestered them with conversation and enquiries, and though her arms ached with holding out the begging-dish and her face felt scorched with strangers' glances, at the day's end her fatigue was almost like refreshment. Unfortunately they were no sooner alone than Dame Sibilla began once more to persuade, expostulate, argue, and lament about the anchoressing. She was so faithful and so noisy that it was hard not to think of her as a little dog.

On the first day their takings were promising enough – considering, the widow remarked, that it was a Friday. By the second day they were already ceasing to be novelties, and those who had given did not give again, so the result of the second day was not so good. Dame Sibilla grew morose, and said that Master Yellowlees could very well afford to give them a new set of altar vessels, and that really it was the least he could do for the memory of poor Sir Ralph whom he had pretended to be so much attached to. On Sunday the number of alms given went up considerably, but when they came to count the day's winnings the bulk of it was in small money and there was a high proportion of clipped coins, tokens, and forgeries; for the increase in the congregation was made up from the city poor, old women, weavers, and day labourers who did not go to mass on ordinary days. Dame Sibilla was much distressed by the bad coins. When Dame Lilias remarked that she supposed their givers felt compelled by courtesy to give something even though that something was known to be worthless Dame Sibilla flew into a rage and delivered herself of a sermon on the theme of comforting Christ in his poor. It was a good sermon; better than the sermon they had heard from the black friar who had preached that morning. But if he had preached like an angel he would have been a disappointment to them, for they had expected to hear the bishop. By the close of the next day Dame Lilias was almost praying for some sort of notice from Bishop de Craye. It had been her terror that by some chance or other Dame Sibilla should get his ear and perform her design of telling him all about the Oby anchoress; but now, seeing Dame Sibilla so quiveringly mortified, so childishly foiled of all her glorious intentions, she felt that she could endure any exposure if it would contribute to Dame Sibilla's peace of mind. But nothing happened, they continued to stand in the porch watching people get quite accustomed to them and able to walk by them with no more concern than they would have felt for two images to which the sculptor had given the posture of beggars.

It was on Tuesday night that Dame Lilias woke up to find herself being half-strangled by her bedfellow. Her first thought was that some murderer had broken in, for she could not believe that Dame Sibilla, so much smaller than she, could grasp her with such force, nor utter such animal-sounding groans.

'You must, you must, you must!'

Half-stifled, and confused by this strange waking, and with the murderer still in her mind, she gasped out: 'Where is he?'

'He's here!'

It was a cry to curdle any blood, and from her bed at the other end of the chamber the widow called out: 'Holy Virgin! Who is here?'

Dame Lilias felt the desperate body beside her relax. Dame Sibilla's voice, prim and awed, said: '*Libera nos!* I have had a terrible dream.'

'I should think so,' said the widow testily. 'You shrieked like a lost soul. *He's here*, you said. And then you yelled as if the wolves had got you. What was the dream, who was it you saw that was so terrifying? God save us all, I feel as if there were someone or something in the room at this moment.'

'Hush, you'll frighten her. She's still only half awake,' said Dame Lilias, feeling the small body beside her convulsed with renewed terror. Interested in her own alarms the widow now got up and unfastened a shutter. The moonlight shone in.

'The door's barred, just as I left it. I don't see how anyone could have got in. There's no one behind the hanging, is there? Or hidden in the chest?'

She poked and muttered about the room. Then she began to snuff and to think of fire, and presently creaked away to make sure of the kitchen hearth. As soon as her back was turned Dame Sibilla clutched hold of Dame Lilias again, and began to whisper.

'Listen! I have had a frightful dream, and in it I saw – I saw the devil, standing on your side of the bed and threatening you. Do you know why? Because of your pride, your pride, you know. You are so proud that you will not do as our Saint Leonard bid you, and all because it may have been Dame Dorothy who struck you and not he. It is quite true what they all say of you, you are eaten up with pride. You are too proud to take anything on trust, you are too proud to ask for anyone's help, you won't stir a finger to become an anchoress. But you must, you must! You have no idea how much hangs on it, you think of no one but yourself, you sulk and do nothing. And all will be lost! I tell you, this is your last chance, your last chance. You must, you must!'

Here the widow came back, munching something she had found in the kitchen, and got into bed, saying Hail Maries and complaining of the cold. For a while she talked about other midnight alarms she had known. When she had fallen asleep and was safely snoring Dame Sibilla began again to threaten and to implore.

'No! Once for all, no,' said Dame Lilias.

There was a silence. Then, in a completely altered voice Dame Sibilla said: 'Very well. I have done all I can for you. Whatever happens now, remember, it is on your head.'

A minute later she was tranquilly sleeping.

Nothing more was said about this. Dame Sibilla appeared to be rather the better for her nightmare. She exerted herself to be agreeable, and instead of grieving over the fall in their takings she dwelt on the good harvest they would get from the pilgrims. During the afternoon the pilgrims began to come into the city. They walked about examining the sights, begging, and making little purchases. One and all, they were marked by a certain manner, an airiness and inconsequence that grew out of their detachment from the everyday cares of life. Perhaps if they had been going to settle, the citizens might not have liked them so well, for their comments were not always flattering and they drove very hard bargains with the shopkeepers, instancing how much cheaper or better such goods had been elsewhere; but as transients they had a cheering effect, and to the two nuns in the south porch they were a most welcome diversion.

That evening the widow's hall and kitchen were full of pilgrims. Some were frying fish for their supper, others patching their clothes or repacking their scrips or doing a little washing. The house was gay with their songs and their stories, and the widow was flushed and boastful as she ran to and fro attending to their needs. These were the people who would take ship at Venice for Jerusalem. In the herring-reek and the bustle Dame Lilias did not at first remember this: recalling it, she loitered in the doorway, wishing that she might pluck up enough audacity to speak to one of the more travelled ones, who had, it appeared, made this voyage once already. But Dame Sibilla pulled at her, saying that she had such a splitting headache that she must instantly lie down. Full of conscience and anxiety and remembering the nightmare Dame Lilias did all she could for her companion. Presently the widow came in and suggested various remedies. But it was balm-water that Dame Sibilla craved for, and unfortunately there were no balm leaves in the house.

'On any other evening . . .' cried the widow. 'But tonight I really cannot leave the house.'

'Never mind, never mind! Better now than tomorrow.'

'Yes, but will you be cured by tomorrow? Tomorrow, too, the great day, when you will need all your wits about you not to let any of the pilgrims slip by without giving an alms. For they'll be sly, you know. They're not like our own quiet, stay-at-home folk. They'd steal the chick from under the fox's paw. That's why I am so loath to leave the house unguarded while I go out for balm leaves.'

'If you will tell me where to buy them, I will go,' Dame Lilias said.

'What! – alone, with the town full of pilgrims? Well, it is not far, only a little difficult to find. But you must ask for Master Peter Hiddlestone, living next to Sim the Glover at the sign of the Bird and Hand. There are other apothecaries, but he is the honestest. Stay, I have a better plan! I will pick out a pilgrim to go with you, nun and pilgrim is the next thing to nun and nun. There is an excellent woman below, she has had thirteen children by the one husband and stuffs pillows, she too has some small shopping to do, and you will be none the slower for going hand in hand. And while you are gone I will make a posset for this poor dove.'

Master Peter Hiddlestone took some finding; the excellent woman, too, had several commissions and was a most scrupulous buyer; by the time Dame Lilias returned Dame Sibilla had somewhat recovered and was eating supper off a tray. The balm-water eased her wonderfully, and she soon fell asleep. But in the morning her headache was worse than ever and she felt such dizziness and such intimations of vomiting that she was compelled to let Dame Lilias set forth alone.

'On this morning, of all mornings!' lamented Dame Sibilla.

'Well, she must rattle the dish so much the louder, and stand well forward, and look them in the face, so that they will be ashamed to sneak by her,' said the widow. 'But it's a pity.'

'Why, where's the other one? Sick? You'll need to look sharp, then,' said Lambert the sacristan. 'For six who'll give there will be half a dozen who'll take. Here they come.'

'Who? The pilgrims? Already?'

'No, no. The executioner's servants, and the men with the faggots for the pitch-barrel. There's a thief being punished this morning. They will chop his hand off and dip the stump into pitch, you know. Yes, and you'll see the bishop. He's going to bless the pilgrims.'

'Are they punishing the thief near by? Shall I hear the screams?' Dame Lilias asked apprehensively. His glance fell on a boy who was filching a candle-end, and he hurried off without answering her.

Because of the headache Dame Lilias was a little late. She scarcely had time to feel the wretchedness of being alone and reflect on the screams of the mutilated man before the first mass-goers began to pass by. As awkwardly as if she had never begged till this hour she held forth her dish, wagging it up and down and saying: 'An alms, good people. An alms for God's poor nuns at Oby.' Her look was so piteous that one or two kind-hearted people gave her a good alms, and others paused to encourage her and to advise her to beg louder. But while these were talking more slipped by, and in her conscientiousness she went too far, leaving her place to run after them. Then one of these said crossly that he had given her an alms but the day before and that she might have the gratitude to remember it; but these nuns had no more consideration than the horse-leach. Abashed she went back into her corner again, and stood there biting her lip and with such shamed cheeks that Lambert came bustling up to ask who had offended her.

'No one, no one.'

'Then what are you making such a pother about? The other

one, Dame Sibilla, isn't too proud to beg. And she is blood-kin to a bishop.'

Now the pilgrims were arriving, spruced up for their mass and their blessing. Inside the cathedral the first disconnected noises of a congregation were amassing into a steady purr, and the newcomers felt themselves to be late comers, and hurried by without stopping to give alms. Presently she heard like a gnat's noise the voice of the officiating priest, and the responses of the quire following it like a caress. She did not dare look at the contents of her dish. Holding it under her veil she went to the cathedral door. Never in all her life had she seen so many people gathered together, and this was more marvellous to her than the quantities of the incense, the amplitude of the ritual. Bishop de Craye was sitting on his tall throne, her short sight could just discern him. Ah, poor Dame Sibilla! But her thoughts only brushed Dame Sibilla's dejected ambitions, going back to the pilgrims, to their incalculable journey, the fatigues and the dangers they must undergo, the long leagues, the mountains, the strange cities and unknown languages. So they would come to Venice, and take ship for Jerusalem.

She was still on her knees when Lambert came up and jogged her.

'Here, Dame Nun! Are you having a vision? Don't you see that they have had their blessing, that they are coming away? Don't let them slip through your fingers this time.'

She hurried back to her station. The shuffling feet approached and the voices, taking hold of the tune, sang more loudly and fervently. Singing, they streamed past her. Though she held out her dish and now and then a coin was dropped in it, the business of begging was quite out of her mind. These people going by her now, so many of them and all unknown and none to be met with again, dizzied her imagination, and it seemed to her that inevitably she would be drawn to go with them as a tuft of dry grass is pulled from the river-bank and carried with the travelling waters to the sea. To Venice, and thence to take ship for Jerusalem; and in Jerusalem to lay her empty sorrows in the empty Sepulchre . . .

But her dream depended on their going by, and now they slowed down and stopped, some block beyond the porch impeding their progress. Her dream snapped, she remembered herself and held out the dish.

'An alms, good people. An alms for God's poor nuns at Oby.'

A sense that she was being scrutinised made her look up. The pilgrim who had been halted just in front of her was examining the contents of the dish, and Dame Lilias received an instant impression that this pilgrim had a cast of countenance which she very much disliked. In the same moment she saw that the pilgrim was Dame Sibilla.

Their eyes met. Dame Sibilla gave a little nod, as much as to say: I told you so. Dropping an alms into the dish she leant forward and said rapidly:

'Do not betray me. Do not say that you have seen me here among the pilgrims.'

'But you will be sought for. And if they find you, you will be brought back, an apostate nun, and . . .'

'I shall not be sought for. And no one will ask you what has become of me, not for a long time, not till I am beyond seeking. I have seen to all that. It will be no trouble to you, you will only have to keep your own counsel. I have written a letter, and by now it is being carried to Oby, telling the prioress that my aunt Anna, the nun at Ramsey, the one who sent us the mock ginger, is dying a slow death, and that her convent has sent for me to nurse her. And that I met their steward here, coming in search of me, and have gone with him, because of the escort, and the saving of expenses. You will find everything arranged when you get back. One of us had to go, you would not be an anchoress, so I am a pilgrim. I see you do not understand, but I assure you, it is all God's will. I am a pilgrim, I am inexpressibly happy. I shall pray for you in Jerusalem. And you can rely on the widow. She understands everything, she will arrange . . . '

The procession began to move forward.

'Remember, I trust you,' said Dame Sibilla.

Joining in the hymn she moved on. The stoppage had been caused by the executioners going past with the man who was to have his hand struck off. Now they had turned aside, and the pilgrims swept on unimpeded. Their singing swelled out like a banner on the wind as they fell into step and marched southward.

OTHER NEW YORK REVIEW CLASSICS

For a complete list of titles, visit www.nyrb.com or write to:
Catalog Requests, NYRB, 435 Hudson Street, New York, NY 10014

J.R. ACKERLEY We Think the World of You*
HENRY ADAMS The Jeffersonian Transformation
RENATA ADLER Pitch Dark*
RENATA ADLER Speedboat*
AESCHYLUS Prometheus Bound; translated by Joel Agee*
ROBERT AICKMAN Compulsory Games*
LEOPOLDO ALAS His Only Son *with* Doña Berta*
CÉLESTE ALBARET Monsieur Proust
DANTE ALIGHIERI The Inferno
KINGSLEY AMIS The Alteration*
KINGSLEY AMIS Dear Illusion: Collected Stories*
KINGSLEY AMIS Lucky Jim*
ROBERTO ARLT The Seven Madmen*
U.R. ANANTHAMURTHY Samskara: A Rite for a Dead Man*
IVO ANDRIĆ Omer Pasha Latas*
WILLIAM ATTAWAY Blood on the Forge
W.H. AUDEN (EDITOR) The Living Thoughts of Kierkegaard
W.H. AUDEN W. H. Auden's Book of Light Verse
ERICH AUERBACH Dante: Poet of the Secular World
EVE BABITZ Eve's Hollywood*
EVE BABITZ Slow Days, Fast Company: The World, the Flesh, and L.A.*
DOROTHY BAKER Cassandra at the Wedding*
DOROTHY BAKER Young Man with a Horn*
J.A. BAKER The Peregrine
S. JOSEPHINE BAKER Fighting for Life*
HONORÉ DE BALZAC The Human Comedy: Selected Stories*
HONORÉ DE BALZAC The Memoirs of Two Young Wives*
VICKI BAUM Grand Hotel*
SYBILLE BEDFORD A Favorite of the Gods *and* A Compass Error*
SYBILLE BEDFORD A Legacy*
SYBILLE BEDFORD A Visit to Don Otavio: A Mexican Journey*
MAX BEERBOHM The Prince of Minor Writers: The Selected Essays of Max Beerbohm*
STEPHEN BENATAR Wish Her Safe at Home*
FRANS G. BENGTSSON The Long Ships*
WALTER BENJAMIN The Storyteller Essays*
ALEXANDER BERKMAN Prison Memoirs of an Anarchist
GEORGES BERNANOS Mouchette
MIRON BIAŁOSZEWSKI A Memoir of the Warsaw Uprising*
ADOLFO BIOY CASARES The Invention of Morel
CAROLINE BLACKWOOD Corrigan*
CAROLINE BLACKWOOD Great Granny Webster*
LESLEY BLANCH Journey into the Mind's Eye: Fragments of an Autobiography*
RONALD BLYTHE Akenfield: Portrait of an English Village*
NICOLAS BOUVIER The Way of the World
EMMANUEL BOVE Henri Duchemin and His Shadows*
EMMANUEL BOVE My Friends*
MALCOLM BRALY On the Yard*

* *Also available as an electronic book.*

ROBERT BRESSON Notes on the Cinematograph*
ROBERT BURTON The Anatomy of Melancholy
MATEI CALINESCU The Life and Opinions of Zacharias Lichter*
CAMARA LAYE The Radiance of the King
GIROLAMO CARDANO The Book of My Life
DON CARPENTER Hard Rain Falling*
J.L. CARR A Month in the Country*
LEONORA CARRINGTON Down Below*
BLAISE CENDRARS Moravagine
EILEEN CHANG Love in a Fallen City*
EILEEN CHANG Naked Earth*
JOAN CHASE During the Reign of the Queen of Persia*
UPAMANYU CHATTERJEE English, August: An Indian Story
FRANÇOIS-RENÉ DE CHATEAUBRIAND Memoirs from Beyond the Grave, 1768–1800
NIRAD C. CHAUDHURI The Autobiography of an Unknown Indian
ANTON CHEKHOV Peasants and Other Stories
JEAN-PAUL CLÉBERT Paris Vagabond*
RICHARD COBB Paris and Elsewhere
COLETTE The Pure and the Impure
JOHN COLLIER Fancies and Goodnights
D.G. COMPTON The Continuous Katherine Mortenhoe
IVY COMPTON-BURNETT A House and Its Head
IVY COMPTON-BURNETT Manservant and Maidservant
BARBARA COMYNS The Juniper Tree*
BARBARA COMYNS Our Spoons Came from Woolworths*
BARBARA COMYNS The Vet's Daughter
ALBERT COSSERY Proud Beggars*
ALBERT COSSERY The Jokers*
ASTOLPHE DE CUSTINE Letters from Russia*
JÓZEF CZAPSKI Lost Time: Lectures on Proust in a Soviet Prison Camp*
LORENZO DA PONTE Memoirs
ELIZABETH DAVID Summer Cooking
L.J. DAVIS A Meaningful Life*
AGNES DE MILLE Dance to the Piper*
MARIA DERMOÛT The Ten Thousand Things
DER NISTER The Family Mashber
ANTONIO DI BENEDETTO Zama*
ALFRED DÖBLIN Berlin Alexanderplatz*
JEAN D'ORMESSON The Glory of the Empire: A Novel, A History*
ARTHUR CONAN DOYLE The Exploits and Adventures of Brigadier Gerard
CHARLES DUFF A Handbook on Hanging
BRUCE DUFFY The World As I Found It*
DAPHNE DU MAURIER Don't Look Now: Stories
ELAINE DUNDY The Dud Avocado*
ELAINE DUNDY The Old Man and Me*
G.B. EDWARDS The Book of Ebenezer Le Page*
JOHN EHLE The Land Breakers*
MARCELLUS EMANTS A Posthumous Confession
EURIPIDES Grief Lessons: Four Plays; translated by Anne Carson
J.G. FARRELL The Siege of Krishnapur*
J.G. FARRELL The Singapore Grip*
THOMAS FLANAGAN The Year of the French*
SANFORD FRIEDMAN Conversations with Beethoven*

CARLO EMILIO GADDA That Awful Mess on the Via Merulana
BENITO PÉREZ GÁLDOS Tristana*
MAVIS GALLANT The Cost of Living: Early and Uncollected Stories*
MAVIS GALLANT Paris Stories*
MAVIS GALLANT Varieties of Exile*
GABRIEL GARCÍA MÁRQUEZ Clandestine in Chile: The Adventures of Miguel Littín
LEONARD GARDNER Fat City*
WILLIAM H. GASS In the Heart of the Heart of the Country and Other Stories*
WILLIAM H. GASS On Being Blue: A Philosophical Inquiry*
THÉOPHILE GAUTIER My Fantoms
GE FEI The Invisibility Cloak
JEAN GENET Prisoner of Love
ÉLISABETH GILLE The Mirador: Dreamed Memories of Irène Némirovsky by Her Daughter*
NATALIA GINZBURG Family Lexicon*
FRANÇOISE GILOT Life with Picasso*
JEAN GIONO Hill*
JEAN GIONO A King Alone*
JEAN GIONO Melville: A Novel*
JOHN GLASSCO Memoirs of Montparnasse*
P.V. GLOB The Bog People: Iron-Age Man Preserved
NIKOLAI GOGOL Dead Souls*
EDMOND AND JULES DE GONCOURT Pages from the Goncourt Journals
ALICE GOODMAN History Is Our Mother: Three Libretti*
PAUL GOODMAN Growing Up Absurd: Problems of Youth in the Organized Society*
EDWARD GOREY (EDITOR) The Haunted Looking Glass
JEREMIAS GOTTHELF The Black Spider*
A.C. GRAHAM Poems of the Late T'ang
JULIEN GRACQ Balcony in the Forest*
HENRY GREEN Back*
HENRY GREEN Caught*
HENRY GREEN Loving*
HENRY GREEN Nothing*
WILLIAM LINDSAY GRESHAM Nightmare Alley*
HANS HERBERT GRIMM Schlump*
VASILY GROSSMAN Everything Flows*
VASILY GROSSMAN Life and Fate*
VASILY GROSSMAN Stalingrad*
LOUIS GUILLOUX Blood Dark*
OAKLEY HALL Warlock
PATRICK HAMILTON Twenty Thousand Streets Under the Sky*
PETER HANDKE Slow Homecoming
THORKILD HANSEN Arabia Felix: The Danish Expedition of 1761–1767*
ELIZABETH HARDWICK The Collected Essays of Elizabeth Hardwick*
ELIZABETH HARDWICK The New York Stories of Elizabeth Hardwick*
L.P. HARTLEY The Go-Between*
ALFRED HAYES My Face for the World to See*
PAUL HAZARD The Crisis of the European Mind: 1680–1715*
ALICE HERDAN-ZUCKMAYER The Farm in the Green Mountains*
GILBERT HIGHET Poets in a Landscape
RUSSELL HOBAN Turtle Diary*
JANET HOBHOUSE The Furies
YOEL HOFFMANN The Sound of the One Hand: 281 Zen Koans with Answers*
RICHARD HOLMES Shelley: The Pursuit*

GEOFFREY HOUSEHOLD Rogue Male*
WILLIAM DEAN HOWELLS Indian Summer
BOHUMIL HRABAL Dancing Lessons for the Advanced in Age*
DOROTHY B. HUGHES In a Lonely Place*
RICHARD HUGHES A High Wind in Jamaica*
RICHARD HUGHES In Hazard*
MAUDE HUTCHINS Victorine
YASUSHI INOUE Tun-huang*
DARIUS JAMES Negrophobia: An Urban Parable
HENRY JAMES The New York Stories of Henry James*
TOVE JANSSON The Summer Book*
TOVE JANSSON The Woman Who Borrowed Memories: Selected Stories*
RANDALL JARRELL (EDITOR) Randall Jarrell's Book of Stories
UWE JOHNSON Anniversaries*
JOSEPH JOUBERT The Notebooks of Joseph Joubert; translated by Paul Auster
FRIGYES KARINTHY A Journey Round My Skull
YASHAR KEMAL Memed, My Hawk
WALTER KEMPOWSKI All for Nothing
MURRAY KEMPTON Part of Our Time: Some Ruins and Monuments of the Thirties*
RAYMOND KENNEDY Ride a Cockhorse*
DAVID KIDD Peking Story*
ROBERT KIRK The Secret Commonwealth of Elves, Fauns, and Fairies
ARUN KOLATKAR Jejuri
DEZSŐ KOSZTOLÁNYI Skylark*
TÉTÉ-MICHEL KPOMASSIE An African in Greenland
GYULA KRÚDY The Adventures of Sindbad*
GYULA KRÚDY Sunflower*
SIGIZMUND KRZHIZHANOVSKY Autobiography of a Corpse*
K'UNG SHANG-JEN The Peach Blossom Fan*
MARGARET LEECH Reveille in Washington: 1860–1865*
PATRICK LEIGH FERMOR Between the Woods and the Water*
PATRICK LEIGH FERMOR The Broken Road*
PATRICK LEIGH FERMOR A Time of Gifts*
SIMON LEYS The Hall of Uselessness: Collected Essays*
MARGARITA LIBERAKI Three Summers*
GEORG CHRISTOPH LICHTENBERG The Waste Books
JAKOV LIND Soul of Wood and Other Stories
H.P. LOVECRAFT AND OTHERS Shadows of Carcosa: Tales of Cosmic Horror*
DWIGHT MACDONALD Masscult and Midcult: Essays Against the American Grain*
CURZIO MALAPARTE Kaputt
CURZIO MALAPARTE The Kremlin Ball
JANET MALCOLM In the Freud Archives
JEAN-PATRICK MANCHETTE Fatale*
JEAN-PATRICK MANCHETTE Ivory Pearl*
JEAN-PATRICK MANCHETTE Nada*
OSIP MANDELSTAM The Selected Poems of Osip Mandelstam
OLIVIA MANNING Fortunes of War: The Balkan Trilogy*
OLIVIA MANNING Fortunes of War: The Levant Trilogy*
JAMES VANCE MARSHALL Walkabout*
GUY DE MAUPASSANT Afloat
GUY DE MAUPASSANT Like Death*
JAMES McCOURT Mawrdew Czgowchwz*
WILLIAM McPHERSON Testing the Current*

JESSICA MITFORD Hons and Rebels
NANCY MITFORD Frederick the Great*
KENJI MIYAZAWA Once and Forever: The Tales of Kenji Miyazawa*
PATRICK MODIANO Young Once*
FREYA AND HELMUTH JAMES VON MOLTKE Last Letters: The Prison Correspondence*
MICHEL DE MONTAIGNE Shakespeare's Montaigne; translated by John Florio*
BRIAN MOORE The Lonely Passion of Judith Hearne*
BRIAN MOORE The Mangan Inheritance*
ALBERTO MORAVIA Agostino*
JAN MORRIS Conundrum*
PENELOPE MORTIMER The Pumpkin Eater*
MULTATULI Max Havelaar, or the Coffee Auctions of the Dutch Trading Company*
L.H. MYERS The Root and the Flower*
DARCY O'BRIEN A Way of Life, Like Any Other
SILVINA OCAMPO Thus Were Their Faces*
IONA AND PETER OPIE The Lore and Language of Schoolchildren
IRIS ORIGO A Chill in the Air: An Italian War Diary, 1939–1940*
MAXIM OSIPOV Rock, Paper, Scissors and Other Stories*
LEV OZEROV Portraits Without Frames*
RUSSELL PAGE The Education of a Gardener
ALEXANDROS PAPADIAMANTIS The Murderess
CESARE PAVESE The Selected Works of Cesare Pavese
ELEANOR PERÉNYI More Was Lost: A Memoir*
DAVID PLANTE Difficult Women: A Memoir of Three*
ANDREY PLATONOV Soul and Other Stories
J.F. POWERS The Stories of J.F. Powers*
ALEXANDER PUSHKIN The Captain's Daughter*
QIU MIAOJIN Notes of a Crocodile*
PAUL RADIN Primitive Man as Philosopher*
FRIEDRICH RECK Diary of a Man in Despair*
JULES RENARD Nature Stories*
JEAN RENOIR Renoir, My Father
GREGOR VON REZZORI Abel and Cain*
TIM ROBINSON Stones of Aran: Labyrinth
GILLIAN ROSE Love's Work
LINDA ROSENKRANTZ Talk*
LILLIAN ROSS Picture*
WILLIAM ROUGHEAD Classic Crimes
SAKI The Unrest-Cure and Other Stories; illustrated by Edward Gorey
TAYEB SALIH Season of Migration to the North
JEAN-PAUL SARTRE We Have Only This Life to Live: Selected Essays. 1939–1975
JAMES SCHUYLER What's for Dinner?*
SIMONE SCHWARZ-BART The Bridge of Beyond*
LEONARDO SCIASCIA The Day of the Owl
ANNA SEGHERS Transit*
GILBERT SELDES The Stammering Century*
VICTOR SERGE Conquered City*
VICTOR SERGE Notebooks, 1936–1947*
VARLAM SHALAMOV Kolyma Stories*
SHCHEDRIN The Golovlyov Family
ROBERT SHECKLEY The Store of the Worlds: The Stories of Robert Sheckley*
CHARLES SIMIC Dime-Store Alchemy: The Art of Joseph Cornell
MAY SINCLAIR Mary Olivier: A Life*

NATSUME SŌSEKI The Gate*
DAVID STACTON The Judges of the Secret Court*
JEAN STAFFORD The Mountain Lion
GEORGE R. STEWART Names on the Land
STENDHAL The Life of Henry Brulard
JEAN STROUSE Alice James: A Biography*
HOWARD STURGIS Belchamber
HARVEY SWADOS Nights in the Gardens of Brooklyn
A.J.A. SYMONS The Quest for Corvo
MAGDA SZABÓ The Door*
ANTAL SZERB Journey by Moonlight*
ELIZABETH TAYLOR Angel*
ELIZABETH TAYLOR A Game of Hide and Seek*
ELIZABETH TAYLOR A View of the Harbour*
ELIZABETH TAYLOR You'll Enjoy It When You Get There: The Stories of Elizabeth Taylor*
TEFFI Tolstoy, Rasputin, Others, and Me: The Best of Teffi*
GABRIELE TERGIT Käsebier Takes Berlin*
HENRY DAVID THOREAU The Journal: 1837–1861*
TATYANA TOLSTAYA White Walls: Collected Stories
LIONEL TRILLING The Liberal Imagination*
MARINA TSVETAEVA Earthly Signs: Moscow Diaries, 1917–1922*
KURT TUCHOLSKY Castle Gripsholm*
IVAN TURGENEV Virgin Soil
RAMÓN DEL VALLE-INCLÁN Tyrant Banderas*
MARK VAN DOREN Shakespeare
SALKA VIERTEL The Kindness of Strangers*
ELIZABETH VON ARNIM The Enchanted April*
EDWARD LEWIS WALLANT The Tenants of Moonbloom
ROBERT WALSER Girlfriends, Ghosts, and Other Stories*
ROBERT WALSER Jakob von Gunten
MICHAEL WALZER Political Action: A Practical Guide to Movement Politics*
SYLVIA TOWNSEND WARNER Lolly Willowes*
SYLVIA TOWNSEND WARNER Mr. Fortune*
SYLVIA TOWNSEND WARNER Summer Will Show*
LYALL WATSON Heaven's Breath: A Natural History of the Wind*
C.V. WEDGWOOD The Thirty Years War
SIMONE WEIL On the Abolition of All Political Parties*
HELEN WEINZWEIG Basic Black with Pearls*
REBECCA WEST The Fountain Overflows
EDITH WHARTON The New York Stories of Edith Wharton*
KATHARINE S. WHITE Onward and Upward in the Garden*
T.H. WHITE The Goshawk*
JOHN WILLIAMS Augustus*
JOHN WILLIAMS Nothing but the Night*
JOHN WILLIAMS Stoner*
ANGUS WILSON Anglo-Saxon Attitudes
RUDOLF AND MARGARET WITTKOWER Born Under Saturn
GEOFFREY WOLFF Black Sun*
FRANCIS WYNDHAM The Complete Fiction
JOHN WYNDHAM Chocky
BÉLA ZOMBORY-MOLDOVÁN The Burning of the World: A Memoir of 1914*
STEFAN ZWEIG Beware of Pity*
STEFAN ZWEIG The Post-Office Girl*